for t, n, and m, whom kismet brought to me

Sandhya Menon

When

Dimple

Met

Rishi

First published in the USA by Simon Pulse,
an imprint of Simon & Schuster Children's Publishing Division

First published in Great Britain in 2017 by Hodder & Stoughton
An Hachette UK company

1

A CIP catalogue record for this title is available from the British Library

Paperback ISBN 978 1 473 66740 2
Ebook ISBN 978 1 473 66741 9

Printed and bound by CPI Group (UK) Ltd, Croydon, CR0 4YY

Hodder & Stoughton policy is to use papers that are natural,
renewable and recyclable products and made from wood grown in sustainable
forests. The logging and manufacturing processes are expected to conform to the
environmental regulations of the country of origin.

Hodder & Stoughton Ltd
Carmelite House
50 Victoria Embankment
London EC4Y 0DZ

www.hodder.co.uk

CHAPTER 1

Dimple

Dimple couldn't stop smiling. It was like two invisible puppeteers, standing stage left and stage right, were yanking on strings to lift up the corners of her mouth.

Okay, or maybe something less creepy. The point was, the urge to grin felt irresistible.

Dimple clicked on the e-mail again and read it. *Stanford*. She was going to Stanford. Even though the acceptance letter had come in the mail weeks ago, she hadn't allowed herself to really, fully believe it until her student log-in details had come via e-mail. She'd thought that, at the last minute, Papa would have second thoughts and renege on the deposit. Or that Mamma would call and tell them Dimple had changed her mind (and if you didn't think Mamma would do something like that, you'd never met her).

But no, it had all actually worked out. Everything was settled. She was officially enrolled.

Now, if only . . .

Dimple clicked over to the other window she had open, her smile fading just a tad.

Insomnia Con 2017:

A fabulous opportunity for rising high school seniors or recent grads! Come learn the basics of web development on the sunny SFSU campus this summer!

Just shut up and take my money, Dimple thought.

But it wasn't that easy. It would be an incredible opportunity—this was true. She'd have a leg up on everyone else when she started Stanford in the fall. And think of the contacts she'd make! Some of the biggest names in web development had gone through Insomnia Con: Jenny Lindt, for instance. The woman was a genius. She'd basically designed and coded the billion-dollar Meeting Space app and website from the ground up. It made Dimple salivate just to think of sitting through the same classes, participating in the same activities, walking the same campus as she had.

But she didn't know if she could push her luck with the parental unit.

The summer program cost a thousand dollars. And while Papa and Mamma were solidly middle class, they weren't exactly flush. Not to mention she'd already stretched her luck about as far as it could go, she was sure, by asking—nay, haranguing—them to let her go to Stanford. She was sure the only reason they had agreed was because they were secretly hoping she'd meet the I.I.H. of her—no, *their*—dreams at the prestigious school.

I.I.H., for the uninitiated, stood for *Ideal Indian Husband.*

Uggghh. Just thinking about it made her want to banshee-scream into a pillow.

"Diiiiimpllllle?" Mamma sounded screechy and frantic as usual.

2

When Dimple was younger, she'd go running downstairs, heart pounding every single time, terrified something awful had happened. And every single time Mamma would be doing something mundane like rummaging in the kitchen cupboard, greeting her casually with, "Have you seen my saffron?" Mamma never understood why it made Dimple so livid.

"Just a minute, Mamma!" she shouted back, knowing full well it would be more than a minute. Dimple now knew better than to rush when she heard her Mamma call. They'd arrived at an uneasy truce—Mamma didn't have to modulate her tone if Dimple didn't have to drop everything and rush to her aid for saffron emergencies.

She clicked through the photo gallery on the Insomnia Con website for another five minutes, sighing at the building's giant glass and chrome structure, at the tech nerds grouped together in inviting clusters, at the pictures of previous, jubilant winners of the legendary talent contest that gave them extra seed money for their apps or websites. Dimple would kill to be one of them someday.

Participants of Insomnia Con were tasked to come up with a concept for the most groundbreaking app they could conceive during their month and a half at the SFSU campus. Although no one could actually code an entire app in that time frame, the idea was to get as close as possible by the judging round. There were rumors that, this year, the winners would get the chance to have their concept critiqued by Jenny Lindt herself. Now *that* would be epic.

Dimple said a little prayer that she'd win a thousand-dollar lottery, turned off her monitor, adjusted her ratty gray *salwar kameez*, and made her way downstairs.

• • •

"Woh kuch iske baare mein keh rahi thi na?" Papa was saying. *Didn't she mention this?*

Dimple stopped, ears perked. Were they talking about her? She strained to hear more, but Mamma pitched her voice too low, and Dimple couldn't make out anything else. Of course. When she actually *wanted* to listen, Mamma decided to be quiet and reserved. Sighing, she walked into the living room.

Was it her imagination or did her parents look a little flushed? Almost . . . guilty? She raised her eyebrows. "Mamma, Papa. Did you need something?"

"Dimple, tell me again about—oh." The guilty look disappeared as Mamma pursed her magenta lipsticked mouth, taking Dimple's appearance in. "Wearing specs?" She pointed to Dimple's glasses, perched on the end of her nose like usual. Mamma's eyes roamed, squinting with disapproval at Dimple's unruly black curly hair (which she refused to let grow past her shoulders), her face so completely unadorned with makeup, and sadly, in spite of Mamma's optimistic naming, nary a dimple in sight.

She should be thankful I brushed my teeth this morning, Dimple thought. But Mamma would never understand Dimple's aversion to makeup and fashion. Every other week one of the aunties from the Indian Association came over to help Mamma dye her roots black while Papa was at work. He was under the impression she still had her youthful color.

"Where are your contacts? And remember when I showed you how to do *kaajal*?" *Kaajal* was the potted eyeliner that was hugely popular in Mamma's youth, a trend which she apparently hadn't noticed had died away sometime in the '70s.

4

"Vividly," Dimple muttered, trying to tamp down the annoyance in her voice. From beside Mamma, Papa, ever the peacemaker, was making a surreptitious *please let it go* face. "I just graduated three days ago, Mamma. Can't I have this week to relax and be lazy?"

Papa's face now resembled a roti that had been left in the pan too long.

"Relax and be *lazy*!" Mamma thundered. Her glass bangles jangled in synchrony. "Do you think you're going to find a husband by being *lazy*? Do you think, for the past twenty-two years since marrying your father, I've had a minute to myself to be *lazy*?"

Of course not, Dimple thought. *Because you've been too busy hovering.* She bit her tongue and sank down on the sofa, knowing that once Mamma got started, she'd be at it for a while. It was better to let her talk until the words petered out, like those windup chattering teeth you could buy at the joke store. There were a million things she could say in acerbic response, of course, but Dimple still hadn't ruled out asking to enroll in Insomnia Con if the opportunity presented itself. It was in her best interest to hold back.

"No, I haven't," Mamma continued. "'Lazy' shouldn't be in a woman's vocabulary." Adjusting the violet *dupatta* on her gold and pink *salwar kameez*, Mamma settled against the couch. She looked like the brilliant Indian flower Dimple knew she herself would never be. "You know, Dimple, a grown daughter is a reflection of her mother. What do you think others in our community will think of me if they see you . . . like this?" She made a vague gesture at Dimple's person. "Not that you aren't beautiful, *beti*, you are, which is what makes it even more tragic—"

Dimple knew she shouldn't. But the flare of temper that overtook her made it all but impossible to stop the flood of words leaving her mouth. "That is *such* a misogynistic view, Mamma!" she said, jumping up, pushing her glasses up on her nose. Papa was muttering something under his breath now. He might've been praying.

Mamma looked like she couldn't believe what she was hearing. "Misogynistic! You call your own mother misogynistic?" Mamma darted an indignant look at Papa, who appeared to be extremely invested in a loose thread on his kurta. Turning back to Dimple, Mamma snapped, "This is what I'm worried about! You lose sight of the *important* things, Dimple. Looking nice, making an effort . . . these are the things girls value in our culture. Not this"—she made air quotes, which up until now Dimple hadn't realized she knew how to use—"'misogyny' business."

Dimple groaned and clutched her head, feeling like that ancient pressure cooker Mamma still used when she made *idli* cakes. She was sure there was an actual chance she would explode. There was no way she and Mamma were related; they may as well have been two entirely different species. "Seriously? That's what you think I should be relegating my brain space to? Looking nice? Like, if I don't make the effort to look beautiful, my entire *existence* is nullified? Nothing else matters—not my intellect, not my personality or my accomplishments; my hopes and dreams mean nothing if I'm not wearing *eyeliner*?" Her voice had risen incrementally until it echoed off the high ceilings.

Mamma, caught up in the moment, stood to meet her glare. "*Hai Ram*, Dimple! It is not eyeliner—it is *kaajal*!"

Dimple's temper flashed, the heat tempered only slightly by the dampness of disappointment. This was an argument they'd had so many times, she and Mamma could probably say each other's lines. It was like they were constantly speaking two different languages, each trying to convince the other in an alien lexicon. Why couldn't Mamma make the *smallest* effort to understand where Dimple was coming from? Did she really think Dimple had nothing valuable to contribute besides her looks? The thought made Dimple's pulse sky-rocket. She leaned forward, face flaming, ready to speak her mind about how she really felt—

The doorbell chime echoed through the house, bringing them to a standstill. Dimple's heart still raced, but she felt all the million old arguments stall, unspoken behind her lips.

Mamma adjusted her *dupatta*, which had begun to fall off during the argument, and took a deep breath. "We have guests," she said demurely, patting her hair. "I trust you will behave for them, Dimple?"

Papa looked at her with big, pleading eyes.

Dimple managed a curt nod, thinking, *Saved by the bell, Mamma. You don't know how lucky you are.*

CHAPTER 2

Dimple

Mamma bustled out of the room in a cloud of sandalwood perfume to open the door. Dimple tried to take deep, calming breaths. Stanford was only a few months away, she reminded herself. And if she could swing Insomnia Con, freedom would be hers very, very soon.

"Helloooo!" Dimple heard after a moment. The word trilled and echoed like a small, annoying bird's song.

Papa grimaced. "Ritu auntie," he said, half resigned, half annoyed. He reached over and grabbed the phone. "Important phone call," he murmured as he disappeared around the corner.

"Traitor," Dimple called softly at his retreating back. She stood and pressed her palms together just as Ritu auntie rounded the corner in her wheelchair, pushed, as usual, by her silent, watchful new daughter-in-law, Seema. "*Namaste*, Ritu auntie, Seema *didi*."

Technically, Ritu wasn't her aunt, and Seema wasn't her *didi*— older sister. But it was customary to always be respectful of your elders, a lesson that had been drilled into her since she was a baby. And yet, somehow, Dimple found herself questioning them—and really, everything—all the time. Mamma often lamented that her first word had been "why."

"*Namaste!*" Ritu auntie said, beaming up at her. Behind her, Seema watched unsmilingly through a curtain of long, sleek black hair.

"Please sit, Seema," Mamma said. "Can I get you some chai? Biscuits? I have ParleG, bought specially for you from the Indian market." Mamma was constantly on a mission to make Seema feel at home. It was her opinion that the reason Seema was as withdrawn as she was, was because Ritu auntie hadn't done a good enough job making her feel welcome in her *sasural*—bridal home. This had created a strange rivalry between Ritu auntie and Mamma. Dimple pitied Seema, caught like a helpless fly in the web of their crazy.

"Oh, Seema and I found something she likes better," Ritu auntie said. "Milanos. Isn't that right, Seema? Tell her how much you like those."

"They're delicious," Seema said dutifully. After a pause—perhaps awaiting another directive—Seema sat in the empty armchair next to Ritu auntie. Dimple sat down too.

"Oh, we have those also!" Mamma announced triumphantly. "Let me go and get. And some chai for everyone."

Left alone with the visitors, Dimple pushed her glasses up and attempted to rack her brain for something to say. Thankfully, Ritu auntie had majored in small talk in college. "So! All ready for Stanford, Dimple? Your mamma can't stop talking about it!"

"Really?" Dimple smiled, touched. She hadn't heard Mamma say much about Stanford besides to lament the price tag of a private school education. It just went to show, Mamma *was* proud of her only daughter's intellect, deep down. Maybe, in spite of Dimple's doubts, Mamma really did want her to get the best education, even if she pretended to be—

"Yes! So many boys go there for engineering. You'll have the pick of the litter." Ritu auntie looked at her with an expectant gleam in her eyes.

Of course. Dimple should've guessed. It was the I.I.H. nonsense again. She suspected the entire community of aunties was in on it. It was like some bizarre version of a geocaching club; the minute somebody's daughter turned eighteen, all the aunties began to scheme the shortest route from her parents' home to the ultimate prize—her *sasural*.

"Right . . . but I'm really more interested in their technology program," Dimple said, forcing herself to stay polite.

Seema shifted in her seat, uncomfortable with this show of assertiveness, but Ritu auntie only waved her off, as if she thought Dimple was being demure—who on earth went to college with anything *but* the aspiration of landing a marriageable partner? Dimple thought of Insomnia Con, of Jenny Lindt, of SFSU, of Stanford. Of all the things she'd jeopardize if she called Ritu auntie a backward, anti-feminist blight on democratic society.

Thankfully, Mamma returned then, arms trembling from holding a heavy silver tray laden with a teapot, teacups, and cookies and plates. "*Chalo, chai aur* snacks *ho jayen*! And, Seema, I brought you extra *shakkar* for your sweet tooth!" She guffawed overjovially, and Dimple had to bite the inside of her cheek to keep from laughing at Seema's frozen expression. The woman was so uncomfortable with Mamma's interest in her, and yet she had no idea how to put a stop

10

to it. Dimple felt bad for the other girl, but not bad enough to say anything—attention on Seema just meant less on her.

Mamma set the tray down on the coffee table, and everyone helped themselves.

"So, where is Stanford, exactly?" Ritu auntie said between bites. "San Francisco?"

There was a strange sort of stillness from Mamma's side of the couch, which Dimple tried, and failed, to decipher. "Um, not quite," she said, turning back to Ritu auntie. "It's about forty minutes south of San Francisco proper."

"Pity," Ritu auntie replied, grabbing another cookie just as Seema was reaching for the same one. Seema's hand seemed to shrivel, and she straightened up, giving up on cookie retrieval completely. Mamma, smiling smugly, put two cookies on a plate and handed them to Seema. Ritu auntie, oblivious to the entire exchange, went on. "San Francisco is supposed to be such a beautiful city. Full of opportunities for the young."

Okay, Dimple could not have asked for a more perfect opportunity if she'd crafted it from rainbows and sunbeams herself. She cleared her throat. Perhaps with Seema in the room, Mamma might want to appear more magnanimous. "Actually, it's interesting you bring that up," Dimple said. She took a sip of hot tea to bolster herself. "There *is* an opportunity in San Francisco this summer I'm interested in. Do you remember me telling you about it, Mamma?" She forced herself to keep her face calm and slack, like asking her parents to drop a grand on this sort of thing was something she routinely did, NBD.

"Mmm?" Mamma looked distracted, blowing on her tea. "Oh, something about . . . web development?"

11

Wow. Dimple had underestimated Mamma—maybe she really did pay attention. "*Haan*, that's right!" She smiled encouragingly. "Insomnia Con at the SFSU campus. It starts in three weeks, and it's such a fantastic program. Some of the greatest minds in technology have been through it. It's six weeks long, and you learn so much. It would really help me prepare for Stanford. But it's pretty expensive . . ." She trailed off, reddening when she noticed Ritu auntie watching with interest. Even Silent Seema seemed to be studying Dimple's reflection in the silver tray.

"It sounds worth it to me, if it will help your career," Ritu auntie said into the silence. Dimple looked up in surprise. Not that she wasn't thankful for the help, but she had to wonder at this sudden interjection. Since when did Ritu auntie think in terms of benefiting a woman's *career*? "Why don't you discuss it with Vijay, Leena?"

Dimple looked at Ritu auntie in disbelief, and Ritu auntie winked at her.

After a moment, Mamma bellowed for Papa to come over. "Vijay! *Idhar aayiye!*"

Papa came in, a wary expression on his face that he quickly converted to a warm smile for the visitors. "Ritu, Seema, hello."

Seema *didi* immediately shot to her feet and pressed her palms together. "*Namaste*, Vijay uncle."

"Please, sit, sit." He took a seat by Mamma, and then, after the briefest of pauses, reached out and snagged a Milano.

Mamma and Dimple both said, "No!" but he stuffed the cookie into his mouth before they could stop him and then grinned sheepishly.

Dimple put two fingers to the bridge of her nose. "Papa, you're a diabetic!"

Mamma sighed overdramatically. *"Kya aap mujhe vidhwaa chodna chahte ho?"*

Dimple rolled her eyes at her mother's words. "It's diabetes, Mamma. I don't think he's going to die and leave you a widow anytime soon." Ritu auntie was watching this little family drama with interest, but Seema looked like she'd rather be anywhere else but here.

"If he doesn't take his medication like he is supposed to, he will! Checking his blood sugar, eating a balanced diet—he doesn't want to do any of this!"

The tips of Papa's ears began to turn pink, and he cleared his throat. "Okay, okay. Now, why did you call me?"

The air in the room tensed. Mamma adjusted her *salwar kameez* and looked at Dimple. "Tell him what you told me."

Barely daring to breathe, Dimple repeated verbatim what she'd told Mamma. "I have the link to the website, if you want to look at it," she finished.

Papa and Mamma looked at each other. It always amazed her, how they could seemingly communicate without speaking. She wondered what that was like, that level of intense bond. Though she'd take to wearing *kaajal* every day before she'd admit it, Dimple sometimes felt a pang at the thought of never having that. Because, she was sure, the kind of bond Mamma and Papa had would require a self-sacrifice she would never be okay making.

Finally, Papa turned to her. "Yes, I would like to see the website. But I think your Mamma and I both feel that you should go." His cheeks were tinted vaguely pink, as were the tips of his hairy ears, like he was embarrassed by this show of caring.

A beat, two beats, three. Dimple blinked, not quite sure what had happened. And then her body caught up with her brain.

"Oh my God, thank you both!" she squealed, throwing her arms around them.

Seriously? Was that all she had needed to do this entire time? Ask Mamma for things while Ritu auntie and Seema *didi* were present?

Her parents chuckled and patted her on the back. She pulled back and grinned at them, still not able to completely believe it. They were letting her go to San Francisco to attend Insomnia Con, just like that. It felt unreal. She should buy Ritu auntie a present.

"This is *toh* great news!" Ritu auntie clapped her hands together. "Leena, before she goes, you must take her to buy some new *salwar kameez*." The older woman appraised Dimple's current outfit with pity. "Clearly she could use the help, *na* . . ."

"Good idea. And *kaajal*, of course," Mamma said, nodding sagely.

Okay, maybe no present for Ritu auntie.

CHAPTER 3

Rishi

The girl was scowling. Literally *scowling*.

She was pretty, with wild black hair and huge brown eyes she hid behind square frame glasses. And petite, a perfect match for his five-foot-eight-inch frame. But that scowl . . .

Rishi handed the picture back to his parents. "She doesn't look too . . . happy, does she?"

Ma put the picture away in the envelope and handed it back to him to keep. "Oof oh, don't worry, *beta*. They probably just clicked it at a bad time."

Pappa put his arm around her and laughed. "Remember how Ma and I met?"

Rishi grinned, misgivings receding. The story was legendary in their family. Within minutes of meeting each other, Ma had beaten Pappa with her umbrella because he took her seat on the bus. He maintained that, in his defense, he hadn't seen her in line (she *was* rather short). And in her defense, she said it had been a long, wet day schlepping through monsoon floods. That seat on the bus was the only thing she'd had going for her. What made it funnier was that Pappa had been on his way to her house to meet her parents to arrange their marriage.

"You ended up giving her the seat after all," Rishi said. "Even after she beat you up with her umbrella."

"Or maybe *because* of it," Ma said knowingly. "You men are all the same—you need a strong woman to keep you in place."

"But not too strong," Rishi said thoughtfully, looking back down at the envelope on the counter. "Dimple Shah looks . . . fierce."

"*Na, beta*, we've known Leena and Vijay Shah for decades. You might even remember them from some weddings we've all attended over the years," Pappa said, though Rishi had no memory at all of this girl. And he definitely would've remembered her. "Hmm, maybe not . . . you were so young. Anyway, they are a good family, Rishi. Solid. From the same part of Mumbai as us. Give it a chance, *toh, beta*. And if you don't get along . . ." He shrugged. "Better to find out now than in ten years' time, no?"

Rishi nodded and drained the last of his chai. This was true. What was the harm, anyway, in attending a program in San Francisco for a couple of weeks to meet Dimple Shah? Obviously, she'd already agreed, so she must think it was a good idea too.

Everything looked good on paper, he had to admit. She'd just graduated high school like he had, and had apparently gotten into Stanford. Which, of course, was across the country from MIT, where he'd been accepted, but he was sure they could work something out. Their parents already knew each other and felt their personalities would be compatible. She'd been born and brought up here too. They probably had a lot in common. Besides, when had his parents ever led him astray? Just look at them, arms around each other, eyes twinkling with anticipation for their oldest son. They were the poster children for arranged marriage.

"Okay, Pappa," Rishi said, smiling. "I'm going to do it."

Rishi whistled as he walked into the den, his heart lifting like a helium balloon in spite of himself. He fully believed romantic comedies were idiotic. There were no insta-love moments in real life that actually lasted. Rishi had watched dozens of his friends—of all ethnicities—fall in love at the beginning of the school year and become mortal enemies by the end. Or worse, become apathetic nothings.

Rishi knew from watching his parents that what mattered were compatibility and stability. He didn't want a million dramatic, heart-stoppingly romantic moments—he wanted just one long, sustainable partnership.

But in spite of his immense practicality, he could picture *her* in his life. He already knew the first time he saw Dimple's picture that their story would become a sort of legend, just like Ma beating Pappa with that umbrella. She'd have some cute, funny quip about the day that picture was taken that would totally endear her to him. Maybe her parents picked that one to send because they wanted to convey her playful personality.

And if it all worked out? If they found that they were, in fact, as compatible as their parents predicted? Rishi's life would be on *track*. Everything would fall into place. He'd go to MIT; maybe she'd transfer there or somewhere close by. They could hang out, date for a couple of years through college and maybe grad school, and then get married. He'd take care of Dimple, and she'd take care of him. And a few years after that . . . they'd make his parents grandparents.

But he was getting ahead of himself. First, he'd have to feel her out, see where she was with things. Maybe she wanted to get married before grad school.

He stopped short when he saw Ashish sprawled on the couch, mantislike legs splayed out so he took up every inch of space on the love seat. His hair had grown out, and it curled over his forehead and into his eyes. He was dressed, as usual, in his basketball uniform.

It didn't matter that it was summer: Basketball and Ashish had been in a serious relationship since he was in elementary school. Now, eight years later, he was good enough to be the only rising junior on the varsity team. He'd been training at a special camp for athletic prodigies like him all summer.

"Dude, get your nasty feet off the pillows. How many times does Ma have to tell you before you'll listen?" Rishi thumped his little brother's shoe, but it didn't budge.

On the TV someone scored, and Ashish groaned. "Ah, man. You're bad luck, *bhaiyya*."

"That may be, but I think *my* luck's about to change, my friend. I'm doing it. I'm going to San Francisco." Rishi's stomach swooped. If he was telling Ashish, it must really be happening. Whoa.

Ashish muted the game and sat up slowly. Rishi tried not to be too jealous of his little brother's bulging muscles; they just had very different interests, he reminded himself. "Tell me you're kidding."

Rishi shook his head and flung himself into the empty spot next to Ashish. "Nope."

"You're actually going to go meet that . . . girl dragon?"

Rishi punched Ashish's arm and tried not to wince when his fist stung. "Hey. Don't forget, the first time Ma and Pappa met—"

Ashish groaned and sank back against the couch. "Yeah, I *think* I have the gist of that story after hearing it four million times." More seriously, he said, "Look, man. I know you . . . you and I don't always see eye to eye on everything. You're, like, some weird thirty-five-year-old teenager. But don't you think you're rushing things? First MIT, and now this girl and Insomnia Con . . . I mean, what about your comics?"

Rishi's shoulders tensed before his brain had fully processed what Ashish was saying. "What about them?" He was careful to keep his voice light, casual. "Those are just a hobby, Ashish. Kid stuff. This is real life. It's not high school anymore."

Ashish shrugged. "I know. I just think, I mean, college doesn't have to mean you just let go of everything, does it? Like, I plan to play ball in college. Why can't you do what you want too?"

Rishi smiled a little. "What makes you think this isn't what I want?"

His brother's eyes, the same color of dark honey as his own, searched his face for something. Finally, apparently not finding it, Ashish looked away. "Whatever, man. As long as you're happy."

Rishi felt a pang of something, looking at his little brother. Ashish was now taller than him by a full inch. They were so fundamentally different. And to Ashish, he was just some weird relic, something that belonged in their parents' time in India, not here in modern America. *Maybe this is the beginning of us growing apart*, Rishi thought, and his heart hurt. But he forced himself to get up, because he knew they'd said all there was to say for now.

He made his way up to his room, to pack for San Francisco. For Dimple Shah, whoever she was.

CHAPTER 4

Dimple

"What about this one? The color will really suit you, Dimple."

Dimple couldn't resist rolling her eyes at the voluminous *salwar kameez* Mamma was holding up. It was swaths of gold brocade, with a vibrant peacock blue *dupatta*. It looked like a costume for a Bollywood movie. "Sorry, Mother, I *cannot* wear that to Insomnia Con."

Mamma lowered the offending garment, looking outraged. "Why not? You should be proud of your heritage, Dimple." From around the tiny shop full of imported Indian clothing, parents gave Mamma approving looks. Dimple could see her practically preening for the crowd. "Papa and I have held on to our culture, our values, for a quarter century! When we came to America, we said we would *never—*"

"Yeah, but I didn't come to America," Dimple interrupted, darting a defiant glance at all the shoppers. "I was born here. This is my home. *This* is my culture."

Mamma clutched the gold *salwar* to her bosom. *"Hai Ram,"* she said faintly.

Dimple sighed and grabbed a few kurta tops hanging on the rail next to her. They were all variations of the same color and pattern: black with grayish-silver accents. "What about these?" she said. She could pair them with her skinny jeans and Chucks and look almost normal.

Mamma made a face, but Dimple could already see she was going to agree. "I suppose that will do, but a little bit of color would really be nice for your complexion. Since you refuse to wear makeup . . ."

Dimple hurried Mamma to the counter to pay before she could begin looking around the store for *kaajal*.

Back at home Dimple texted Celia. *Leaving tomorrow 8 AM! Should take me about 4 hrs from Fresno.*

Celia was one of the few other girls who were attending Insomnia Con. They'd met on the forums and decided to room together for the month and a half.

Of course Dimple hadn't told Mamma and Papa about that. They'd worry that Celia would turn out to be a fifty-year-old man with a shovel and a van if they knew that Dimple met her online. (She wasn't. Dimple had checked her out on Facebook.) It had been hard enough to convince them to let her drive herself. Dimple wasn't completely sure they grasped the concept of college—that, in just a couple of weeks, she'd be living apart from them, making decisions for herself. Alone.

Her phone beeped with an incoming text.

I. Cannot. Wait.

Celia, who'd also just graduated high school, lived in San Francisco with her parents. She would start at SFSU in the fall.

Me either! Do you want to meet up for lunch when I get there?

Sure! How about on campus? They have a great pizza place.

Sounds awesome.

After they'd settled the details, Dimple sank back in her bed and smiled. It was all falling into place. Her life was finally beginning.

Rishi

Ma performed the ritual in the driveway. She'd set a bowl of *kumkum* powder dissolved in water on a silver tray, and she circled it around his face and shoulders. Her lips moved feverishly in prayer to Lord Hanuman as she asked that good fortune smile on her oldest son. When the ritual was completed, she stepped back and smiled up at him, tears glistening in her eyes.

Pappa put his hand on Rishi's shoulder and squeezed once, briefly, before letting go. "You have everything you need?"

Pappa said "everything" with a meaningful weightiness, and Rishi nodded solemnly, knowing what he meant.

"Call us the minute you get there," Ma said.

"We're in Atherton. It'll take him, like, an hour to get to SFSU. He takes longer baths." Ashish was a few feet away, shooting hoops while he waited for his friends to swing by and pick him up for whatever fun weekend activity they had planned—contracting hep C or maybe alcohol poisoning.

His mother glared over her shoulder. "Yes, but this is a special trip. He could be meeting your future *bhabhi*, Ashish. Have some respect."

"Don't worry, I'll call as soon as I can," Rishi said quickly. Then he bent down and touched their feet. "Bye, Ma, Pappa."

He felt his chest swelling with emotion as he got in the car and drove off, his parents waving like mad in the rearview mirror. Something bigger than him threatened to flatten Rishi, something bigger than all of them. He could swear, as he drove down the tree-lined street in the late morning light, that he saw dozens and dozens of flickering ghosts—his grandparents and their parents and *their* parents—watching him, smiling. Escorting him to his destiny.

Dimple

Dimple stretched out her stiff muscles as she made her way to the cluster of stores and restaurants across from the parking garage. The afternoon sunlight was luxuriant on her skin; she'd been sequestered in her car for the past three hours. The open air of the city felt positively therapeutic after all that inhaled air-conditioning.

Dimple had gotten here faster than she'd anticipated, so she'd texted Celia to tell her that she was here, but to take her time. She would explore the campus a bit while she waited. But first—Starbucks.

She needed some caffeine in her system before she called home to tell her parents she'd arrived. Mamma was sure to have another litany of questions and warnings about American college boys. Dimple had to actually roll up the car window *while* Mamma was talking this morning so she could leave on time. Even Papa had given up and gone inside after twenty minutes. The woman was relentless, with the jaw muscles of a jungle predator.

The upside was that because she'd been so worried about being late, Dimple had driven ten above the speed limit the entire time, refused to stop for breaks, and made it early.

"An iced coffee, please," she told the cute male barista with the septum piercing. The coffee shop buzzed, college students mingling like showy tropical fish with their brightly colored hair. The sheer scope and number of tattoos and piercings would have Mamma fainting. Dimple adored it.

Clutching her iced drink, she made her way outside and meandered over to a stone fountain of the SFSU gator (which was turned off; thank you, drought conditions). Dimple sat on the lip of the bowl and tipped her face up to the sky, soaking up the sunshine and thinking about how she'd spend the next hour. Should she go by the Insomnia Con building now or do that with Celia later? She wanted to stop by the library, too, to see if they had the new Jenny Lindt memoir. . . .

Man, the freedom made her feel almost drunk. She really did love her family, *so* much, but being at home was starting to feel like wearing an iron corset, painful and breathless and pinchy in all the wrong places. Although, she had to hand it to them: sending her here was unprecedented.

Dimple didn't know what had brought on her parents' sudden change of heart about Insomnia Con, but maybe she was having more of an influence on them than she thought. Maybe they were *finally* beginning to realize she was her own person, with a divergent, more modern belief system that renounced the patriarchal dynamics of their time—

There was a sort of scuffling sound nearby, and Dimple opened her eyes, startled. An Indian boy about her age was gazing down at her with the weirdest, goofiest grin on his face. His straight, jet-black hair flopped onto his forehead.

"Hello, future wife," he said, his voice bubbling with glee. "I can't wait to get started on the rest of our lives!"

Dimple stared at him for the longest minute. The only word her brain was capable of producing, in various tonal permutations, was: What? *What?*

Dimple didn't know what to think. Serial killer? Loony bin escapee? Strangely congenial mugger? Nothing made sense. So she did the only thing she could think to do in the moment—she flung her iced coffee at him and ran the other way.

CHAPTER 5

Rishi

Oh, crap. Oh, no, no, no. He'd been *kidding.*

As Rishi watched the rapidly retreating back of his possible future wife, he realized he'd totally freaked her out because of his poorly executed joke. This was why he usually left the humor to Ashish.

Wringing out the cold coffee from his shirt, he considered running after her, explaining himself. But he knew by the mileage she was clocking right then that she was probably not in the head space to really listen.

Shoot. What if she called her parents to tell them what a psycho the Patel boy was, and then they called *his* parents? Rishi whipped out his cell phone and dialed home to warn Ma and Pappa.

"Hello?" His mom answered, breathless, anticipatory.

"Ma?" Hearing her voice made him feel even guiltier, more ashamed at how he'd handled the first meeting. All that hard work they must've put into arranging this . . .

"*Haan, beta!* Did you arrive safely?"

"I did, but—"

"Wonderful!"

"No, no, it's not." Rishi hung his head, inhaling the smell of coffee wafting off him. He sank down on the sunbaked lip of the fountain where a moment before, his future had been perched.

A pause. *"Kya hua?"*

"You might get a phone call from Dimple Shah's parents soon. I just met her." Rishi's voice was a croak. "And it didn't go well. I totally blew it."

He heard a scuffling sound and his mom saying something softly to someone else. Then his dad was on the phone. "Rishi?"

Rishi squeezed his eyes shut. "Pappa, I'm sorry. Vijay uncle and Leena auntie are probably going to call you, and they're not going to be happy."

"Tell me what happened."

"I saw her; Dimple Shah. So I walked up to her and made a totally stupid joke about us beginning the rest of our lives together. And she . . . she threw her coffee at me and ran away."

A lengthy pause. "I see. And . . . did you introduce yourself before you made the joke?"

Rishi's eyes flew open. Dammit. Was he *really* that much of a moron? "No. No, I didn't."

"So a perfect stranger approaches her on the street, tells her he wants them to begin the rest of their lives together. It doesn't seem to be much of an overreaction to panic, does it?"

Rishi's heart lifted, just a smidge. Could it be that that was all it was—she'd needed context? Dimple hadn't even known who he was! He smiled a little. "No, I guess not." Then his smile fell again. "She's not going to want to talk to me again after that."

His mother said something in the background, and Pappa replied,

"*Haan*, that's not a bad idea." To Rishi, he said, "Do you have . . . the special gift?"

Rishi frowned a little. "In my duffel bag in the car, yeah. But you don't think it's a little soon?"

"It might be in the usual circumstances, *beta*, but now it's the perfect way to show her who you are. Apologize for your mistake. She's probably a very traditional girl, Rishi, if Vijay and Leena are any sort of indicator."

Rishi's brow cleared. He could handle this. "Okay. You're probably right."

"One minute. *Ma se baat karo.*" A scratching sound as he handed the phone to Ma.

His mother's voice was eager, bright. "Tell me, Rishi, what did you think of her?"

Hmm. What *had* he thought of her? To be honest, he'd been too crazy nervous to really process everything he'd seen. He'd gotten out of the parking garage and was thinking about getting a bottle of water at Starbucks. And then she was just *there*, right in front of him, like some sort of huge cosmic coincidence personified. Sitting on that fountain, face upturned, drinking in the sunshine like a flower, looking completely beatific. Her curls had been wild, desperate for a comb. She'd been dressed in a kurta top, which he liked.

But the way she'd looked at him—at first aghast, then hostile. And after that, totally and utterly murderous.

Rishi was really lucky all she'd done was throw iced coffee at him. She looked like she'd be capable of much more, like breaking his nose or a brutal fishhook. "Uh . . . she seemed . . . spirited."

His mother's peals of laughter traveled down the phone line.

28

"Spirited! Good, good. Pappa would have said the same thing about me twenty-five years ago."

Sure, Rishi thought. But Ma's spirit had a soft, tender underside. Dimple Shah he wasn't so sure about. Something about the way her brown eyes spit fire behind those huge glasses . . . "Yeah. Maybe I should go, try to find her at the dorms." The prospect made him uneasy, but the longer he waited, the worse this was going to be. Maybe once he explained himself and showed her what he'd brought, she'd be flattered. Maybe they could have a laugh about the whole thing.

Dimple

If this was San Francisco, Dimple would have to invest in some heavy-duty pepper spray. She'd barely been in the city fifteen minutes and already she'd been accosted by a predator. Maybe she and Celia could take some Krav Maga classes on the side, learn how to use their attacker's size against them. Not that that dude had been very big. He was sort of built like Chris Messina, on the shorter side and slim, but strong-looking. She wondered what his deal was. In any case, iced coffee or not, Dimple could've taken him. She was no delicate flower.

Adjusting her messenger bag, Dimple made her way to the coed dorms. She supposed she could bring her small suitcase in at some other time; she was too tired right now. (Thank you, psycho mugger, for the lack of caffeine.) She could set her stuff down, look into getting a map of the campus, and then head over to that pizza place to wait for Celia.

The dorm was a tiny rectangular room, just big enough for two twin beds and two desks. The inexplicable scent of wood shavings hung heavy in the air. The walls were institutional gray-brown; the carpet, ditto. On the headboard of one of the beds, some past student had inscribed, with a Sharpie and a careful hand: *ipsa scientia potestas est.* Dimple loved it, *all* of it, instantly and with an unadulterated passion.

It was beginning. Her freedom, her independence, her period of learning—about herself, about the world, about her career. She was finally doing it. Here she wouldn't be Dimple Shah, wayward, Americanized daughter of immigrant parents; she'd be just Dimple Shah, future web developer. People would judge her on her brain, not her lack of makeup. There would be no cliques like high school. Everyone was here of their own volition, to learn, to teach, to work together.

She sent a quick text to Mamma and Papa:

Got here safely! Dorm is nice. Papa, please take your medicine—and no more sweets today!!

Then, smiling, she shut the door behind her and made her way past chattering students, here for various summer programs, down to the main lobby.

Rishi spotted her again in the main lobby, looking at the rack of dusty campus maps. He hadn't even checked into his room yet; he was so nervous he was going to miss her, he'd run to his car to get the gift and then run back here to find her. All the Insomnia Con students had been given rooms in the same dorm, so it wasn't hard to figure out where she would be.

But now, standing in the somewhat empty lobby, he wondered if she'd freak out again. She didn't seem to be holding beverages of any kind, which was good. This time, Rishi thought, he'd be sedate. Chill. Breezy.

Rishi smoothed his hair back, adjusted his shirt collar, and started forward.

Dimple

The maps all looked ancient, but Dimple supposed they would have to do. She grabbed one at random and turned around.

And there *he* was again, mouth open, staring at the back of her head.

"What the heck?" Before she'd even fully thought about it, Dimple had reached out and sliced him with the edge of the map.

"Ow!" Clutching his forearm, the psycho staggered backward a few steps.

Huh. Not much of a predator if all it took was a paper cut to deter him. "Why are you following me?" Dimple took what she hoped was a menacing step forward, map held out as a weapon.

The boy eyed it warily, letting his arms drop. He was dressed pretty sanely for a psychotic attacker, Dimple thought, in a button-down blue shirt (sporting a wet patch still; her coffee, she guessed proudly)

31

with the sleeves rolled up and well fitted jeans. His eyes, the color of deep caramel, were almost innocent-looking. It just showed, you could never trust appearances. "Well, I was about to explain that when you attacked me."

"*I* attacked *you*?" Dimple said slowly, eyebrows raised at his indignant tone. "Are you serious? You've been following me, being totally creepy—"

He hung his head a little, the tips of his ears pink, the same way Papa's got when he was embarrassed. "I'm sorry. 'Creepy' wasn't what I was going for."

"Sure, buddy, whatever." Dimple stepped carefully around him, alert for any lunging. "Just stay away from me, or I'll call the campus police."

"No, wait!"

"I mean it!" She turned again, brandishing the map.

"Dimple, please, just let me explain. This isn't what—"

She lowered the map and frowned. "How do you know my name?"

Rishi

Man, she was taking a really long time to put two and two together. Weren't Stanford students supposed to be bright?

"That's what I'm trying to tell you," Rishi said patiently. "It's me. Rishi Patel." He waited for the light to dawn, for her to smile, smack her forehead, and say, *Of course!* But she just continued to frown at him, thick eyebrows knitted together. She was actually kind of scary.

"Oh . . . kay. Is that supposed to mean something to me?"

Rishi stared at her. This was a joke. Right? Or maybe she was just incredibly embarrassed and didn't want to admit she'd made a mistake. Maybe he should make this easier for her. "Hey, it's okay." He smiled. "This is all a little out there, I know."

She shook her head. "Look, I don't know what you're talking about."

She looked too sincere to be messing with him. He felt the beginnings of doubt begin to creep in. "You're Dimple Shah, right? From Fresno? The daughter of Vijay and Leena Shah?"

Her eyes widened and she stepped back. "You know an awful lot about me."

Oh great. Now he was freaking her out again. He should just say it. "That's because we . . . we're supposed to be getting married."

Dimple

Not this nonsense again with the marriage delusions. But, she had to admit, he seemed genuine. Sincere. Something dark and heavy began to squirm just under her diaphragm. "Wait. *How* do you know about me and my parents?"

He looked totally confused. "Because our parents are childhood friends. They set this whole thing up. Your parents mailed my parents a picture of you, and vice versa." Then his face cleared. "And . . . this is the first you've heard of any of this." It wasn't a question.

Dimple was afraid she might be sick. If she actually had anything in her stomach, she would've been. The world tilted and spun, and there was a ringing in her ears. *This* was why Mamma and Papa had been so open about letting her go to Insomnia Con. *This* was what all the weird, guilty looks were about. And that damn Ritu auntie had probably been in on it too.

"Hey, are you okay?" The boy—Rishi—came forward and put a gentle hand on her elbow, steadying her.

Dimple wrenched her elbow away from him, heat flooding her cheeks. She really wanted to slice him with the map again, but managed to resist. "This is ridiculous. Okay? I can't even *believe*—how do I know you're not making this up, huh? Maybe this is just some sort of cheap, twisted pickup line." Dimple couldn't help it; all the anger and fury she should've been directing at Mamma and Papa was being misplaced and directed at Rishi instead.

She saw his cheeks color, his jaw harden. But instead of lashing back at her, he reached into his pocket and pulled out an envelope, from which he extracted a small picture. It was her.

Dimple remembered that . . . it was from last Diwali, when Mamma had insisted she go to the celebration put on by the Indian Association. She'd wanted to go to a local showing of the documentary *Bridegroom* instead. Hence the scowl. Now that she thought about it though, all her pictures pretty much looked like that.

"And . . ." Rishi reached into his pocket again and pulled out a small jewelry box.

Oh God, no. Please don't let that be what she thought it was. He snapped it open. Nestled inside was a ring made out of gold so pure it looked almost orange.

"My great-grandmother's ring. My parents have kept this for me since I was born." Rishi paused, looking down at the small, square ring. His expression was solemn, like he was holding something that could shape fortunes and mold destinies. When he looked back up at Dimple, it hit her how much this really meant to him. This wasn't just an arranged marriage to Rishi; this was the rich fabric of history, stretched through time and space. "Believe me, I wouldn't use this for a cheap, twisted pickup line." He was speaking slowly, his words and tone measured, but she could tell he was angry.

God, now she felt like a total jerk. It wasn't his fault they were in this heinous situation. Dimple felt the anger drain out of her. She blew out a breath. "I'm . . . I'm sorry. I just, I was totally caught off guard."

He was staring at her openmouthed.

She frowned. "What?"

"I just didn't expect you to apologize. You're so . . ."

Dimple waited, one eyebrow raised.

"Spirited," Rishi finished, in a way that implied he'd considered, and then decided against, using a much less complimentary adjective. He put the ring back in his pocket, and after a moment, held out the picture to her. She took it. Rubbing the back of his neck, he said, "So . . . ah, this is awkward."

"Yeah," Dimple began. And then she stopped. "You know what? Why is this awkward for *us*? The only people it should be awkward for are my parents." She pulled out her cell phone right there in the lobby. "I'm going to give them a piece of my mind."

Rishi nodded slowly. "Okay, well, I guess I'll leave you to it then."

She grabbed his arm. "Oh no. You stay right there. You're their victim too."

Dimple dialed home and wasn't surprised when it went to voice mail. "So. You two think you're being clever, do you?" she said in her most biting voice, her breath coming hard and fast. "What did you *think* was going to happen? That I'd get here and fall into his arms?" She saw Rishi blush and hurried to add, "I'm sure he'll make some girl very happy someday. But that girl is not me." She jabbed righteously at her own chest. "So I hope you know you've ruined *everything*. I hope you're ready to tell your friends—" She covered the cell phone mic and spoke to Rishi. "What are their names?"

"Kartik and Sunita," he whispered back.

Dimple turned back to the phone. "—Kartik and Sunita that you've effectively ruined your decades-long friendship because you decided to *deceive* your only daughter. Good-bye."

She hung up, heart still racing, adrenaline coursing through her veins. "Ridiculous," she muttered, hands on her hips. Then, looking up at Rishi, she said, "So, what, do you live in San Francisco?"

He shook his head. "I live in Atherton, with my parents and brother. I'm here for Insomnia Con, like you."

"Oh." At least he wasn't here solely for her. "So what are you going to do now?"

Rishi shrugged. "I had planned for us to get to know each other, but obviously that's not going to happen." He smiled a little crookedly, and Dimple saw the strain in it. He was trying hard not to show how disappointed he really was. She felt a stab of sympathy for him and a harsher, meaner stab of anger at her parents. "I'll probably hang out in my room for a while." He raised his hand stiffly in good-bye and began to walk away toward the elevators.

Something inside her sank at the sight of his retreating back. She didn't want him to go just yet. Dimple heard herself call out, "Wait!"

Rishi turned, eyebrows raised.

"If you want, you could, you know, come to lunch with me and my friend Celia. If you're hungry, that is." She stopped short, unsure where, exactly, the invitation had come from. It was obviously just that she felt some sort of kinship with him because of what had happened, Dimple told herself quickly. They were like two trauma survivors, the victims of her parents. She was just being a decent human being. Nothing more.

Rishi smiled again, but *fully* this time, unrestrained. It was like watching the sun rise, Dimple thought, or the streetlights come on at dusk. Gradual, powerful, brilliant, in a way.

"Thanks," he said, walking toward her. "I'd like that."

CHAPTER 6

Rishi

They walked to Little Gator Pizzeria side by side, the silence stretching on. Rishi was hyperaware of everything; the way Dimple felt walking beside him. How he could see the top of her head. How the curls on her left side were invading his personal space, and how he didn't mind, not one bit. When the breeze blew, he could smell her shampoo, like coconuts and jasmine. Oh gods. He'd just inhaled deeply, and now she was looking at him funny.

Rishi tried to smile casually. "So, who's this friend? Do you know each other from Fresno?"

Dimple shook her head and adjusted her messenger bag. "No, we met in the Insomnia Con forum and decided to room together."

He stared at her, waiting for the punch line. "You're kidding. Right?"

She raised an eyebrow. "No?"

"You seriously met a stranger online and decided you'd live with . . . 'her' for two months, sight unseen?"

She sighed. "It's six weeks. And there's no need to make the air quotes around the word 'her.' It really is a she. I checked her out on Facebook."

Rishi huffed a laugh, incredulous. He was beginning to doubt Stanford's reputation. "Do you honestly not see the logical fallacy there? You're checking to see if this person's online persona is fake . . . online."

"Well . . . ," Dimple said as they rounded the corner and came to a stop in front of the Little Gator Pizzeria. The smell of grease and cheese clotted the air. Her eyes widening behind her glasses, she leaned in closer. "Either we're about to get hacked to pieces by a serial killer or we're about to enjoy some pizza. Only time will tell."

Rishi reached out to get the door for her, but with a flourish, she opened the door herself and walked in.

A girl in the corner with a trendy, caramel-colored, two-foot-tall mass of curls and huge hazel eyes grinned and stood, grabbing Dimple in a hug she clearly hadn't been expecting. She wore giant heels that made her tower over Dimple, but without them, Rishi guessed they'd be about the same height. "Dimple! You made it!"

Dimple pulled back and grinned. "How did you know it was me?"

"Facebook, of course," the girl said, laughing.

Dimple tossed a triumphant look Rishi's way. He sighed and made his way over.

"Oh, hello." The girl smiled a little suggestively. "Who's this? You didn't tell me you were bringing a *friend*." Somehow, she made the word "friend" sound naughty.

Dimple sat, and, after a moment, scooched over so Rishi could sit next to her in the booth. He tried to ignore the way his pulse stuttered a bit at that. "That's because I didn't know," she said. "Celia Ramirez, this is Rishi Patel. Rishi, this is Celia."

"*Enchanté*," Celia said, taking his hand. "I ordered a large pepperoni pizza; hope that's okay with the two of you."

"Totally," Dimple said, just as Rishi said, "I don't eat meat."

They looked at each other. "I'll go order a cheese," he said after a beat, sliding back out of the booth. *Add another item to the "1,001 ways we're incompatible" list,* Rishi thought. As he ordered at the counter, he watched Dimple, totally relaxed in a way she hadn't been with him, talking to Celia. And not for the first time in the past hour, Rishi wondered how his parents could've made such a big mistake.

Dimple

"Seriously?" Celia said, ogling Rishi openmouthed.

"Stop staring at him," Dimple hissed. "And yes, seriously. My parents are so deranged it's not even funny."

"And he brought his great-grandmother's ring. To your first meeting." Celia, clearly not well versed in the way of certain Indian families, could not seem to wrap her head around this fact.

Dimple sighed. "I really just feel kind of bad for him. I mean, it's got to be embarrassing. But he's taking it like a champ. He's a lot calmer than I am. I cannot *wait* to rip my parents a new one." She shredded her straw wrapper with gusto. "They can't hide from me forever."

"It's sort of romantic," Celia said, smiling a little, turning back to Dimple. "Don't you think?"

"Romantic!" Dimple sputtered on her sip of water. Setting her glass back down, she said, "Please. I'm freaking eighteen years old. Marriage is the last thing on my mind."

"Well, I'm seventeen, so right back at you," Celia said. "But still. I mean, just the fact that, you know. He *could* potentially be the one. There's a kind of magic in that."

Dimple tossed a glance over at Rishi. He was walking over to the soda fountain. Every movement of his was sure, calm, confident. "I don't know," she said, finally, just as the waiter brought their pizzas over. "I guess I just don't see it."

Rishi

When Rishi sat down, there was a weird sort of hesitant, crackling silence in the air. He sighed and looked at Celia. "She told you, didn't she? About the arranged marriage thing?"

Dimple stiffened beside him, and Celia nodded. "She did."

"And you think it's crazy," he said.

"Uh-huh." Celia chewed the giant piece of pizza she'd bitten off before speaking. "I also think it's romantic." She grinned. "A predestined romance."

Rishi smiled. Maybe this girl wasn't a serial killer after all. "Sort of. But arranged marriages are more about practicalities than romance. Compatibility, a long-term partnership. That sort of thing."

Beside him Dimple snorted. He turned to her. "I'm guessing you don't agree."

"Compatibility may be what it's ostensibly about," Dimple

41

responded, pushing her glasses up on her nose. "But it's really just a way for our parents to control us. I mean, that's even how the institution of marriage was born. So fathers could form alliances and use their children—especially their daughters—as pawns in their battle for power." She ripped off a piece of pizza and chewed angrily.

Jeez, did she ever relax? "Well, since our parents aren't rajas and ranis, I don't think that's what it's about."

Celia laughed. "'Raja'—that's *king*, right?"

"Right." Rishi smiled. "And 'rani' is *queen*."

"So you're bilingual?" Celia asked.

Rishi nodded. "Yeah, I learned Hindi first, before English. My parents were really adamant about that. They're technically from Gujarat, but they're third generation Mumbaiites, so they speak Hindi. Mumbai is, like, this huge melting pot of people from other Indian states, so apparently everyone speaks this special version of what my parents call 'Bombay Hindi.'" His eyes were far off and he had this small smile on his lips. It was obvious he loved talking about this stuff.

"That's so cool," Celia said. "I wish I knew more than, like, five words of Spanish. Have you ever been to Mumbai?"

"Are you really interested in web development, or are you just here for this?" Dimple interjected, gesturing between herself and him. If Rishi didn't know better, he'd say she was irritated at how he and Celia were hitting it off. *Jealousy?* he wondered hopefully. But he had to be practical—she likely had just wanted to have an impassioned discussion about the evils of arranged marriages and controlling parents and was disappointed it wasn't coming to fruition.

Rishi shrugged and ate another bite of pizza. "Both. I mean, I'm starting at MIT in the fall for computer science and engineering, so this is a good thing to have on my CV."

"But web development isn't your passion." Dimple's eyes narrowed. "It's not your dream."

"No," Rishi said slowly. "I guess not."

"You spent a thousand dollars on something that you're not passionate about?" She stared at him, seemingly dumbfounded.

"So he wants to expand his horizons; don't be so judgy," Celia said.

"Whatever. You just better not be my partner," Dimple muttered, turning back to her pizza.

"Believe me, that sounds totally fine to me," Rishi said. He felt the stirrings of irritation. Why did she have to be so . . . intense? What did it matter to her whether or not he wanted to marry web development and have its babies? "You know, I think I'm going to head back to my dorm," he said, wiping his hands on his napkin. "I need to unpack and all that."

"Aw, are you sure?" Celia said, and he got the feeling she genuinely liked his company.

"Yeah." He smiled. "But I'll see you both tomorrow in class."

The silence was heavy while Rishi stood and left a hefty tip on the table so they wouldn't have to. He knew they were just waiting for him to leave so they could talk about him. Sighing, he headed to the door and stepped out into the afternoon sunshine.

CHAPTER 7

Dimple

The bell above the door clanged shut as Rishi disappeared onto the sidewalk. Dimple continued munching on her pizza, ignoring the tiny pit in her stomach, even though she could feel Celia's gaze heavy on her face.

"A-hem."

Dimpled rolled her eyes. "No one says 'ahem.' You're supposed to just clear your throat."

Celia waved an insouciant hand. Her many wooden bangles clattered together. "So pretend I just cleared my throat. Did you have to be so mean to him?"

"I wasn't mean, just . . . honest. Wouldn't it be crueler to make him think there was some hope that I'd come around and just embrace all of this?" She took a sip of water, feeling the pit in her stomach grow. Guilt, she thought. It was guilt. Celia had a point: Rishi was a perfectly nice guy, and Dimple had sentenced him to a thousand lashes of her sharp tongue. *Speak first, think later*, that was her default setting, no matter how she tried to control it. Dimple sat up straighter, quashing those thoughts. She'd sent Rishi Patel away—there was no reason to be all weak and second-guess her choices now.

Celia wound one of her long curls around her finger. "I guess." Dimple wondered how she could stand having hair that fell to her waist. She'd have to be careful not to mention this to Mamma, or she'd probably phone Celia for tips on how to convince Dimple to grow her hair out too. And it wouldn't matter that they'd never spoken to each other before in their lives.

"Okay, I'm done talking about boys." Dimple leaned forward and smiled. "What do you think the prize is going to be for this year's Insomnia Con?"

"Ooh." Celia rubbed her hands together, eyes shining. "I don't know, but it's definitely something epic. There were rumblings that they really went all out this year. Everyone thinks it's going to be a personalized letter with feedback from Jenny Lindt, but I'm guessing a cash prize of, like, ten grand."

Dimple shook her head. "No, I bet it's something way crazy cooler than that. They don't generally do cash prizes with Insomnia Con; that's usually what they do for the talent show about halfway in, remember? Maybe it'll be, like, feedback and a signed copy of Jenny Lindt's next memoir or something."

Celia laughed. "Your Jenny Lindt obsession knows no bounds. You know what your big project's going to be yet?"

"I have a pretty solid idea," Dimple said, trying not to show how ridiculously excited she was about it. She'd thought of it last year. And honestly, she was going to code this app somehow whether or not she came to Insomnia Con, but the idea of doing it on such a large scale was even more thrilling. She'd checked—there was nothing on the market quite like it. She couldn't share it with Celia; that was one of the rules of Insomnia Con. Only your partner could know what you were working on. "I haven't fully fleshed it out, though. You?"

"I'm still thinking about it; nothing's really jumped out at me. I wouldn't mind working with you on your idea." Celia grinned. "Do you think they'll make us partners?"

"I've heard roommates don't generally get made partners," Dimple said, pushing her empty plate aside. "But fingers crossed."

When her phone rang early the next morning, Dimple was dreaming that she was accepting an award onstage from Jenny Lindt. Jenny beamed at her as she said something that Dimple was sure were effervescent compliments, but every time Jenny opened her mouth, all Dimple could hear were beeps. "Sorry?" Dimple kept saying, in her dream. "Can you repeat that?"

Finally, Celia called out from across the room, "Dimple, it's your phone! For the love of God, answer it before I lose my mind!"

"Sorry," Dimple mumbled, reaching for her phone on her nightstand. She silenced it and looked at the screen. Anger shot through her, red-hot. Suddenly she was very much awake. Grabbing it, she strode out into the hallway, shutting the door quietly behind her. "Mamma."

"Dimple!" her mother said, sounding forcefully jolly. "*Kaisi ho, beti?* Did you unpack? How is the campus?"

"Oh no, no. You don't get to wake me up and ask me about the campus. Let's talk about the *real* issue here, shall we?"

"I woke you up? But why you're not already awake? It's the first day!"

Dimple squeezed the phone tighter. "Because the seminar doesn't start at the butt crack of dawn! Besides which, that is not even the point. Can you please focus, Mamma? What the heck is up with Rishi Patel?"

"Up with him . . . ?" Mamma feigned ignorance to slang, which just infuriated Dimple more. Seriously, where did she get this stuff? "I don't know what you mean, Dimple—"

"Mamma, please! Why did you and Papa do this? Why are you trying to set me up with some dude I've never heard of before in my life? You know that's not why I'm here! You know how important this is to me!" Dimple felt tears rising, pressing hot and furious against her eyelids. For once, why couldn't her parents just be on the same page as her?

"Dimple, *beti, math ro.*" Mamma sounded genuinely upset now. "Don't cry. We just wanted you to meet him. He is a good boy, from a good family. You have a lot in common."

Dimple swiped at her eyes, ignoring the looks of a couple of early risers probably headed out to coffee. They were all blurry to her anyway, without her glasses on. "Don't you see? I. Don't. Care. He could be crafted from unicorn dust and jelly beans, and I still wouldn't want to have anything to do with him. I'm not interested in a marriage partner, Mamma, now or ten years from now!"

There was a shuffling, like Mamma was holding the phone away from her. She heard her mumble in Hindi, "Vijay, you talk to her." A pause, and then, "I don't know. Something about unicorns. I don't understand."

Dimple rolled her eyes and sighed, waiting for Papa to come on. "Dimple *beti*?"

His voice, deep and soothing, comforting and familiar as a

cotton T-shirt, made the lump rise in her throat again. How could two people who loved her so much simply not *get* her on such a basic, essential level? "*Haan*, Papa." She drew in a shuddering breath. "I don't understand why you lied to me. Both of you. You pretended you were agreeing to Insomnia Con for me, but this is . . . it's ridiculous, Papa. I'm not getting married."

"No one wants you to get married now, Dimple. We just wanted to know if you and the Patel boy would be compatible. Down the road, who knows what might happen? It's not easy finding a good Indian family here in the States, *na*." He paused, and a hard edge had crept into his voice when he spoke again. "*Usne kuch kiya?*"

Dimple sank down against the wall, the fight going out of her. Papa's voice, his gentle, calm, reasonable demeanor, often had that effect. "No, he didn't do anything bad. He was perfectly fine, a gentleman." The truth was, her parents had done a good job picking someone who wasn't a total douche nozzle. "But, Papa, I'm just not in that place of thinking of him—or any boy—in that way. Can't you understand that?"

Papa's breath crackled down the line. There was no judgment or anger in his voice when he said, finally, "I understand."

She blinked. Was it going to be that easy? "Really? What about Mamma?"

She heard Papa's footsteps as he walked somewhere, likely away from Mamma. "She will understand also. We just want your happiness, Dimple. That is the most important thing."

The lump was back. Dimple had to swallow a few times. "And what about Insomnia Con? Can I still stay even if there's no chance of me and Rishi becoming a thing?"

She heard the smile in Papa's voice. "Of course. When I said I think it's a good career decision, I meant it."

Dimple hung her head, relief and love and joy overpowering her. "Thank you, Papa."

"*Mujhse bas ek vada karo*, Dimple. Promise me just one thing."

Warily, Dimple said, "What's that?"

"Win the Insomnia Con."

She grinned. He must've really read the website she sent him. "Oh, I plan to," she said. "Don't you worry, Papa."

CHAPTER 8

Dimple

Dimple felt a weird energy pulsing through her as she and Celia walked to the Andrew G. Spurlock building, where Insomnia Con was hosted every year. In spite of the heavy fog rolling in, it was like some filmy gauze had been cleared from the atmosphere, or like a particularly nauseating stench had been done away with. Everything felt fresh and bright, swept clean. There were no expectations on her anymore except to conquer the heck out of Insomnia Con. And that was exactly how she liked it.

So she hadn't exactly spoken to Mamma again; she was sure that wasn't going to be a fun conversation. And whenever she thought of Rishi—whom she hadn't seen at all today, in spite of being hyper-aware and spotting about a dozen different guys of his same build and height—she felt a twinge deep inside her. Because he wasn't a bad guy. In fact, he seemed to be really nice. There was an easy flow to their conversations; a sort of instantaneous shorthand, maybe because they came from similar backgrounds. If they'd been intro-duced under any other circumstances, they might've been friends. Maybe. Even with their similarities, they were just different enough that things could've been interesting. Or, you know, totally annoying. Whatever. Why was she even wasting brain space on this?

"Look at them," she whispered to Celia, refocusing her attention on the dozens of other Insomnia Con students milling in the same general direction as her and Celia, 98 percent of whom were male. "We can totally take them, right?"

Celia made a sort of grunting noise from behind her Starbucks that sounded like "toma," but Dimple was fairly certain was meant to be a "totally." It was eleven o'clock in the morning, and the girl was barely awake. Dimple got the impression that Celia was even less of a morning person than she was. Celia blinked and looked around, a little bit more animatedly. "Hey, I don't see your friend Rishi."

Dimple didn't want to admit it, but she'd noticed that too. "Me either."

"Huh. Maybe he dropped out."

Dimple wondered why that thought sat like a ball of lead in her stomach.

Rishi

He'd watched her go out the front doors with Celia, waited five minutes, and then headed out after them. He didn't want to be a pain in the ass; Rishi knew when he wasn't wanted.

Ma and Pappa had called for an update, and it had been so difficult to tell them the truth: that it probably wasn't going to work out with him and Dimple. She just . . . wasn't where he was. He could tell they were disappointed, but they'd tried to put on a brave front. And when they'd asked if he wanted to go back home, he'd seriously considered it. But then he'd decided to stay. It was too late to get a refund anyway, and besides, he didn't want Dimple Shah to think he'd come all this way simply for her. Even if in a way he had. So his plan now was to go to Insomnia Con, learn a bit about web development, and then head off to MIT. He had nothing to lose.

He walked in the weird misty fog listening to the students around him chatter like mockingbirds. He wondered how it could be that he just never fit in with his peers. It had always been that way; apart from a few friends in the comic book fan community, he'd never really been able to relate.

And it wasn't just that he took things so seriously when it came to being a good son or following the path his parents had so carefully laid down for him. It was something inside *him* that felt different. Off. Like he never truly showed the world who he was except when he was making art.

But he'd known since the beginning that being an artist was a phase. It had to be. Creative pursuits had no place in the practicalities of real life. That's just how things worked, and Rishi was fine with it. Perhaps it was the burden of being the first son; Ashish certainly didn't have similar compunctions about his sports. But the thing was, there was already a framework for athletes to make it. Ashish could use his skills to put himself through college, to really make a name for himself, to open more doors. He was that good. Rishi was good too, but who really took comic book art seriously? People didn't tune in en masse to watch comic book artists sketch on

TV, did they? They didn't have Super Sketch parties. Exactly.

Rishi looked up—and blinked. Was this some weird conjuring of his imagination? But no, up ahead was a giant banner on which someone had drawn the manga characters Madoka and Sayaka from the anime *Madoka Magica* as students with SFSU T-shirts and satchels. SFSU ART DEPARTMENT, it said underneath. At a table in front of the banner, students with hipster glasses and uncombed hair hung out, talking about whether Ferd Johnson was really the genius behind the 1920s comic strip *Moon Mullins*. Rishi blinked again. As if by some weird art law of attraction, he found his legs carrying him forward.

The male student, reedy and tall with a healthy smattering of acne across both cheeks, looked up and smiled. "Hey, man. Interested in a degree in art or graphic design?"

No, Rishi thought. *Absolutely not.* "Maybe," he found himself saying instead. "I'm into comic book art."

"Cool, me too." The reedy guy grinned in a *now we can be pals* way. "Hey, you should come to Little Comic Con. SFSU art students put it on, and it's open to the public. Some of our professors will be there too, and we're going to have a few big names." He thrust a flyer at Rishi. "My name's Kevin Keo. Just look for me at the manga booth."

Rishi raised his eyebrows. "Cool." He looked down at the flyer. Little Comic Con was a week away. "I'll try to be there."

"Great. I think you'd really enjoy it. That's what convinced me to apply to SFSU's art program." Kevin smiled.

"Thanks." He glanced at his watch. "Crap. I gotta go." Rishi hurried toward the Spurlock building. Argh. He was going to be late.

Dimple

Dimple was having a crisis. The *good* kind, if such a thing even existed.

All around her, people sat, waiting expectantly for the man at the front of the lecture hall to begin talking. Some of them looked cocky—like that group over there, with the two boys who looked like they'd stepped out of a hipster clothing catalog, and the blond girl who wore a perpetual sneer as if she were too good for all of this. One of the guys, the Indian one, caught her eye and made a creepy-gross gesture with his tongue, then burst out laughing when she looked away, heart thumping. Others, like the group of boys in the very back, all about her height or shorter and some with their baby fat still intact, looked terrified.

Dimple glanced over at Celia and wondered how she and Celia appeared to others. She felt electrified, ready. "Isn't this exciting?" she said for the sixth time since they'd sat down. The instructor at the front, with a full beard and dressed in a colorful vest, was fiddling around with the mic on his podium. There must be about fifty people in here, easy.

"Yes." Celia smiled, a little indulgently, Dimple thought. She definitely wasn't as fired up about all of this as Dimple was.

Dimple had the feeling almost everything came easily to Celia. Her parents were extremely rich, so they'd paid for this without a second thought. It was just another way, like the sailing class Celia had taken already, to fill up the time until college began. "And I spy hot-teeez," Celia added in a singsong, looking right at the group of hipster, model-beautiful people, ogling all of them, boys and girl. This time they didn't notice Dimple looking.

"Welcome to Insomnia Con!" the bearded man boomed from the front of the class, beaming congenially around at all of them. The hall went instantly silent. "My name is Max Framer, and I'm your instructor for Insomnia Con. Please call me Max, not Mr. Framer. It helps us old folks feel young." A few people laughed. "I'm delighted to see another year of shiny new faces, and I'm so psyched to see what you guys come up with this year. Now, before we go on to what I know all of you *really* want to know"—he paused, grinning—"i.e., Insomnia Con's grand prize, I want to go over some basic info and ground rules first. That'll ensure you guys actually listen to the words coming out of my mouth."

There were groans and titters all around. Dimple was sure she'd go nuts if he didn't spill the beans soon.

"So, first, welcome to San Francisco to those who aren't from our wonderful city. A couple of things of note: This may be summer, but the temperature can drop to the sixties or lower at night. You'll also become well acquainted with Karl." A few people like Celia chuckled, but Dimple just frowned, confused.

"What?" she whispered to Celia. "Who's Karl?"

Celia whispered back, "Fog. It's the fog that comes off the water."

Dimple began to nod and then shook her head. "No, that's still confusing. You guys *named* a natural weather phenomenon?"

Celia grinned. "Welcome to San Francisco."

At the front of the room Max was still speaking. "So, next: I'm going to pair you guys up. I don't want you to pair with people you're rooming with, but if you indicated a preference on your application, I've taken that into account." Dimple hadn't met Celia until after she'd already put in an application (well before Papa and Mamma had actually said yes—she had to save her spot, just in case), so they hadn't requested each other. She wondered whom she'd be paired with. Hopefully not that frosty blond girl who looked like she ate little kids for dessert, though Celia probably wouldn't mind, judging from the way she was still darting glances over at that group.

"Secondly," Max continued, "once you find out who your partner is, I want you to begin sitting together so you can start working on your concept right away. Some of you may already have a notion of what you want to do; others won't. That's okay. All we'll focus on for the next two to three days is fleshing out your fledgling ideas. And then we'll get into the fun part—actual development."

There was a noticeable frisson through the room. Everyone was chomping at the bit to get started. Dimple was sure most, like her, knew exactly what they wanted to do.

"Okay," Max said. "Now, for the part you're all waiting for. The grand prize for this year's Insomnia Con." He paused, and the entire lecture hall held its breath. "Jenny Lindt will consider partnering with the winning team to make their app market ready *and* fund the advertising. Your app could go out into the world with the power of Meeting Space, Inc., behind it. Let that sink in."

The latter part of Max's words were swallowed by the pandemonium that erupted. Dimple turned to Celia, her eyes wide. She was in shock; she couldn't think of a single thing to say.

"Well, it's settled then," Celia said casually. "You're just going to have to kick some major butt."

Dimple shook her head. Her mouth was so dry her lips stuck to her teeth. Her head swam until she could barely see. Was this real? "I can't even— Oh. My. God. They've—they've never done anything like this before." This was everything. She had to win.

"All right." Max raised his voice, and everyone calmed down a bit, though there was a new energy in the room, buzzing, thrilling, churning through each of them. "I'm going to begin calling out the partnerships. When I say both your names, come to the front row and have a seat."

The door opened right into the silence. Dimple turned.

Of course. It was Rishi.

CHAPTER 9

Rishi

It was clear he'd missed something vital. Everyone's eyes were bright, their cheeks flushed. Fifty pairs of eyes took in his presence, but forty-nine pairs of them didn't really seem to register him before they swiveled away.

He saw Dimple instantly. Hers were the only pair of eyes that were attempting to incinerate him. He thrust his chin out and stepped forward. He had just as much right to be here as she did.

"Oh, hey, hold on before you take a seat," the dude with the exuberant red beard at the front of the class said. "I'm just about to call out partners, so you may as well take a seat with yours. What's your name?"

"Rishi Patel."

"P . . . Patel . . . ah, there you are. You're with Dimple Shah." The instructor looked up, into the sea of faces. "Dimple Shah?"

Rishi didn't dare look at her. Crap. He'd totally forgotten he'd requested her on his application. It had seemed a good idea at the time, and he'd fully expected her to do it too. He'd thought it'd give them more time together, see how they worked in a partnership.

She stood, and they walked to the front row together, Dimple's back straight, her shoulders set. Her body conveyed anger like a second language; she must have had a lot of practice. As soon as they sat down, she turned to him, eyes flashing. "You requested me, didn't you?"

Rishi rubbed the back of his neck, his cheeks warming. "Yeah, but I thought you might request me, too. Look, I'm going to go up there at the end of class and talk to the dude about reassigning us, okay? So just chill."

"His name is Max. Which you'd know if you'd bothered to be here on time. You even missed the announcement of the grand prize." She looked at him like she was accusing him of torching the redwood forests.

"Oh yeah? What is it?"

Rishi watched as the corners of her lips tugged upward in spite of herself. Her eyes shone behind her glasses, brilliant, fiery. "The winning partners will have a chance to pitch Jenny Lindt their idea. If she likes it, she'll partner on marketing and development!"

Dimple's voice was two octaves higher than usual when she finished, so Rishi knew whatever she said must be a big deal. He racked his brain trying to remember who the heck Jenny Lindt was and came up empty. Okay. He could fake it for now and look her up later.

"Great!" He grinned and tried to mirror her excitement. "That's so cool!"

Dimple leaned in closer, and Rishi caught a waft of that maddening, amazing shampoo again. "Really? You're a Jenny Lindt fan too?" Her face was open, her eyes wide and soft in a way Rishi hadn't seen yet.

"Oh, *totally*," he said, thinking, *I will be by the end of today if it makes you look at me like that.*

Dimple laughed. "I know, she's so great! What's been your favorite part of her success story so far?"

Crap. He kept the smile on his face. Okay, success stories. What did they all have in common? "How she came from nothing and became, you know, *Jenny Lindt.*"

Rishi thought he'd done pretty well, but Dimple was frowning. "She didn't exactly come from 'nothing.' Her parents are both lawyers; they gave her the seed money for Meeting Space. It's in all her interviews." Rishi felt his cheeks heat. Traitorous body.

Dimple's brow cleared. "You don't know a single thing about her, do you?" she asked, leaning back and crossing her arms. "Had you even heard of her before today?"

"You know what? I'm, uh, going to go talk to the instructor guy—Max," he hurried to add, "about reassigning us."

"Yeah." Dimple's eyes were now flat marbles behind her glasses. She would make a good serial killer. "You go do that."

Dimple

He had some nerve, lying to her like that. "The way she came from nothing," Dimple muttered mockingly. What a jerk. Maybe Max would make an exception this one time and reassign her to Celia. Celia knew how important it was to Dimple to win this thing. She'd work her butt off.

Dimple glanced over her shoulder and saw Celia deep in conversation with one of the hipster-model boys, tossing her curls and laughing throatily at a joke. Huh. Or maybe she wouldn't want to be partners anymore.

Dimple turned back around to see Rishi taking a seat beside her again, his cheeks still pink. "What happened? Who are we getting reassigned to?"

"Um, well . . . nobody," he said, wincing a little as he met her gaze. "He said it's too late now. We're just going to have to stick together."

"What? Did you tell him requesting me was a mistake?"

"Yeah. Didn't work."

Dimple stood. "Oh, it's going to work. I'll take care of it myself."

She stalked over to Max. "I'm sorry, I absolutely need to be reassigned," she said as soon as he met her eye, feeling slightly guilty. By doing this, Dimple was effectively saying she couldn't bear to spend a minute with Rishi. Ambition and kindness were warring inside her, and she was choosing ambition . . . again. But she wanted this so badly. So, so badly. "Rishi Patel knows absolutely nothing about Jenny Lindt. I doubt he knows much about web development."

Max smiled. "Well, we're all here to learn, Dimple."

"Right, but he doesn't care about it as much as I do. I need to partner with someone who wants to win just as much."

Max stroked his beard thoughtfully. "Or maybe you need someone who can teach you something, hmm? Maybe Rishi is the universe's way of teaching you how to take a breath and just roll with the punches."

Oh dear God, he was an honest-to-goodness hippie. Curse you, San

Francisco. She could tell he was going to be implacable, so Dimple forced herself to nod and smile. "Mmm. Good point. Thanks anyway."

When Dimple returned to her seat, she tried not to bite Rishi's head off right away. She could tell he was side-eyeing her, trying to figure out how to ask.

"No," she finally bit out. "He won't let us swap partners at this point."

He sighed, and sounding genuinely sympathetic, said, "That sucks. I'm sorry."

"Yeah." Dimple felt that familiar fury boiling inside her, the same one that flowed when Mamma or Papa didn't understand why she wanted to do the things she did. "Sure. I'm sure you're really sorry."

There was a pause. "Look, I don't get why you're so annoyed at me. We already talked about this yesterday." She could tell Rishi was trying to tamp down his own irritation. He got this little crease between his eyebrows when he was mad, Dimple noticed. And then tried to unnotice. "I didn't know your parents were keeping you in the dark about all of this. Heck, I thought you'd be requesting me as your partner too. I thought you were totally on board. So your anger is a little misplaced, don't you think?"

"Misplaced?" Dimple tried not to yell, though with the noise and activity level in the room, she doubted they could attract much attention even if they began flinging things at each other. Which definitely hadn't crossed her mind. Definitely not. "Oh, I don't *think* so. You have no idea, do you? You don't know what this has been like. My mom and dad, they just don't get me, okay? My mom doesn't know why I want to do anything besides get married to the Ideal Indian Husband and settle down. She thinks college is basically just this big

mating ritual. So for me to even *be* here is nothing short of a miracle. For me to even get this chance to follow in Jenny Lindt's footsteps—to actually get a chance to talk to her about my idea? It's the stuff of my wildest fantasies. But even here, where it should just be about me and my career and the things I want to do in this world, I have to contend with you. I have to remember, every single second that I have to look at you, that the only reason I'm here is because my parents expect me to finally fall in line. To become that dutiful Indian daughter they always wanted. I thought this was going to be my chance to just be me, for this whole six weeks to just be about my skills and my talent and my intellect. But it turns out the joke's on me. And you know what? I'm tired of it. I'm tired of it and it *sucks*." She stopped, out of breath, and pushed her glasses back higher onto the bridge of her nose. Her heart pounded; her throat was tight with anger and unshed tears, but she was determined not to let it show how close she was to crying.

Rishi looked . . . well, the scientific term might be "gobsmacked," Dimple supposed. It almost made her want to snort with laughter. His eyes were wide, his face completely frozen in shock.

Yeah, she'd unleashed the fury. But she'd needed to. Problem was, with Rishi and his utter guilelessness, she felt guilty for her ferocity, for subjecting him to an entire lifetime of pent-up rage that had little to do with him. She would never admit that out loud though. Sighing, she sat back and crossed her arms. "Well, you asked," she mumbled.

CHAPTER 10

Rishi

Whooooa.

Obviously, she'd had a lot she needed to get off her chest. Rishi didn't know quite what to say. This was all so much heavier for Dimple than it was for him. He was disappointed that she was so pointedly, decidedly, against this, yes. But mostly he felt bad for his family. All the effort and hopes they'd put into this had clearly been for nothing.

"Hey," he said finally, cautiously. "I can see how that would suck. I had no idea. Look, I'll leave. I'll go back home, and he'll have to reassign you. Maybe you can be in a group of three with someone."

Dimple looked at him, slightly disbelievingly. "You'd do that. For me."

"Sure." Rishi shrugged. "It means way more to you than it ever did to me. And, you know, I get it. This is your passion."

"You won't get a refund," she said sharply, and he tried not to laugh at the suspicion in her voice.

"It's okay," he said. "My parents are totally cool with me going home early. I'll just finish out the day and tell Max I have a family emergency or something."

Dimple opened her mouth to respond, but Max spoke from the front of the room, interrupting her. "I trust you are all getting to know your partners. But I want us to take this to the next level. This being our first day together, I thought we could all use a jump start on breaking the ice. I want you all to reach under your chairs."

Abuzz with curiosity, they did. Rishi looked at the contraption in his hand for a few seconds before realizing what it was.

"A Polaroid camera," Dimple said at the same time. "Wow. I think my parents have one of those in our attic."

"What are we supposed to do with these?" Rishi asked, looking around the room. An obnoxious group of well-manicured people—a white girl and boy, and an Indian boy—were already trying to take pictures of one another. One of the boys, the white one, seemed to be paired with Celia, he saw.

"Okay, boys and girls," Max said again from the front of the room. "For those of you who may not know, you hold in your hands a forgotten treasure. This is the Polaroid camera, and as an amateur photographer, I find it to be one of the most honest artistic mediums for the capture of everyday moments. I want you to go forth and capture a few such moments today. To that end, I've come up with a few items for your photo scavenger hunt." He began to pass out sheets of paper with enumerated lists on them. "You'll see I've given each team a sheet with five items on it. I want you to capture all five items and bring your photos back to class in two hours. It is my hope that you will all get to know your partners much better this way than if we were all just sitting in this horrendous recycled air, firing questions at each other. The only rule is: No collaboration with any other teams. The teams who successfully complete this exercise will be awarded ten extra points toward their final score in Insomnia Con." A buzz went around the room. Max made a shooing motion with his hands and spoke louder. "Off you go. Good luck! I'll be outside napping in my hammock. Just wake me when you're back."

Rishi looked at Dimple as they both got up. She looked about as pleased as he felt; her lips were pursed tight, her eyes fixed longingly on Celia's retreating back. As he followed her out, he said, "If you want, I could bow out now."

She slowed down so they could walk outside together, and nibbled on her bottom lip. "No," she said finally, looking up at him. "Let's do this thing together."

Rishi frowned, not sure what was up with the total change of mood. "Are you sure?"

"Yeah." Dimple took a deep breath and looked at him. "It's really cool of you to volunteer to bow out. Not a lot of people would do that." And then she smiled a smile so dazzling, Rishi tripped over his own feet.

Dimple

"Are you okay?" Dimple reached out to grab his arm, but Rishi steadied himself against the wall and blushed a bright and furious red.

"Yeah, fine," he said, not meeting her eye. "Shoelaces," he added vaguely, looping the Polaroid camera's strap around his neck.

They walked along in relative silence, their classmates melting off onto various paths and striding over grass to go to the places where their pictures beckoned. It was cool enough, in spite of the sun, that Dimple had to pull her hoodie tighter around her.

She glanced sideways at Rishi through her curls, feeling like a jerk. She'd really unleashed a bunch of crap on him, and he'd been so . . . adult about it. So empathetic. Dimple really wished she could do this ice breaker thing with someone else, someone she'd be working with for the rest of this project, but asking him to leave right away would just be cruel. It was like saying she couldn't stand to be around him for the length of a stupid project. And given how decent he'd been, there was no need for that. So she'd deal. It wasn't like he was bad company, from the little she'd seen of him, anyway.

"Okay." Dimple glanced down at the list as they meandered toward a patch of green field where a few students were tossing around a football. "Our list is: *Funny, water, yellow, blur,* and *Buddha.*" She looked up. "Where do you want to start?"

Rishi grinned. "Definitely with Buddha. Come on, check this out." He quickened his pace, the Polaroid camera bouncing against his chest, and Dimple hurried to keep up.

"Want to tell me where we're going?"

"Oh, you'll see, my friend," he said happily.

Dimple shook her head. "All right," she said slowly. "Hey. What's that on your T-shirt?" His jacket was unbuttoned, and the graphic on his T-shirt was only just visible. It looked like a comic drawing of a young Indian boy in an embroidered kurta, holding something—a sword?—above his head.

Rishi colored a little, but she couldn't tell if that was from the pace they were keeping or her question. "Just a comic book character."

Dimple rolled her eyes. "You're pretty cryptic today, aren't you?

Obviously, I know it's a comic book character. I meant, which one?"

Rishi glanced at her sideways. "You know comics?"

"Eh, just the major ones. Wonder Woman is sort of my girl crush."

He smiled. "Yeah, she's cool." Glancing down at his shirt, he opened his jacket a bit more. Dimple could see now that the boy held a golden *gada*, or mace, in one hand, not a sword. "This is Aditya," Rishi said, a smile cupping his words. "He's a young Indian super-hero who draws his power from the sun. I based him vaguely on Hanuman—hence the *gada*. I was a huge Hanuman fanboy grow-ing up; my mom used to make me watch those *Ramayana* series with her on the Hindi channel when I was little. Aditya's one of my earliest creations from about three years ago. I was so proud of him, I had him put on a T-shirt." He snorted.

"Wait, wait, wait, you drew him? Like, from scratch?" Dimple ogled the drawing, the rich detail of the boy's brocade kurta and pants, the intricate metal work on the *gada*. "That's amazing. And you were what, fifteen?"

Rishi nodded. He barely met her eyes when he spoke, but there was a blooming happiness in his voice that belied how pleased he was at her compliments. "Yeah, making my own comics was the big thing back then. I had a little studio space set up in my room and everything."

"What do you mean, 'back then'? You don't do it anymore?"

He shrugged as they came to a light and then began to cross the street. The air was getting mistier, heavier. Rishi's words got muffled. "I don't know. I guess when I have the time, which isn't very often these days."

Dimple pulled her hoodie up. "But . . . why? I mean, you obviously love it, and you're good at it." She couldn't wrap her head around it. She lived and breathed coding; she couldn't imagine giving it up for anything.

He laughed a little, but there was something guarded about it, like there were things he was keeping hidden away in a mental lockbox. "It's not the most practical pursuit. Art is a nice side hobby, for when you have the time. But it's not something you pursue for itself." A pause and then, "Stupid fog."

"Karl," Dimple confirmed, distractedly. "Apparently San Franciscans name their weather patterns." They rounded the corner, and Rishi began to slow down. "But anyway, I just don't believe that," Dimple said. "So what if your art's not practical? If you love it, you should do it. What's the point of anything otherwise?"

She nearly ran into him when he stopped. Surprised, she looked up at the peeling green façade of an ancient-looking store tucked among many other abandoned seeming shops. WANDA'S WORLD TREASURES, the hand-painted sign out front said. "What is this place?"

"This is where we'll find Buddha," Rishi said, grinning as he pulled open the door for her.

CHAPTER 11

Rishi

The smell of sandalwood and cloves enveloped them like a soft, unfurling curtain. The wind chimes on the door sang gently, and Rishi found himself nervous. He wanted Dimple to like this place, he realized.

To be honest, they could've found a statue of Buddha in virtually any store around campus. This was San Francisco, after all. But he'd specifically dragged her over here to see this, to delight in it. Rishi wanted to give her a reason to smile. But he wasn't sure if this was Dimple's thing at all. What if she found all of this old, used stuff totally gross?

Rishi gestured around at the dimly lit, cluttered interior. Everywhere they looked, piles of *things* teetered—books with leather and gold covers, gold and silver trays, bead necklaces hanging out of chipped teacups, old, creaking furniture of all kinds. Overhead, strings of globe lights were looped around tall mirrors, bedposts, and the odd nonfunctional chandelier. "I stumbled on this place yesterday, after we'd had lunch. I don't know, I guess I thought it was kind of cool—"

"I love it," Dimple breathed, the lenses of her glasses reflecting the lights as she swiveled her head to look at every corner. She walked to a painted horse head and stroked its opalescent mane. "Amazing."

"Welcome," a middle-aged lady with short hair said from behind a teal desk in the corner. "I'm Wanda. These are all things I've found on my travels around the world. Some are from flea markets; others were gifts. Take a look around and let me know if you have any questions!"

"Will do!" Dimple called. Then she looped a gaudy set of necklaces laden with gold discs the size of her palm around her neck and put a hand on her hip. "What do you think? Definitely me, right?"

Rishi held up a finger. He grabbed a silver rhinestone-studded headband with a peacock feather sticking out of it and set it on Dimple's head. "There you go. Now *that's* simply fetching."

She pretended to strut around, and, on impulse, he raised the Polaroid and took a picture.

"Hey!" she said when the flash popped. "What was that for?" She reached out and punched him in the ribs, seemingly as an afterthought.

"Ow!" Rishi said, rubbing his side. "What the heck?"

"Sorry," Dimple mumbled, and it sounded only half true. "But seriously, why'd you take my picture?"

"I think we may have just crossed *funny* off the list," he said, referring to item number one on their scavenger hunt list. He flapped the photograph a few times, and then held it out for her to see. She looked like a turkey wearing jewelry.

At first Rishi thought Dimple might rip up the photograph. A look of abject horror passed over her face. But then her eyes crinkled and she snorted. "Okay. Point taken." Pulling the necklaces and headband off, she looked around the store, hands on hips. "So where's Buddha?"

"Aha. This way." Rishi beckoned, winding his way around a few room dividers and coffee tables. When they emerged into the far corner of the store, he gestured with a flourish. "Ta-daaaa!"

He watched her face closely as she took in the nearly eight-foot-tall, gold-plated statue in the corner. Dimple's eyes widened, and then she turned to him, grinning. *Oof.* It was like getting punched in the diaphragm when she turned the wattage to full on that thing. Rishi tried to smile normally in response. "Isn't it cool?"

In response Dimple laughed and ran over to it. "Cool? This is fan-freaking-tastic! My mom would flip out. She loves Buddha statues, especially laughing Buddhas. She has, like, this whole collection in the *puja* room at our house." She ran one hand over the statue's arm. "It's really beautiful, in a way, right?"

Rishi raised an eyebrow and pulled the camera up to take a picture. "If by 'beautiful' you mean 'tacky' . . ."

Dimple chuckled. "It's my turn to take a picture." She reached out and grabbed the camera he was holding in his hands, apparently forgetting that the strap was around his neck. When she yanked on it, she pulled him closer, his head automatically inclining toward hers.

Rishi froze, his eyes gazing down right into hers. They weren't more than three inches apart. Strange things were happening in the pit of his stomach. Fun things.

● ● ●

Dimple

His eyes reminded her of old apothecary bottles, deep brown, when the sunlight hit them and turned them almost amber. Dimple loved vintage things. She followed a bunch of vintage photography accounts on Instagram, and old apothecary bottles were a favorite subject. So it was a kind of magic, being here in this antiques store with a boy whose eyes were just the right shade of honey.

For about two seconds.

Dimple pulled away, coughing, and let go of the camera so it bounced back down against his firm chest. "Er, sorry. I thought, um, that—I didn't know the strap was still around your neck." She was having a hard time meeting his eye. And was that a tiny coating of *sweat* on her upper lip? Yuck. Dimple pretended to be pulling at an errant curl and swiped a hand across it.

Rishi must not be feeling the tumult of weirdness that she was. His voice was perfectly calm as he replied. "No problem. Here." He pulled the strap gracefully from around his neck and held out the camera to her. There was a flicker of something in his eye when he looked at her, but it was gone so quickly, Dimple wondered if she'd imagined it. "It is your turn, you're right."

The laughing jokiness of the past few minutes was completely gone as Dimple pointed the camera at the statue and took a picture. "Thanks." She handed the camera back to Rishi as she flapped the picture, and, wordlessly, he looped the camera back around his neck. "So," she said, slipping the photograph into the envelope that the list had come with. "Where to next? We've done *Buddha* and *funny*. That leaves *water, yellow*, and *blur*."

Water was easy. They were both thirsty, so they decided to be totally unimaginative and head to the café across the street for bottles of water. But they'd drunk them in the courtyard outside at a fog-wrapped wrought-iron table, the camera on the tabletop between them. That's when Rishi had decided to begin stealth-spraying her with drops of water.

Dimple had totally thought it was the fog, somehow melting onto her. Tipping her head back, she'd looked up at the swirling mist. "Weird. I could've sworn I felt water drops. Does this fog just randomly turn to rain?"

"Huh. I don't think that's possible." Rishi's face had been totally impassive, his hand circled casually around the water bottle. "But maybe a bird drooled on you."

Dimple laughed. "A bird *drooled* on me? What are you smoking?" But when she took another sip of her water, she felt more drops. And when she looked up, she saw a flock of birds flying by.

"Told ya," Rishi said, still totally serious. "It's a thing not many people know about. But birds are one of my hobbies. Some species, like *Avius borealis* above, drool to release scent. It helps the other birds follow them better through foggy areas."

"The only *scent* around here is BS." But Dimple's voice lacked conviction, even to her own ears. Everything he was saying sounded totally stupid, but he was so serious. . . .

Rishi lifted an earnest hand. "Swear to God." But there was a glint in his eye that gave him away.

"Interesting." Dimple bit her lip to keep from smiling and then very deliberately looked down to pull out the scavenger hunt list. And when she felt the next drops of water begin to splash against her skin, she grabbed the camera and took a picture of Rishi.

She caught him red-handed, laughing surreptitiously as he flicked water at her. The picture was really cool, the drops of water catching the sun and twinkling like little diamonds. They were headed right at her, frozen in space, with a blurry Rishi grinning right behind.

Dimple held out the evidence, one eyebrow raised. "So. Bird drool, huh?"

They stared at each other for a moment before bursting out laughing.

"I had you going for a minute, admit it," Rishi said, once he'd caught his breath.

Dimple stuck her tongue out at him. "Never." She wouldn't admit it to him, of course, but Rishi Patel was sort of a fun guy. She might even miss him when he left tomorrow.

Yellow and *blur* turned out to be the easiest when Rishi snapped a picture of a yellow cable car going by while they walked. "Boom. We're all finished. And we still have"—he consulted his watch, a Gucci; she remembered reading once that when they were that expensive, they were *timepieces*, not watches—"seventeen minutes to go." He handed her the picture, and she slid it into their envelope as they began to walk back toward the Spurlock building, now about three quarters of a mile away.

"Awesome." Dimple glanced sidelong at him. The oblique late afternoon rays turned the ends of his hair a chocolate brown. "So what do your parents do?"

"My parents?" Clearly confused at the question, he said, "My dad's a corporate executive, and my mom's a housewife. Why?"

Dimple wondered if the Patels' wealth had been a reason her parents had chosen Rishi for her, and then was immediately ashamed. Mamma and Papa were many things, but they weren't mercenary. "Just curious. Do you think our parents will remain friends, even after you leave tomorrow?" Dimple kept her tone light, but the question felt like jagged rock in her mouth. She tried to imagine goofing off with another partner like she had today with Rishi and supposed it was possible. She could possibly be matched up with someone whose sense of humor she'd also instantly get, whom she found just as easy to be around. It was definitely in the realm of possibility. And yet.

"Oh, I think so," Rishi said. "I get the feeling that when you're bound by decades, a couple of foolish kids aren't enough to dissolve that."

She heard the smile in what he was saying, but there was a hint of regret, too, tinting all his words blue. Was she being foolish? Rishi had already agreed that they weren't going to be an item. Papa had already said he didn't expect anything of her except that she win Insomnia Con. So why did she want Rishi to go away? What would that accomplish, really? Who said that if she got reassigned to a partner, they'd be anyone better or more invested in her idea than he was?

"So what are—"

"I think you should stay."

They'd both spoken at once, and Dimple turned to face Rishi. He frowned a bit, a wary hope shining in his eyes. "What?"

"Don't go. Tomorrow. I think you and I should be on this team together." Dimple realized she was twisting the envelope as she spoke and forced herself to hold still.

"Really?" A smile began to edge around his lips.

"Well, I mean, as friends." Dimple looked down at her feet and then up at his open face. Crap. She hadn't meant to give him the wrong impression.

His face crumpled. "But . . . but I thought you meant you wanted to get married!"

She stared at him, her heart sinking. And then Rishi burst out laughing, apothecary bottle–colored eyes crinkling up at the corners. Her hands itched for the camera, but she swatted him with the envelope instead. "You're not funny, Rishi Patel."

Rishi laughed again, running an easy hand through his hair as they resumed walking side by side, sleeves brushing lightly. "Be that as it may, I would love to be your Insomnia Con partner, Dimple Shah."

CHAPTER 12

Rishi

When Dimple and Rishi walked back into the lecture hall, they first noticed the throng of people milling around on the east side of the cavernous room. Someone had hung up long, thin steel cables, on which were mounted clothespins. Poster boards hung at equal intervals with signs that read, GROUP 1, GROUP 2, and so on all the way to GROUP 25 with the partners' names listed right below. A few groups had already hung up their five pictures.

Rishi returned the Polaroid camera to Max's desk at the front of the room and then jogged back up to where Dimple stood, studying group 8's (Tim and José's) pictures. "These are really good," she said, pointing to a close-up of a banana. The pits and bruises looked like craters on a large yellow planet.

"Pah. Photographing a banana for the prompt *yellow*? That's so cliché."

Dimple turned to him and raised an eyebrow. He was beginning to see it was one of her talents, the imperious eyebrow. "We combined two pictures. What if they think we're lazy?"

He shrugged and led them over to the sign that said GROUP 12:

DIMPLE AND RISHI. "So what if they do? I think Max will see our artistic genius."

She pulled their Polaroids out of the envelope and began fastening them to the clothespins. He saw her lips twitch at the picture of the funny face she'd been making in the antiques store—glasses askew, mouth contorted into a grimace, nostrils flaring. Pointing to it she said, "Oh yeah, totally. That's sheer artistic genius right there."

"Jesus Christ, put a bag over it." Braying laughter punctuated the comment as the hipster Indian guy went walking by, joined by the goateed white guy Celia was paired with, who was high-fiving him. Their eyes alighted on the picture, then Dimple's face in real life, then over Rishi as they passed.

Rishi turned toward them as they brushed past, surprise slowly burning away into anger. "What did you say?"

Dimple put a hand on his arm. "Don't worry about it."

"But they—"

"Don't." Her eyes flashed, and he saw she was serious. "It just makes it worse. Let them be. They're just big jerks with micro penises anyway."

He frowned. The practiced way she said it, the rehearsed-sounding lines . . . "What do you mean, 'It just makes it worse'? Have they bothered you before?" The thought sent molten geysers of fury pulsing through his veins.

Dimple sighed and leaned against the wall next to the pictures, crossing her arms over her chest. "Not *them*, specifically. Just guys like them. I'm not conventionally pretty. I like techie things." She shrugged easily. "I guess that makes them think it's open season or something." She took a breath. "Like I said, micro penises."

Rishi felt his frown deepen. "Who says you're not conventionally pretty?"

Dimple rolled her eyes. "So not the point."

Rishi opened his mouth to respond, but Max was standing next to them then, stroking his beard. It glistened under the lights and smelled like oranges, as if he'd just smoothed it out with oil. "These are excellent." He leaned in to study the picture that Dimple had taken of Rishi flicking water at her. Then he moved over to look at the one with the both of them standing next to the Buddha. Wanda had snapped it right when they'd been looking at each other—Rishi had kept making bunny ears behind Dimple, and she'd been giving him a warning glare. "What I notice in a majority of these is a sense of easy camaraderie. As if your spirits are already friends." He smiled at them. "Did you know each other from outside of this class?"

Rishi felt something hot pressing its weight against his diaphragm. *Your spirits are already friends.* That was it, he thought. Even though this was the first day he'd spent any kind of extended time with Dimple, he felt like he already knew her. Like they were continuing a conversation they'd left off.

Rishi found he couldn't bring himself to look at her when he said to Max, "No." He cleared his throat. "We just met yesterday."

"Well, then, I think you will work fabulously together. But you probably already know that. Good work." Max smiled kindly at the two of them and then moved on to the next group.

• • •

Dimple

Dimple glanced sideways at Rishi, but he was gazing at the picture of the yellow cable car like Max was going to give them a pop quiz later.

Your spirits are already friends. What a load of hippie BS.

Except . . . maybe Max had a point. It wasn't often that Dimple found people she could relate to easily. Her guard was always up, like Mamma was fond of telling her when she sat alone at a table during the *garbha* dance while the other Indian boys and girls danced together: *If you always look like you're going to bite them,* beti, *no boys are ever going to want to talk to you.* That was kind of the point, though, which is what Mamma didn't get.

Dimple wasn't fishing for compliments when she told Rishi that she'd been bullied by guys like those two jerks who'd walked by earlier. She was flat chested, insisted on wearing glasses and no makeup, refused to grow out her hair, and commonly occupied spaces—like Insomnia Con—that seemed to be implicitly reserved for men. Even when she was in elementary and middle school, she always chose computers as her choice of centers while all the other more popular girls seemed to cluster together in art or reading. All of that seemed to make the boys think there was something wrong with her. For a time people had assumed she was gay. Because, you know, maybe that made it, and her, safer.

But it wasn't like that with Rishi. It was like he'd found a chink in her armor and had squeezed through, insisting with his easy laughter and his goofy jokes that she like him. That they become friends.

And were they? Dimple wondered, darting a quick glance at him. Were they really becoming friends?

"So you want to meet up later, talk about where you want to begin with the app concept?" Rishi asked, pulling her out of her internal cogitations.

"Um, yeah, sure." Dimple scratched the back of her neck, feeling suddenly out of sorts. If Rishi wasn't the enemy, did that mean she had to forgive Mamma? "Let's meet at the pizza place again, and we can outline our plan of attack."

Rishi smiled at her, excited, his eyes shining. And Dimple was put out to realize she didn't exactly hate the thought of spending more time with him.

CHAPTER 13

Dimple

Celia was sprawled diagonally across her bed in their dorm room, texting someone on her phone. She glanced up when Dimple walked in. "Heeey. There you are. Feel like I haven't seen you all day."

Dimple felt her guard go up, that unbreachable wall laid with bricks of cynicism and aloofness that kept people at bay. Celia hadn't exactly done anything. She was just becoming friends with people Dimple had spent her entire life alternately avoiding and being made fun of by.

But Celia wasn't culpable, she reminded herself. So far, she had been nothing but unfailingly nice. She couldn't help it if she'd been assigned to the goateed boy any more than Dimple could help being assigned to Rishi. "Hey." She set her bag down and flopped down on her bed, sighing in contentment at just being there.

Celia set her phone facedown on the bed and sat up, crossing her legs. "Soooo," she said, and Dimple heard the eyebrow waggle in her voice, "I saw you got paired up with Rishi."

Dimple picked up the pillow and dropped it on her face. "Yeah," she said in a muffled voice. "He requested me when he applied."

Celia laughed merrily. "That's so cute! So, how is that going? Did he ask you to marry him again? Give you any other family heirlooms?"

Dimple groaned and pulled the pillow off her face. Rolling to her side, she propped her head up with a hand. "No, thank God. We had a chat, and I think he gets that I'm just not interested. He was actually kind of cool about it. We ended up having fun on our scavenger hunt." She held up a hand at Celia's gleaming eyes. "As *friends*. We had fun as friends. So I think we'll be okay working together."

Celia waved a hand. "Eh, work today, bone tomorrow."

"Gross!" Dimple threw her pillow at her, and, laughing, Celia tossed it back. "So . . . how is your partner? I saw you got paired with one of the grotties."

Celia raised an eyebrow. "You mean 'hotties'?"

"What did I say?" Dimple asked, feigning confusion.

Celia shook her head. "Anyway, yeah, I did. His name's Evan. The other hottie is his friend Hari, and the girl is, like, a friend of theirs from high school who also happens to be Evan's third cousin or something. Her name's Isabelle. She and Hari are partners. They've all known each other since kindergarten." She smiled and leaned forward, playing with the edge of her bell-sleeved peasant top. "They're so cool. I knew people like them in high school, but it was different then, you know? I never really . . ." She made a gesture with her hands like she was putting two blocks together. "Fit in. But I feel like it'll be different with these guys. They seem to get a lot of things about private school and growing up in Nob Hill with insane parents. And apparently Isabelle is, like, one-sixteenth Dominican or something. Which is cool, because I think I told you, right, my dad's Dominican?"

"Yeah . . . cool," Dimple said faintly, mostly because she didn't know what else to say.

Celia cocked her head, buoyant curls scraping her bedspread. "That sounded less than enthusiastic."

Dimple pushed her glasses up on the bridge of her nose. "No, they just seemed sort of . . . superficial." She couldn't, *wouldn't*, tell Celia about the comments the boys—she supposed Evan and Hari—had made. She didn't know her that well, and she didn't want any pity. It was bad enough that Rishi had heard.

"Oh, they're not." Celia said it quickly, in a rush, before Dimple had even finished her sentence. Her phone rang, interrupting their conversation, and she picked it up. "Hey, Isabelle!" she said cheerily. Dimple heard a high-pitched squawk and imagined Isabelle speed talking.

"Dinner sounds great!" Celia said. "What about Italian?" She listened for a minute. "No, that's fine, we don't have to do Italian. . . . What were you guys thinking?" Celia made a face at Isabelle's response. "Elm? No, I'm just not crazy about their food. . . ." After a pause, she said in a hurry, "No, no, that's totally fine! I think I was just having an off day when I went there last time. I'm sure I'll find something good tonight." Celia listened some more and then laughed, the sound pressured and fake. "Okay, see you then. Bye!" She hung up and looked at Dimple, forcing a smile. "Look, I'm having dinner with them. Why don't you come? Get to know them." Seeing Dimple's expression, she added, "Bring Rishi, too. Then at least there'll be two people you know there."

Dimple sighed. On one hand she had no desire to see those people again outside of class. On the other hand Celia would be there, and

Rishi, if he wanted to come. Maybe she could put this whole thing to bed and Evan and Hari wouldn't bother her again if they knew she was with Celia. They could all just forget about the stupid comment they'd made and move on, no awkwardness necessary. Plus, she didn't want Celia to think she was judging her new friends without even giving them a chance. That'd make for an awkward six weeks living together.

"Okay," she said finally. "Where are we going?"

"This place called Elm on Piazza Ave, about a ten-minute walk from here." She itched her ear, and in a not completely believable way, added, "Their mac and cheese is supposed to be killer?"

"All right, I'll be there. Do you want to walk together?"

Celia pulled a face and held up her phone. "Wish I could, babe. I have to run home really quick though. Apparently my grandma decided on a three-day surprise visit, and she flips if she doesn't get to see me." Celia stood and slung her bag onto her shoulder. She'd switched out her multicolored, patchwork-adorned backpack for a more demure taupe leather handbag. The interlocking *C*s glinted in the overhead lights. "But I'll see you there at seven, okay?"

"Sounds good." As the door thundered shut behind Celia, Dimple sat back and looked up at the ceiling. It was one stupid dinner, and then she'd be home free. No big deal. She reached over and grabbed her phone out of her bag. Max had made all the partners exchange phone numbers, so she had Rishi's in her contacts already. For some reason, her palms were slightly sweaty as she texted.

Hey, it's Dimple. Want to come to dinner with Celia's new friends tonight instead of doing the pizza place? 7 pm.

Wait, the Aberzombies?

Dimple snorted, only slightly surprised that Rishi's nickname nailed exactly what she felt about that group. *Yeah, unfortunately. I promised to give them a chance, though. It's at Elm, on Piazza.*

Sure, I'll be there. Pick you up or meet there?

Dimple paused, heart stuttering a bit. Was this a weighted question? If she said he should pick her up, would that give him the wrong idea? But if she didn't, would that sound like she didn't want to spend any more time with him than absolutely necessary? Dimple quietly thunked her forehead on the screen a few times and then typed, *Pick me up at 6:50.*

Rishi's response was immediate. *See ya then.*

Promptly at 6:49, there was a knock on Dimple's dorm room door. She opened it to find Rishi on the other side, dressed in a neatly pressed burgundy button-down (the color actually looked really good on him—brought out the red in his lips, not that she was *looking* looking) and khakis. He looked very much like Boy on a First Date. At least he hadn't brought a flower.

Rishi

Rishi had considered bringing a long-stemmed flower—he knew this wasn't a date, so maybe a carnation rather than a rose?—but had nixed it at the last moment. Seeing Dimple's face now, taking in his business casual attire, he was kind of glad.

• • •

Dimple

She'd say this for him: He had no guile. There were no mind games, no trying to be cool or appearing to be something else. Rishi was unabashedly himself. She felt a tug of endearment and coughed to cover it up. "Oh, er, hi. I feel underdressed."

"You look fantastic." He smiled, and she could tell he really meant it. "Ready?"

Outside, the sun had streaked the fog a molten pink and gold. Karl wafted lazily, toying with their hair and whispering wetly in their ears. Dusk pulled their shadows long, and a slight breeze ruffled the leaves on the eucalyptus trees they passed. Dimple pulled an errant, damp curl off her face. "So do you want to talk really quickly about the idea I had for Insomnia Con? Since we're not going to hash it out over pizza?"

Rishi tucked his hands into his pockets. "Sure."

Dimple's pulse quickened. She'd been thinking about this for so long, and now it was finally here. The chance to make this into a reality. "So the first thing to understand is that Papa's a diabetic. He really struggles to take his medication and stay on the straight and narrow with his diet. He's always saying how much of a pain in the butt it is to remember each little thing that comes with being a diabetic. There's the shot, the medication, the special diet, the exercise. . . . That got me thinking, what if there was a way to make it easier and more fun for sick people to stick to their routines? What if there was an app that turned it into a sort of game with a reward system?"

"Interesting. I just recently read an article about the psychology of gaming. How even the simplest or most repetitive of games can be made addictive if the person is rewarded enough or something?"

Dimple nodded, excited that he'd heard of it. "Yeah, it's called a compulsion loop. When we repeat a certain behavior and get rewarded for it, we want to keep repeating that behavior. So if that behavior is inputting that they took their medication or stuck to their diet—something that'll be visually represented and give them a reward—they'll want to keep repeating it. But it has to be simple enough that even older people like Papa can do it easily from their phones."

Rishi looked at her, impressed. "That is really cool. I love this idea already."

Dimple flushed and ducked her head. "Thanks. I hope the judges do too."

"We'll just have to work extra hard so they do."

Dimple smiled at Rishi, at his open enthusiasm. Softly, she said, "By the way, thanks for coming to this thing."

"No problem." A pause. "So . . . why are we going, again?"

She noticed the "we" in place of the "you," and felt a warmth in her belly. Rishi was a naturally good friend, she could tell, the kind of guy who thought your every fight was his as well. "Mainly because it's important to Celia, and I think this month and a half will be a whole lot less awkward if I make an effort to like her friends. I'm sure they'll be coming over to our dorm room and stuff." Dimple thought of the way Celia turned pink when she talked of Evan. "Besides, if I can just spend some time with them, maybe—" She broke off, not able to believe she'd actually been about to tell Rishi her thought process.

"Maybe they won't bother you again," he finished mildly. "Makes sense."

They walked along, both looking straight ahead until they got to the light. Dimple turned to look at him while they waited for a WALK sign. "Does it really? Make sense to you, I mean?"

"Sure." Rishi's eyes were clear and genuine.

Dimple smiled a half smile. "No *don't appease the bullies* sentiment?"

Rishi shrugged. The WALK sign beeped, and they started across. "There's a place for that. But if you want to try appealing to their friendly side, I see nothing wrong with it."

Dimple nodded. She didn't need his approval; she knew her strategy was a good one. And still, somehow, she felt vulnerable in a way that was totally unfamiliar to her. Her usual style was ignoring the haters, pretending they didn't exist.

It worked, for the most part. They usually got tired of it and went away, eager to pick on the next victim, preferably someone who'd give them what they wanted—blood and tears. But this time she was striding right into the mouth of the beast. She was going to have dinner with them.

But you don't know they're really bullies, she told herself. Sure, they'd made that obnoxious comment about her face. But maybe . . . maybe they were having an off day.

Even as she thought it, she was annoyed at herself. No off day justified making fun of someone's appearance or being as cruel or vulgar as they had been. She knew that.

I'm afraid, Dimple realized, with a bit of a start. This was new to her. She had no idea what would come of eating dinner with people like these, and in a way, it was terrifying.

She glanced down and saw Rishi's feet clad in their black lace-up oxfords right next to her Chucks, and felt a thud of gratitude toward him. At least she wasn't walking in there alone. And who knew? Maybe by the time tonight was done, she wouldn't have anything to worry about with Evan and Hari.

CHAPTER 14

Rishi

There was something different about her that sat uneasily with Rishi, like a scratchy tag against the back of his neck. He didn't know Dimple very well, obviously, and yet tonight she was just . . . off, a faded print of her former vibrant self. It was like someone had left a photograph out in the sun too long. She was sort of folded into herself, arms crossed across her gray kurta tunic, curls hiding her face like a makeshift curtain.

Rishi clenched his fists against his sides and tried to breathe. Okay, so they were doing dinner with these dirtbags tonight. Fine. That didn't mean he had to just sit there while they laughed at Dimple. If anything close to what he'd heard before came out of their mouths, he'd lose it. It wasn't Dimple's preferred way of handling things, but seriously. There was only so much you could take before you had to shut it down. Besides, he knew people like those Aberzombies; he'd gone to school—private school—in Atherton. And 99 percent of the time, they were all bluster and no balls.

He glanced at her again, worry niggling at him. He wished she'd just turned Celia down. Was it really worth it?

Dimple

Anxiety's cold fingers pressed against Dimple, trying to find a way in. She took a deep breath as they approached Elm. It had a super trendy exterior, she noted in surprise, the shiny silver letters glinting in the fading sunlight. The windows were covered with heavy gold fabric. Anxiety's fingers became claws.

Turning to Rishi, she said, "Uh, is this, like, a *fancy* place?" She whispered the word "fancy" like it was something illicit, as a smartly dressed couple in their fifties walked by. Before he could respond, the twenty-five-ish-year-old hostess (dressed in a slinky black dress and gold high heels) who'd opened the door for the couple smiled at them. "Hello! Table for two?"

Dimple noticed the girl's eyes hitch just slightly on her dark-rinse skinny jeans and Chucks before moving on smoothly. "We're actually meeting some people," she said, her voice small. "Celia Ramirez?"

The hostess tapped something into her tablet and smiled. "Ah yes. Please follow me."

Oh great. When they walked into the restaurant proper, it became clearer and clearer why Rishi was dressed the way he was. Everywhere, couples and groups who looked like they were either heading off to conferences or cocktail parties smiled and laughed over candlelit tables. On every gold clothed table was a glass bowl full of pale yellow flowers. In the center of the space, an actual fountain gushed. Dimple was the only person there in a faded kurta, jeans, and Chucks.

As the hostess wound deeper and deeper into the restaurant, Dimple turned to Rishi. "Why didn't you tell me?" she said. "I'm *so* underdressed. You said I was fine!"

"Sorry!" The anguish on his face from seeing her discomfort was clear. "They're more casual in the afternoons, so I figured you'd be fine. I've never done dinner here before."

Dimple sighed. "Celia said they did a mean mac and cheese. I was expecting some small, down-home kinda place." Another thought occurred to her, and she paled. "Crap, I can't afford this." She could, but only if she used the emergency credit card Mamma and Papa had given her. Which she really, really didn't want to do. The bill went straight to them.

"Don't worry about it," Rishi said immediately. "I got it."

She turned to him, her cheeks burning. "Absolutely not."

"But—"

"I don't take handouts. Besides, I'm not going to be the only one not able to pay for myself, Rishi. That definitely will not help my case with the others."

He sighed and, after a moment, nodded.

Rishi

The hostess led them to their table, a large one in the corner that had its own carved wood chandelier hanging above. It was empty.

"First ones here," the hostess chirped. "Please have a seat and your server will be right with you."

"Thanks," Rishi said.

Dimple sank into a seat and he took one next to her. She looked even more despondent than before. Her phone beeped, and she fished it out of her bag and looked at the screen. "Great," she muttered. "Celia got stuck watching a movie with her grandma. She's going to be thirty minutes late."

"It'll be interesting to see if the Aberzombies beat her here. At least she texted."

Dimple smiled, a wilted thing. "Well, if they don't come, that'll be good for my wallet, at least." She pulled the menu to her and opened it, scanning the items with what could only be described as fear.

Rishi cleared his throat. "Hey, um, I'm going to run to the restroom. Be right back."

He walked quickly to the back of the restaurant, where the double doors led to the kitchen. A middle-aged waiter in a bow tie approached him, smiling. "Hello, sir. Can I help you with something?"

"Yeah, hey. I'm at that table over there." He gestured vaguely in the direction. "It's a table for seven, reserved under 'Ramirez.' I'd like to pay for everyone's food at that table."

The waiter smiled kindly. "Okay, sir. What we'll do is bring you the check and—"

"No." Rishi shook his head. "You don't understand. I want to pay anonymously, in advance."

The waiter stopped, his mouth slightly open, brows knitting together. "Anonymously?"

"Yes." Rishi tried to keep his tone patient. Had no one ever done this before? Well, now that he thought about it, maybe not. "I'd like to pay now, and for you or whoever our waiter is to not mention that it was me who paid. Maybe you guys could just say someone decided to pay our bill. You know, like those *pay it forward* things. Okay?"

The waiter adjusted his bow tie, still looking totally lost. "But, sir, how will we know how much it's going to be in advance?"

"Well . . ." Rishi reached in his wallet and pulled out a wedge of bills. "This should cover seven full course meals, right? Plus tip? Just keep the change."

The waiter took the money and discreetly slipped it into a bill holder he pulled from the pocket of his apron. "Of course, sir. I shall be taking care of your table myself."

Rishi grinned at him, and after a moment, the waiter grinned back.

Dimple

Oh, no. Oh, no, oh, no, oh, no.

Dimple heard and smelled them before she saw them. The Aberzombies. Instead of death rattle moans, they were known for their piercing laughter (girls), forced guffawing (boys), and excessive expensive perfume (both). She craned her neck and scanned desperately for Rishi, but he wasn't visible. He'd left to go to the restroom only a minute ago, so she was just going to have to handle this on her own.

Dimple turned as Evan, Hari, and Isabelle sauntered up, laughing and talking loudly, impervious to the glares of the older diners. Evan was a paler, taller version of Hari, but otherwise they were dressed almost identically, in understated plaid button-down shirts with a little Ralph Lauren emblem on the chest, khaki pants, and loafers. On each of their wrists gleamed a heavy gold watch. Unlike Rishi's, these were made to proclaim, *Look at me!* Evan's watch caught the light and seared Dimple's retina. Blinking, she looked at Isabelle. In spite of the chill outside, she was dressed in a barely-there strapless blue dress that complimented her tanning bed complexion. A thin white belt snaked around her narrow waist, and a small diamond cross glinted in the hollow of her neck. Her blond hair had been teased into curls that hung past her shoulders.

They all sat down without so much as a glance at Dimple, still engrossed in their conversation about some dude named Corey on their lacrosse team back home. Dimple sipped her water, trying not to feel small and irrelevant. *I don't care about them,* she kept reminding herself. *I'm here for myself.*

Finally, a good five minutes later when the conversation began to peter out, Isabelle turned her blue eyes on Dimple. "Hi," she said, smiling a tight-lipped kind of smile. "It's Dimple, right?" She said "Dimple" with a slightly distasteful grimace. As if Dimple's name were Pus Filled Cyst or Male Pattern Baldness instead.

"Right," Dimple said, forcing herself to smile. "And you're . . . Isabella?" she couldn't help adding.

"Isabelle," the girl said, in the tired manner of someone who'd said it a thousand times before, which, of course, was exactly what Dimple had been counting on.

"Right. Sorry." She forced herself to turn to the boys, who were silently studying their menus. "And you guys are Evan and Hari, right? Celia's told me about you all." She pronounced Hari the correct way, rolling the *r* and saying it sort of like *Hurry*.

Evan just nodded and went back to his menu, but Hari turned to her with an orthodontically enhanced smile that made her feel sticky all over. "It's pronounced *Harry*, actually."

Evan snorted.

No, actually, Dimple thought. *Why should he get to act all high and mighty when he was wrong?* "But it's not," she responded, before she could stop herself.

Hari's gaze was all ice and venom as he said, "Forgive me if I don't want to take advice on names from someone called *Dimple*."

Dimple felt her shoulders hunch into themselves even as she tried not to let them. She shouldn't give someone like Hari so much power, but she couldn't help it. She felt utterly dumpy and completely put in her place, which, of course, was exactly what he'd been going for.

Evan guffawed showily and said, "Dude . . ." into a closed fist that he held in front of his mouth.

Isabelle glanced at Dimple out of the corner of her eye. A slight flush was working its way into her cheeks. "Chill," she mumbled. "She's just interested in a connection with someone from her own country." Dimple tried not to roll her eyes at Isabelle's well-intentioned defense. She needed a sandwich board that said, *America is my country too.*

Evan grinned. "Yeah, don't worry about Hari." *Harry.* "He's not as well traveled as some of us."

Isabelle snorted and played with her cross, clearly uncomfortable. "Sailing around in your daddy's yacht doesn't mean you're well traveled."

Evan leaned back in his chair. "Excuse me. I've been to Manila,

Bombay, *and* Haiti on missions. And here's my proof: As soon as you hit the airport, you can *smell* the third world countries. That's something they don't tell you in travel books. Ask anyone. Ask Dimple here. Isn't it true?" he asked, his green eyes wide. "Can't you just smell them as soon as you land?"

Dimple tried not to let her anger show. "Um, I haven't been to India since I was a little kid, so I don't remember." They were just dumb rich kids who knew nothing about anything. She knew that. And yet, somehow, it was amazing how conversations like these made her feel so *other*. Hands shaking a bit, she picked up her glass and took a sip of chilled water.

Dimple began to wish she hadn't accepted this dinner invitation.

CHAPTER 15

Rishi

As soon as he rounded the corner back to the table, Rishi saw the Aberzombies had arrived. He picked up his pace, wanting to get back to Dimple. And when he saw her, cheeks red, teeth nibbling on her bottom lip, he knew they'd already said something. And he'd missed it. Crap.

He sat down and smiled at Dimple. "Sorry I took so long. There was a line."

"No problem," she muttered, her eyes on her menu.

Rishi began to study his. "What looks good to you?"

"Um, hi?" a female voice said. "I'm Isabelle?"

Rishi raised his eyes, making sure to wear the "bored mask" he'd perfected at private school. "Rishi." He didn't acknowledge the guys before he began to study the menu again.

"Rishi," Isabelle said, pronouncing it *Ree-shee*, even though he'd just told her how to say it. "You guys have such interesting names." The way she said "interesting" made it clear she meant "weird."

Rishi looked up, feigning confusion. "'You guys'? You mean people at Insomnia Con? Because I haven't noticed that."

He heard Dimple's sharp intake of breath and looked to see her bite the inside of her cheek to keep from smiling. His heart sang.

"No, not . . . I meant, well, *Hari*'s name is . . . but you . . . ," Isabelle began, but clearly her upper-class manners made it hard for her to explain what she *had* meant.

They talked about inconsequential, safe things for about fifteen minutes. The guys were pretty silent except for perfunctory replies to Isabelle's string of inane chatter about which sorority she wanted to join. She wanted everyone to know how her mom would just *die* if Isabelle wasn't also a part of the Alpha Omega Toe Jam legacy like her grandmas on both sides.

Eventually, thankfully, conversation looped to Insomnia Con.

"Hari and I think we're going to win it, don't we?" Isabelle smiled and leaned toward him, and he rubbed her shoulder, his face slack as he stared down the front of her dress.

Rishi raised his brows and turned to Dimple. "I don't know; I think we have a good shot. Your idea is really good. Innovative, just ambitious enough . . . I think we're going to kill it."

Evan looked up, his eyes showing the merest interest. "And what's your idea?"

Rishi looked at him, forcing himself to feign a bit of surprise, as if he hadn't noticed Evan perched on his chair like he was king of the table, the restaurant, and the world. "Oh. Well, I don't want to give it away. You know, 'inspire' you guys inadvertently." He laughed uproariously and watched in glee as Evan and Hari turned red. "It's just that good."

"You don't have to worry about that, bro," Hari said, glancing at

Evan. "Our ideas are popping. Too bad we have to share them with a couple of girls. Can't believe they split us up even after my dad made that donation."

Evan, at least, had the decency to look slightly discomfited while Isabelle whined, plaintively and squeakily. "Heyyy. We're just as good as you guys." She stuck her tongue out prettily, but there was a stiffness about her that belied a deep discomfort. She looked so much like someone playing the part of spoiled rich girl that Rishi wondered if she practiced it in the mirror to fit in better.

Beside him, Dimple sat up straighter. "If anything, having girls on your team will just make your idea better." She pushed her glasses up on her nose, like she did when she was feeling especially fired up about something, Rishi had noticed. "Research shows that women are better coders—"

Hari yawned, loudly and long, cutting her off. Dimple's cheeks felt like they were on fire; she fell silent.

Rishi turned to him. "Well. I guess that just goes to show you. All of Papa's money can't buy good manners."

In his peripheral vision, he saw Dimple's jaw just about come unhinged. Isabelle went strangely still, and Evan looked up slowly from his menu. Hari leaned forward toward Rishi, his tawny cheeks a healthy fuchsia. "What. Did. You. Say. To. Me?"

Rishi smiled congenially. "Oh, you heard me. If you have to be nasty to prove you're better than others, then . . . well. Let's just say breeding isn't everything."

Hari's hand clenched into a fist on the table, and Evan put a hand on his forearm. "Chill, bro. Don't let him get under your skin."

A taut tension stretched over the table. Dimple sat, rigid in her seat, refusing to look at anyone, gazing into the middle distance. Rishi felt a beat of guilt. He hadn't listened to her. She'd wanted to make this a reconciliatory thing, and he'd been the exact opposite of reconciliatory, whatever that was.

"I'm sorry I'm late! Once Abuelita begins talking, she doesn't stop. And then she foisted all of this *food* on me; I don't even know where I'm going to store it. . . ."

They all turned at the husky voice. It was Celia. She had two bags of stuff with her, including her purse, and her purple *just for show* glasses were pushed up, holding her curls back. She paused, looking at all of them in turn. "What'd I miss?"

Dimple

Dimple wanted to die.

She couldn't believe Rishi. What was he thinking? Hadn't she specifically told him not to interfere? He was supposed to just hang out, not basically challenge Hari to a duel. Her fist itched with the urge to punch something, and his ribs were so close. . . .

If she didn't feel like it'd make it worse (ha, as if that were even possible), she'd leave right then. Just tell Celia she felt sick and take off. But instead she forced herself to smile a little. "Nothing. You didn't miss anything. So what movie did she rope you into watching?"

Celia handed her bags to the solicitous waiter in a bow tie and sat down, sighing mightily. As she launched into the trials and tribulations of watching *Little Women* with her seventy-two-year-old

Dominican grandmother, Dimple allowed herself to tune out.

She glanced at Hari, who looked like he wanted to be anywhere but here. He was on his phone, texting someone furiously. Isabelle was enraptured with Celia's story, which was interesting. Maybe she really did like her. Evan was smiling politely, but Dimple could tell by the way he kept glancing at his cell phone screen that he wasn't totally into the story. If she had to guess, they were probably here just as a favor to Isabelle.

Finally, she stole a look at Rishi—and felt her cheeks heat when she saw he was looking at her, too. Then she sat up straighter, remembering she was mad at him for what he'd said to Hari. She tried to show her fury through her eyes, but he just smiled at her. She shook her head at him, and he raised his eyebrows, like, *What?* But she saw the tips of his ears turning pink. Oh, he knew what he'd done.

The waiter, somehow intuiting the pause in Celia's story, melted back into view. "Are we ready to order?" he asked, smiling around at them. Dimple would say one thing for these ridiculously expensive places: The service was impeccable. She couldn't imagine this ever happening at Bombay Bistro, a tiny Indian buffet place that was her family's idea of a fancy dinner out.

Once they'd all ordered (Dimple was the only one who'd ordered a cup of tomato basil soup, in spite of Rishi pressing her to order something more filling. What part of "I can't afford this place" didn't he understand, anyway? Dumb rich people.), conversation inevitably turned to where everybody "summered" when they weren't doing peasantlike things like Insomnia Con. Isabelle swore by Boca Raton, where her family had a home, but Evan liked Prague, and Hari said the girls in Bermuda couldn't be beat (eww).

Rishi glanced at her, and Dimple stiffened. There was something in his eyes . . . she could tell whatever he was going to come up with she wasn't going to like. Before she could open her mouth to stop him, he was off, like some unstoppable rocket. "So, tell me, Hari, which part of India are your parents from?"

Hari looked up slowly to glare at Rishi, but Dimple saw the corner of his mouth twitch. He was uncomfortable. "My parents are from San Mateo."

Rishi nodded, unperturbed. "Right . . . so what about your grandparents?"

Hari raised both glossy eyebrows that looked like they'd been waxed and powdered. "I can print out a family tree chart for you later, if you'd like."

Evan began his mindless guffawing, but Rishi cut him off, speaking loudly and clearly. "Let me tell you something—I'll never forget last summer, when I visited my family's ancestral home in Gujarat."

Everyone was staring at him. But if Rishi felt the heat of their gazes, he didn't show it. "It was amazing," he said, beaming at them all as if he were totally clueless that they'd find this anything *but* amazing. "All of those decades—over a century!—of history. When you stood on the courtyard in the rain, you felt like the gods were singing in the heavens."

Celia looked confused, like she sensed a strange undercurrent but didn't know what it was or how it had come to be. Hari snorted, but he didn't say anything. He looked a little embarrassed now—all the Aberzombies did, actually, Dimple noticed—like they didn't know what to do with someone who was so obviously at home with his uncoolness. Someone who had the audacity to feel like *he* was the cool one when he so obviously wasn't.

Dimple cleared her throat. "That's really awesome." She forced herself to speak up, firmly and clearly. Smiling at Rishi, she said, "I bet that's a more meaningful vacation than going to Bermuda and sleeping with a bartender whose name you can't remember." She darted a glance at Hari and almost laughed out loud at his expression. He looked like he was choking on a fish bone.

The waiter came by with their orders then, and everyone's attention turned to food.

CHAPTER 16

Dimple

"So, just based on first day impressions, who do you guys think is going to win Insomnia Con?" Celia asked between bites of her $42 mac and cheese. Dimple couldn't help calculating the value of each bite. *There goes $2. And another $2. She didn't even properly chew up that $2.*

"Like it's even a question," Hari said. "It's either going to be Evan's team or mine."

Dimple tried not to roll her eyes at that. Didn't a partnership mean it wasn't just either of their teams? "I think José Alvarez and Tim Wheaton have a good chance," she said, slurping up a bit of her tomato basil soup. For $25, it tasted like tomato paste diluted in water. "They had spreadsheets of what they were going to do on what days of the week and everything. José had already even written a script for some stuff he wanted the computer to do at night, while they slept." She'd never admit it, but Dimple felt a pang of jealousy at that kind of dedicated foreplanning. Why hadn't she thought of it?

"Yeah, they've probably been planning for this since freshman year of high school," Rishi laughed. "My money's on Marcus

Whitman and Simon Terrence. After Dimple and me, of course."

"They're solid," Dimple agreed. "But they lack that single-minded dedication that José and Tim have. They, like, breathe this stuff."

"Mmm-hmm," Celia said. "I even heard they paid off their roommates so they could move in together to work on this stuff twenty-four/seven." Deals like those were pretty common within Insomnia Con, and the organizers usually just looked the other way, probably because it was too hard to control.

"I wouldn't mind moving in with Dimple," Rishi said, laughing, and everyone whipped their heads around to look at him. And her.

Dimple felt herself turn bright red. "What?" she bit out.

The tips of his ears flamed, and his face slackened as he realized what he'd just said. "I meant because we could really kick everyone's butts. If we had more time like that. If we were living together." Rishi sighed when he saw that she wasn't convinced. "Never mind."

Celia giggled. "That is so cute."

"Yeah." Evan smiled a strangely plastic smile. "So . . . cute."

Before it could get more awkward, the waiter came forward. "Would anyone like dessert?"

Dimple groaned inwardly. Why couldn't they just give them their checks? Now she'd have to pretend she was all filled up on tomato water while everyone else ordered $50 desserts and ate them around her.

Celia looked at her. "The Nutella crepes are supposed to be good. Split one with me?"

The Nutella crepes. Those were $28. Half of that was fourteen, which meant her bill would be just about $40, plus tip. Dang it. She only had a twenty, so she'd have to put the rest on the credit card.

Would it be weird to pay half in cash and half on a card in a place like this? Yes. It would. She'd have to put it all on the card and find a way to explain it to Mamma and Papa later.

"Excuse me, sir," Rishi asked the waiter, who turned to him, beaming. "Can you tell me how much the Nutella crepes are?" He raised his eyebrows. "I want to make sure I'm not exceeding my budget here."

What? Why was he saying that? Mr. Gucci obviously didn't have a budget. He was doing this for her benefit, wasn't he?

The waiter nodded and smiled. "An understandable concern, sir. But not to worry. An anonymous donor has very generously paid for all of your meals already. To include desserts."

Dimple looked up sharply. "What? Who was it?"

The waiter held up his perfectly manicured hands. "Now, that wouldn't make it very anonymous, would it, miss? The donor asked not to be identified. But please order whatever you choose."

"Well, that is really cool of this donor person," Rishi said.

Dimple glanced at him suspiciously, but he was studying the dessert menu with a renewed interest. The others looked dumbfounded.

"We can afford to pay our own bill," Hari said finally, sounding mortally offended.

"Indeed, sir," the waiter said. "The donor was simply attempting to do something good, I think. One of those *pay it forward* things."

Isabelle was pink as she said, "Yeah. Or, like, it was a guy and he wanted to pay *my* bill and didn't know how to do that without paying for everyone's." She looked at the waiter. "Did he leave a number?"

The waiter frowned. "No, miss. The donor left nothing except money. Do you wish to order a dessert?"

Miffed, Isabelle blew out a breath. "Well." After a pause, she said grudgingly, "Yes. I suppose I'll have a caramel brownie."

The rest of the dinner wasn't very eventful. Everyone mainly talked about the upcoming week, how they were going to position themselves going into Insomnia Con proper, and how difficult it was going to be. Some people, they'd heard rumors, even brought caffeine pills to stay up through the night.

Celia shuddered. "I couldn't do that. Give me a Red Bull any day of the week." Then she paused and looked around. "Seriously. Any day of the week, I'm willing."

Everyone laughed, even Dimple, who laughed with a hysterical edge to her voice because she was just so glad this thing was winding down. She wanted nothing more than to go back to the dorm, take a scalding hot shower, and wash her hair. There was something about washing out her hair that calmed her.

Dimple and Rishi finished their desserts at the same time, and Rishi immediately threw down his napkin and stood. "Well, I'm off." Dimple tried not to laugh; he wasn't even pretending like he wanted to suffer their company a moment longer than he absolutely had to. With a hand on the back of her chair, he said, "Are you coming, or would you like to stay a bit longer?"

Dimple tossed her napkin on the table and pushed her chair back. "Oh no. I'm definitely done." She smiled at Celia. "I'll see you later."

And then they walked toward the doors, leaving a heavy silence behind them.

● ● ●

Outside, the evening had turned even colder. The stars were erased by the fog, and Dimple felt a pang. That was one thing she loved about her backyard in suburbia—she could always make out at least a few stars.

"So," Rishi said, buttoning up his jacket. "That was interesting, no?"

Dimple snorted but remained silent, cinching her hood tight around her head.

"Come on, Dimple Shah," he said, gently hitting her shoulder with his. "What'd you really think?"

"Were you the donor?" she asked quietly.

There was an infinitesimal pause, just one tiny breath. Then: "You must think I'm way more generous than I am. Did you see how much those Aberzombie boys ate? And they didn't even have brains on the menu."

"Har har," Dimple said, thinking, *You didn't answer my question.* She wondered if it should bother her more, if she should challenge him. But she realized, even if the donor had been him, she was just grateful that Mamma and Papa wouldn't be footing the bill.

She switched tack. "Okay, so answer me this, then: Do you really believe all of what you said? About your family's ancestral home in Gujarat? Seeing all the history? Or was that all just for their benefit?" She rubbed her arms against the chill, and Rishi, seemingly unthinkingly, scooted closer so they were touching arms. She'd protest, but the boy put off an insane amount of body heat, even through layers of fabric.

"You ask a lot of questions, don't you?"

Dimple laughed.

"What?"

She shook her head. "It's just, my mom. She says the same thing. 'No one likes a nosy girl, Dimple.' 'You'll never land a boy with that mouth of yours.'"

"Huh." Rishi cocked his head to the side and studied her face as she watched him in confusion. It was sort of hard to do while they walked, but they managed somehow. "I don't know . . . I think your mouth is perfect the way it is."

CHAPTER 17

Dimple

The air between them felt suddenly charged somehow. Heat rushed to Dimple's cheeks. Suddenly, she wasn't so cold anymore, and she moved away from Rishi. His face went blank for a second, and then mortification overcame everything. Even his eyebrows looked embarrassed, somehow. Dimple felt a little bad for him. But not that bad, because he was the one who'd said it.

"I didn't mean—I meant, your questions—"

Dimple waved her hand, keeping her eyes steadfastly on the sidewalk. "Anyway. Answer my question."

"Right." He rubbed the back of his neck, which she found strangely endearing. "Yeah, I do. I totally believe that."

"For real." She raised an eyebrow at him.

He chuckled. "For real. When you think about it, our families are back in India, about eight thousand miles away. And they're still so intricately connected to us. We have their names, their rituals, their traditions. Their dreams sit behind our eyelids. I think it's beautiful."

Dimple was silent as they rounded the corner to the stoplight. "I don't know. I guess I think it's sort of stifling. All those rules. You can't date people who aren't Indian. You can't date, period, until you're thirty." She gave him a look and said, "Unless, of course, your parents are trying to set you up with a marriage partner. Girls can't be interested in a career more than they're interested in marriage. Wear makeup. Grow your hair out."

When the WALK sign beeped, they began to cross. Rishi laughed. "That does sound annoying. I guess I haven't been through those rules, except for the first and second. But the thing is, those are tangential things. I'm talking about the big picture. The idea that we're connected by this thread to people who live in the place where we came from. Where our parents came from. We have a blueprint for our lives. I think that makes it all seem comforting somehow. Safe." He pushed a hand through his floppy hair before stuffing it into his pocket, like he was embarrassed for all he'd said.

"I think having a blueprint makes life boring. Maybe I don't want to get married or have kids or any of that. Maybe I just want a career and that's all."

Rishi looked at her, frank and open. "And that doesn't sound lonely to you?"

Dimple paused, considering it. She'd never thought of it that way. With her relentless pursuit of freedom, she'd never actually stopped to think about what the day-to-day of it might be like. Eventually, she shook her head. "When you've had a mother who does a great impersonation of a helicopter, any kind of solitude sounds like heaven." But saying it made her think of Mamma, at home. If Dimple were home, Mamma would be bustling around, cleaning the kitchen while Dimple sat at the counter nearby and drank her tea. They'd probably be bickering about something inconsequential. Dimple

114

would be considering taping Mamma's mouth shut. Mamma would probably be considering putting Dimple up for adoption. But they'd be together. It was their ritual, sort of.

Dimple wondered what Mamma was up to right now. She imagined her sitting in the living room, alone, doing her crossword puzzle. Or watching the Hindi channel by herself. And it made her sad. It made her almost miss home.

Almost.

"I guess we just look at it differently," Rishi said. They passed a man ensconced in fog and playing the guitar. Rishi tossed in what looked like a twenty-dollar note. The man tipped his head at them and kept playing, something that sounded like the saddest love song ever.

"Why aren't you like them?" Dimple asked.

"Huh?"

"The Aberzombies. Why aren't you more like them?"

Rishi shrugged. "I don't know." He jammed his hands in his pockets. "I guess I never really got why the kids in my private school thought they were such hot stuff. I mean, it's our parents who did all the hard work. We were just born into it. It's like being proud that you're tall or have thick hair or perfectly spaced eyes. Absurd."

Dimple laughed a little. "It's neat that you were able to see that, though. So many people don't. Obviously."

Rishi grunted in response. Softly, he said, "I'm sorry if I overstepped in there. I just got really frustrated that they were talking to you like that. They're just such little d-bags, you know?"

"I guess." Dimple played with the zipper on her hoodie. "Don't you . . . care that you're making it worse? You're not smoothing

115

things over with them. They're probably going to be even bigger jerks to us in class now."

Rishi ran his hands across the leaves of some bush with brilliant blue-violet flowers as they walked, releasing that green plant smell. "I think they're going to be like that no matter what. They'll find a reason. If you smooth things over, it'll be because they think you're weak. If you don't, it'll be because their egos are hurt. I like to just confront it head-on."

Dimple looked at him sidelong.

"What?" he asked.

"Nothing." A curl that hadn't been contained by her hood blew into her eyes, and she pushed it away. "You surprise me, that's all. I would've pegged you for a much more *go with the flow* kind of personality."

"I am," Rishi said. "Mostly. But not when it comes to people who try to step all over things that are too important."

"Fair enough." Dimple would never admit it, but she felt a grudging admiration for his kind of no-BS bravery.

They wound their way around the green to the dorms. Rishi held the lobby door open, and she chuckled.

"What?" he asked, looking self-conscious.

"You're so chivalrous. Is that your desi breeding or your millionaire breeding?"

He rolled his eyes. "It's my Patel breeding. We Patel boys are very well behaved, you know. Ma wouldn't have it any other way."

"So you have a brother?" Dimple asked as they strode across the chilly lobby and showed their IDs to the residence hall desk assistant, who barely looked up from the text she was furiously tapping on her phone. Dimple hadn't really thought about Rishi having siblings. "Older or younger? Is he a lot like you?"

She saw Rishi suppressing a smile and said, "Sorry. Too many questions." She jabbed at the elevator button, knowing she should feel embarrassed. But somehow, strangely, with Rishi, she didn't.

"Not at all." It sounded like he meant it. Leaning against the wall, he crossed his arms and said, "My brother, Ashish, is sixteen. You couldn't find two blood relatives more different than we are. Sometimes I think Ashish wishes he'd been born into another family. He's like a different species than the rest of us."

Dimple pulled a face. "Ashish and I would probably have a lot in common, then."

The elevator doors dinged open and a few girls got out, talking animatedly about some poetry reading they were going to for their summer literature program. Rishi and Dimple were the only ones going up.

As the doors slid closed, enveloping them in solitude in that tiny metal chamber, Dimple's mind somehow kept reverting back to that moment in the antiques store. When she'd tried to take the camera and they'd ended up so close together. The way the air had shifted.

She tried to think about more important things, like the upcoming Insomnia Con prep they had to do in the morning, but her mind stubbornly kept interjecting that scene, playing over and over the memory of her pulse quickening, the way Rishi's smile had slowly faded. . . .

● ● ●

Rishi

He watched her surreptitiously. She was lost in thought, and the emotions on her face were sort of amusing. There was something dreamy, and then a flash of irritation, and then more dreaminess before irritation erased it again. His lips twitched; he wondered what she was thinking about.

Rishi cleared his throat. "Hey, it's, uh, only nine thirty. We could work on a little bit of the prep if you want. Or, you know, do it tomorrow morning too, if you have other stuff going on." He didn't want this night to be over. Which was ridiculous, because he was sure there were about a thousand other nights they could both name that would probably have ranked much higher than this one, thanks to the Aberzombies.

Dimple glanced at him, her lips parting a bit, like he'd caught her out at something. Now he really wanted to know what she'd been thinking. "Um, no, yeah. That sounds good. I'm just going to go take a shower and change into some comfier clothes. I can meet you at your room, if you want. I'm not sure I'm ready to face Celia when she gets home."

He grinned, his heart singing that she'd said yes. To a *study session*, Patel, he reminded himself. To her, he said, "Yeah, that's cool. I imagine I'm not her favorite person right now anyway, so she probably wouldn't be too thrilled to see me in your room."

The doors pinged open on the fourth floor. Stepping out, he

put one hand against the slot so they wouldn't close. "So, say ten fifteenish?"

She nodded and smiled. "Works for me."

And Rishi, gods help him, thought, *I could look at that smile every day and never get tired of it.*

CHAPTER 18

Dimple

Back in her room, Dimple loaded up her shower caddy and took a quicker shower than she strictly wanted to. She didn't want to be there when Celia got back. She hadn't fully processed all that had happened at Elm, and she needed some time to do that. When Celia asked her why she and Rishi had been so hostile to her friends, she wanted to have a proper response. Dimple was excellent at arguing with Mamma, but when it came to confrontations with other people, her backbone somehow became jellylike. One way to fix it, she'd learned, was to take her time thinking of responses to various arguments.

Sorry, Celia, but those Aberzombies can suck it.

Nah, too confrontational without any constructive stuff in there.

I'm sorry you thought I was unfriendly, but you didn't see all the stuff they said before you got there.

Too "telling Mommy on you."

Sighing, Dimple shampooed her curls, taking care to massage her scalp. It was something that could consistently lower her blood pressure and erase the crap out of any day. If she had the money, she'd just go sit in a salon and have them shampoo her hair for a full day.

As the smell of coconuts and jasmine filled the shower stall, she thought about the anonymous donor who'd paid for the meal. She was 95 percent sure it was Rishi, though he'd never admitted it. He was different from what she'd expected. Rich but not showy about it. Goofy and easygoing, but with a backbone. Utterly sure of himself in a really comfortable way. There was something about people who were that secure; they made you feel better about yourself, like they accepted you for everything you were, imperfections and all.

Dimple rinsed her hair out and got out of the shower, making her way back to the room in her gray terry cloth robe. She opened the dresser drawer and looked at her pajamas. All she'd brought were some ratty old T-shirts and sweatpants she'd had since freshman year of high school. For just a beat, she felt intensely self-conscious and considered going through Celia's drawer for something more . . . girly. But then the rest of her brain caught up to her and annoyance replaced self-consciousness. Seriously? Rolling her eyes at herself, she threw on her *Silly Boys, Coding Is for Girls* T-shirt and plain gray fleece pants. They'd lost their drawstring eons ago and were baggy in all the wrong places, but whatever.

Dimple was finger-combing her hair when her phone rang. Frowning, she walked over, hoping Rishi wasn't canceling. But her parents' faces flashed on the screen.

She grabbed the phone and slid to answer. "Papa?"

"Dimple?"

She straightened up, gearing for an argument. "Mamma." Papa had probably told her about their last conversation; that she and Rishi Patel weren't going to happen.

121

"*Kaisi ho?* I . . . miss you, *beti.*"

"I talked to you this morning," Dimple said, but she knew what Mamma meant. They'd barely talked. And Dimple had been too angry to have a real conversation.

Dimple sank down on her bed, a lump forming in her throat. Mamma's voice was soft, defenseless like she'd never heard it. It reminded her of being sick when she was little, how Mamma used to come sit on the edge of her bed, smooth her hair back off her feverish forehead, and give her milk with turmeric in it. *Haldi doodh,* Mamma's magic fix for every situation. It usually worked. Dimple would kill for some right now. "I miss you too, Mamma," she said thickly.

"Did you eat dinner already?"

Ha. If only you knew. "Yeah, I ate dinner. At a new restaurant, Elm."

"*Kaisa tha?* You liked?"

Dimple blinked. *No, I hated,* she wanted to say. *The people sucked. My roommate has new zombie friends, and they all think I'm a freak. But at least I didn't have to pay.* Swallowing, she said, "Eh, it was okay, I guess. Nothing like your prawns curry."

Mamma laughed, obviously pleased. "There is no cooking like home cooking!"

Dimple snuffled a laugh. That was one of Mamma's mantras. Anytime Dimple kvetched about wanting to order a pepperoni pizza because she was tired of eating something Mamma was cooking, Mamma would bust out with that. "Mamma, did Papa tell you about . . . Rishi?"

She heard Mamma's deep breath. "*Haan.*" A long silence followed. Dimple imagined little crystals of disapproval forming along the phone line.

"I know you're not happy. But honestly, I just—"

"*Beti.*" Dimple stopped. "It's okay. No problem."

But she didn't sound convinced. There was something guarded about Mamma's voice.

"It's not that I don't like him," Dimple said. "He's nice. I just . . . I need some time, Mamma. To be by myself. To find out what I want from life."

Another silence as Mamma processed this. "Okay." From the slow, heavy way she said it, Dimple knew what a Herculean effort it must've taken.

"Okay? Really?" Shut up, Dimple, she told herself. If the woman says okay, just run with it! "Thanks, Mamma."

She knew Mamma didn't understand what time had to do with anything. In her eyes, women went to college just to make themselves more marketable to guys. For her to say that just showed how much she was willing to take into account the changing times. And her strange daughter.

"Tell me, Dimple, are you remembering to wear makeup to class?"

Dimple sighed and flopped backward so she was lying flat on the bed. And now that they were done with that, apparently it was on to more important topics. "Um, no? I didn't even bring any makeup with me, Mamma."

"What! What about the contacts?"

"Mamma . . . I'm here to learn."

"You can't learn with lipstick? You can't read with contacts? What, Dimple." *What, Dimple.* The Indian way of saying, *Get your life together, Dimple.*

Dimple sat up. "Okay, I have to go now."

"Beauty sleep time, *na?*" Mamma said. "You have Pond's cold cream?"

Dimple paused, confused.

"*Hai Ram.* I bought from Walmart for you, *na?* Dimple, Pond's will make your skin soft. Just put it on at night and—"

"Oh yeah, I remember. I, uh, already did that." She yawned showily.

"Okay, okay. Good night, *beti.* Papa already went to sleep, but I'll tell him tomorrow you send your regards."

"Thanks, Mamma. Sleep tight."

"You also, *beti.*"

CHAPTER 19

Rishi

At 10:19 Rishi walked around the minuscule space once again, making sure everything was in order. The thought of Dimple, here, made him feel strangely ebullient, like he was filled with champagne bubbles. Obviously he knew nothing was going to *happen*. He wouldn't try anything anyway, not when he knew how she felt. It was his damn fool heart. Ever optimistic, always looking for a sliver of sunshine in a sky clotted with thunderclouds. He shook his head and fluffed his pillow.

At 10:20 Rishi laid out a bowl full of sweet and sour *khatta meetha*, some *baadam* that Ma had packed for him, and water. He wiped the screen of his laptop with his shirtsleeve, then had to change his shirt because the sleeve turned gray from the dust.

At 10:22 Rishi seriously began to worry that Dimple wouldn't come. Should he text her? Nah, that would be too needy. If she wasn't going to show up, then he'd have to give her some space. *But who decides to just not show up?* he thought in annoyance. At least she should text him. Or tape a note to his door. He glanced at his door. Maybe there was a note taped to the other side.

At 10:23, as he was walking across the room to check for the note, there was a knock. He exhaled.

She stood on the other side, hair somewhat damp, smiling. "Hey. Sorry I'm late. My mom called."

Wow, she smelled good. Rishi made a concentrated effort not to inhale deeply. "No problem." He held the door open and spread his arm out. "Come on in."

Dimple walked in, her eyes sweeping across his room. "You don't have a roommate? How'd you swing that?"

He shrugged and rubbed the back of his neck. "Ah, my parents insisted on springing for a private suite."

She looked at him, smirking, but when he raised his eyebrows in question, she just looked away, resuming her inspection of his dresser top, his bed, his desk. "Oh, *khatta meetha*! It's my favorite."

He grinned. This fact made him irrationally happy. "Awesome. Help yourself."

"Did you bring it with you? Or did you find an Indian grocer?" she asked, stuffing a small fistful of the peanut and rice-flake mixture in her mouth.

"My mother packed it for me. But that's a good idea—we should find an Indian grocer. Stock up on some of our favorite snacks to energize us while we write."

Dimple nodded. "Good idea. We should find an Asian grocer too. I need some Pocky sticks. Those are, like, my go-to snacks during finals." Apparently seeing Rishi's confused face, she gasped and held a hand to her chest. "Do you not know what Pocky sticks are?"

He shook his head. "Sorry. No idea."

"We have to remedy that." She grabbed a few *baadam* and tossed them into her mouth, playfully side-eyeing him as she chewed on the almonds. Rishi felt his heart lift; she seemed happier than before, like she'd managed to wash off the crap laid on her by the Aberzombies over dinner. Good. They weren't worth a millisecond of her time.

Dimple looked around for a second and then awkwardly perched on the edge of his bed, toward the foot, close to his desk. "Is it okay if I . . . uh, sit here?"

He felt his cheeks heating. "Yeah, sure. I'll sit here." He plonked himself down on the cheap wooden chair at the desk. In this tiny room, it was about as far away as if he'd sat right next to her on the bed, but the distinction between chair and bed somehow felt safer, less scandalous.

"So." Rishi moved a finger across his trackpad so his laptop would come to life. "I know you told me briefly already what your idea is, and we'd decided to get into more details later. Where do you want to start?"

"I was thinking we should approach this top-down. Let's think about the high-level functions we want—what's the heart and soul of the app? And then we can drill down from there. What do you think?"

"Sounds good to me." Rishi opened up a Word document. "I'll take notes as we talk."

"Okay, great." Dimple hopped off the bed and began pacing, her T-shirt and pants hanging off her like she was wearing her big brother's clothes. Rishi felt a tug of affection that he attempted to cover by scratching the back of his neck and looking away. "Let's see . . . so I want to make sure that people know this is a serious product. You know? Like, it can be lifesaving. But that it's also fun. Taking care of your health, taking your medication, or checking your sugar levels or whatever doesn't have to be a drag. That's always the main thing for Papa . . . he feels like managing diabetes is too heavy. I think he'd rather not think about it because of that. So if people could see the lighter side of it, maybe it'd help make it a little less scary."

"Okay." Rishi nodded and typed up the gist of what Dimple was saying. "So we want to convey health care with a twist."

"Exactly. Serious but fun. It works, but it's not scary to use. It makes you *want* to use it. You get points the more you track. And then, at the end of like, five sessions, you get to go to the store where you can buy stuff."

"Right." Rishi tapped a pencil against his chin. "But maybe we could tap into that compulsion loop you talked about a little more. So people can go to the store if they keep tracking the times they successfully take their meds or whatever it is, right?"

Dimple paused in her pacing and nodded.

"But what about if they don't track? What's the impetus for them to begin tracking regularly in the first place?"

"I guess just the points?" Dimple shrugged, frowning slightly. "But I see what you're saying. That's not a big enough push, is it? Not if they're already sort of iffy about tracking that kind of thing."

"Right. It should be our job to make it an addictive game, to make it seem not at all threatening, so they actually want to open the app."

Dimple paused, thinking, her eyes bright and sparking as she worked. Rishi watched openly and perhaps a little too closely, intrigued. "Ooh." She looked up at him, and he looked away, flushing, but she didn't seem to notice, caught up as she was in her idea.

"Okay, what about if it's like something advancing on them? Like, the reward is that you get to stave off some big, bad boss guy coming for you the more you track. And if you get lazy or careless, you get killed."

Rishi grinned. "Yes." He grabbed a scrap piece of paper and a pencil off his desk and began to sketch. "What about something like this?"

He felt Dimple, standing behind him, observing. Instead of making him nervous like he usually felt when Ashish or Ma tried to watch him, he felt more confident. The more he sketched, the closer she leaned in, seemingly mesmerized, until she finally knelt down to be closer, the tips of her curls brushing his arm.

Rishi forced himself to concentrate on his sketch, to ignore the tingling heat that was running up and down his arm. There was nothing but this sketch. *Focus, Patel.*

Dimple let out a breath. "Wow."

Rishi moved his arm out of her way, shifting uncomfortably, and she realized she'd just breathed on him and probably grossed him out.

"Oh, sorry." She moved away a bit, but not so far that she couldn't see what was going on. This was fantastic. Rishi had drawn a hoard of about seven zombies, all nuanced and gross in the goofiest way. Some of their eyeballs bulged out while others were missing teeth or had wavy lines of bad smell coming off them. Others oozed slime from between their toes. They were all advancing on a tiny circular fox with huge eyes and a bushy tail curled around itself.

"See?" Rishi said. "So maybe there's this huge gang of roving zombies, and your user gets to pick an avatar, and the zombies are going to eat the fox if they don't track fast enough or regularly enough. You know? Kind of like 'Plants vs. Zombies' but with more tracking action." He turned to look at her. "What do you think?"

Dimple nodded sagely, her heart thumping in her chest. This was good. This was very, very good. She could already see that. "I do have one serious concern."

Rishi waited for her to continue, a small wrinkle between his brows.

"Can we make them aliens instead of zombies? Zombies are so overdone."

"Aliens?" Rishi rolled his eyes. "You totally don't have my artistic vision."

Dimple punched him in the ribs, lighter than she wanted to, but he still winced. "Ow. You know, most girls just slap guys playfully on the arm or something. They don't actually hurt them."

"Well, maybe you need to expand your idea of how girls behave," Dimple replied, grinning.

Rishi laughed. "Fair enough. And yes, I can totally do aliens, since they seem so important to you."

"Awesome. Then we're totally going to kick Insomnia Con's butt!"

They high-fived, and Dimple grabbed the sheet of paper and sat on the bed to look at it. "You're an amazing artist. Will you do the preliminary artwork for the concept?"

He nodded. "Of course. I don't want anyone else coming in and stealing my vision, you know."

Dimple snorted. "Totally. By the way, do you have any samples of your comics? Like, your old work or anything?"

Rishi immediately began to click around on his laptop screen, as if he'd discovered something of immense importance that had to be done right away. "Uh, no. Nothing like that."

"Hmm." *Interesting,* Dimple thought. *I think Rishi Patel is lying.* She flipped over the paper he'd drawn the zombies on; it was a flyer of some kind. "Oh, cool. Little Comic Con. Are you going to this?"

Rishi rubbed the back of his neck. "Ah, I don't know. It was just a thing I picked up on impulse."

"The thirteenth, from six to ten," Dimple read. "Hey, that's this weekend." She looked up at him. "We can go together. I mean, if you want to. Since you were nice enough to come to the Aberzombie dinner with me."

Rishi

Had Dimple Shah just asked him out on a date?

CHAPTER 20

Dimple

"I mean, not like a date or anything," Dimple rushed to put in. And then felt like a total jerk because his face fell, just the tiniest fraction of a bit. "But, you know, as a friend. Which is even better, in my opinion."

He smiled, though she saw it wasn't his usual vibrant, full-on sun smile. "Yeah, cool. Let's do it."

They put in another two hours researching the market, designing the UI, and getting started on the wireframe and storyboard. The process frequently sent a frisson of excitement up Dimple's spine. This was her idea they were talking about implementing. In six weeks it would be an actual *thing* out there in the world, about halfway to completion, not just an abstract concept. Key people would be looking at it, judging it. And if it passed muster, maybe Jenny Lindt would want to work with her to finish it. It would go on to save lives.

Finally, around one a.m., Dimple stood and stretched. "I think I should head back to my room. See you in the morning?"

Rishi stifled a yawn as he closed his laptop. "Yeah, sounds good. Want me to swing by and pick you up?"

Dimple gathered her hair into a loose bun and looked down at her feet. "Might as well. We're going to the same place, right?"

Rishi

It shouldn't have, but it made Rishi's heart lift. When would he ever learn?

You're setting yourself up for heartbreak, Patel, he told himself.

But no matter how true he knew that was, he couldn't stop the grin from spreading over his face.

Dimple

Dimple was so keyed up over all they'd accomplished—and, a tiny voice inside her said, from the fact that she and Rishi had a non-date that would let her see more of the comic book persona he liked to keep hidden—that she didn't even notice Celia until she'd taken off her shoes and climbed into bed.

Celia sat on her bed, propped up against her pillows, staring at Dimple reproachfully. Her phone lay facedown on her lap.

"Oh, hey," Dimple said, suddenly remembering in a mild panic that she hadn't come up with any good responses.

"What the heck happened at dinner?" Celia said, and it was more a wail than an angry accusation. "I thought you guys would hit it off!"

Dimple sighed and climbed under the covers, turning on her left so she could face Celia. "That's what I hoped too. But I think your friends and I are just too different." She shrugged, like, *c'est la vie*. Celia didn't have to know how much Dimple had been hoping for some kind of olive branch, even though Dimple wasn't the one who'd done anything wrong.

"And Rishi was kind of rude," Celia went on, fiddling with her phone. "What was his deal?"

Dimple thought of how Rishi had stuck up for her, over and over again. How he hadn't been the least bit cowed by the rude remarks or digs of the night. She felt anger flash through her; she always did find it easier to stick up for people other than herself. "Sorry, Celia, but you missed about forty minutes of conversation while you and your grandma were bonding. Your friends deserved everything they got, and more. I mean, I know you think they're cool and they get you and whatever, but let's not try to force something that's never going to happen."

Celia raised her eyebrows, like, *wowza*. "Fine." She picked up her phone, and there was a prickly silence in the room.

Dimple pulled the covers around her shoulders. "But I still want to be your friend. I think we should still stick together and be each other's moral support. But maybe it's okay if we're not friends with each other's friends."

Celia continued to surf for a moment. Then she set her phone down again and looked over at Dimple. There was a smile in her eyes. "I like that idea."

Rishi

The weekend came at a breathtaking pace. Dimple and Rishi had spent every day in between fine-tuning Dimple's initial wireframe prototype, making sure they were ready to begin working on the backend of things.

Rishi loved the way she seemed lit from the inside when she talked about her plan for the app, how much she wanted her Papa's approval. Whether she liked to admit it or not, her parents were important to her, and Rishi respected that.

He combed his hair in the mirror, pulling his fingers through the floppy part Ashley Sternberger in eighth grade had once called "adorable." She'd batted her baby blues at him while she said it too, so Rishi knew it wasn't the kind of adorable you think your baby brother is.

His gaze fell on the Little Comic Con flyer on the dresser, and he felt a strange warmth come to his cheeks when he remembered Dimple asking if she could come with him. She'd asked about his comics so many times now, and each time he'd deflected. The truth was, he'd love to show her.

He'd seen the fire in her eyes when she talked about developing that app; he knew she'd understand exactly what Pappa and Ma didn't. She'd get how it made him feel, how the characters became an extension of himself, how he could lose himself for hours as he sat there, hunched over a sheet sketching in panels, watching the characters slowly begin to blink and breathe and laugh and live.

Rishi walked to his bag, and digging behind the paperbacks he'd brought with him, he reached to the thing he'd packed at the last minute, without really letting himself think about it—his sketch pad. He felt that sense of love and attachment and warm familiarity envelop him as he pulled it out.

The cardboard cover was falling apart, and the pages were bent and soft from age, especially the ones in the front. It was like a flip book of his talent—at the front were the sketches he'd done about three years ago, still a bit blocky and dull from their creator's lack of experience. As the months progressed, they'd morphed into something warm and alive, liquid and vibrant. He'd gotten pretty good at keeping his characters consistent, at developing their unique characteristics and his own style. He smiled at the iterations of Aditya as the months went on. Silly and inconsequential as all of this was, drawing had always been a tempering balm. Art was a way to quiet his brain and lose himself in a place where he didn't even really exist.

Rishi slipped the sketch pad back into his bag and then slung the bag over his shoulder. Maybe going to Little Comic Con later tonight wouldn't be the worst thing ever. He could figure out what people who went into this looking for careers as comic book artists actually did. His bet was that most of them ended up teaching in programs like this or working in advertising, neither of which appealed to him on any level.

He wasn't going to lie, though, he thought, as he grabbed his dorm key and let the door shut behind him—the idea of Dimple Shah accompanying him to the Con made it all that much more alluring. He had one more stop to make, and then he'd pick her up at her dorm room.

The thought of seeing her again made his stomach flip in a very impractical way.

Dimple

"What are you wearing?" Celia said from in front of the dresser/vanity where she'd just finished slathering foundation all over her face and neck with a sponge.

Dimple looked up from her computer and shrugged. "Jeans?"

Celia groaned and clutched at her hair before meticulously smoothing it back down. Popping on a black headband with a big glittery bow on it, she said, "This is Little Comic Con. I'm guessing people dress up in costumes? Go all out?" It was Friday night, and apparently the Aberzombies had invited her to some party.

Dimple chewed on her lip. She hadn't even really thought of that. "You think so?"

Celia began drawing on her face with what looked like a chubby brown crayon. Seeing Dimple's quizzical look, she said, "Concealer. And yes, I definitely think so. Why don't you Google it? See what they've done in the past? The flyer says 'third annual,' so I bet they have pictures online."

"Good idea." Dimple pulled up the website for the art department and groaned. "Oh no." She clicked from picture to picture. People didn't just go all out—they went freaking crazy. There was a write-up on a guy who'd actually built his own Iron Man costume out of junkyard parts and then spray-painted them an amazing iridescent pink. Another student made her own Predator costume, and it took her an entire year of hand-sewing everything. It was Oscar-worthy. Or, you know, whatever the award was for costumes. There were group costumes, and costumes made out of interesting materials, and eco-friendly costumes, and glow-in-the-dark costumes. . . . Dimple stared. "Why the heck didn't Rishi tell me?"

"Um, maybe he doesn't know? You should probably text him." Celia smoothed a mermaid-hued eyeshadow on her lids. It looked amazing with her hazel eyes; even makeup averse Dimple could appreciate that.

She grabbed her phone.

Did you know everyone is going to be wearing costumes? Really elaborate ones?

Her phone beeped a few seconds later. *Yeah, it's like Comic Con, no? Only smaller.*

Dimple groaned. Did everyone know stuff like this automatically?

Her phone beeped again. *But you don't have to dress up. You're my guest.*

Well, what are you going as?

Aha. That's for me to know and you to find out.

Dimple rolled her eyes. Great. She looked at Celia. "Do you have anything in your closet I could wear that would pass as a costume?" Celia had brought virtually everything from her closet back home. She was actually using part of Dimple's closet because all her stuff wouldn't fit.

She made a face as she applied a pale gold lipstick using a brush. Who applied lipstick with a brush? No one Dimple knew. "You can look. All I have is regular clothes though. . . . Who are you planning on going as?"

"I don't know!" Dimple threw her hands up. "The only cartoon I even remember being interested in—" She stopped, a thought forming. "Celia, do you have anything green and long sleeved?"

"Hmm . . ." Celia set her lipstick and brush down and turned to her closet. After a second she pulled out a long-sleeved hoodie with a zipper. "What about this?"

Dimple smiled slowly. "I think that'll do really well. And can I borrow a short black skirt too?"

CHAPTER 21

Dimple

When Rishi knocked on her door at seven, Dimple wasn't even nervous. She knew her costume kicked butt. He stared at her for less than half a second before he grinned. "I love Daria."

"Right?" She grinned back. Celia had even helped her straighten her hair. It hung shiny and long, well past her shoulders. "Who doesn't? I think it would've worked better if Celia could've been here to be Quinn, though."

Rishi laughed. "Oh, man. Where did you get those '90s combat boots, though?" His laughter faded as he saw that she was glaring at him.

"Those are mine. I wear them sometimes."

"Oh, I, uh, those are really great—"

Dimple smiled. "You don't have to pretend to like them. I like them, and I don't care that they're not in style or whatever. So. Are you who I think you are?"

He did a little manly twirl. "Yep. Aditya the Sun God/superhero, at your service."

"That is so cool! Where the heck did you get that *gada*?" She closed the door behind her and they began walking together to the elevators.

"Well, you might remember our old friend Wanda. I went back there and told her the nature of my inquiry. It turns out her husband is quite the welder. So he helped me put this together out of some recycled metal parts in his shop, and I spent the afternoon painting on some of the finer details. Kevin Keo, this dude I met before from the art department, was cool about letting me go down there and use some of their supplies when I told him what it was for."

"That's awesome," Dimple said, looking him up and down in appreciation while also not letting him see just how appreciative she was. He was wearing a tight fitting kurta with his jeans, and every time he swung the *gada*, she could see his biceps flex through the flimsy material.

Outside, the air was warmish in spite of the fog, with the faint tang of perfume and cologne as college students made their way off campus to various events. Dimple loved the buzz of energy, a slightly drunken, heady thing. The twinkle of city lights barely broke through the fog, making the air look just gold-hued enough to be magical. She inhaled deeply—and sneezed. Stupid allergies.

"Gods bless you," Rishi said.

Dimple arched an eyebrow. "Gods?"

He nodded sagely. "As a Hindu, I'm a polytheist, as you well know."

Dimple laughed. "Yes, and I also know we still only say 'God,' not 'gods.' We still believe Brahma is the supreme creator."

Rishi smiled, a sneaky little thing that darted out before he could stop it. "You got me. It's my version of microaggressing back on people."

"Explain."

"So, okay. This is how it works in the US: In the spring we're constantly subjected to bunnies and eggs wherever we go, signifying Christ's resurrection. Then right around October we begin to see pine trees and nativity scenes and laughing fat white men everywhere. Christian iconography is all over the place, constantly in our faces, even in casual conversation. *This is the bible of comic book artists . . . He had a* come to Jesus *moment*, all of that stuff. So this is my way of saying, *Hey, maybe I believe something a little different.* And every time someone asks me why 'gods,' I get to explain Hinduism."

Dimple chewed on this, impressed in spite of herself. He actually had a valid point. Why *was* Christianity always the default? "Ah." She nodded, pushing her glasses up on her nose. "So what you're saying is, you're like a Jehovah's Witness for our people."

Rishi's mouth twitched, but he nodded seriously. "Yes. I'm Ganesha's Witness. Has a bit of a ring to it, don't you think?"

They cut across the lawn and headed west, toward the building marked by a star on the Little Comic Con map Rishi was holding. In the distance someone honked.

"I can't tell if you're exceptionally eccentric or just really passionate about the cultural stuff," Dimple said after they'd walked a little ways in silence.

Rishi chuckled. "My brother, Ashish, and I have had that conversation many times." He said it lightly, but something hard and dark flickered beneath the surface. "I don't know how I can explain it . . . it's just this need inside me. I guess I just feel it stronger than most people our age. I feel like I need to speak out, because if no one speaks out, if no one says, *This is me, this is what I believe in, and this is why I'm different, and this is why that's okay*, then what's the point? What's the point of living in this beautiful, great melting pot where everyone can dare to be anything they want to be?" He shrugged. "Besides, haven't you gone to India and just stood among your relatives and listened to their stories and felt like . . . I don't know, like you wanted to tell more people?"

Dimple fiddled with the zipper on Celia's hoodie, avoiding Rishi's eyes. "I don't know. I haven't been to India since I was twelve; the tickets are too expensive for my parents. But even when I did, the thing I remember most is feeling like I didn't belong. I mean, I was already going through that phase at my school where I felt like my family was weird and different and I just wished they'd be like all the other parents. But then I went to Mumbai and realized that to all the people there, I was American. I was still the outsider, and still strange, and I still didn't belong."

She tucked a curl behind her ear, feeling that pinch of realization again, just like when she was twelve. It had really been driven home when her cousin Preeti, who was the same age, had introduced Dimple to her neighborhood friends as her cousin from America. One of the girls, hearing Dimple's accent, had laughed and called Dimple *firang*, which Preeti had explained, red-faced, meant *foreigner*. Preeti stuck up for her, but she could see it was halfhearted. Even Preeti thought Dimple was a *firang*. She just didn't belong.

"Interesting," Rishi said, a small breeze lifting a tuft of his hair so he looked, adorably, like an Indian Dennis the Menace. "I guess I'm the opposite. I feel like an Indian American here, and when I'm in India, like just an Indian. I see them both as equal and valid for me."

"How are you so well-adjusted?" Dimple grumbled.

Rishi snorted. "It's taken time, I swear. I went through this whole emo phase in middle school where I played with the alias 'Rick.'" He winced. "I'm just glad it didn't stick."

Dimple laughed. "Yeah, I like Rishi much better."

"To be honest, even if I feel like I culturally belong, I don't really feel like I socially belong. I mean, just like you were saying . . . I've never belonged with the private school crowd. I've never really had good friends in high school I wanted to keep in touch with. There's no one I'll miss."

Dimple didn't want to admit how much what he was saying resonated with her. Loneliness. That's what he was describing. And she'd felt it so much it had become like a constant presence in her life, curled up against her like a sleeping cat. "I know what you mean," she said softly. "Unfortunately."

"I don't think it's unfortunate. It's probably why we get along so well. Even if you *did* viciously attack me when we first met."

Dimple laughed, and Rishi beamed at her, the way he seemed to every time she laughed. It was like he was basking in her happiness. Instead of looking away like she usually did, she smiled back.

Something flickered in his eyes. She itched her elbow and dropped her gaze. "What?"

"Nothing." He looked away, but a small, secretive smile played at his lips.

Dimple punched him lightly in the ribs. "*What*, Rishi?"

"Ah . . ." He rubbed the back of his neck and looked at her sidelong. "That's just the first time you haven't pretended to be oblivious to the fact that you have a certain . . . effect on me when you laugh."

Dimple felt her cheeks burning, and she looked down at her boots. "I have no idea what you're talking about."

Rishi chuckled quietly. "Yeah, I think you do, but I'll let it go, since you clearly don't want to talk about it."

And Dimple found herself feeling just the slightest bit disappointed.

CHAPTER 22

Rishi

Little Comic Con was going to be held in the lobby of the art department main building. As they passed another quad, Rishi saw it looming on the corner. It was a huge, modern structure, and the lower floor consisted of mostly windows. Inside, Rishi could see a bustle of colorful activity: squirming clots of costumed people and booths and banners and demonstrations. He felt a pinprick of nerves along his spine—he'd had no idea it was going to be so busy. There was a massive sculpture of a fortune cookie outside, made from what looked like old clothes. As streams of people walked past, they reached out and grabbed a "fortune" from the opening.

"What is that?" Dimple asked, and she picked up the pace.

"I don't know," Rishi mumbled, trailing a little bit behind, wishing he'd just said he wasn't interested when he met Kevin Keo last week. *Are you interested in a degree in art? No, thank you.* How hard would that have been, Patel?

As they approached the sculpture, Rishi saw a sign in front of it that said SARTORIAL FORTUNE COOKIE BY YAEL BORGER, 2017. "The body of the cookie is constructed out of PVC pipe, over which padding is attached. Sanitized clothes from the landfill cover those. A strip of cloth, which has been printed with each viewer's 'fortune,' can be pulled from the hollow center of the structure. Yael Borger is a senior in the SFSU fine arts program and hopes to raise awareness of clothing waste and its impact on the environment."

"Cool." Dimple whistled and reached over to pull a fortune out. She arched her eyebrow at Rishi when she saw he wasn't. "Come on. You have to too."

He sighed and reached into the large slit in the center of the cookie to pull out a strip of fabric. "This is just awkward."

Dimple laughed. "Just read yours." She unfolded her strip, a piece of sky blue denim with fraying edges, on which words had been printed in white. "Hmm. *Extinction is near.*" She looked up at him. "What's yours say?"

He turned his black-and-yellow-polka-dotted strip of fabric around. In red, it said, *This will not end well.*

"Wow." Dimple laughed. "Ominous."

Rishi crumpled up his strip and stuck it into the recycling bucket provided. "Man, Yael Borger is probably a ton of laughs. Can you just see her at a dinner party?" Putting on a cheerful voice, he said, "Hi, Yael, how are you today?" And then, in a sepulchral intonation meant to be Yael, "You will die."

Dimple snorted. "At least she's getting people to think and talk about the issue she wants them to think and talk about. Mission accomplished, I'd say. Isn't that the point of art?" They wound their way around a group of students chattering in the doorway. "I mean, why do you make your comics, for instance?"

"Release," Rishi answered, before he could really consider censoring himself. To Pappa and Ma, he was careful to always say comics were just a fun hobby, inconsequential. They were more magnanimous about them that way. "It's like taking a giant helium balloon full of your worries and just letting it go."

The lobby was huge, marble floored, and echoing with excited chatter from all the students and exhibitors. A giant banner, similar to the one at the table Kevin Keo had been manning the other day, hung in the center of the space and said, WELCOME TO LITTLE COMIC CON! YOU CAN TURN YOUR ART INTO A CAREER. LET US HELP!

There was a gigantic poster of Naruto Uzumaki hanging from the stair banister. Someone in the department obviously loved anime. Booths with giant banners showcasing various other famous comic characters dotted the space—Rishi saw everything from Pokémon to Harley Quinn to the Hulk. Across the floor, Rishi spotted someone at a crowded booth. His breath caught in his throat. "Oh my gods." Heart pounding, he grabbed Dimple's hand without thinking and then immediately let go. "It's Leo Tilden."

"Who?" Dimple followed his gaze. "Who's that?"

"He made this totally amazing character, Platinum Panic, for a series of graphic novels. I read them all when I was, like, ten. It's sort of what got me started on comics. He has these amazing YouTube videos too." He rubbed the back of his neck. It felt surreal, to see the man standing not ten yards away from him, after having hero-worshipped him from afar for nearly a decade, after having laughed at every YouTube joke. After having sent him embarrassing fan mail when he was eleven—not that he was about to divulge that piece of information to Dimple. Or the fact that he kept the postcard Leo had sent back, stapled to the last page of his sketch pad. It said, *Semper pinge—Keep drawing always* in Latin. Platinum Panic's catchphrase was *Semper sursum—Always upward.*

"Well, come on, let's go wait in line and meet the guy." Dimple grabbed his hand again and started toward the line.

Rishi didn't quite have time to process that (a) she'd grabbed his hand of her own accord and (b) how nice it felt, because he was beginning to freak out.

"Um, I don't know," Rishi said, pulling back.

All of this was happening too fast. It was too much. He'd said yes to Kevin Keo when he should've said no, now he was at this huge con, and his idol was right in front of him. He was slipping down some comic book rabbit hole. It was, he thought, like trying to stay away from the girl you desperately loved but who you knew was bad for you. You kept your distance, because that was the only way to save yourself. You kept your distance, because you knew if you didn't, you'd be helplessly and hopelessly caught up in everything you loved about her. Distance was the promise of safety. Without distance, Rishi knew the inexorable love for his art, for creation, would suck him in and never let go.

Dimple turned to him, eyes narrowed. "What do you mean, you don't know? You just said this guy's your idol, right?" Something in his expression softened her. She put a hand on his arm. "What's up?"

"I wasn't expecting all this." Rishi waved a hand in the general direction of Leo Tilden. "This was supposed to be small." He pointed to the welcome banner that said LITTLE COMIC CON. "See? *Little.* It's even in the name." He smiled, but his heart wasn't in it.

Dimple studied him for a second. "Are you afraid that you don't belong here? Or that you do?"

He looked at her, startled. How had she so quickly, so succinctly, verbalized everything he was feeling? "What are you, some kind of mind reader?"

Dimple smiled. "Look, we'll just go meet Leo Tilden, and then we can leave. You don't even have to let on that you draw or anything. You can pretend your costume is from some Indian comic they haven't heard of." She shrugged. "What do you have to lose?"

She was right. When he looked back on this in a year, when he was at MIT, he wouldn't remember any of these feelings. He'd remember meeting Leo Tilden. He'd always have that.

He nodded. "All right, Daria. And maybe after that we can go get some gelato or something."

Dimple grinned. "Let's do it."

CHAPTER 23

Rishi

"Hi." Leo Tilden's distinctive voice, in real life. Wow.

Rishi smiled, but he wasn't fully sure he was smiling in a socially appropriate way. Meaning, he was baring his teeth. But the tall muscular man next to Leo Tilden—his assistant, Sven, probably—looked fairly perturbed. Dimple elbowed him in the side. "Um, h-hi. I'm, I'm a big Rishi." He heard Dimple snort. Oh my gods. Had he just said, *I'm a big* Rishi? "Fan," he corrected, feeling like his entire face was about to burst into flames. "I'm a big fan. My name is—"

"Let me guess," Leo said, grinning. "Rishi." He held out his hand. Beside him, burly Sven relaxed. "Nice to meet you, my man."

"You too," Rishi said, feeling like he was in some sort of bizarre dream. He made sure to enunciate and face Leo the entire time. He knew from Leo's YouTube videos that the artist was fitted with a cochlear implant, which allowed him to hear, but not quite at the level of a hearing person. "I read *Platinum Panic* when I was ten. It's what got me into comics. I still remember finding out that you were the only deaf comic book artist to have ever made it so big. It felt . . ." He shook his head. "Momentous. Like it was okay to break the mold."

Leo nodded. "Totally. It's even *necessary* to break the mold. We need more people shaking things up. This is where I got my start, at SFSU. They're pretty great about letting diverse voices be heard." He pointed to Rishi's outfit. "Who're you dressed as?"

Rishi looked down. He'd honestly forgotten he was wearing the costume. His mouth felt like the Rajasthan desert. "Um, n-no one."

Leo raised a bushy eyebrow. "No one?" He pointed to Rishi's *gada*. "Do you regularly just carry that around with you?"

Dimple elbowed him again. He ignored her. "It's just . . . it's not . . ."

"It's Aditya the Sun God/superhero. He created the character himself, a couple years ago." Dimple darted Rishi a spiteful, triumphant look. He was going to have a Very Serious talk with her later. He tried to convey this through his gaze, but she didn't seem to get it. Or if she did, it didn't seem to make her very nervous.

"Really?" Leo leaned forward. "You have any panels on you?"

The messenger bag weighed heavy on Rishi's shoulder. His sketch pad was in there. Years of work. He even had a few recent panels he'd done, all inked in and everything. They were good enough to show Leo Tilden. It wouldn't be embarrassing or anything.

But . . . it felt weird. Like a betrayal of Ma and Pappa. They thought he was out here for Dimple, for experience before he went off to MIT. This was exactly the kind of thing they wouldn't want him doing. Showing his sketches to a major graphic novelist felt like a step. A step he wasn't sure he wanted to take. "Not on me, no," he said, finally, the words like jagged pieces of glass in his mouth. It hurt. It really hurt.

Leo looked genuinely disappointed. "Oh, that's too bad. Maybe next time."

There will never be a next time, Rishi thought. He knew this with complete certainty. Somewhere inside him, something soft and creative and vulnerable hardened, a mockingbird turning to stone.

"Yeah, sure." Rishi forced a smile and held out his hand again. "It was nice to meet you. I'd love to buy a signed copy of your latest."

Sven had one at the ready.

Dimple

Dimple darted glances at Rishi as they made their way to the various booths. He smiled, placid, as he observed some art student doing a live demonstration of pottery. Something had shifted in him from thirty minutes ago. Something vital. But Dimple didn't know what.

"Are you . . . okay?" she asked as he took a proffered flyer and then put it down at the next table without looking at it.

"Yeah." He looked down at her and smiled. It was the fire in his eyes, she realized. It had blazed when he'd first seen Leo Tilden, but it was gone now. "Why?"

Dimple shook her head. "I don't know. You seem different. Subdued. Was it because you didn't have your sketches to show Leo Tilden? Because I bet you can ask him if you can e-mail them to him later—"

"Nah, it wasn't that." They walked up to an exhibitor booth where a pretty dark-haired woman in bright fuchsia lipstick was demonstrating some new range of markers to a group of guys who were watching her more than her product. Rishi picked up a pack of markers and then set them down again. "I think I'm ready to get out of here, though. What about you?"

Ugh. It was so frustrating how he was doing that. Dimple didn't know what, exactly, he was doing, but it was definitely frustrating. "Um, yeah. I guess."

They began to loop around a group of people lining up for free popcorn when someone shouted out, "Hey! Yo! Rishi, right?"

They turned to see a wiry guy at a booth a few yards away. He was about Rishi's height, with spiked black hair and red wire-rimmed glasses, and was grinning, waving effusively. He was very obviously dressed as the manga character on the banner right behind him.

"Who is that Energizer Bunny?" Dimple asked as they began to make their way over.

"That's Kevin Keo, the guy who invited me," Rishi said. "He's pretty cool. If it's okay with you, I'll just say hi really quick, and then we can go."

"Yeah, sure." As they got closer, Dimple saw that Kevin's booth was dedicated to comics and manga. There was even a sketchbook open in front of him, and he looked like he was drawing a cross between a space alien and a girl in yoga pants. It was actually really cool; the whole thing looked 3-D, like it was climbing out of the page. Dimple glanced at Rishi, but he was looking at everything in that weird, impassive way again, as if none of this had anything to do with him. What was his deal?

Even Dimple thought the sketch was extremely cool, and she wasn't really into artsy stuff. "That's amazing," she said, leaning over to study the detail. From up close, she saw that the alien creature's tentacles were actually made of words, tightly packed together, loop-ing lazily over each other.

"Thanks!" Kevin said. "It's dialogue from *One Piece*." He ges-tured to the banner behind him and then his own costume. "I'm dressed as Monkey D. Luffy, the main character. It's one of my favorite shows of all time. Do you watch it?"

Dimple shrugged. "Sorry. I know absolutely nothing about manga." She glanced at Rishi. "Have you heard of *One Piece*?"

"Yeah." He nodded, but it was halfhearted, like he was already itching to go. "I watched a few episodes one summer."

Kevin, oblivious to Rishi's lukewarm mood, rubbed his hands together. "I like how your *gada* turned out, man. Really sweet." He paused, and when Rishi muttered a faint "thanks," he powered forward. "So? What do you think of LCC so far? Meet any cool people?"

Rishi smiled, a closemouthed thing. "Yeah, Leo Tilden. That was neat." He held up the graphic novel he'd bought. "Got a signed copy."

"Dude is sick!" Kevin said, his entire face lit up with passion and excitement and fire. "Are you subscribed to his YouTube channel?" When Rishi nodded, he went on, "I tune in every week. I heard he might start taking user subs, and if you go here in the fall—"

"Listen, man, this has been cool, but I gotta say, I don't think I'm gonna be going here. I'm already in at MIT." Rishi shrugged. "Just don't want to lead you on."

"Oh." Kevin's face fell. Then he frowned. "MIT? But I thought you were into comic art."

"I am." Rishi paused. "I was. It was more a passing hobby in middle school and high school. But I'm not going to have time for all that. I have a real career to focus on, you know?"

Something passed over Kevin's face. More coolly, he said, "So what are you going to be studying at MIT?" The way he said it, Dimple could tell he thought Rishi was a pretentious douche nozzle. *But he's not!* She wanted to yell. *I have no idea who this weird, serious zombie is!*

"Computer science and engineering," Rishi said.

Kevin nodded. His eyes flickered over Rishi's kurta and *gada*. "So you didn't go into details before, when I saw you. Who are you dressed as?"

Rishi looked down. For a moment, he seemed like he wanted to tell Kevin about Aditya. There was a look, almost like longing, that passed over his features like a soft cloud. Then his expression cleared. "No one. Just an obscure Indian comic from when I was a kid."

CHAPTER 24

Dimple

Kevin looked over at Dimple. Clearly, he'd dismissed Rishi. "So." He smiled. "Are you into comics or any kind of art? I don't recognize your costume."

"This is Daria, the '90s cartoon. You should check it out if you get a chance. But as far as creativity goes . . ." Dimple made a face. "I think I was out sick when the artsy genes were being doled out. The extent of my creativity is app development and some website design. Coding is sort of like telling a story, I guess, but nothing other than that. Seriously though, I think what you've got going on here is pretty sweet." She gestured around at the building. "I love all the color! And everyone's costumes are just amazing." A girl in a gorgeous gold retro dress, blue braids, and makeup that looked airbrushed on walked by, proving her point.

Kevin beamed, clearly pleased that at least one of them was in their right mind. "Well, do you have any major plans tonight after this?"

Dimple shook her head. "No, I don't think so. Why?"

"The art department students always put on an awesome after

party. You should check it out. It usually gets started around nineish."
He scribbled an address on a paper in his sketch pad. Ripping it out,
he handed it to Dimple. Reluctantly, he turned to Rishi, who was
watching the whole exchange impassively. "You can come too."

"Thanks," Rishi said, "but I don't—"

"We would love to," Dimple said firmly, ignoring Rishi's glare.

Outside, the air felt cool and revitalizing after the mugginess of
Little Comic Con. Dimple inhaled deeply as they walked away,
leaving the noise and the heat and the laughter behind. The world
was dark and cold, the stars still obscured by fog. They walked in
silence for a few minutes, the breeze rustling the leaves overhead
and playing with Dimple's hair. She pulled it up into a bun. "So,"
she said lightly, "what'd you think?"

"I'm a little hungry. You up for some of that gelato we'd talked
about?"

Dimple nodded slowly. "Yeah. But, um, are you going to tell me
what happened in there?" She glanced at Rishi; she couldn't read his
expression. "I mean, if you want to."

For a moment his expression stayed like that—stonelike and
unyielding. But then he took a deep breath. It seemed to begin at
the soles of his feet and travel up to his mouth, like he was carrying
a weight he was glad to set down for a moment. But when he spoke,
his voice was temperate and controlled, mild. "I just don't see the
point in wasting time—mine and other people's—on something
that's never going to happen." Rishi looked at her and said, almost
defiantly, "I am never going to be a comic artist."

Dimple wondered whose benefit he was stating it aloud like that for. "So what if it's not going to be your career? You still love it, right? Why can't you just do it as a hobby?"

"It's too time-consuming," Rishi said, but even he didn't sound convinced. "And it all snowballs. You saw that—Kevin wanted me to apply there. Leo Tilden wanted to see my sketches. Much ado about nothing."

"They're excited for you," Dimple said, shaking her head. "I think it's great that there are people who want to see you succeed. You keep saying you're not going to be a comic artist, but I think the point is that if you wanted to be, you could."

Rishi laughed, but there was no joy in it. "It's not that simple. I mean, it's great for Kevin Keo that he just knows he wants to be a comic artist and feels free to pursue it. But I'm not like that. Do you know the odds of someone becoming the next Leo Tilden or Stan Lee? A million to one. I know what's important to me—I want a life. I want to get married and have a family. I can't support a family working as a waiter and hoping to break out as a comic book artist."

"You're eighteen." Dimple looked at him, wondering if this were some weird universe where Rishi would turn out to be a two-thousand-year-old vampire instead. "You don't have to worry about all of that yet."

Rishi sighed and kicked a small rock in his path, sending it skittering off into the night. It lay glittering under a tree. "I know I don't *have* to, but I want to. I'm never going to be that crazy eighteen-year-old party animal, you know? It's just not my scene."

Dimple smiled. She loved a challenge. "Really? Have you ever been to a party? Like, in high school?"

"Sure I have."

Dimple raised an eyebrow. "Like, a legit party. One a parent didn't organize."

There was silence. She laughed. "You were thinking of Diwali parties, weren't you?"

"Hey, they're legit parties!" Rishi said, but he was laughing too.

"Okay, we're totally going to this party." Dimple held up the piece of paper on which Kevin had scribbled the address.

Rishi made a face. "Really?"

"Really. You don't have to be a 'party animal' to go to a party and have a good time. I've been to a few small ones with friends in high school, and I swear they weren't so bad. It's a chance to hang out, that's all." Seeing him open his mouth to argue, Dimple rushed on. "Besides, just look at it as a social experiment. You have to go to at least one college party, right? It's like a rite of passage. You can just get it out of the way now, with me as your guide."

After a moment, he shut his mouth. "Oh, fine."

Dimple jostled him with her shoulder. "Good. You might even have some fun."

Rishi

"This is insane." Rishi and Dimple stood across from the house where the party was.

There was no mistaking they were at the right location. The front yard was decorated with what looked like a DIY glow-in-the-dark bowling set made from plastic water bottles with glow sticks inside them. People were trying to knock down the pins while screeching with laughter. What Rishi was pretty sure was a life-size doll sat in a tree like she was watching the proceedings, her lips, hair, and dress glowing from the black lights strung in the tree branches. The front door was open, and the music pouring out of it was so loud that the bass shook the ground under Rishi's feet. "We can't go in there. Those people look drunk off their butts."

"Oh, come on. You can't even see them from here. Besides, look at this place. This is a real college experience." Dimple grabbed his wrist and pulled him across the street. Her eyes, Rishi saw, were glued to the bowling pins.

On the tiny front porch was a cooler filled with drinks, both adult and not. Dimple grabbed two Cokes, and handed one to Rishi.

"Was that beer in there?" he asked, shaking his head, as she shut the top.

Dimple gave him a look. "Yeah, some people here are twenty-one." Seeing his unconvinced expression, she added, "You know, one beer won't land a person homeless on the streets."

Rishi popped open his Coke and followed her into the house. "Ha-ha. You know, I watched this documentary one time . . ."

Dimple

Dimple walked in and peeked around the corner while Rishi talked at length about how addiction could wrap itself around you like a python and squeeze you dry if you weren't watching out for it. There was a small kitchen, she saw, and people were bustling around, getting things ready for the party. A tall boy poured lemonade out of a carton into tiny plastic glasses on a tray. A girl with multiple piercings in her lips and ears and nose put a fresh batch of brownies into the oven.

Dimple smiled to herself, an evil thought taking root as the boy brought out the tray of lemonade and set it down on a table near where she and Rishi were standing. Glancing at Rishi, she confirmed what she suspected: He hadn't seen any of this. He was still talking about the documentary and how heroin was the new drug of choice for suburban kids.

Her smile widening, Dimple reached out for the tray full of pink drinks and downed one quickly.

CHAPTER 25

Rishi

"You don't even know what was in that!" Rishi said, trying not to let his voice reach the crescendo it wanted to. Was she *crazy*? He'd never drink anything that he hadn't made himself or at least seen someone pour. She didn't even know these people!

Turning around, Dimple put her hands on his elbows and leaned in so he could hear her over the thumping music. It was dark inside, with just a few black lights and glow sticks strung up around the place, and Rishi found his heartbeat quickening just a bit. "Relax," she yelled. "It was just pink lemonade, I promise." Then, grinning, she picked up another pink lemonade and drank it. "I'm going to keep doing that until you drink something too. Loosen up!"

A throng of people came by hooting and hollering as they rushed outside to bowl. There were only three drinks left, and, raising her eyebrows, Dimple reached for another.

"Okay, okay," Rishi said. He grabbed one of the little plastic cups and downed one. It was tart and sweet and slid easily down his throat. To be honest, it really didn't taste like anything more sinister than strawberry lemonade. Maybe this party wasn't as *completely* out of control as he'd thought. "There," he said. "Happy?"

Dimple grinned. "It's a start. Come on, let's see what they're doing." She pointed to a bunch of people who were clustered around a redheaded boy and a girl in braids who sat on the couch across from each other, sketch pads poised on their laps.

Rishi followed Dimple as she pushed through the crowd, slipping easily between people who were much taller and bigger than her. Rishi followed with a few "excuse mes" and "pardons."

"Okay, another one!" a tall boy who was clearly playing the role of MC said, looking out at the small crowd. The boy and girl on the couch switched to blank sheets on their pads.

"What's going on?" Rishi asked a tall, thin guy standing next to him, and Dimple leaned in to listen.

"They're having a sketch-off," the guy said, grinning. "People in the crowd call out suggestions of crazy things for them to draw, and then they do it."

"Miley Cyrus and Darth Vader's child!" someone in the crowd called out, and someone else added, "With Gothic flair!" Everyone laughed and hooted their approval.

Dimple

Both the sketchers put in a valiant effort. It was hard to see in the dim black light and whatever outside light filtered in through the windows, but on the pad of the guy nearest her Dimple could make

164

out a hilarious rendition of Darth Vader's helmet atop a sexy woman riding a giant ball. In an attempt to make it Gothic, the guy was drawing spires along the top of the page.

"You should do that next," Dimple said.

"What?" Rishi looked at her in alarm, his thick eyebrows almost disappearing into his floppy hair. She had a sudden urge to giggle. So she did.

"I think you should compete next," Dimple explained. She pointed to the two artists.

"I don't think so," Rishi said, giving her an *okay, crazy lady* look.

"And—time!" the MC guy shouted, and the artists set their pencils down. One of them wiggled his fingers as people began to vote on who won, which consisted of them shouting out either "Vinnie!" or "Lola!" Someone, obviously too excited for his own good, said, "Lolinnie!" They counted that one as one vote for both artists. At the end Lola was declared the winner. Vinnie slammed his sketch pad closed and proceeded to disappear into the darkened rooms of the house with a girl from the audience.

Lola, a small woman with blue (or burgundy or yellow—it was hard to tell in the light) braids looked around at everyone, smiling too widely. "So? Who's next?"

Dimple pushed Rishi, harder than she'd meant to, and he went stumbling forward so his shins knocked against the table.

"All right!" Lola said, looking up at him. "Have a seat!" She grinned wider. "And get ready to lose."

Rishi tossed Dimple a baleful look over his shoulder, but he sat down and pulled out his sketch pad.

"Okay, contestants, introduce yourselves to each other," the MC said.

"I'm Lola," the girl said, holding out a hand.

"Rishi." He shook her hand.

"Great! Now let's hear some suggestions, guys!" MC boy looked around at the swarming, grinning, chattering crowd.

Someone in the audience yelled, "A sloth in a dress doing ballet!"

There were hoots of approval, so the two of them nodded at each other and began to draw.

Dimple had been to a magic show before. She'd been eight, and her elementary school principal had hired some dude named Amos the Amazing to entertain them. She remembered sitting in the auditorium with all the other sweaty second graders, neck craned to look up at the stage while Amos pulled out orange silk scarves from his sleeves, made a bunny appear out of thin air and then disappear again, and pushed a penny through his own palm. She'd been totally enthralled. For two weeks afterward she'd even decided she wanted to be a magician when she grew up. Her stage name would be Dimple the Dazzling.

But that complete rapture was nothing compared to what she was feeling now.

As Rishi sat there, hunched over his sketch pad, the stub of a pencil in his hand, the other hand curled around the corner of the paper, Dimple knew he wasn't *really* there. He'd checked out; he was on some floating island made of graphite and paper where this reality didn't exist. The only thing he saw was the bizarre ballerina sloth in his head, the one that was taking shape pencil stroke by pencil stroke on paper. His lines were confident and sure, the emerging picture comical and twisted and breathtakingly mesmerizing all at the same time.

Dimple noticed people nudging each other, leaning in to get closer, to really take in the little details. Like how the sloth was wearing a monocle. Or the fact that Rishi was drawing it with a perfect ballerina's bun, except the bun happened to be a croissant.

A few minutes later, the MC called out, "Time!"

Rishi set his pencil down and flexed his fingers. His eyes searched for Dimple's in the crowd, and when they locked gazes, he grinned, big and happy. Dimple felt something flutter in her chest as she smiled back.

It was almost unanimous—Rishi won. Lola stood. "Great work," she said, nodding seriously. "You go here?"

Rishi shook his head. "No, I'm just here for a summer program." He darted a glance at Dimple.

"Too bad," Lola said as she gathered her sketch pad and adjusted her skirt. "You kick butt."

"Who wants to go head-to-head with our new champion, Rishi?" MC boy asked, but Rishi stood up and shook his head.

"No, thanks, man. I'm done."

People groaned and booed, but Rishi held up his hands—sketch pad and all—and made his way over to Dimple.

She felt suddenly shy. It was weird, but it was like . . . like she'd seen a part of him she'd never knew existed. Most people wouldn't have this kind of reaction to a sloth in a monocle doing ballet, she knew. It was hard to explain, even to herself. Rishi had a gift. A serious gift that he didn't seem to like to share with people. Dimple knew why now . . . it was so intimate. He became someone else, stripped down, unself-conscious, unaware. She'd seen what his soul was made of. And she'd liked it.

"So," he said, smiling at her, tucking his sketch pad into his messenger bag and snapping it shut, "what do you want to do next?"

She rubbed her arm. "Um, I'm not sure. . . ."

"Dimple!"

They both turned at the voice to see Kevin Keo coming into the house, followed by three other artsy types. One of the girls, Dimple saw, was the one with the piercings she'd seen earlier, putting brownies into the oven. "You came!"

She smiled. "Yeah. Thanks for inviting us. This is a cool party." She nudged Rishi. "He just won a sketch-off."

"Really?" Kevin eyed him a little warily. "Great."

The girl with the piercings set the plate of brownies on the table where the lemonade was. "You guys want one?" she asked, taking a square herself.

"Sure!" Dimple said, reaching for it.

Rishi grabbed her elbow. "Um, Dimple, are you sure those brownies are safe to eat?" he whispered in her ear.

She tried to ignore the tickle of his breath in her ear, or the way it sent a little delicious shiver up her spine. "Yes, it's fine," Dimple said, aware that her voice was two octaves too high.

Rishi didn't seem to notice. "But you don't know for sure," he repeated, raising his eyebrows for emphasis.

Kevin Keo watched this interaction in interest.

CHAPTER 26

Dimple

Stifling a laugh Dimple reached for one of the totally innocent brownies and took a bite. "Mmm. It's good."

"My favorite mix," the girl said. "Made from scratch."

"You're a really talented baker," Dimple said, and the girl flushed with pleasure.

Rishi leaned in to Dimple as Kevin and his friends began to disperse into the crowd. "How can you just eat and drink things in a place like this?" He looked around at all the people hooking up and shouting and laughing in near darkness.

Dimple took another bite, chewed, and swallowed. "Are you serious right now?"

He looked at her blankly.

"You need to relax and let go a little." Rishi opened his mouth, and she said, "And *please* don't say I need to watch out for the date-rape drug." *Because I already saw these were completely safe,* she thought but did not say. She was enjoying watching Rishi worrying about her, though she didn't want to admit it.

He snapped his mouth shut. "Okay, I won't. But seriously, aren't you worried? Didn't you ever pay attention in any of those D.A.R.E. presentations?"

Dimple snorted and took another bite. "No. Did you?"

Rishi rubbed his jaw. "Th-that's not the point. Look, you can't just wander around a strange party drinking and eating from unattended containers. It's not safe. People will take advantage—"

He stopped talking when Dimple leaned closer to him and brushed his lips with the rest of her brownie. "You know you want to. It's *delicious*."

Looking down at her, he shook his head and made an "uh-uh" noise in the back of his throat without opening his mouth. Oh my God, he was so cute. Dimple batted her eyelashes at him and said, in a sultry voice she had no idea she was capable of, "Please, Rishi Patel?"

Something glittered in his eyes at her words, and Dimple felt herself flushing at whatever was going on, practically rippling in the air between them.

After a pause, Rishi obediently did as she asked. Dimple felt a thrill that he'd actually listened to her. That somehow, some way, she seemed to have power over this boy.

Rishi

It was important not to panic. So, okay, he'd just downed a brownie that might potentially contain something illegal. That he'd done it because of Dimple's petite, chocolate brownie–scented hand near his mouth (and because she was standing so close to him he could feel her body heat) just made it worse.

But Rishi wouldn't think about that. He wasn't going to worry about the possibility of a SWAT team bursting through the door, throwing him to the ground, and handcuffing him either. He wouldn't think about writing letters home from his prison cell while his somewhat flirty, six-foot-three-inch roommate, Bozo, watched.

Dimple giggled—giggled! A sound he'd never imagined leaving her mouth—and let her hand drop. Rishi was immediately bereft. "You should see your face."

"I bet it's nothing compared to my brain waves. They're probably crying out, spiraling into years of addiction."

Dimple shook her head and sighed. "There's nothing in that brownie except sugar and fat." She gave him a sidelong glance. "I saw them make it, okay? I peeked into the kitchen when you weren't looking."

Without talking about it, she and Rishi began to make their way to the sliding back door. The dark backyard beyond looked mostly empty. Rishi opened his mouth and feigned being aghast at her, his heart lifting when she trilled a laugh.

"Sorry, sorry," she said, lifting her hands in front of her. "You're just too easy with your paranoia."

"It's not paranoia, Dimple. I think it's idealistic to trust people so completely. That's why I don't like going to parties." He could feel her watching him in that sardonic, Dimple way she had—eyes calculating, eyebrows slightly furrowed. "Yeees?"

She stepped through the sliding door, and he followed, pulling it shut behind them, hoping to deter any wasted college students from following. They made their way to a grove of bushes off to the right, the breeze just cool enough to provide some respite from the thick, soupy heat of bodies inside. "Well, see, I don't think it's idealistic. People go to parties all the time to just kick back and chill. For me it's about getting away from the constant pressure I felt at home to be someone I wasn't. Didn't you ever feel the need to let go of stress?"

Rishi laced his hands behind his head. There was a small bench beyond the grove of bushes, sheltered from the rest of the yard and the house. He went to it, and Dimple followed.

There was a soft quietness in his head now, as if the world was at a remove. His voice sounded muffled in the fog. "Sure I did. That's why I drew." He sat on the cold stone bench, and put his messenger bag down by his feet. "I never felt the need for anything else."

Dimple sat beside him, her arms and legs stiff, as if she were afraid of encroaching on his personal space, of touching him. He knew how she felt. Before, scraping elbows together or grabbing her hand had seemed benign, just exciting enough without being serious or scary. But here in this private little alcove in the dark, things felt more. Bigger. And Rishi wasn't entirely certain he wanted to go down that path. Mainly because he wasn't certain *she* did.

"Hmm."

When Dimple didn't say anything else, he tipped his head back, drank in the air. The fog coated the sky and filtered through the trees around them so it felt like they were encased in a tiny gray bubble. Just him and Dimple. His heart beat faster at the thought of that, but he felt fine about the unknown of it all. He felt fine about everything, he thought, with a small smile. She had that effect on him.

"Show me your sketch pad."

The fine feeling disappeared. Rishi looked at her, big eyes shining in the dark behind those glasses. Some of her wild hair, curly again thanks to the humidity in the air, was brushing his shoulder in spite of her careful posture, as if it had a life of its own. "Huh?"

"You must have some sketches in there, right? You lied to Leo Tilden."

Leo Tilden felt like forever ago. Thinking back to that moment made something unpleasant and bitter squirm in his stomach. "Yeah. But . . . I don't know. It's just, they're not that great."

"Don't do that." Dimple turned toward him completely, her face eager in the dim light. "Don't downplay your talent. If you don't want to show me, just say so. But I saw what you're capable of in there"—she gestured toward the house—"and it was remarkable. Aditya, what I've seen of him, is amazing. So it's clear you have talent; lots of it. I don't know why you don't want to show people, though. If it were me, I'd be diving into it whole hog."

"Is that what you're doing?"

Dimple nodded, her face small and vulnerable. "Trying to. And it's crazy scary, but you know, what's the alternative? Just forget about it? I can't." She leaned forward. "You shouldn't either, Rishi. Just because it's scary—"

"It's not because it's scary." He sat back, taking a deep breath. It still wasn't easy to talk about this, even with Dimple's presence turning everything pink and soft around the edges. But looking at Dimple's open face, hearing her earnest questions, his usual inhibitions turned to puffs of cloud, insubstantial, floating away as he tried to grasp them. Rishi found himself being honest. "I would love to do what you're doing. To immerse myself in the work, to think, breathe, eat, and sleep art. But that's how it'd have to be. See? There's no in between for me. I can't be an engineer *and* a part-time comic book artist. It can't be a hobby. I love it too much; it means too much to me. It's like, like having a child, I guess. How I imagine that would be—all consuming."

"Well, then, that's easy, isn't it?" Dimple sounded genuinely confused. "Do it. Do what you love, what you're passionate about. So what if it's not the most practical thing? You're eighteen, you don't have to be practical for a long, long time—maybe not ever, if you choose not to be. There are people who live very frugally, who just keep plugging away for years because they can't think of doing it any other way."

"That's not going to be me." Rishi shifted, uncomfortable, suddenly done talking about it.

"Why not?"

"I told you. My parents, I made them a promise. I'm their oldest son. It's just not going to happen. I have duties, obligations."

Dimple sighed, soft and slow.

Rishi looked at her for a second, touched at how much she seemed to care. Then, without giving himself too much time to think about it, he reached down and unsnapped his messenger bag top. Sliding his sketch pad out, Rishi held it out to her.

CHAPTER 27

Rishi

Dimple smiled, a lantern in the night. "Really?"

Rishi nodded, and she took the sketch pad, setting it carefully on her lap. She pulled her cell phone out of her pocket, turned on a flashlight app, and set it on the bench between them. Then, almost reverentially, she began lifting the cover.

"Wait." Rishi put a hand on hers. She looked at him quizzically, her face and glasses tinted a silver blue from the phone. "So, these aren't finished sketches. Well, some of them are, but some aren't. More just like . . . blocking. Like, ideas."

"Okay." Dimple nodded, and he let go of her hand. She began to flip the cover open again. He put a hand on hers. She looked at him, one eyebrow raised.

"One more thing. Don't look just at what's happening; look at the nuance. Like, notice the backgrounds in each panel. That's important information; it'll tell you more about what I had planned for the story. It'll set the mood and everything."

Dimple nodded again. "Okay." Rishi let go of her hand, and she began to open the cover.

"Oh, and another th—"

"Rishi," she said, turning so she could look him in the eye. "I have no expectations. Okay? None. Whatever's in here, I'm not going to be judging. I just want to take it in."

He studied her, the honesty in her eyes, the frank openness of her face, and his shoulders relaxed. "Okay."

Dimple opened the sketch pad, and as she studied each panel, each sketch, each line he'd made, Rishi studied her. She smiled quietly at some sketches, others seemed to arrest her. Her gaze would travel over each line, over and over, and sometimes she'd pull the book closer. One she stopped and squinted at, the most curious mixture of disbelief, amusement, and wonder on her face. Rishi leaned in to see what she was looking at.

It was a panel he'd done around two years ago, of a boy of about ten or eleven making paper flowers out of a heap of crumpled pages while rain poured outside his window.

Rishi chuckled, the sound slow and deep in his head. "Paper flowers. I used to make those when I was that age. I don't know why, but I was obsessed with them for a while. That panel was more like an exercise. I was feeling sluggish and empty that day." It wasn't nearly his best; he didn't know why Dimple seemed so enthralled with it.

She turned to look at him, that same strange expression still on her face. Her entire body was frozen, still. "You made paper flowers. Out of magazines."

He nodded, surprised. "How'd you know I did them out of magazine pages?"

"Don't you remember?" Dimple shook her head, her eyes wide as she studied him. *"Keep it. Remember me. And don't tattle."*

And just like that, the memory slammed into him.

He'd been dragged along by Pappa and Ma to some Indian acquaintance's wedding in San Diego. It was hot, and the wedding was outside. Ashish was being a baby, whining about being hungry, and his parents were bickering about something, and there were absolutely no activities for the kids to do, so Rishi told his parents he had to go to the bathroom and wandered off. His kurta had been a thick gold brocade, he remembered, and itchy as heck. His plan was to get inside the big hotel where it was cool and air-conditioned and find a T-shirt or something to wear. Maybe he'd steal it from an open room—that always seemed to work in the movies.

But when he got inside, Rishi saw the guests had commandeered the interior lobby too. There was no way to get past them and to the upstairs—there were caterers and waiters and nosy aunties and uncles everywhere. So he'd ducked into a room with a sign that said CONFERENCE ROOM A, whatever that was, and sat down on a chair in the semidark (just one lamp in the corner of the big room was on), grateful for the cool and quiet. There was a pile of magazines on the table in front of him, and Rishi began methodically ripping out pages as he sat, folding and turning them into flowers that he set in a line in front of him.

He'd gotten into the habit just months ago, having seen some special on TV. Rishi first tried it with one of Ma's Bollywood magazines and found it weirdly compelling, not even minding that his fingers were constantly covered in paper cuts. Now he made roses and mums and lilies, the repetitive, familiar motion soothing.

He was on his third rose when he heard someone clear their throat. Startled, Rishi looked up at a small girl with wild hair. She sat on a high-backed armchair he hadn't noticed in the corner of the room. A copy of *A Wrinkle in Time* was facedown in her lap, and her feet, sticking out from underneath her bright blue *lehenga*, didn't touch the floor. She was staring at him through glasses that were too big for her narrow face. "Why are you ripping up those magazines? They're not yours." Her voice was high-pitched. It reminded him of Tinker Bell, a cartoon Ashish loved to watch, though he didn't like to be teased about it. Rishi had learned that the hard way. He still had the bruise on his shin.

Rishi sat back, letting the rose fall from his fingers, and studied the tiny girl. She must be around his age, he decided, in spite of her unimpressive size. "You're not a *tattletale*, are you?" he asked, in a way that implied (a) there was little he could think of that was worse than being one, and (b) she definitely looked like one.

"No," the girl said immediately, almost before he was done speaking, pushing those oversize glasses up on her nose. "I was just asking."

Rishi looked at her for another long moment, appraising. Then he said, "I'm bored." And went back to rolling the paper for his next flower. "Why are you in here reading?"

The girl studied him for a minute before replying. "I'm bored too."

Rishi nodded, but kept his eyes on his lily.

After a pause, the girl hopped off her chair and came up to the table, sidling into the chair across from him. Rishi watched her through his peripheral vision. She set her book carefully down, dog-earing a corner of her page with love. When that was done, she picked up a chrysanthemum and studied it closely, turning it this way and that. "I like it," she pronounced finally, setting it back down and looking up at him. "How do you know how to do that?"

Rishi shrugged nonchalantly. "Picked it up."

She nodded, curls bobbing. "Cool. Maybe you could teach me."

"Nah, it'd take too long," Rishi said. "Besides, your hands are too small." Rishi wasn't entirely sure this was true, but it wasn't like the girl would know any better.

"Hey, that's not—"

"Diiiiimple!"

The girl froze, looking toward the door. "That's Mamma. I have to go." She grabbed her book and began to slide off her chair, but right before she was completely out of reach, Rishi grabbed her wrist. She looked at him, confused.

He pressed the chrysanthemum into her small, sweaty hand. "Keep it," he said, his gaze boring into hers like he'd seen Shah Rukh Khan do to a dozen different actresses in a dozen different Bollywood movies. "Remember me." He paused. "And don't tattle."

The girl glanced down at the flower, and then up at him again. She nodded solemnly, like she understood the gravity of this moment. She wouldn't tattle. Then, closing her fingers around the flower, she slipped out of the conference room, shutting the door quietly behind her.

CHAPTER 28

Rishi

On the cold stone bench, Rishi exhaled. "That was you?" he asked, staring at Dimple. His brain delighted at the impossibility of this, at the sheer coincidence that that tiny, serious girl in the blue *lehenga* now sat opposite him, looking at his sketch pad.

Dimple laughed, shaking her head. "I know. Crazy." Shrugging, she added, "I mean, not *crazy* crazy. We do both live pretty close to each other, and our parents are part of the Indian community in NorCal, which isn't that huge. . . ."

"No." Rishi rubbed the back of his neck. "Still crazy." Softly, he said, "Kismet."

She looked at him, big eyes luminous and almost black in the light from the phone. "Kismet." And then Dimple Shah put her hands behind his head and pulled him in for a kiss.

• • •

Dimple

In retrospect, Dimple wasn't quite sure how it happened, exactly. One minute they were talking about the crazy coincidence of having met about eight years ago at some random wedding. And the next she was attached to Rishi's face.

Her heart pounded in her chest; it echoed around the world. Her blood was fire, flames licking at her skin—

Oh God. He wasn't kissing her back.

Why wasn't he kissing her back?

Rishi sat rigid as a statue while her mouth moved against his. The minute Dimple realized this, she pulled back. Cheeks flaming, she forced herself to look him in the eye. "I'm sorry. I didn't realize . . . um, I don't know what happened there. Exactly."

Rishi cleared his throat, his eyes slightly glazed. Dimple turned away, back to his sketch pad, although she wasn't seeing a single sketch anymore. "I'm sorry too," he said, and her heart sank, dripping in a sad, cold puddle to her feet. "I'm sorry you stopped."

She turned, hope quickening her pulse. "What—"

And then he grabbed her around the waist and pulled her to him, one hand moving up to cup her cheek, thumb just under her jaw while his fingers tangled in her hair. Rishi kissed her with purpose, with meaning, like he believed this was exactly where they were supposed to be in this moment. He kissed her till she believed it too.

Rishi

Some moments in life were intensely disappointing. You waited and waited and waited and then . . . Summer vacation turned out to be boring. Your big trip to NYC was awful because people were rude and it rained the entire time. The movie you'd been waiting to watch for months sucked when it finally came to theaters.

This moment was nothing like that. This moment was like Diwali and Rishi's birthday and a new Leo Tilden YouTube video all rolled into one. No, scratch that. It was way better than all of those things combined. Rishi was fairly sure he lacked the lexicon to put into words what was happening in his brain—and his body—right then.

Rishi felt clearheaded, bright, delighted, amazed. Dimple's mouth was soft and small and full against his, her body was warm as it pressed into him, and the smell of her skin and hair flooded him like a thousand stadium lights. He was kissing her. He, Rishi Patel, was kissing her, Dimple Shah. And *she'd* initiated the kiss. How the heck had this happened? How the heck could one guy get so lucky?

When they finally pulled apart, Rishi's mouth tingling still, Dimple smiled shyly and looked down at their hands, entwined between them on the bench. "So," she said softly. "That was unexpected."

He leaned over and kissed her forehead, like it was the most natural thing to do. Was this going to be their thing now, casual kissing? He hoped so. "Unexpected but awesome." Rishi paused. "Right?"

She laughed and looked up at him. "Definitely."

He grinned, his heart soaked in happy.

Her smile fading a little, Dimple looked down at his sketch pad, still in her lap. "Rishi . . ." She took a breath, apparently steadying herself for whatever she wanted to say next. Rishi felt that familiar guard come back up around his heart, like some electric fence. "You should show these to Leo Tilden. Really. These are . . . they're just amazing. We can go show them to him right now."

He saw in her eyes that she truly believed it, that she felt he had this great gift to offer the world and how it'd be a tragedy if he didn't, and a surge of affection threatened to flatten him. He tucked an errant curl behind her ear. "I think it's probably too late."

Dimple shook her head, the set of her jaw stubborn. "We can find out from Kevin what hotel they've put him up at. There has to be some way to—"

Rishi ran a gentle thumb over her bottom lip. "Can we just sit here instead? Can I look at you?"

Silently, she nodded. Rishi studied everything there was to study in her face—every curve and line and shade of color. Then he reached over and took his sketch pad from her lap.

"What are you doing?"

Flipping it open, he grabbed a pencil from his bag and began to draw. "Oh, you'll see, my friend," he said. When Dimple tried to peek, he turned, shielding the page from her view.

She laughed. "So it's like that?"

Rishi grinned but didn't respond. In another minute he'd finished the sketch. He ripped out the paper, folded it, and passed it and the pencil over to her. It was silly, but his heart beat faster. This moment felt more serious than it had any right to feel.

• • •

Dimple

Dimple opened the paper. It was an amazing sketch, which, if she hadn't seen Rishi do in about a minute, she would have believed had taken a lot longer. It showed a boy, hair flopping in his eyes and bulging muscles ripping his shirt sleeves—Dimple snorted—handing a fierce-looking girl a paper flower. He'd captured her so perfectly in just a few strokes—her oversize square glasses, her wild hair, the furrow in her brow. Underneath the sketch, he'd written:

Will you go on a date with me?

Yes

No

Dimple took a deep breath as an uneasy pulse beat within her. He was trying to make it official, and she wasn't sure she wanted official. She wasn't sure what she wanted, really.

Underneath the "no," she wrote in:

Other

And handed it back to Rishi.

He studied the paper, and she could see the slight disappointment tint his features. But when he looked back at her, he had rearranged his expression to reflect just curiosity. "Care to explain?"

Dimple reached over and turned off the flashlight app on her phone. Somehow it was easier to say things under cover of darkness. The foggy night worked as a salve, taking the sting out of words. "Rishi, I can't be your girlfriend."

A beat of silence. "Why not?" He said it softly, not as a judgment but simply in an effort to understand.

Dimple's heart hurt. "It's not why I'm here," she forced herself to say firmly. She refused to be one of those girls who gave up on everything they'd been planning simply because a boy entered the picture. "You know I'm not looking for a relationship right now."

"Even if the relationship feels right?"

She paused, listening to the sound of some distant partygoer screech in laughter. "Especially if."

She saw Rishi nodding in her peripheral vision. In the quiet, she wondered if he was so hurt that he couldn't bear to speak. Then, he turned to her, grinning. "Okay. So what? We don't have to do the whole relationship thing. You can just go out with me, and we'll call it a . . . a non-date."

Dimple arched an eyebrow. "Rishi . . ."

"No, listen, it's just like you and Celia going out, right? No strings attached. Neither of us has any expectations. We'll just hang out."

Dimple looked at his eager, open face, at the optimism and cheerfulness there, and felt her resolve melting. Sighing, she said, "I don't want to hurt you."

Rishi's grin broadened. He could taste the "yes" in the air, apparently. "You won't. Just friends on a non-date." He scribbled something on the paper and handed it back to Dimple.

It now said:

Will you go on a non-date with me?

Laughing, she checked the "yes" and hoped to heck they knew what they were doing.

CHAPTER 29

Dimple

It was the Friday after the Big Kiss, as Dimple and Celia had dubbed it.

To her credit, when Dimple mentioned it, Celia had squealed in delight, ordered pizza from the twenty-four-hour place around the corner, and made Dimple tell her every single detail, ad nauseam, so she could help dissect everything. Dimple had tried to explain that she didn't need to do that—that Dimple, in fact, was the one holding back in the non-relationship, but Celia seemed unable to grasp the concept.

After a couple of minutes of silence she'd said, "You guys are like Raj and Simran."

Dimple had stared at her. "Raj and Simran? Like, in *Dilwale Dulhaniya Le Jayenge*?"

Celia nodded. "Mmm-hmm."

"How do you know that movie?"

"When you and I began to talk on the boards, I thought I should watch a couple of Bollywood movies on Netflix, figure out how to be sensitive to your culture and all that." Celia grinned, hanging her head upside down off the bed, her massive pile of curly hair brushing the floor. "Course, that was before I knew you were more American than me."

Dimple snorted. "Well, it was a nice thought anyway."

"You guys are just, like, fated to be together, y'know?"

Dimple sighed and lay down. "I don't believe in fate," she said, although she and Rishi had talked about kismet at the party. "I believe in logic. And logically, I shouldn't go out on this non-date with him."

In class now, Rishi beamed. "This is what I have so far. What do you think?"

Dimple looked at Rishi's sketches, her excitement tempered by the nerves that had begun manifesting themselves every time she looked at him after that night. It was like her body immediately remembered he was the one she'd locked lips with, even though it had been a week, and tried to turn her into a gibbering, flirtatious idiot. Well, she wasn't a gibbering, flirtatious idiot. She'd just have to remember that and forget the kiss had ever happened. Or the fact that their non-date was tonight.

The butterflies in her stomach began beating their restless wings again at the thought, and Dimple tried not to groan. What the heck was wrong with her? "These are amazing," she said a little too loudly, hoping to distract her own brain from its traitorous thoughts. And truly, Rishi had done a remarkable job. He'd sketched out a detailed layout for their app, using the placement Dimple had suggested. Every button was vibrant, humorous, exactly what she'd wanted.

"I'm glad you like it," Rishi said, leaning closer to point out something. Dimple got a waft of his cologne, something subtle but deeply male that reminded her of oak trees in the summer sun. Her head almost swam with the memory of their kiss, and she had to blink several times to get her thoughts back on track. " . . . can do that, if you'd like?"

He was looking at her now, those gorgeous honey-brown eyes warm and expectant. Dang. She had no idea what he'd asked. "Um, yeah, sure," she said, itching the back of her neck.

He smiled quietly to himself, like he knew where her mind had been, and put away the sketch. Stretching his long legs out in front of him, Rishi folded his hands behind his head, a lock of shiny black hair flopping into his eye. "So," he said, a mischievous flicker in his smile, "you ready for our non-date?"

Dimple caught herself wondering again if this was a bad idea. It's *fine*, she tried to convince herself for the millionth time. It was a non-date, and she wanted to go on it. That wasn't a big deal. She wasn't compromising any of her values. "Yep." She fiddled with the wheel on her mouse. "Where do you want to go? I don't really know this area too well. . . ."

Rishi waved a hand. "I've got it all taken care of. I spoke to a few of the guys on my floor, and they recommended a couple of places. Then I Googled stuff, and voilà. Non-date is all planned out." He grinned.

Those stupid butterflies surged up again at his smile. And the way he was looking at her. And the fact that his hair was so sexy-floppy-messy. "Great." Dimple heard the wobble in her voice and tried not to wince. "Can't wait."

"Pick you up at seven?"

Before she could respond, Isabelle—whom they hadn't talked to since they'd eaten together at the restaurant almost two weeks ago—came over. Her presence was preceded by the smell of her perfume, something fruity and bubbly that threatened to choke Dimple with two hands. She muffled a cough.

Isabelle stood in front of Rishi, hands clasped before her as she fiddled with one of many rings she wore. Her booty shorts barely covered her booty. Wasn't she cold? It was foggy and damp outside. But Isabelle's midriff looked tan and happy beneath the sheer white tank top she wore. Before she could stop herself, Dimple found herself glancing at Rishi to see if he noticed. She also couldn't stop the surge of vindication when all she saw was annoyance splashed across his every feature.

He looked at Isabelle for only a brief second before he looked away, as if he had much more important things to get to.

"I, um . . ." Isabelle tucked a wavy lock of blond hair behind one ear and looked from Rishi to Dimple and back again. "At Elm, the guys . . ."

Dimple waited, curious. Rishi had his casually bored expression on.

But whatever Isabelle had started to say, she obviously decided she couldn't finish. Instead, she cleared her throat and said to Rishi, "My dad knows your dad."

"Okay," Rishi said, still seeming less than enthused.

"You never said your dad was the CEO of Global Comm. My dad, like, totally wants to invite your parents over for dinner. He says Kartik Patel's a total legend." Isabelle said this last part wonderingly.

Dimple could see her trying to fit the two pieces together: The respect that Rishi's dad obviously garnered combined with the fact that Rishi was absolutely the dorkiest guy she'd ever known. There were cracks in her perceptions, and she was trying to make sense of them. It was almost fascinating, like watching the part of a wildlife documentary when the gazelle realizes it's being stalked by a lion. *How will it respond? What will it do next?* Dimple thought, in a documentary narrator's deep, polished voice.

And then what Isabelle had said sank in. Dimple glanced at Rishi sharply. CEO of Global Comm? They, like, provided Internet services to basically the entire nation. And his dad was the freaking CEO? When she'd asked before, he'd only said his dad was "a corporate executive." But the CEO was the big boss, basically. Of a multibillion-dollar company.

Dimple studied him closer while he talked to Isabelle, but couldn't see it. She'd always assumed the ultrarich kids were like Evan or Hari, but Rishi was so . . . Rishi. Goofy and funny and talented and sweet and so serious about his culture. Rishi seemed so much more like Dimple than like Isabelle and the rest of them.

Immediately, before she could stop it, that famous Emily Brontë quote popped into her head: "Whatever our souls are made of, his and mine are the same." Dimple blushed and coughed to hide her embarrassment at having had such a gooey, stupid thought.

"I'll pass on the message," Rishi said nonchalantly, and then turned to Dimple, effectively dismissing Isabelle. "So, I heard about this movie playing at the IMAX theatre . . ."

Isabelle hesitated, looking from Rishi to Dimple and then back again in a slightly frustrated way. As if there was more she wanted to say. But, like before, she decided against it. Dimple watched her walk away before turning to Rishi.

"What movie?" she asked, since Rishi had never completed his sentence.

"Nothing. I was just done with that conversation."

Dimple laughed. Really, it was sort of refreshing to have a boy prefer her company to a girl like Isabelle's. That literally had never happened before.

Rishi smiled and shrugged. "So, about tonight. Pick you up at seven?"

"Sure." Dimple *reeeally* hoped he didn't notice how weirdly high-pitched her voice sounded.

CHAPTER 30

Dimple

Dimple pulled at the hem of the kurta she'd bought with Mamma. The thing had frayed in the wash, so the silvery gray now just looked gray, a total noncolor, like something she'd washed and worn for a decade. She almost wished she'd taken Mamma's advice and bought something a little more colorful.

Almost. Times weren't that desperate yet.

And anyway, Dimple thought, straightening her shoulders and adjusting her glasses, she didn't need to look pretty for this . . . nondate. It was irrelevant what she looked like, really.

When Dimple turned around, Celia was sprawled on her bed watching, chin propped up on one hand. "You need something sexier."

"Aren't you supposed to be sexting Evan?" Dimple grumbled.

It was Celia's new thing, sexting Evan at all hours of the day and night. When Dimple asked why she didn't just go to his dorm room, she always said, with a sparkle in her eye, *Pour cultiver le mystère.* Whatever that meant. From what Dimple had heard in the bathroom and elevators from other girls, Evan was developing a reputation as a player. She'd tried to broach the subject with Celia, but Celia just changed the subject, as if she willfully didn't want to know. Was she so desperate to fit in with the Aberzombies that she was ignoring the fact that Evan was playing her? Or was she really cool about Evan seeing other girls in a way Dimple could never imagine being?

Mainly Dimple tried not to be jealous that not only was Celia smart and glamorous and rich and beautiful, but she also spoke passable Spanish, excellent French, and fluent English. While Dimple struggled with both her Hindi and her Serengeti-wild hair.

Celia sighed dramatically and dropped her head to the mattress, pressing her cheek against the sheet as her curls cascaded adorably all around. She could be the main character in a children's book series, Dimple thought. "That's a little complicated right now," Celia mumbled, her words muffled by her hair. "He's being . . . difficult to read. And I'm not sure I want to read him."

"Oh." Dimple picked awkwardly at a loose thread on her sleeve. She was awful at dispensing romantic advice, being so inexperienced in the field herself. "Sorry."

"Ah, whatever. I'll figure it out." Apparently filled with a sudden surge of energy, Celia hopped off the bed and pranced over to her closet. After a minute she pulled out a sheer . . . something and held it out to Dimple, triumphant. "Wear this."

Dimple took an automatic step back. "Um, what is it?"

Celia looked wounded and outraged at the same time, her mouth hanging open. "It's a dress! It's this season's Elie Tahari!"

Dimple wondered if she looked as blank as she felt. "Is that . . . a brand?"

"Is that a—" Celia clutched the floaty dress/shirt contraption to her chest and rolled her eyes to the ceiling, in a remarkably on-point imitation of Mamma. Finally, looking at Dimple again, she sighed. "Trust me. You need this in your life and on your body."

Dimple picked up a billowy something that was probably a sleeve. "I don't even know how to get this on."

"I'll help you."

"Um, no. I'm not undressing in front of you."

"Oh, for God's—" Celia turned abruptly to her dresser, rummaged in a drawer, and thrust a silky slip at Dimple. "Here. Put this on and you can wear the dress on top of that. Okay? Can I see you in a slip or does that go against your virgin sensibilities too?"

Dimple snatched the slip and gestured for Celia to turn around. When she'd slipped off her kurta and jeans and put the wayyyy too short slip on, she said, "Okay."

Celia helped her, pushing her arms into certain holes and her head into another one. Then she smoothed the fabric over Dimple's hips and stood back, smiling. "There. Look in the mirror."

Dimple felt a flurry of nerves as she spun around. And whoa. She didn't even look like herself. The dress was snug across her waist and chest, but the slip kept anything too revealing from . . . being revealed. The bell-shaped sleeves hung loose around her arms, and the floaty hem stopped a few inches above her knees.

"Here." Celia came up behind her, and using the hair tie she always wore around her wrist, twisted Dimple's hair into a messy-sophisticated bun, leaving some of her curls cascading down.

Dimple stared at herself as Celia stood off to the side, smiling like a proud mom watching her kid go off to prom. She couldn't believe she looked like—like this. She looked like a girl in a magazine, someone who should pose beside a vintage bike with pastel-colored flowers and balloons. She belonged on a greeting card.

"I knew you'd like it," Celia said, smug. "Now, do you want to borrow some makeup? Because I could do your eyes in, like, a soft mauve and your lips in—"

"No," Dimple said, firmly breaking eye contact with her mirrored self. "Definitely no makeup."

"But—"

Dimple turned to Celia and pushed her glasses up on her nose. "I'd like to look at least somewhat like me." She was already afraid Rishi would think she was trying to impress him or something. *Was* she trying to impress him? The thought was mildly disturbing, but not enough to change out of this magical, someone-else dress.

"Okay, fine. But that dress goes with these boots." Celia reached into her closet and pulled out a pair of trendy, pseudo cowboy boots. "I mean, they're like a set. You'll wear them, right?" She looked genuinely concerned Dimple might say no. "I just want you to have a good time. And I know you're going to rock his socks off as you are, but this would really complete the ensemble."

Dimple smiled, touched at the realization that Celia really thought of them as friends. This was her way of showing she cared; she was 100 percent invested in this non-date. Dimple had never had a friend quite like her before—a generous, glamorous fellow coder. "Sure, I'll wear them. Thanks, Celia."

• • •

Rishi

Rishi smoothed over his hair. Did his floppy front bang things look better tilted to the right or the left? He flipped them one way and then another. Would Dimple even notice something like that? No, definitely right. Left made him look like an engineer. The kind with pocket protectors, not the cool kind. And for gods' sake, why was he wearing this shirt again? He was fairly sure he'd been wearing it the first time they met, and, well, that wasn't exactly the best association, was it? He was unbuttoning the top button when there was a knock at his door.

"Who is it?" he called, moving on to the next button.

"Um, it's me. Dimple. Sorry, I know we said you were going to pick me up, but I got done early and thought . . ."

Crap, crap, crap. She was *here*? She was here. Too late now. Rishi buttoned up again and pulled the door open, his heart in his mouth. But the minute he saw her, it thumped back into his chest, where it began thundering at warp speed.

Holy hotness, Batman.

She. Looked. Phenomenal.

Rishi couldn't form a coherent thought.

"Wow." He breathed out and rubbed his jaw, feeling his cheeks heat up when he realized he was staring at her thighs. Eyes up, Patel. "You look, um, just . . ."

"Yeah." Her cheeks were staining a dusky purple as she tugged the hem of her dress, as if she could will it longer simply by sheer physical strength. "Celia sort of bullied me into this and I don't know. It's really not me, but—"

"No, no. You look amazing." He gestured at her, making sure to keep his eyes on her eyes this time. Hard as that was to do. "Good job, Celia."

She blushed even deeper, which made Rishi want to gather her in his arms. And then Dimple bit her lower lip and his brain immediately reminded him what it felt like to kiss that mouth, how soft her lips were, how silky her tongue felt that night at the party. Great. Thanks for that, brain.

With a lurch Rishi realized his brain was also diverting blood flow to other parts of his body. He immediately began to think of Nani, his grandmother with the hairy mole on her neck jowls. Yep. That did it. Whew. Crisis averted.

"So, are you ready?" Dimple asked, looking back at him.

"Yeah. Let's do it." He closed the dorm door behind him and stepped out into the hall with her.

Even under the sickening fluorescents of the hallway, she was beautiful. The ugly gray walls did nothing to mar her perfect cinnamon complexion, although it made most people look like walking zombies. How was that possible? Was it lust?

Rishi had heard once you were attracted to someone, your brain could actually rewire itself and make you think all kinds of sucky things about them were perfect. And then, once you'd been together awhile, bam. The gauzy lust-curtain fell away and you realized you'd married an alligator with bad breath.

Dimple glanced at him sideways, in that sneaky yet piercing way she had. "What are you thinking?"

Crap. He could not tell her he'd been engrossed with thoughts of halitosis-suffering marine carnivores. Not on their first date. Nondate. Whatever. "Just, you know. The brain. It's an amazing organ, don't you think?"

Dimple twisted her mouth to one side. "Yeah. Sure. You looked like you'd eaten something really gross though."

Okay, time to change the subject. "Speaking of gross, you know who I heard from today? My little brother, Ashish."

"Oh yeah? How's he doing?" They arrived at the elevator, where a group of guys were noisily discussing the merits of wet T-shirt contests. Morons. Dimple, looking uncomfortable, pressed the down button, even though it was already lit.

Rishi glared at the group, but they were oblivious to anyone else except their own obnoxious opinions. "He's doing great," Rishi said loudly, hoping to drown them out. "He got some interest from an SFSU basketball scout, so my parents want him to come up here, maybe check out the campus and meet with some of the team. They're here for practice, I guess. Ashish was here last summer for a camp, but this would be different, since he might actually go here for school."

Dimple looked genuinely impressed. "That's really great!"

The elevator doors pinged open, and the group of obnoxious guys stepped in.

"Wait for the next one?" Rishi murmured, and Dimple nodded gratefully. One of the guys held his hand out so the door wouldn't close, but Rishi smiled brightly. "Oh no, you go ahead," he said jovially. "Our brains need a break from all the unchecked, casual misogyny."

The guy immediately smiled and waved in response, but as the doors closed, they heard him say, "Wait, what'd he say?"

Rishi looked at Dimple, and she burst out laughing. He thought he could maybe listen to that music all of his life. "You always surprise me," she said, shaking her head.

"In a good way?" he asked, smiling too, not wanting to show her how much he cared.

"In a really good way," she said, holding his gaze just a moment longer than she had to before turning to push the down button again. "So, you think Ashish is going to come stay with you?"

"Probably. To be honest, I think he's mostly just interested in ogling college girls rather than checking out the merits of the campus." Rishi rolled his eyes.

"Oh, like that thought never occurred to you when you were coming here," Dimple said.

The doors opened to an empty elevator, and both of them stepped in. Rishi turned to her as the doors closed. "It didn't," he said seriously. "I was only thinking of you."

CHAPTER 31

Dimple

Without thinking, Dimple leaned in closer just as Rishi inclined his head toward hers. Some faint, still coherent voice inside her intoned that this was already feeling a lot like a date and absolutely nothing like a non-date. Before they could kiss, Dimple's phone began to play "Ride of the Valkyries." Perfect.

She jerked back and pushed her glasses up on her nose, registering the way Rishi's face fell as he backed away too. Dimple knew how he felt; the ringtone had doused stomach acid on the butterflies fluttering pleasantly in her stomach. "Sorry." She rummaged in her bag, noting with alarm that she was mostly disappointed, and only a *very little bit* relieved, that the mood in the elevator now lay shattered in a thousand pieces at her feet. Seriously. She needed to get a grip on this thing, whatever it was, before it got out of control. Sliding the screen to silence the noise, Dimple took a deep breath and said, "Mamma. Can I call you back?"

"What's so important that you can't speak to your own mother? I have to tell you what that Ritu auntie did to Seema. You know she wanted to see that Hrithik Roshan film, *na?* Vishal was about to take Seema for a date night, and then Ritu decided she was going to go with them! At the last minute! Can you believe it? I told her, Ritu, give the kids some private time—"

Dimple rolled her eyes. Rishi was biting the inside of his cheek to keep from smiling. Of course he could hear Mamma, Our Lady of the Voice Like a Dentist's Drill. "*Mein* friend *keh saath hoon*, Mamma. So I'll call you later, okay?"

"Friend? Who's this friend?"

She sighed and looked at Rishi. He raised his eyebrows, like, *Well, now you have to say it*. Dimple wished she were a better liar under pressure, but she knew if she lied now, with no preparation, Mamma would instantly be able to tell, and then she'd just get even more unbearable. Better to get it out of the way. "Okay, it's Rishi Patel. But please don't get any ideas—"

"Rishi Patel! *Kartik aur Sunita ka beta?*"

Dimple flushed, sweat prickling at her hairline. God, she couldn't even bear to look at Rishi now. "Mamma, please. It's not a big deal," she mumbled, squeezing the phone in her sweaty hand. Why had she even answered her phone? Seriously, what had she been thinking?

"Where are you going? *Akele uske kamre mein math jaana*, Dimple—"

"*God*, Mamma, I have to go. And of course I won't." She hung up, feeling a stab of guilt at cutting off Mamma's well-intentioned advice. But jeez. *Don't go to his room alone?* Like she hadn't embarrassed Dimple enough in front of Rishi already. She was probably on the verge of talking about Dimple's sacred virginity.

Slipping her phone back into her bag, Dimple forced herself to meet Rishi's eye. He was still chewing on the inside of his cheek.

"What?" she said, a little more savagely than she'd meant to.

He raised his hands. "I didn't say anything." Then he began humming under his breath.

Dimple recognized the song just as the elevator doors slid open on the first floor. *Hum tum, ek kamre mein bandh ho, aur chaavi kho jaaye. . . .* It was a popular old Hindi song, about a couple who're shut away in a room when the keys go missing. Dimple slapped Rishi on his upper arm as they walked toward the doors. "Very funny."

He burst out laughing, and her heart lifted in mirth in spite of her still bubbling irritation. "Oh, come on. It's not that bad. She's just being your mom."

"Exactly," Dimple mumbled as they strode across the lobby and outside. It was sort of nice that she didn't need to explain the hovering, how it really came from a place of love. Rishi got that this was just what moms and dads did in their world.

Dimple took a deep breath, acrid smog and wet mist and herby eucalyptus all mixing together in her lungs. Groups of people and a few couples milled around, all laughing and joking and calling out to each other, some obviously already intoxicated, heading off campus for the weekend.

Dimple began to climb the steep road off to their right that led off campus, imagining that they were going to a restaurant nearby, but Rishi put a hand on her arm.

"Wait a sec." Casually, Rishi grabbed Dimple's hand and they crossed the road.

She tried not to show how flustered she felt, or how much she liked the feel of his big, warm, blunt fingers loosely grasping hers. "Um, where are we going?"

Rishi gestured to a glossy black convertible with the top down. As they got closer, the doors beeped. "Our chariot awaits."

Tossing Rishi a dazed look, Dimple climbed in. When Rishi had shut her door and hopped in his side, she asked, "You drive a *Beemer?*"

Rishi looked at her innocently. "What?"

Dimple snorted. "Nothing. It's just that normal people usually take the bus when they want to go somewhere far."

He looked genuinely uncomfortable as he pulled out of the space. "The bus. Right."

Feeling a little sorry for him, Dimple adjusted her tone from *mocking* to *gently teasing*. "This is really flashy for a non-date."

Rishi grinned and rubbed the back of his neck, accelerating as they climbed a steep hill. "What are you talking about? Yesterday I ordered a stretch limo when I wanted to run to the store to buy a pack of gum. Isn't that what everyone does?"

Dimple laughed. "Totally. Sometimes I'll even order a private jet."

They were quiet for a moment, feeling the wind in their hair, and then Dimple said, "So, where are we going?"

Rishi shook his head. "Still a surprise. I think you'll like it, though."

There wasn't a single place, Dimple realized, that she *didn't* want to go right now. Not because she wasn't picky, but because she could go pretty much anywhere with Rishi and enjoy herself. The realization was alarming. Concerning. And not altogether unwelcome.

The glitzy car dipped and reached, engine purring as it climbed the ubiquitous San Francisco hills. Rishi had turned on the seat warmers when he saw Dimple shivering lightly in the wind, so she was now perfectly comfortable. Dimple watched the buildings of the campus recede as they wound deeper into what looked like a residential district. Squat houses in pastel colors lined the road like rows of sidewalk chalk. Little potted plants decorated their stone porch stairs. An elderly man walking a little white dog looked curiously at them as they passed.

They came to a stop at a red light. "I feel like a celebrity." Dimple smiled and turned—and found Rishi watching her, unabashed. When their gazes locked, he flushed, the tips of his ears turning pink. But he didn't look away. And Dimple didn't look away. She . . . couldn't.

The moment stretched out, soft and gauzy tangling with dark and heavy. Dimple began to notice other things; how close her bare arm was to his. The heat his body was putting out. The way he smelled—like sunshine and something woodsy and boy.

Rishi rubbed the back of his neck and somehow shifted subtly forward. The only reason she really noticed was that his arm was now rubbing against hers. Something inside her went melty and warm. His eyes were all she could see as he leaned forward. Dimple found her lips parting, involuntarily, even as she thought, *This is distinctly* not *non-date behavior.*

The SUV behind them honked. The light had turned green. Rishi started and turned away, the moment gone.

CHAPTER 32

Dimple

Rishi cleared his throat as they sped down the road. Dimple adjusted her dress awkwardly, wondering if he was just as disappointed as she was. That was twice that a kissable moment had been thwarted.

A moment later Rishi signaled left and pulled up to the curb. Hopping out of his seat, he ran over to open her door, ever chivalrous. Neither of them said anything. There was a little charge of electricity in the air, that feeling of pressure right before a storm. Dimple's pulse raced. Did Rishi feel the same? His face was impassive; she couldn't say.

Silently, they crossed the little street together, heading toward a bank of narrow storefronts—mostly clothing and record stores—on the other side. Rishi led her toward a greenish-blue storefront. The sign outside read TWO SISTERS BAR AND BOOKS.

"Bar and books?" Dimple pushed her glasses up on her nose, feeling fingers of curiosity tap their way along her skin. "What does that mean, exactly?"

Rishi twinkled at her. "You'll see."

• • •

Rishi

The place was just as amazing as when Rishi had come here earlier in the week to scope it out. The vintage, Victorian-style red-and-tan wallpaper, the smell of old book glue, the clink of glasses and hum of quiet conversations and occasional laughter . . . it was just quirky and different enough to be worthy of Dimple. It was exactly what he'd wanted for their first non-date. Now that it was dusk outside, the store had turned on the hanging lights, and thanks to them and the pink wallpaper, everything was cast with a pink-gold glow.

Dimple was staring at the bar and the bookshelves, openmouthed. Rishi suppressed a self-satisfied chuckle. Oh, yes. Dimple's mind could be considered 100 percent blown. Well done, Patel. "So is this a bar? A restaurant? With *books* inside it?"

Rishi grinned. "Yeah. The owners get these really cool editions from all over the world. So you can just sip, eat, and read, I guess."

Dimple raised an eyebrow and smiled. "You know we're not old enough to drink, right?"

"They can make everything virgin," Rishi said. "I asked."

Dimple got a funny look on her face as her smile faded. "You asked? When?"

"A few days ago, when I came in here to check it out."

There was something in Dimple's eyes he couldn't read. She looked away, fiddling with the strap of her bag, and Rishi wondered if he'd said something wrong. When she didn't say anything, he continued, less surely. "So you can look around at the books, pick something up if you like. But ah, I also . . ." He paused, wondering if he should actually tell her. Her face, her expression . . . something was off. Did she think he was overplanning it? Putting too much thought into it? Was this all too much for her?

Dimple looked back at him, questioning. "You also what?"

Rishi felt the beginnings of panic. Crap. Here came the waiter, Willie, Rishi had made the arrangement with, smiling his toothy smile. Rishi tried to tell him with his eyes—since Dimple was still looking at him—that they needed to abort the plan. Abort. The. Plan. But Willie just smiled wider and added in a little wave. Double crap.

"Hello, folks!" Willie said, and Dimple spun around to face him. "You must be the lovely Dimple I've heard so much about," he said, taking her hand and pumping it enthusiastically. Dimple's eyes widened as she looked from Willie to Rishi. It was not happiness Rishi saw there.

Oh, no, no, no. Rishi glanced longingly out into the street. If it didn't mean abandoning Dimple, he might consider running to the car, jumping in, and taking it all the way home to Atherton.

The oblivious, obnoxiously cheerful Willie continued to talk. Why hadn't Rishi noticed before how effervescent the dude was? "Why don't you guys follow me this way? We have a table set up for you already." He beamed not so subtly at Rishi, totally not getting the vibe that he was trying to put off.

Dimple and Rishi followed him to the back, where it was quieter and emptier. He gestured to their table, already adorned with the few books Rishi had specifically ordered and requested to be placed there.

"Thanks," Rishi mumbled, and pressed a tip into Willie's palm.

Finally looking slightly bewildered at the lack of enthusiasm, Willie had the good sense to take the tip and leave quietly.

They took their seats in the heavy dark wood chairs, Rishi barely daring to look at Dimple. She looked down at the books, realization slowly seeping into her expression. She pushed her glasses up on her nose and picked up one of the small, clothbound editions. *"A Wrinkle in Time,"* she said softly.

"Yeah, it's, um, a 2009 special edition. Eight years ago, you know, because—"

She met his eye. "That's the year we met at the wedding."

Rishi felt a little surge of relief. At least she got it. But he didn't know, looking at her, whether she was freaked. Or flattered. Or just confused. Dimple touched the two other books on the table.

"Those are just some of my favorite graphic novels," Rishi explained. Both of them had first love as their theme, though Rishi didn't think he'd tell her that right now. "I thought you'd, uh, enjoy them. Maybe. If you wanted to read them." He rubbed the back of his neck. This was excruciating. Why the heck had he done all this? How had he thought this would be a good idea? She'd gone out of her way to make sure he understood that this was a *non-date*. Which meant Rishi was now officially a member of Camp Trying Too Hard.

Uggghhhh.

"Are you okay?"

He jumped a little and looked at her. "What? Why?"

"Why'd you just groan like that?"

Crap. He'd done that out loud? "Ah . . . no reason." Rishi exhaled.

"Look, if this is too much, if you hate it, we can go somewhere else."

But Dimple put a hand on his hand. When he looked up at her, hope blooming painfully in his chest, she was smiling at him, soft and sure. "I definitely don't hate it. Thanks."

Rishi exhaled. "You're welcome." At least Dimple didn't hate it. It still didn't mean he could check out of Camp Trying Too Hard yet, but she didn't hate it. So there was that.

CHAPTER 33

Dimple

"'Underneath Mrs. Murry's chair Fortinbras let out a contented sigh.'" Dimple closed the book and sat back to look at Rishi, smiling slightly. It was crazy how words—just black squiggles on a page—could bring memories rushing back. She remembered lying in bed under the covers, long after she was supposed to be asleep, her flashlight shining on these same pages. "I love this book," she said, stroking the cloth cover that was so much fancier than the $2 paperback she'd had. "I still remember feeling so . . . so cozy, thinking of the giant Murry family. How they all loved each other, how they looked out for each other no matter what. It used to make me wish my parents had popped out a few more."

Rishi leaned in, eyes wide. "Okay, but what happened to the dad? Does he ever come back?"

Dimple snorted and reached for the last bite of her salmon slider. Rishi had pretty much inhaled his French onion soup while she read. "I can't believe you've never read *A Wrinkle in Time*. It's a classic."

"I guess I was too busy reading comics. But seriously, does he ever come back?"

Dimple pushed the copy of her book forward. "Tell you what. You read that, and I'll read your comics." She paused, frowning. "Oh, wait. We can't take these out of the store, can we?"

The tips of Rishi's ears went pink. He dropped his gaze to where his thumb was tracing patterns in the woodwork of the table. "Ah, not usually. But these are, um, my books. I ordered them and had the waiter put them here for us. So we can."

Dimple's heart fluttered. Rishi had made a real effort for their non-date. He'd scoped out a place he knew she'd love—and she did; if she could live here under one of the tables forever, she'd be perfectly content to do just that. He'd bought books that meant something to her and to him. She knew she should discourage him. She also knew she didn't want to. If this was how Rishi Patel showed his interest in her, if this was him wooing her, she wanted more. More, more, more.

Dimple took a sip of her virgin cosmo and set it down, forced herself to meet his eye. "Rishi . . ."

He looked up, every muscle taut. "Yeah?"

"I, um, just wanted to say . . ." God, why couldn't the legal drinking age be eighteen in the US? European teens didn't know how good they had it. Then again, you had to be twenty-five to drink in Mumbai, so maybe they didn't have it that bad. Why the heck was she thinking of drinking laws now? Dimple forced herself to refocus. "I . . ." She swallowed. "I'm making headway on the coding. I got past that snag we were talking about yesterday." Ugh, coward.

His face fell, and her heart followed. "Oh yeah." He forced a smile like watery chai. "Good."

Willie the waiter came over then, that eager, toothy smile still plastered on his face. "Hi! How was everything, guys?"

"Great." Dimple smiled at him. "We're ready for the check."

"Okeydokey!" He slipped the leather check holder from his pocket, and Rishi reached for it.

"We can split it," Dimple said immediately.

But he just shook his head, put in a few bills, and said to the waiter, "Keep the change."

"Are you ready to go?" He was smiling, but it was that same watery chai smile. He'd lost his luster. He'd lost his luster because of her.

Dimple's chest felt tight. She should say something to put this right. To tell him how much she appreciated what he'd done. For once she should just lay out her feelings. She opened her mouth—and then closed it again. "Yeah. I'm ready."

They walked outside, the air heavy and pulsing with all the things left unsaid.

This is your chance, Dimple. Say something. Tell him you're having fun, at least. But she found she couldn't overcome the silence.

At the Beemer, Rishi opened her door, like before, and Dimple slid in. Rishi hopped in his side. The air felt different from the first time they'd gotten in . . . emptier, stiffer. Colder.

Rishi glanced at her. "I thought we might go watch a movie or something, but if you want to go back to the dorms, that's totally fine."

Dimple began to say that the movies sounded fine, but the thought of this continuing silence, this hurt/awkward mixture of pauses and emptiness, was too much. She took a breath. And another. "Actually," she said, "if you're up for it, there's somewhere else I'd like to go. It's about fifteen minutes away. Bernal Heights?"

Rishi raised his eyebrows. She saw the hope there, and it made her happy. "What's in Bernal Heights?"

"Oh, you'll see, my friend," she said lightly, even though her heart was hammering in her chest.

He smiled and started the car, pulling into the street. "Okay."

Dimple's mouth was dry. She'd never, ever done something like this before. To give herself something to do, she glanced sideways at Rishi and said, "You forgot the book." She set *A Wrinkle in Time* in the center console. "You're not going to look it up on the Internet and read the CliffsNotes, are you?"

He laughed. "No, I'm really looking forward to reading this. I have a theory: Charles Wallace is a killer robot."

Dimple stared at him. "A . . . killer robot."

"What? You said it's sci-fi, right?"

Dimple groaned. "*Hai Ram,* not every sci-fi has to have a killer robot in it, Rishi Patel. Just read it."

"I don't see the point if there aren't any killer robots, but okay," Rishi said, and Dimple thought, *I love the way your eyes twinkle when you're messing around.*

Rishi

About fifteen minutes later, Rishi pulled over. "This is it, Bernal Heights." Across the street, an old homeless man was yelling at thin air in a flat Boston accent. Rishi wondered what his story was; how someone from Boston ended up there, a fifty-something-year-old street person. His story would probably make an interesting comic. *Everything's not a story, Rishi*, Pappa would say. *Your head is in the clouds again.*

Rishi got out of the car and held Dimple's door open. Her face shone, pink-and-gold-tinged in the setting sun. She looked . . . excited. Rishi tried not to get his hopes up.

He'd obviously read this whole thing wrong. He'd thought the kiss meant that Dimple was conflicted; that maybe he could win her over even though she'd said this was a non-date. That obviously hadn't worked to his advantage. She'd been aloof on and off through dinner, and he was fairly sure she saw his gifts as over the line. Ugh. Rishi still felt the echo of the sting of rejection, even though she hadn't said anything outright. Well, he wasn't going to give her the chance. From now on he'd be friendly and nothing more. That was his new motto: Friend. Amigo. *Dost.*

"It's this way, I think . . . ," Dimple said, walking forward, looking down at her phone.

Rishi looked around. They were walking along a winding path on one of the many hills in San Francisco, bordered on one side by green grass and on the other by squat houses, a road, and parked cars. Karl the Fog swirled, ever present. "So now are you going to tell me where are we? What's here?"

Dimple smiled at him and put her phone away. Pushing a curl off her forehead, she said, "Just keep walking."

CHAPTER 34

Rishi

That was easier said than done. Bernal *Heights* definitely lived up to its name—Rishi's thighs were burning from scaling the thing. It felt like they should have special equipment. But Dimple apparently wanted them to climb this giant hill, so Rishi did, with minimal grunting.

By the time they got to the top the sun was dipping lower, smearing the sky with color, and Rishi was trying his best not to look like he was dying. Which, you know, was hard to do when he was bent over, wheezing, with sweat dripping into his eyes. Crap. He was sweating. Did he smell? Rishi was dipping his head in what he hoped was a surreptitious way to sniff at his armpit when Dimple grabbed his arm and said, "Look!"

He straightened up. "Ho-ly crap." They had a 360-degree view of San Francisco's seven-by-seven-mile beauty.

It looked like chaos at first—buildings and homes and roadways and other unknown structures all jostling for this tiny parcel of forty-nine square miles. But if you looked closely, like Rishi was doing, it all began to coalesce into this design. Wavy lines of white houses and a bridge (he thought it was the Bay Bridge, but he wasn't familiar enough with San Francisco to say for sure), rectangular strips of buildings interspersed with strips of green-black trees, the Pacific in the distance, encroaching on it all. And the sky like an overturned bowl of rose gold above them.

"It's beautiful, isn't it?" Dimple stepped forward, toward the edge of the hill. Rishi's instinct was to tell her to please step back before she fell off, but he didn't. She looked . . . peaceful there, the sunset making her black hair glow with red, like she was holding lava inside her instead of blood. Rishi smiled to himself. The fire she had, that passion? Yeah, he could definitely see her being born with lava in her veins.

She glanced over, and he averted his eyes, so he was looking out at the sunset too. "It's definitely something else," he said, answering her question just a few seconds too late. "How did you find out about this place?"

"Celia." Dimple walked closer to him, and Rishi felt his heart speed up merely at the proximity of her. Idiot. He forced himself to count to three before he looked over. She paused, uncertainty passing over her face. And then, in the next moment, she'd extended her hand out. It sat there between them, fog swirling in the spaces between her fingers.

Rishi was pretty sure his mouth had fallen open, so he concentrated on forcing it closed. Was she . . . reaching for his hand? He placed it in hers, no questions asked. And waited, because it seemed like she had something to say. Rishi could tell the words were practically squirming, trying to get out.

"Um . . ." Dimple blew out a breath, and with her free hand, tucked a curl behind her ear. The breeze just blew it out again, but she didn't seem to notice. "Rishi, I'm sorry if I seemed ambivalent at the restaurant before. What you did, that gift . . ." She shook her head. Her eyes burned into his. "It's the most thoughtful thing anyone's done for me. I really liked it. I really like . . . you." Dimple dropped her gaze again. Her hand was shaking slightly in his, and Rishi covered it with his other hand. Looking back up at him, she said, "I have a hard time with all the feelings stuff sometimes. But I think—I think I want this to be a real date. If you do, I mean." Her eyes widened slightly. "I mean, I'm not even sure if you're on the same page. I said I really like you, and you didn't really respond, and now you're just kind of looking at me—"

Rishi couldn't help the chuckle that escaped his lips. But when he saw her face fall, he dropped her hands and cradled her face instead. She was so close he could smell that coconut jasmine shampoo. He felt the warmth of her rushing over him, through him. Her eyes were huge behind her glasses, luminous even. "Dimple Shah . . . I really like you, too." He pressed his lips lightly against hers as he kept talking. He felt her shiver again, and he smiled against her mouth. "And I would be honored if this turned into a real date."

Her lips parted against his. And then he was lost in her.

Oh my God. Or as Rishi would say, Oh my gods. They were *kissing*. Again. Finally. Dimple sighed in perfect bliss, and Rishi's arms

217

wrapped around her waist in response, pulling her body snugly against his.

He wanted her. He wanted her just as much as she wanted him. It was unbelievable. Dimple had never thought her life would include a boy like Rishi. Was it kismet, like he'd said? Then she felt his tongue against hers, and all coherent thought flew out of her head.

Eventually they broke apart so they could breathe, but Rishi kept his arms circled loosely around her waist. His lips were swollen and red in the fading light. He smiled and rubbed her nose gently with his. "It's too bad we can't keep doing that indefinitely. Oxygen is so overrated."

Dimple's arms were resting against his chest, but she moved them down to his waist too, so her arms were crossed behind his back. "So is eating."

"And going to stupid web-development classes."

"Hey." She smacked him, and accidentally whacked the top of his butt. There was something ridged and hard like a notebook in his back pocket. "Those classes are my ticket to Jenny Lindt, let's not forget."

"Oh yeah. Her. What's so great about her again?" Rishi pulled away from her, but kept one hand clasped loosely around hers, which made Dimple happier than she wanted to admit. He pulled her down to the ground, and they lay facing each other, heads propped up on their elbows, lower legs tangled with each other's.

Dimple clasped her free hand to her heart. "Are you serious? Jenny Lindt is a pundit. A beacon. A herald of the coming age of Women in Tech."

Rishi smiled and tucked her hair behind her ear. That was quickly becoming her Favorite Thing. Besides kissing him, obviously. "She's your Leo Tilden, huh?" He lay down all the way and stretched out his arm under her head.

Dimple glanced at him, her heart hammering. Rishi's eyes were hopeful, but respectful. He didn't expect it. After a pause, Dimple lay down and put her head on his chest. Rishi sighed, a deep, humming thing that echoed in his chest and her ears.

Dimple smiled up at the sky. "Yeah. She's my Leo Tilden." They listened to the wind in the eucalyptus trees awhile. Somewhere below them, a dog barked. "Speaking of Leo, was that a notebook I felt in your pocket before? My hand brushed against it."

"Observant. Yes, it is. I always have to have a sketch pad with me. I left the big one at the dorm, but I had to bring this one."

"So . . . can I see it?"

Rishi laughed. "Yes, but on one condition."

She frowned. "Okay . . ."

"You have to let me sketch you."

Dimple sat up and looked at him. "What the what?"

Rishi grinned and rolled over onto his side again, propping his head up on one hand. She could barely see him now; the light was fading fast. "Let me sketch you, and you can look at my book."

Dimple gestured to the sky. "It's dark. How are you going to sketch?"

"Well . . ." Rishi pulled out his phone. "Someone gave me the great idea to install a flashlight app."

Dimple groaned. "I'm not the most photogenic person." Her

cheeks heated as she said the words. She didn't exactly want to call attention to that fact right now, on their first date.

Rishi put his fingers under her chin until she met his eye. "You. Are. Beautiful. *Lajawab*. My only worry is that I might not be able to do you justice."

CHAPTER 35

Dimple

Dimple rolled her eyes, even though the butterflies in her stomach began to flutter up a tiny tornado. *Lajawab.* Translated literally it meant *without answer.* "Okay, fine. But only because I get to see your sketchbook after." Self-consciously, she adjusted Celia's gauzy dress over her thighs. "How do you want me?"

Rishi jerked his head up to look at her, and she blushed, realizing the double entendre of her words. Thankfully, he looked just as flustered as she felt. Rubbing the back of his neck with the hand that held his pencil, he said, "Ah, just . . . maybe just lie down like you were. You can prop yourself up on your elbows if you want. Whatever's most comfortable."

Dimple lay down again, supremely aware of every movement she was making. The damp grass had cooled even more with nightfall, and it tickled under the backs of her knees. She turned over on her side so she was facing Rishi, one hand supporting the side of her head as she watched him smooth out the small sketch pad. In the blue-white light of the flashlight app, his hands shook just the slightest bit as he picked up his pencil.

Rishi looked at her, his gaze sweeping from her eyes to her lips to her collarbone to her chest, her waist, the curve of her hips. Dimple felt warm in spite of the cool breeze; the gauze of Celia's dress seemed to cling tighter to every part of her body.

Rishi made the first strokes, his hand dwarfing the stub of charcoal pencil that had obviously been sharpened many, many times. The more he drew, the more his expression became intent, focused, consumed. He wasn't sitting there next to her anymore, she knew. He looked up every so often, but he didn't really see her as Dimple. The thought was strangely disquieting, like she didn't really know him. Rishi the artist and Rishi Patel, whom she was on a date with—were they the same person?

When he turned the page, Rishi looked up and smiled, his face relaxed again. Dimple felt a tremor of relief to see him back. *This*, she thought. *This is what he meant when he said he couldn't do it as a half measure. He* lives *his art. If he did it full-time, there might not be time for anything or anyone else.*

"Still comfortable?" Rishi asked her, his voice gentle. "You can move if you need to—it won't bother me."

Dimple adjusted her body a little and tried to peek. "Can I see what you have yet?"

Rishi laughed and shielded his notebook with his hand. "Not yet. Soon, I promise. I want to do a small series of things. Okay, now you can just talk to me."

"Talk?" She frowned slightly and pushed up her glasses. Rishi began to sketch again. "Talk about what?"

"Anything at all." Rishi looked up at her, briefly, and then back down at his page again.

"Hmm, okay." Dimple played with a blade of grass. She knew what she wanted to say, but it caught in the back of her throat like a fish bone. "You, um . . ." She cleared her throat. In her peripheral vision, Rishi looked up at her and then back down again. "I don't want to get married anytime soon. Maybe not ever. This date doesn't change that."

She did look at him then, and his hand paused. He looked up at her. "I know. You said that already. I didn't think this date changed anything." He smiled and looked back down, resuming his sketching.

Dimple should let it go. Right now. Just. Let. It. Go. "So then what's the point?" She heard herself ask instead. "I mean, wasn't that why you talked to me that first day? That's why you decided to come, right? Because you thought I knew about this whole thing our parents had arranged."

Rishi frowned slightly; his pencil stopped moving. He looked up at her with those honey eyes. "What are you asking? Why would I want to go out with you if it doesn't involve marriage as the end result?"

Dimple was grateful for the misty darkness. "Yeah," she said quietly. "I thought that was the whole point for you. Marriage, following your parents' wishes, all of that. And if it is, then I'm definitely not the girl who's going to get you there."

Rishi set his notebook and pencil off to the side. He looked up at the stars, thinking, and Dimple felt her heart banging in her chest, afraid of what he was going to say. But also just wanting him to say it, to just rip the Band-Aid off. The scent of eucalyptus wafted at them in soft swaths. "I'm not going to lie. Culture and tradition are important to me." He looked at her, his eyes shadowed. "Very important. It's how I was raised, you know? It's an incredible responsibility, being the first child . . . the first son. Especially since Ashish is so . . . Anyway. The point is, I don't think he'd really respect Ma and Pappa's wishes the way I will. The way I want to. So, yeah. Getting married is important to me. Giving my parents grandkids someday is important. Taking care of them in their old age, ditto." Then, in one fluid motion, Rishi lay down on his belly so his face was near hers. He crossed his hands and put his chin on top of the backs of them. Their faces were no more than an inch apart. Dimple couldn't breathe. He looked straight into her eyes as he spoke. "But you're showing me that other things are important too. The point of dating you, Dimple Shah, is to get to know you. To spend time with you. To see the way you push your glasses up on your nose when you're especially moved by whatever you're saying. To smell your amazing shampoo. To feel your heart beating against mine. To see you smile. To kiss you." He leaned in and kissed her gently on the lips. When she opened her eyes, he was smil-ing. "So maybe all that other stuff that's important to me can take a backseat for now. And maybe I'm totally fine with that . . . if you are?"

Dimple's heart slowed down. She felt every muscle relaxing. "I am. I'm very fine with that." She leaned in and kissed him again, tasting his lips, smiling when she heard the way his breath caught when their tongues met.

When they pulled apart, Rishi grinned and sat back up, picking up his notebook and pencil again. He began sketching. "So. Now that we've put that issue to rest, tell me the truth. What'd you think of me when you first saw me?"

"At the wedding? Or at Starbucks, when you randomly accosted me?" Dimple raised an eyebrow.

Rishi laughed. "Both. Start with the wedding."

"At the wedding I thought you were cool. Like, how you sat there, just ripping up magazines that didn't even belong to you. That would never even have occurred to me. At first I thought you were just some destructive, crazy *boy*, but then you began to make those flowers, and I was totally impressed. I was doubly impressed when my mamma's voice didn't make you flinch."

Rishi smiled, looking up at her quickly before looking back down again. "Want to know what I thought?"

Dimple leaned forward. "Yes."

"I thought you were the loveliest bookworm I'd ever seen in my life."

She laughed and threw a blade of grass at him. "Oh please. You thought nothing of the kind."

"I did too!" he said, indignant. "Why else do you think I gave you my best flower?"

Dimple didn't know whether to believe him or not, but she flushed with pleasure anyway. "So, now tell me what you thought of me at the Starbucks. You know, right before I flung my coffee at you."

CHAPTER 36

Dimple

Rishi smiled wryly at her before looking back down at his drawing. "I thought you looked peaceful. You were sitting on the edge of that fountain, your face turned up to the sun. You looked like a flower, with that angelic halo of curls around you. Of course, I quickly realized how mistaken I was."

Dimple reached over and slapped his knee, but she was laughing too. "Shut up. You totally creeped me out with that whole *future wife* line! You should be glad I didn't have pepper spray or throwing stars on me." It was incredible, she thought, that they were laughing about this now. When it first happened, she'd been so sure that Rishi and she would have absolutely nothing to do with each other. But that was Rishi . . . he was like a pop song you thought you couldn't stand, but found yourself humming in the shower anyway.

"Noted," he said, sketching away. "In my defense, I thought you were here because you knew about our parents' nefarious plan too."

Dimple sighed. "Yeah. My parents are a whole other matter. You're lucky you get along with yours so well." But maybe it wasn't lucky at all, she thought. Rishi agreed with everything his parents said or planned. Dimple didn't. There was a fundamental difference in how they related to their parents.

"Your mom sounds like she really cares for you." When Dimple snorted, Rishi hurried to continue. "I mean, she's calling you. She's talking to you. She's trying to be a part of your life."

Dimple laughed. "Trying to be a part of my life? You know, the same could be said about head lice. Or termites. Or botulism. Those bacteria are just trying to be a part of our lives!"

Rishi smiled and set his pencil down. "Okay. Are you ready to see?"

Dimple sat up in a hurry. "You're done?"

"Yep." He handed her the notebook, his finger holding a spot between the pages. "Start there, and move forward. I sort of modeled these sketches after a creative exercise comic artists like to do. It's called 'twenty-five expressions.' Basically, you sketch the same character with twenty-five different expressions, to sort of get to know your character better. That's one of the first things I noticed about you. You wear your expressions on your face so plainly."

Dimple took the book, putting her finger in place of his so she didn't lose the page either. "Really?"

Rishi raised one eyebrow, as if to say, *Are you kidding?*

Dimple opened the book. The first image was of her looking . . . nervous. Anticipatory. This was right when Rishi had begun to draw her. He'd captured the tentativeness she'd felt, the anxiety of how she might be perceived. She looked . . . beautiful, she realized.

He'd drawn the entire thing sort of smudgy, to reflect how he saw her through the curtain of fog around them. Still, the details were arresting. There was a glow about her cheeks, a soft sparkle in her eyes. Her glasses made her look intelligent and artsy-nerdy, not geeky like she usually thought she looked. Her bun was a mass of wild curls, but not in the unkempt way she usually saw it in the mirror. She looked like she could be the model for some hair product. Was this how he saw her? She turned the page.

In the second sketch, Dimple was laughing, her eyes squeezed shut at something Rishi must've said. She looked happy, carefree, like she'd forgotten herself. She liked that, to him, she was smart and pretty and funny all rolled into one. She turned the page.

Each sketch showed her with a different expression, and in each one she found the basic essence of herself. He'd captured her in so much vibrant detail, even sitting here in the near-dark with just a flashlight app, that she knew: He'd been watching her even when she hadn't noticed. He'd committed every detail of her face, her hair, her body, to memory. Even before this had turned into a real date for Dimple, this had been a real date for Rishi. He'd just been waiting for her to catch up to him.

And, she realized with a thud, she'd been watching him, too. When she hadn't been thinking of him, all she'd really been thinking about was him. That first day, after she got over the shock of him popping up out of nowhere, he'd caught her eye. Dimple hadn't been looking for this . . . whatever it was between them at all. But somehow she had a feeling that love had found her. It was circling them, waiting for the perfect spot to land.

Dimple didn't know if she wanted it to. She didn't know much beyond the fact that right now, she wanted to kiss Rishi. So she did.

She set the book down, crawled over to him, and climbed in his lap. Dimple didn't know where the courage came from, but she wrapped her legs around his waist, held his face in her hands, and kissed him until her lips were swollen and she couldn't breathe anymore. When they pulled apart, he was looking at her, with his hands wrapped tightly around her, like he couldn't believe his luck. Like she was a gilded winged *apsara* he'd just come upon in the woods.

"Wow," he finally managed to say, his voice breathless. "I should draw you more often."

Dimple laughed, wanting to tell him she'd kiss him even without him doing that, but then their lips met again, and she lost her train of thought.

Rishi

Hours or weeks or milliseconds later (time sort of did its own thing when Rishi was with Dimple, he'd noticed), they were in the convertible, driving back to campus. They'd talked for hours, until Rishi's stomach had growled its impatience, and Dimple had insisted they go get some froyo at one of their favorite places near their dorms.

He looked at her, sitting next to him, the city lights playing across her face and hair. She'd catch his eye and they'd laugh, surprised, disbelieving, that this was happening. That they were here, that this magic was for them, that it was real. At least, that's what Rishi was thinking. Dimple may just have been laughing at the goofy expression on his face.

"Don't forget this," Dimple said, patting *A Wrinkle in Time* in the center console. "Your assignment is to read it so we can discuss it later."

"Right. I'll get right on it. My money is still on Charles Wallace being a terminator, though. Kid's creepy."

Dimple laughed, and he had to stop himself from closing his eyes so he could just let the sound wash over him. *Speaking of creepy, Patel. Jeez.*

CHAPTER 37

Dimple

A couple of days later Dimple and Rishi were sitting in the lecture hall, having a heated discussion (or as Rishi would say, arguing) about their app's data diagram when Celia sank into the empty seat next to them with a sigh and a cloud of citrus perfume.

Dimple looked at her. "Everything okay?"

"Yeah. I'm just taking a breather. You guys carry on; just ignore me." She rummaged in her bag, purposely not meeting Dimple's eye.

Dimple resisted looking over her shoulder at the Aberzombies. Things between Evan and Celia must not be going well. She had walked over with him today after spending the night with him in his dorm.

"Okay, everybody! I know you're all busy cranking out your projects, but listen up for a second. I have something important to say." Max stood at the front of the lecture hall, stroking his beard and smiling benevolently at them all.

When everyone had quieted down, he continued. "All right. So we're just about at the halfway mark of your six weeks here. I trust we're all making good progress with our programs and apps. As you know, right around now is when we announce the fun part of Insomnia Con . . . the talent show. This year's talent show will be held next weekend, on Saturday, at the Little Theater at seven p.m."

There was scattered applause, although some people—those of the introvert persuasion—groaned. Needless to say, the Aberzombies all looked like they might tear off their clothes and dance on the tables right then. Dimple pulled a face at Rishi.

"The talent show is important because it's a chance to really get a leg up on your competition," Max continued, over the noise. "Historically, we've had a five-hundred-dollar prize for the pair of winning partners. However, due to the generosity of a donor this year, the prize has been upped to a cool grand. Remember, the goal is to get your project as finished as possible by the time Jenny Lindt looks at it, and this will go a long way toward helping you put your most polished foot forward."

Celia groaned and stood. "I guess I should go talk to my partner, figure out what we're doing," she said.

Dimple waved to her and turned to Rishi. "Wow. We're almost at the talent show already." Her heart fluttered in a strange, unpleasant way.

Rishi nodded, his face slack. "Yeah. Halfway through. Just three more weeks and we'll be going home."

She waited for him to say more. To acknowledge what they hadn't spoken about yet. What happened when this was all over?

He opened his mouth and leaned in, his eyes serious and sharp. Dimple's heart thundered. But then his eyes dimmed and he sat back. "So . . . do you have any idea of what you want to do for this thing?"

Dimple swallowed her disappointment and nodded. Okay, focus. The talent show. That's what was important now. "Yes," she said firmly. "We're doing a Bollywood dance."

Rishi stared at her. "What? *You* want to get up on a stage in front of a bunch of strangers and dance?"

"I know. It doesn't sound like me. But look at this." Dimple clicked to open a spreadsheet and turned her laptop around. "I went back ten years—since the inception of Insomnia Con—and plotted out all the winners of the talent show. Look: 2007: dance; 2008: dance; 2009 and 2010? Dance. 2011 was a singing year, but 2012 again was dance, followed by magic in 2013, but in 2014, we have another dance! 2015 and 2016 were juggling and singing, respectively." She looked at Rishi. "Do you know what this means?"

"That . . . you're a little too obsessed with Insomnia Con?"

Dimple punched him in the ribs, and it was a testament to him having acclimated to her that he didn't even flinch. "No. This is a dance year! I can feel it in my bones. The judges are clearly biased toward the dance category. And look, about a third of these winners were ethnic dances, but no one's done a Bollywood dance yet. We have to do it."

"Okay, but you do realize this means we'll have to get up onstage? And actually dance?" Rishi leaned forward in his chair. "Because I don't know if you've noticed, but you're sort of an introvert."

"Yeah, I thought about that." Dimple pulled her hair up into a bun and stuck her pen into it, dropping her gaze. "That's why I picked a song where, um, I have a very small dancing part. It's mainly all you." She winced and darted a sidelong glance at him.

"What! So you're just going to sell me down the river so you can ride off into the sunset with your prize?" Rishi laughed. "I don't think so."

"Look." Dimple turned in her chair so he could get the full effect of her eyelash batting. Not that she was very skilled at it, but still. "You just look like one of those people who can dance well." When he opened his mouth, probably to argue, she hurried on. "Okay, so not well, but decently?" He made an *eeeh* face. "You're our big shot, Rishi. I can't dance. I just get too nervous and weird and—I had this one performance, when I was nine? My mom made me do a bhangra dance for the Indian Association's Diwali party. And I puked. Onstage. In front of *everyone*. It was humiliating."

"Oh, okay." Rishi nodded, like he understood, and Dimple relaxed. "So you just want *me* to be humiliated instead." He raised an eyebrow. "No, Dimple. This is your idea. Let's do a dance where you have to do most of it."

Dimple hung her head and scratched at her scalp. "Uggh, then I guess we'll just have to do something else." She looked up at her Excel sheet, her heart sinking. Dancing was what would win the first place prize. She knew it in her heart. It would take her that much closer to Jenny Lindt. She'd been counting on Celia—who loved performing and attention and everything that made people exceptional at talent shows—to do the dance. But Rishi? Rishi was too much like her. She sighed. The truth was, she was still glad they were partners. They'd figure out a way.

"Hey." Rishi's hand was on hers, and when she looked over, he was smiling. "I'll do it."

She blinked. "You'll do what?"

"I'll do the stupid dance." He grinned. "But you owe me."

"Are you serious?" Dimple couldn't help grinning too.

"Totally. Now, tell me what song you were thinking of."

"I can do better than that. I can show you." Still smiling, Dimple pulled out her headphones, plugged them in, and handed them to Rishi. "Thank you." She leaned in and kissed him on the cheek before she could talk herself out of it, and his grin went supernova. Laughing, Dimple queued up "Dil Na Diya" from the movie *Krrish* on YouTube. "We can practice it after we get out of here, in your room."

While Rishi listened to the song, Dimple heard Celia's voice, raised in anger. She turned around in her seat to see her yelling at Evan. "Well, I don't want to do that! That's total BS!" And then she turned and stalked away, slamming out of the lecture hall.

CHAPTER 38

Dimple

Dimple turned to Rishi and mouthed, "I'll be right back." He nodded, apparently not having heard anything.

She got up and raced after Celia, catching up with her in the hallway outside. Celia was splashing cold water from the water fountain on the back of her neck, her curls bunched up in one fist. Her cheeks were pink. When she saw Dimple, she let out a shaky breath. "Did you hear that?"

"Yeah. I mean, just the last part, before you walked out. What's going on? Are you okay?"

Celia leaned her back against the wall, one knee bent, her foot pressed against the wall. Crossing her arms, she blew out a breath. "Evan's being a total jerk. He wants to do a dance to this song, 'Sexy Heat,' with me and Isabelle and Hari. Have you heard it?"

Dimple shook her head and took a seat on the bench next to the water fountain. *It sounds like a real winner,* she wanted to say, but managed to chomp down on her tongue somehow.

"It's total crap. Like, the entire song has the two girls in skimpy outfits dancing together while the guys talk about how hot they are.

I mean, I get it. It's just a talent show, whatever. Isabelle's totally up for putting on a bikini and dancing with me onstage. But I just . . ." Celia mock-gagged. "It makes me feel gross. I mean, Isabelle's *gorgeous*, don't get me wrong."

Dimple nodded to encourage Celia to keep talking. Of course Isabelle was up for it. She'd probably even eat carbs for that amount of attention. Dimple ignored the pinprick of guilt she felt at the uncharitable thought; Isabelle wasn't nearly as awful as the guys.

"I just don't know if I want to be up there onstage on display for everyone to stare at." Celia waved her hands in the air aggressively. "Am I being too sensitive? They all seem to think so." She gestured to the lecture hall.

"No." Dimple reached out and put a hand on Celia's arm. "Not at all. It's totally up to you how comfortable you are with this, you know? It's not up to Evan or Hari or Isabelle. So what if she wants to do it? She's not you, and you're not her." Celia gave her a look, and Dimple chuckled. "I know, I'm very wise. But seriously, don't give in. It sucks that you're in a partnership with Evan, or you could just quit. But will Max even let all four of you do this thing together? I mean, I thought partners were supposed to work just with each other."

"Yeah, I think they worked it out with him. They didn't tell him what song we'd be dancing to, but he seemed to think it was creative. Each partnership would be judged separately, anyway."

"Well, could a partnership split up? Because then maybe you could dance with us, and Evan could be the one in a bikini."

Celia snorted. "Thanks, but I don't think they'll let us do that. I should probably figure out a way to deal with this." She held out her arms and Dimple stood to give her a hug. "Thanks for not thinking I'm crazy. I think I've been hanging out with those three for too long."

"Probably," Dimple said, pulling back. "Maybe you can come to dinner with Rishi and me tonight. We're probably going to be eating at the dining hall."

"Sounds good." Celia smiled, seemingly cheered at this thought. "Thanks."

They turned around and walked back into the lecture hall.

"So you have the gist, right?" Dimple asked after they'd watched the "Dil Na Diya" video for the fourth time. They were in Rishi's room after class, getting ready for their first practice session. "It's not too complicated? I mean, I know Hrithik's, like, this world-class dancer. But you don't have to be. Just get the moves down and it'll be good. I've seen the other talent show winners on YouTube, and it's not like they were all rock stars. We're coders, you know? Not . . ." She trailed off at Rishi's raised eyebrow.

"You're nervous," he said, but not accusingly. He was sort of smiling.

Dimple chewed the inside of her cheek. "I guess. Kind of." But not for the reason he thought. She was nervous because in a moment, he'd see her dancing skills. The video had about two seconds of the girl dancing, but still. She'd never danced in front of anyone since the bhangra puke fiasco. Let alone in front of a boy she actually liked. Whom she'd *kissed*. Dimple felt herself begin to hyperventilate, so she busied herself with putting her hair up in a bun.

Rishi, oblivious to her internal storm of turmoil, had pushed his bed up against the far wall, so they had a clean rectangle of space to work in. He stood in the middle and nodded, satisfied. "Okay."

Dimple hit the play button with a shaking finger, and the song flooded the room. Rishi paused, his eyes closed, apparently trying to let the beat move him or something.

Then he jerked, his hands and legs spasming as he tried to copy Hrithik Roshan. He kept going, occasionally glancing at the screen to make sure he had it down. He was grinning now, enjoying himself as he jumped up and landed with his feet wide, then shimmied across the room, nodding his head with a *heck yeah* expression on his face.

Dimple was sure she was in a dream. That could be the only explanation. She saw her hand float out in front of her and hit the space bar on his laptop, pausing the video.

Rishi stopped thrashing abruptly. "What's wrong?"

Dimple gripped the edge of his desk. The corners of the room swam. Her voice came from a million galaxies away. "That's . . . that's how you dance?"

Rishi looked down at his body, as if to check something. "Yeah?" He looked back at her, confused.

Dimple clutched her head. "But you said—you said you were a good dancer!"

"I did not! I barely agreed that I was 'decent'!"

Dimple glared at him, her temper flaring. She spoke slowly, enunciating the words. "That. Was not. Anywhere *near* decent."

They stared at each other for a minute, Rishi's deep honey eyes boring into hers. And then he burst out laughing. Geysers of "ha ha ha" burst out of him, and watching him guffaw like that, helpless, actually *slapping his knee*, Dimple began to laugh too, just slightly hysterically.

Finally, Rishi sank down on the floor, holding his stomach, alternating groans with laughter. Dimple sat beside him and wiped her eyes, her laughter subsiding to a few hiccups. "Okay, seriously, what are we going to do?"

Rishi looked at her from where he was sprawled on the floor, his arms and legs askew. "Well, do you still want to win the talent show?"

She nodded. "Obviously."

"Then we keep practicing. We have six and a half days to get this down." Rishi hopped up, lithe as a lion. Why couldn't he use that grace in his dancing? He held out a hand to Dimple and pulled her up. Bending down so they were nose to nose, he said, "Show me what you got, Priyanka."

Priyanka Chopra—Hrithik Roshan's partner in "Dil Na Diya"—was equally as good as him. Thankfully, since her part was so minuscule in that song, Dimple didn't have the intense pressure that Rishi had on him. They practiced the part where both Hrithik and Priyanka danced together. Dimple moved her arms around and hoped to God she didn't look like she was convulsing. Like Rishi looked right then.

Panting, Rishi grabbed her arm so she'd stop. "Hey, what about at this part if you, like, hopped up in my arms?"

"What?" Dimple wiped her forehead and went over to pause the laptop. In the silence she said, "Rishi, I don't think *hopping into your arms* is going to improve this routine. Let's just stick with what the Bollywood choreographers, in all their wisdom and experience, deemed good enough for Hrithik and Priyanka."

"No, wait, just hear me out. Here, rewind it a bit? Like, to the part where he points at her?" Dimple did what he asked in spite of her intense misgivings. "Okay, now hit play and come back here."

She did.

"Now, when I point to you, instead of beginning your dance move, what about if you just jump up on me and I'll catch you?"

"Are you serious? I'm not going to just jump—"

"I won't let you fall, I promise. Oh, look, it's coming up, come on!" Rishi held his arms open, and Dimple, giving in to peer pressure in spite of every instinct screaming at her not to, leaped into his arms.

Or rather, she tried to, but her jeans wouldn't allow her the flexibility she needed. So, instead, she kneed Rishi in the ribs, hard.

He yelled out "Ow!" and instead of catching Dimple, used his arms to fend her off with a deftly executed karate chop. Suddenly realizing what he was doing, Rishi scrambled to help her, apparently consumed by a vortex of regret. But Dimple, feeling spiteful, grabbed him around the neck on the way down to take him with her.

They lay in a silent, shocked heap on the floor, arms and legs so tangled Dimple had no idea whose limbs were whose.

She was in too much pain to say anything for a full ten seconds, so she just lay there staring at the ceiling as the merry tunes of "Dil Na Diya" blared into the room. And then Rishi began to laugh again. Dimple wasn't sure she cared anymore for his penchant for finding humor in every situation.

He turned his head, groaning, and said, "Are you okay?"

"I'm fine," Dimple managed, pushing his thigh off her stomach so she could breathe better. "Ouch."

Rishi tried pulling his arm out from under her, but since she was still partially pinned under him, she just rolled toward him. He was looking down at her, their noses almost touching, both her legs under his left one. "Hi," he said, his eyes warm and liquid. "I'm sorry."

She wanted to punch him in the ribs. She wanted to bite his nose. But looking into those eyes, Dimple realized she wanted something else even more. So she lifted her head and kissed him.

And that's when a male voice said, loudly, "Well, well, WELL. What have we here?"

CHAPTER 39

Dimple

They flew apart, struggling to sit up, Dimple's head swimming. Oh my God. They hadn't even heard the door opening, they'd been so deep into their kiss. Dimple blinked and then frowned. Wait. Rishi didn't have a roommate. So who was this boy, with his curly black hair and seemingly never-ending, muscled legs, dressed in athletic shorts and dirty sneakers, standing there with that annoying smirk on his face?

Rishi

"Ashish?"

What the heck? What was his idiot brother doing here, ruining this perfectly amazing moment? Rishi struggled to his feet and held out a hand to Dimple, but she hopped up herself, her eyes wild, looking from him to Ashish and back. Like they'd been caught smuggling diamonds instead of just kissing. It would be comical if

Rishi weren't so irritated. "What are you doing here?"

Ashish breezed into the room and, like he owned it, pushed pause on Rishi's laptop. "Okay, *what* is going on here?" He dumped his gym bag on the floor and sprawled on Rishi's chair, his gigantic praying-mantis legs encroaching into Rishi's space. The stench of Axe body spray was enough to strangle anyone within fifty feet of the boy.

Rishi stepped back and crossed his arms. "Answer my question first."

Ashish rolled his eyes. "I thought Ma and Pappa told you. I wanted to see the campus."

Rishi held out his arms. Were all little brothers this annoying, or was he just blessed with an especially potent member of the species? "And? How'd you get here? Why didn't Ma or Pappa call me first? And how the heck did you open my locked door?"

Ashish reached into his shorts pocket and pulled out a key. "I told the desk attendant that I was Rishi Patel in room 406." He looked at Dimple and said, as an aside, "My mom and dad told me which room he was in." Then, looking back at Rishi, he added, "I said I'd been locked out of my room and needed to borrow the spare." He grinned. "Good thing people think all Indians look alike, huh?"

Dimple cleared her throat and looked meaningfully at Rishi. He pushed a hand through his hair. "Sorry. Dimple, this is my brother, Ashish. Ashish, this is Dimple Shah."

Ashish smiled lazily at her as he shook her proffered hand. "You're a lot less scary-looking in perso—"

"Answer my other two questions," Rishi interrupted loudly just as Dimple crossed her arms and cocked her head, in a *come at me, bro* pose. "How'd you get here? And why didn't any of you call me?"

Ashish let his head fall back over the back of the chair. "Ah, I bummed a ride from someone I know. Ma and Pappa were driving me nuts. I had to get out of there. So I figured why not come now? A few days early, but whatever." He looked at Rishi, smiling, but there was an edge to it. "You don't mind, do you, *bhaiyya*?" He said *bhaiyya* ingratiatingly, cloyingly, making it a mockery of the word.

This was embarrassing. Not only was Ashish being a total punk, like usual, he was also talking about Ma and Pappa in front of Dimple. Rishi would never think to speak about his parents behind their backs. He glanced at Dimple, wondering what she thought about all of this.

"Maybe I should go," Dimple said, slipping on her Chucks. "So you guys can, you know, talk and—"

Ashish crossed his hands behind his head. "Aw, don't leave. I haven't even had a chance to speak with my future *bhabhi* yet."

Dimple's face paled at the Hindi word for *sister-in-law*, and Rishi rushed to correct Ashish. "There are some things you and I will need to talk about, Ashish."

"What were you guys doing?" Ashish said, totally ignoring them. Always on his own schedule. Selfish. He looked at the YouTube video, tilting his head. "Is that *Krrish*?"

"Yeah," Dimple said, ignoring Rishi's very obvious *don't encourage him* eyebrow raising combined with a head shake. "We have this talent show we're doing next weekend, and we decided to do a dance routine with 'Dil Na Diya.'"

"Hey, you guys need some help? I mean, I don't want to brag, but I'm a really good dancer." Ashish smiled again, that smarmy, full-toothed shark smile. "Ask Rishi; he knows."

Dimple turned to him. "Seriously? That would be so awesome if—"

"No," Rishi said. "We don't want your help." He looked at Dimple, half pleading, half annoyed. "Right? We can do this ourselves?"

She raised an eyebrow and pushed her glasses up on her nose. "We were lying in a tangled heap on the floor when Ashish walked in." And then she felt her cheeks heat because she'd thought of just what they were doing in that tangled heap. Rishi knew because he'd automatically thought it too. And now he couldn't stop staring at her . . . and she was staring at him, too.

Ashish cleared his throat loudly, shaking them both from their reverie. "Oh-kay. You guys seem a little . . . conflicted or something, so I'm going to go downstairs and return this." He jangled the spare key. "See ya." He stood and ambled out of the room.

Dimple watched him go. When the door had shut behind him, she turned to Rishi, her lips twitching. "*That's* your brother?"

"Yeah." Rishi sighed. "What? Why is your mouth all quivery?"

Dimple laughed, one hand at her chest. "Oh my God. You guys are so different. Like, I didn't even think that was possible. Aren't siblings supposed to share the same genes and everything?"

Rishi pushed a hand through his hair, feeling slightly put off by how amused Dimple was. Living with Ashish was anything but funny. This entire situation was distinctly unfunny. "Yeah, he's somewhat of an aberration. I'm pretty sure someone stole our nice, sweet boy and replaced him with . . ." He gestured at the door.

Dimple stopped laughing. "Oh, come on. He's not that bad." She toyed with a pen on his desk. "And we really need the help, Rishi.

You know we do. Besides, what are you going to do? Send him back home? He came here to be with you." She shrugged.

Rishi tried not to groan and tear out his hair. Did Dimple have a point? Would he just be a big jerk if he insisted Ashish go back home? There was one person he could always count on for advice.

Rishi pulled his cell phone off his desk and called Pappa.

"*Beta! Kaise ho?*"

"Fine, Pappa. I have a visitor." He raised his eyebrows at Dimple, and she giggled in response.

"*Haan? Kaun?*"

Rishi frowned. Who did Pappa think? "Ashish." He straightened as a thought occurred to him. "No. Please tell me he told you he was coming."

"Ashish! Ashish is with you? In your dorm?" Rishi heard Ma in the background, speaking in rapid-fire Hindi. He caught a few hysterical *kya?!*s and *kyon?!*s.

Rishi sighed and pinched the bridge of his nose. "Yes, he's here. He hitched a ride with someone. I thought you knew."

Dimple clapped her hand over her mouth. Rishi couldn't help but see the slight admiration in her expression.

"*Haan, Pappa, main usko keh doonga.* I'll tell him. *Thikh hai.* Bye." Rishi hung up and looked at Dimple. His face was so creased with worry, he looked at least a decade older. "I better go find Ashish before he gets up to I-shudder-to-think-what. Will you be okay here for a minute?"

"Yeah. I mean, I could go downstairs back to my room if you need a little while with him."

"No, stay. We need to practice. Besides, I'm not ready for you to go yet." Rishi smiled, leaned down, and gently kissed her. Then he was gone.

CHAPTER 40

Dimple

Dimple sank into the chair and fiddled absently with the laptop. This was beyond weird. Ashish was nothing at all like what she'd expected, like what she'd thought Rishi's little brother would be like. He'd said before that Ashish was different from him, but this was so beyond different, Dimple didn't even know how to comprehend it. Ashish seemed like he should've come from a different set of parents. Honestly, he seemed more like he could be Dimple's little brother than Rishi's.

But things made more sense now. That's why Rishi was so adamant about doing exactly what his parents wanted. He'd said it before, but Dimple hadn't really gotten it. He was the only child in the family who was doing what their parents wanted. Ashish was probably such a handful that Rishi wanted to smooth things over, make things better for his parents.

But that's not fair, Dimple found herself thinking, her temper flaring. Why was it Rishi's responsibility to keep their parents happy while Ashish got to do whatever he wanted? Why did it become Rishi's job by default to be unfailingly dutiful and obedient just because his little brother wasn't? Dimple felt a throb of resentment toward Rishi's parents, for not realizing how unhappy they were making him with their unfair, unrealistic expectations.

She got up and began to pace the room to dispel some of the anger before Rishi and Ashish came back. That's when she saw it.

Rishi's messenger bag, hanging open from the bedpost. Peeking out was his sketch pad, full of his art, brimming with his talent. Dimple hesitated for just a second before walking to it.

She ran her fingers along the spiral top, letting the cool metal press into her flesh, turning her fingertips white. Rishi was protective of his sketches. He didn't like anyone to see them, but he was doing such a great disservice to himself and other people. He didn't know how much the world needed his art. Society was practically crying out for people who poured their heart and soul into work that was bigger than them. Besides, he had let her see his pocket-size sketch book. Surely he wouldn't object to this.

She slid out the sketch pad and began to riffle through it. The earliest sketches dated back three years, and as she progressed, Dimple felt like she was holding a guidebook to Rishi's talent, of the time and effort he'd put into carefully and lovingly honing his craft. His characters became more lifelike, more real. Although he sketched a variety of things and people—buildings, his house, what looked like students in a posh school cafeteria—he kept coming back to Aditya. As time progressed, Aditya became more and more fleshed out, more substantial. His expressions changed, became more fluid and dynamic, more complex. In the most recent ones, Aditya had begun to fall in love with a girl with wild, curly black hair. They were dated before Dimple and Rishi had even met. Kismet?

There were fewer sketches as Dimple moved through the sketch-book, and she felt a pang. His art was disappearing. No one was telling him how good he was, how much he needed to keep going, and so he was letting it die. She saw the pain in the pages—when he did come back, he drew detailed scenes, every leaf on every tree vivid and trembling with life.

Aditya looked reproachful in these later sketches, his eyes beckoning the artist to stay with him for just a while longer, to not forget, to not relegate him to these empty pages. Dimple felt an actual lump in her throat. This was wrong. She couldn't, in good conscience, just stand by and watch Rishi's talent wither away like some poor plant in a dark basement.

Before she could talk herself out of it, Dimple pulled out her phone and began to take pictures of Rishi's latest sketches, focusing on Aditya. She was about six pictures in when she heard Rishi's and Ashish's voices in the hallway, raised in argument. Heart hammering, Dimple slid the sketch pad back into Rishi's messenger bag, crossed the room, and sat back down at the laptop. She slid the phone back into her pocket and took a deep breath, trying to rearrange her facial features into a *not guilty of snooping or any other illicit activity* expression.

She shouldn't have bothered. When the guys burst in, they were in such a heated argument, they didn't even look at her.

"You're such a brownnoser," Ashish said, thrusting his hands through his hair as he walked in, leaving it sticking up in every direction. "Did you seriously have to call them the minute I left the room? Tell me, was it like a physical impulse? Goody-goody syndrome manifesting itself?"

"Brownnoser! Really!" Rishi thundered, his eyes flashing with a temper Dimple hadn't seen yet. "You can call me names all you want, Ashish, but our parents had no idea where you were. Do you know how worried Ma is about you? Does it ever even *occur* to you to think about anyone besides yourself?"

Oh God. She seriously should've just gone to her room. Dimple had a sinking feeling they had no idea she was there and that she was witnessing a very, very private fight. She would leave now, but the two of them were right in the middle of the room, blocking access to the door. Should she clear her throat so they knew she was here? Should she get up and leave anyway, just push right through them? Dimple decided on the *clear my throat* strategy, but the sound was swallowed by Ashish's bitter laughter.

"Oh yeah, I'm so selfish for wanting to live my life! For wanting to have a modicum of space without my parents breathing down my freaking neck all the time! So sorry, *bhaiyya*, but not all of us can be self-sacrificing, dutiful sons who belong in one of Ma's cheesy *Ramayan* sagas!"

"Have some respect!" Rishi roared. "Ma and Pappa are our parents! You can't talk about them like that!"

"Says who?" Ashish said, and immediately, Dimple could see them as elementary school kids, having a very similar fight about whose turn it was to pick the cartoon they were going to watch. "This might come as a surprise to you, but you can't control what I do!"

"This might come as a surprise to you, but *I don't want to!*"

In the lethal silence that followed, both brothers glaring at each other, Dimple's phone blared to life. "Crap." She scrabbled in her pocket, aware that both Rishi and Ashish were now watching her, their faces slightly slack, like they'd completely forgotten her existence. Which they probably had.

"Sorry." Dimple smiled sheepishly. "It's my roommate." She pressed answer. "Hello?"

"Hey! I realized we never actually set up a time for when we were gonna do dinner. Or, like, even figured out where we were gonna go get said dinner. You said the dining hall before, right? Is that still the plan?"

Dimple could hear Transviolet playing in the background, which meant Celia was probably moping about Evan, even though she wouldn't admit it. She sighed and mouthed a "sorry" at the guys. Rishi gave her a tense smile, but Ashish just sprawled out on the bed with his own phone. "Um, yeah, I'm not sure. . . . What about sevenish? If you want, you can just come up to Rishi's room. That's where I am right now, 406."

Dimple could almost *see* Celia perking up. "Ohhhh, you're in his room? I didn't know you were going to do that!" She giggled, obviously cheered at the thought. "That's so cool! Are you guys doing it? Like, right now, were you in the middle of—"

Dimple felt her cheeks heat. She couldn't even look at Rishi. "*No,* but I really need to go. We need to practice for the talent show, you know?" Speaking of which, Dimple still wasn't sure what Celia was going to do. When they'd talked last night, she said she hadn't decided, and she hadn't really seemed interested in talking to Dimple about it. As far as Dimple knew, she and the Aberzombies weren't even on speaking terms. "But come up at seven. Okay, gotta go. Bye." She hung up, feeling vaguely guilty. Celia was probably just lonely. But Dimple had the awkwardness of Ashish and Rishi to deal with. "Sorry," she said to them again, gesturing at the phone. "My roommate. She just wanted to know what our dinner plans were."

"Cool," Ashish said, barely looking up from his phone. His thumbs were flying over the keyboard.

Rishi glared at him. "You need to go back home. I'll give you a ride."

Ashish paused in his texting madness and looked up, thick eyebrows disappearing into his hairline. "Are you serious? Like, right now?"

Rishi spread out his arms. Dimple had the sneaking suspicion that if he were the violent type, he'd wrap his hands around Ashish's neck instead. "Yeah, I'm serious. Did you not hear me before? Ma and Pappa are worried sick about you. You can't just walk out on them and think I'll cover for you."

"I'm not asking you to cover for me. I was gonna call them later."

"Later? They could've been calling the police for all you know, but you were going to—" Rishi broke off and rubbed his jaw. "I can't even—" He looked at Dimple like, *Can you believe this BS?*

She managed a weak smile.

"Well, I'm not leaving." Ashish tossed his phone down. "And unless you think you can carry me to your car . . ." He shrugged.

Rishi lunged forward, and Ashish held up his arms defensively.

Not this again. Dimple stood. "That's enough!" she said, more sharply than she'd been intending.

CHAPTER 41

Dimple

Both brothers froze and looked at her, surprised.

"Look, I know you guys hate each other right now." Dimple shoved her hands in her back pockets because they were shaking. This was so not her place. But she just couldn't take the bickering anymore. And if she wasn't going to be able to leave, she was going to take control of this weird situation. "But it's obvious to me that we're at an impasse. We're not going to solve anything by, like, fighting and"—she gestured at them—"whatever you guys were about to do." She took a deep breath. "So what I propose is this." Dimple looked at Rishi. "We can go to dinner around seven, which is in ninety minutes. Let's get a practice session in, really hone our moves. Ashish can give us his feedback if he wants. And then, after dinner, you guys can have another, calmer conversation about the plan for Ashish."

"Really? You'd like my advice?" Ashish grinned triumphantly and looked at Rishi, who rolled his eyes and shook his head.

"Whatever," Rishi said. "She's just saying that to be nice. And fine. Since you're being totally juvenile right now, I guess we're going to have to do that." He glared at Ashish, who was still grinning.

"I'm really not just saying that to be nice," Dimple said, relieved that they both seemed on board. "We need a lot of help, in case you hadn't noticed, Rishi. The talent show's not that far away."

Ashish sat on Rishi's bed and spread out his legs. "So how much longer do you guys have left in this program anyway?"

Dimple felt something hot in her throat and blinked fast. "Um, just over three weeks."

She saw Rishi shift in her peripheral vision, but he didn't say anything. Maybe at the end they'd just . . . leave. Go their separate ways. She'd made it pretty clear she didn't want anything too serious, right? So, why would he want to do anything but that? She should be fine with it. It was for the best.

Dimple turned to Ashish, trying to push the swirling thoughts out. "Just tell us what you think. Where can we improve? What looks too awkward?"

He nodded and held up his phone. "I can even video you guys if you want. Seeing yourself can really help. That's what I do for my games."

"Great." Dimple smiled. She wasn't thrilled about the idea of watching herself, but whatever. She needed the prize money. "Let's do this."

Thirty minutes later, when Dimple and Rishi had fallen on the floor in a big pile yet again, Ashish hit a button on his phone to pause the recording. "Can I give you guys some advice?"

"Yes, please," Dimple said from under Rishi. He rolled off her and helped her up. She rubbed her arm—she'd banged it against his chin, which turned out to be surprisingly pointy and weaponlike.

"Okay, look." He turned his phone so they could all three see it and queued the video to the part where Dimple had her three second solo. They all watched her thrust her hips this way and that, her arms waving through the air. Dimple flushed. Ashish paused the video and looked expectantly from Dimple to Rishi and back again.

"What?" Rishi asked, frowning.

"It's pretty clear to me," Ashish said, looking at them like they were idiots, "that *Dimple* is the real talent here? This isn't working because *bhaiyya*—Rishi—has the majority part. We need a song where Dimple gets to do most of the stuff."

"Um, *no*," Dimple countered right as Rishi said, "Oh my gods, you're right."

They looked at each other. Dimple sharpened her look into a glare. "I'm not dancing on that stage by myself."

Rishi put a hand on her arm; it was hot and sweaty. "You don't have to. We'll just get a song where I get a really tiny part instead."

"That's still people looking at me for most of it." Dimple felt the beginning of stress hives breaking out on her face just from the thought of it. "I can't do that. I can't. I can't." She looked helplessly from Rishi to Ashish.

Ashish looked thoughtful for a moment, and then he smiled. "That's okay. I have an idea."

Rishi watched his brother choreograph the new dance, getting 360-degree video shots of Dimple and Rishi dancing. Ashish even kept the video running when they had stopped dancing to talk about the steps, to "capture this crazy experience," as he put it.

When Dimple wasn't sure she could do something, Ashish took on the role of coach, bolstering her confidence by joking with her, without even letting on that that's what he was doing, until Dimple agreed without knowing she'd agreed—and all Rishi could think was, *Wow*. He hadn't seen his little brother this engaged in something that had nothing to do with basketball in years. He'd never seen Ashish so pumped about something that would net him nothing. He was acting . . . selfless.

The thought caught Rishi so off guard that he stumbled, and Dimple, who'd been about to twirl into his arms, went twirling off into the room without him. "Oops, sorry," he said, smiling in what he hoped was a winning way when she stopped and glared at him.

"Ah, maybe it's time to take a break anyway," she said, the annoyance in her eyes dimming. That was something he'd been noticing more—that he was able to soften her, to rub out those hard edges of hers, when he smiled. The thought made him deliriously happy, mostly because he hadn't thought it possible for Dimple's hard edges to be softened at all, let alone that he'd be the one to accomplish it.

Ashish paused the video. "Great. This is good stuff. We can go over it more later, but I think you guys are really close to having a finished dance on your hands. You just need to practice it a couple of times and you'll be set."

Dimple took a deep breath. "Aah, thank you." She reached out and patted Ashish's arm, somewhat stiffly. She was definitely not big on physical affection, so Rishi knew how much she must really mean it. He wondered if he should feel a stab of jealousy—Dimple bonding so well with his muscled, much cooler younger brother—but all he felt was this warm, almost gooey feeling in his chest. Like his heart was wrapped in microwaved Nutella.

Dimple checked her watch. "Okay, it's twenty till, so I'm going to run down to my floor and take a quick shower before dinner. I can meet you both downstairs in the lobby."

"Wait, wait, wait." Rishi reached out and wrapped his arms around her waist. He kissed her soft and slow and then smiled, his forehead against hers. "Okay, now you can go."

Grinning, Dimple floated off.

When she was gone, Rishi turned to Ashish, who was rolling his eyes at their public display. "We still need to talk about Ma and Pappa." Ashish's face closed off, and Rishi hurried to add, "But thanks. For helping us. That's really nice of you."

Ashish shrugged, that old defensive wall coming back up. Rishi tried to ignore the heavy stone of disappointment weighing him down. "Yeah. Dimple's cool, so, you know . . . Hope you guys win the thing."

He sounded like he was talking to an acquaintance, one he didn't even like very much. Rishi swallowed and rubbed the back of his sweaty head. "Yeah, um, I'm gonna take a shower too. We'll go to dinner, and then we can figure out when I'm going to drive you back."

Ashish sprawled on the bed and began to text. He didn't even look up to acknowledge what Rishi had said.

Sighing, Rishi got his shower caddy and towel and walked to the bathroom down the hall.

CHAPTER 42

It was 7:20 and Dimple was alone in the lobby.

Celia hadn't been in their room, and Dimple hadn't gotten a response when she'd texted her. So now she sat listening to the laughter and chatter of the other students, all getting ready for a Saturday night out (or in, in some cases—José and Tim had just had pizza delivered; they said they were gearing up for a marathon weekend coding session). She'd texted Rishi a minute ago, but hadn't heard back yet. So it was probably now or never.

Dimple took a breath and opened the e-mail app on her phone.

She had a draft saved—she'd written it after her shower, but hadn't had the courage to send it yet. The cacophony of voices faded to a dull hum as she began to read what she'd written.

To: leotilden@leotilden.com
From: codergirl99@urmail.com
Subject: We met at SFSU Little Comic Con

Hi Leo,

I'm not sure if you remember me, but we met at SFSU's Little Comic Con event a couple of weeks ago. I was with a boy, Rishi Patel, who was dressed in a costume you commented on—a thick brocade kurta, silk pants, and a hand-painted mace. You asked him if he had any sketches to show you, and he said no. He said he wasn't dressed as anyone special.

But here's the thing—he was lying.

You've been Rishi's idol forever. He's watched every single video you've ever made and pored over every single comic you've ever drawn. I'm a coder; I love everything to do with coding and technology. It's a passion. But for Rishi, art is so beyond that—it's who he is. It's part of him; ink and blood flow together through his body. And that's what scares him. He thinks he loves his art too much. He's afraid of it consuming him.

But I think for him to let it go to waste—to never share it with the world—is what we should all be really afraid of. Because I truly think his art could change the world.

Anyway, hope that's not too melodramatic. At LCC, Rishi was dressed as Aditya, an Indian Sun God superhero he's been working on since he was fifteen. I'm attaching some of his sketches here. I hope you'll see what I see when I look at them.

Rishi's e-mail address is: platpanicfan@urmail.com

Thanks,
Dimple Shah

Dimple had already attached the pictures she'd taken. All that was left was to press send. She took a deep breath. Her finger hovered over the button. Rishi would freak if he knew what she was doing. But he needed help. He needed a tiny nudge over to the other side, to show him what he was missing, what he could have. His parents weren't going to do it; Ashish wouldn't do it. That left her. Dimple wasn't doing Rishi a favor, she was doing the world a favor.

So she pressed the button and listened to the swoosh that meant it was on its way to Leo. Dimple sat back, trembling slightly, half afraid, half ecstatic, the background noises that had been muted fading back in and crashing over her.

There was no going back now. She'd just have to wait and see how this unraveled.

The line in the bathroom was long, everyone getting ready for the weekend, and by the time Rishi was finished with the shower and brushing his teeth, it was seven thirty. "Crap," he said as soon as he walked into his room and saw the clock on his nightstand.

Ashish sprang up from the bed, stared at him for a moment, and then sat back down. "Dude, where have you been?"

"Did you text Dimple? Did my phone buzz?" Rishi speed walked over to where his phone was charging—as much as one could speed walk in a towel, anyway—and checked the phone. Besides one *Coming down soon?* text ten minutes ago, she hadn't said anything else. "Crap, she's probably mad." He texted her quickly: *Sorry, line in bathroom was crazy. Getting dressed now.*

"Why didn't you get my phone and text her?" Rishi opened the closet door for cover, let his towel slip, and climbed into his boxers and jeans.

"Oh yeah, because you'd be totally fine with me pawing through your phone."

"I wouldn't have cared this once. It's a half hour past when we said we'd meet her, Ashish, come on." Feeling that familiar pulsing annoyance behind his eyes, like an ever present headache when Ashish was around, Rishi pulled on a light sweater and stepped out from behind the closet door. "All right, let's go."

They walked downstairs, Ashish weirdly distracted. He kept looking at Rishi, but when Rishi looked at him, he'd look away quickly. "What?" Rishi asked finally, trying not to snap. "Why do you keep doing that?"

Ashish raised his eyebrows, that perpetual defensive set to his jaw slightly deepening. "Doing what? What am I doing wrong now? Breathing too slow? Blinking too fast?"

Rishi sighed. Sometimes it just wasn't even worth it.

They walked out into the lobby, and Rishi's gaze instantly landed on Dimple, like his body immediately sought out where she was.

She had her phone in her hand and was turning it end on end, her expression halfway between dazed and happy. Her smile was adorable, just barely there, like she had a secret that was too good to keep to herself. She looked up then, saw him, and dropped her phone trying to stuff it in her bag. Rishi couldn't help the smile that broke out on his face. He was so, so glad that he flustered her just like she flustered him.

He loped across the lobby, not waiting for Ashish anymore. "Hey," he said when he was close enough, pulling her up gently by the arm. He kissed her nose. "I'm sorry it took me so long."

"Oh, no problem." Dimple smiled and pushed her glasses up on her nose, her eyes darting away like she was shy. Probably Ashish, making her uncomfortable about the PDA. "I got your text. And actually, Celia isn't here either. I couldn't find her. Did she come up to your room?" She looked from him to Ashish, who had finally caught up.

Rishi shook his head. "No, but I was gone so long. . . ." He turned to his brother, keeping one arm around Dimple. "She didn't come by, did she?"

Ashish shrugged, like he couldn't be bothered with such banalities as figuring out where Dimple's roommate was. Rishi wondered if he practiced that maddening insouciance in the mirror or if it came naturally. None of the rest of them—Rishi or Pappa or Ma—could ever manage casual nonchalance bordering on arrogance. "Can we go? I'm starving."

Dimple frowned down at her phone. "Yeah, I guess. I texted her, so hopefully she'll text me later and let me know what's up with her. Wonder if she got back with Evan."

They walked out into the chill, Dimple pulling her hoodie on, and Ashish blowing out a breath. "Man, it's foggy," he said, looking around.

"That's just Karl," Dimple and Rishi said casually at the same time, like wizened San Franciscans. Rishi looked down at her as they burst out laughing. Her eyes shone like wet black jewels; the hoodie almost completely obscured her face. Gods, he wished he could keep her in his pocket.

"Oh . . . kay," Ashish said, rolling his eyes. It was in his tone; Rishi didn't have to look at him to know he was rolling them. "I don't remember it being like this last year." He said it all affronted, as if Rishi had purposely conjured up the fog to ruin his visit.

Funnily enough, Rishi didn't care so much. Ashish's attitude was as annoying as getting your sleeves wet when you washed your hands, but somehow with Dimple there, it didn't really bother him. It didn't feel as abrasive, as unforgivable.

The truth was . . . Dimple made everything seem softer. She was like a tortillon, a blending brush, melting harsh lines into gentler curves. Rishi put his hand around hers as Ashish trailed behind them, already back to texting and pretending they didn't exist. "Your hands are cold. You nervous?" He grinned at her, arching an eyebrow villainously, expecting her to laugh and swat at him or punch him in the ribs.

Instead, she swallowed. Like, literally gulped. And smiled much, much too brightly. "No! What? Why would you say that? Nervous about what?"

CHAPTER 43

Rishi

Rishi frowned. Was it just him or was everyone acting weird tonight? "I was just kidding." He squeezed Dimple's hand gently. "By the way, I know we were going to do the dining hall tonight, but what do you feel about Portuguese instead? I was thinking maybe Rios. It's a bit of a walk, but Ashish is a total *Caldo Verde* fanatic, and they make it well, so . . ."

"That's fine with me," Dimple said. "Celia was supposed to tell me what she wanted, but I guess she's just going to have to deal. If she ever shows up." She sighed.

"She having problems with Aberzombie number two?" Rishi asked, trying to keep the distaste out of his voice.

"I think so," Dimple said, another gusty sigh making her shoulders heave. "I feel so bad for her. They're being totally awful about the talent show too, and she was all messed up about it. She doesn't take crap, you know, but these people totally unnerve her, I can tell." She glanced up at him, the edge of the hoodie in the way, so he could see only half her eye. "I'll shut up; I know you despise them."

"No, I wanted to know. I care about Celia. Maybe Maximo wouldn't mind letting her be on our team."

Dimple gave him a grateful smile. "I thought about that too, but she didn't want me to ask. Oh well, I'm sure it'll work out. Maybe she needed the night off to think or something."

"Maybe," Rishi said thoughtfully. "Hey . . ." He looked behind them to make sure Ashish wasn't within hearing distance. He shouldn't have bothered; the boy was absorbed in his phone again, thumbs and fingers doing a furious dance on the keyboard. It was possible that this wasn't the best time to have this conversation. But the thought had built and built in Rishi's mind until he couldn't contain it anymore.

"Yeah?" Dimple looked up at him, chewing on the inside of her bottom lip. That lip. Rishi was fairly certain he could write an epic poem about it.

"We're leaving in three weeks." The fog sucked the tremor of inflection in his voice, and the sentence came out sounding flat, lifeless. Rishi tried again. "I mean . . . Insomnia Con's going to be over then. It'll be back to real life."

Dimple's voice was tiny when she spoke. She was pointed forward so Rishi couldn't see her face at all. "Yeah. I've been thinking about that too."

"You have?" He couldn't figure out whether she was happy or sad or what. It felt like there was a rock in his stomach, slowly grinding away at his internal organs. "And what have you been thinking, exactly?"

She glanced at him then and quickly looked away. "I don't know," she said quietly.

"Right." The rock was now on his chest. "You don't know. . . ."

"You're going to MIT. I'm going to Stanford. Those are on opposite coasts." Each sentence she spoke was devoid of emotion. She sounded like she was reading an instruction manual. Karl the Fog burned Rishi's nose, and he felt suddenly, irrationally angry at a weather pattern.

"Right." He swallowed, his hand still loosely clasped around hers. He didn't want to be the first to pull away, but was he making things weirder for her? "So you . . . you're saying . . ."

"I'm saying they're on opposite coasts." Dimple looked at him full on, her eyes searching behind her glasses even as she kept walking. "So it'd be stupid, right? To attempt to continue this?" The way she said it, like she wanted him to argue, made his heart lift. The stomach/chest rock shrunk hopefully. She turned back toward the street. "I mean, everyone says long-distance relationships are the worst. Like, it's just an idiotic way to go into your freshman year at college—attached to someone."

"Right, right," Rishi said, as if he were seriously considering her points. "But, I mean, people say all kinds of stupid crap about college. Like, you've heard about the Freshman 15, right?"

She snorted. "Yeah. Dumb."

"Exactly. *Exactly.*" Rishi grinned. "And what about the whole fraternity/sorority thing? People actually think joining one of those is the only way to go through college."

"That's true," Dimple said thoughtfully. "Like paying to make friends really deepens the college experience."

"Right!" Rishi laughed and looked at Dimple until she glanced at him, too. She was smiling. The rock turned into a blob of warm, gooey honey. He tugged gently on her hand. "So . . . ?"

She shrugged. "I guess, um . . . I guess we can try to make it work or something." But she was smiling so big she couldn't finish her sentence as nonchalantly as she'd started it.

Rishi grabbed her by the arm and pulled her to him, lifting her up by the waist while she shrieked indignantly. He set her down again and cupped her cold face in his hands, aware that Ashish was now watching them, most likely with a judgy expression on his face. "So we're doing it? We're making a serious go of this thing?"

"As long as 'this thing' doesn't involve *shaadi* for the next decade," Dimple said, pushing a finger into his chest.

He laughed and kissed her softly, breathing in jasmine and coconut. "Dimple Shah," he said, his mouth still against hers, "if I get to do this with any regularity, I'll gladly put marriage on the back burner for the next *century*."

Dimple

Rios was a cozy restaurant with blue and white ceramic tiles lining the walls, cork floors, and windows that looked out over the city streets. Lamps were lit on all the wooden tables, and Dimple sighed happily in the warmth as she fluffed out her damp hair and sank into the velvet booth. Rishi sat beside her, and Ashish plonked into the seat opposite.

A small, almost hysterical thrill ran through Dimple as she looked at Rishi's and her hands on the table, side by side. They'd agreed to date long-distance. *Long-distance.* She'd come to San Francisco so relieved to get away from it all—Mamma and Ritu auntie's constant prattle about makeup and clothes and the I.I.H.—and now she was leaving with a serious boyfriend. One her *parents* had actually chosen for her. One whom she'd flung a cold beverage at the first time they'd met. It felt like forever ago, but really, it had been less than a month.

Are you sure about this? a tiny, annoying voice asked, slithering around in the back of her head.

Of course I am, she thought, smiling at Rishi in the flickering lamplight. *This is good. This is perfect.*

You just lied to him. That's not what I'd call "perfect," the voice said, with a definite passive-aggressive edge this time.

But she hadn't really lied so much as withheld information. Sending those drawings to Leo Tilden was a *good* thing. Rishi would thank her later, when Leo wrote back to confirm what Dimple already knew—that Rishi was a genius.

Even if we put aside the lie—which I don't think we should—there's still the matter of this relationship, which you never wanted in the first place. Do you honestly think this is ever going to be a casual thing? For you or for Rishi? Are you ready for this? Really *ready?*

Dimple wished the voice would choke on its own spit and die.

"You okay?" Rishi asked, tucking a damp curl behind her ear.

"Yeah, sure," she replied, sitting up straighter and forcing herself to smile. "Why?"

"You just seem a million miles away. You have, since we left the dorm." He frowned, thick eyebrows knitting together, and turned to Ashish. "As have you. What—is it something in the water? Something I'm doing?"

Ashish glanced at his phone and then drummed his fingers on the table. "What?" he asked suddenly, snapping his head up to look at them. He obviously hadn't heard a single word Rishi had said.

CHAPTER 44

Dimple

Now that Rishi mentioned it, Ashish did seem weirdly out of sorts. Dimple might assume it had something to do with the fact that Rishi and he were fighting and he might have to go back home when he clearly didn't want to, but he hadn't really started with the weirdness till they were walking to Rios. She frowned and watched him check his phone again.

Dimple's phone beeped.

Where are you?

"Celia, finally!" she said to Rishi as she typed back:

At Rios. Where have YOU been??

Her phone beeped again.

Long story.

Dimple waited, but there didn't seem to be more forthcoming. Curiouser and curiouser.

Come join us, she typed. *Rishi's brother is here too. Warning: He's very . . . teenagery.*

Be there in 5.

Five minutes? Had Celia been walking around the neighborhood?

Dimple set her phone facedown and turned to Rishi. "She'll be here in a couple of minutes."

"Oh." He took a sip of his water. "Was she already out with the Aberzombies? Everything okay?"

Dimple shrugged. A small part of her was glad to have this mystery to distract her from the tiny, annoying voice. "I have no idea, but I guess we'll find out."

Ashish was watching them intently from across the table, but when she met his eye, he looked away.

The door dinged and Celia walked in, looking harried. Her face was flushed from the damp cold, her hair unkempt. She still looked fabulous as ever, in a long fuchsia trench coat and wedge peep-toe booties. Huge beaded hoop earrings sparkled at her ears. She smiled when she saw Dimple and Rishi and made her way over, unbuttoning the trench coat. She looked so effortlessly "movie star," Dimple wanted to hate her. But she looked so on edge—her eyes darting every which way, landing on Ashish for a brief second, and then on Rishi, and then lifting off—that Dimple couldn't bring herself to. "Hey," she said instead. "There you are!"

Celia hovered by the booth instead of sitting next to Ashish. She walked a step forward and then half turned back toward Dimple. "Um, can you—can you meet me in the bathroom?"

Dimple frowned. "Are you okay?"

"Just . . ." Celia pointed in the general direction of the bathrooms, a pained smile on her face. "Please?"

Dimple nodded and watched her scurry off.

"What the heck was all that about?" Rishi asked, staring after Celia.

"I have no idea. . . ." Dimple slid out of the booth after Rishi. "I'll be right back." She hurried to the right corner of the restaurant and walked into the tiny bathrooms.

Celia stood watching her in the mirror, her caramel-colored hair all shiny in the recessed lighting. Dark shadows pooled under her eyes. She turned around slowly, her hands in a nervous tangle before her.

"What's going on?" Dimple asked, hurrying forward to put her hand on Celia's arm. "Are you okay? Are you hurt? Did Evan do something?"

"AshishandIhookedupdon'thateme." Celia looked at her, eyes huge, expression tense.

Dimple wondered if she was supposed to understand that. Was it French? And then Celia's giant nonsense word began to break apart into smaller, more intelligible ones. *Ashish and I hooked up. Don't hate me.* Dimple's hand fell off Celia's arm. She stared at her friend, who was easily five inches taller in those ridiculous heels. "What?"

"It's true." Celia paced the length of the bathroom like an upset hen, her open trench coat flapping behind her like a large wing. "I'm sorry. It just . . . happened."

"But . . . you don't even know him." Already Dimple knew this wasn't true. How did she know this? Because Celia, a non-Indian, had pronounced his name right. Not *Ash-ish* like it was written, but *Ah-sheesh*. Also, and a bigger point, Dimple was fairly sure she hadn't even told Celia Ashish's name.

Celia stopped her pacing and looked at Dimple. "Except I do. We've met before."

Rishi

"What the heck are you talking about?" Rishi said, staring at his brother. His sixteen-year-old brother, who was apparently getting more action than him, with girls he barely knew. Who even *was* this kid?

Ashish pushed a hand through his floppy hair. When a curl fell into his eye, he didn't push it away. Rishi wanted to slap it off his head. "Dude, you know I've come to the city before for basketball camp. And that girl's, like, a party animal. She was at every party I went to last summer."

Rishi threw his hands up. "So, obviously, when you saw her again, the appropriate first response was to hook up with her. *In the time it took me to take a shower.*"

Ashish looked up at him defensively. "We didn't actually do *it*. There wasn't time for that. We just did other stuff. You were gone almost forty minutes!"

Rishi groaned and put his head in his hands.

Dimple

"How fast did that have to happen?" Dimple asked. She was genuinely curious. How did that even work? "Did you just, like, say hi and then latch on to each other's faces?"

Celia groaned and let her head fall back, curls brushing the back waistband of her skinny jeans. Her trench coat was lying discarded on the counter. "I guess! I mean, we'd had a spark last summer when we met at all those parties, talking and laughing and flirting and texting, but we hadn't acted on it. I had a girlfriend at the time—not serious, but still. So it just felt like we were picking up where we left off. And we knew you guys were expecting us, so that just added, like, an extra thrill. . . ."

Dimple made a face. "Oh God. Really not interested."

There was a silence, and Celia sighed. "I'm sorry. I know it's not cool to hook up with people your friends are related to, even tangentially."

Dimple shook her head. "I mean, I just feel sorry for you." She laughed a little. "Ashish is a little . . . moody."

Celia frowned a bit. "I hadn't noticed that. Besides, don't feel sorry for me. I mean, I'm not planning on doing it again or anything. It's just so awkward. He kept texting me, because after we hooked up for a bit, I freaked and realized what was happening and ran away. I couldn't respond except to tell him I was fine. I've just been walking around since, trying to clear my head. I feel so guilty."

Dimple wondered if she'd missed something. "Guilty about what? I told you, I don't care."

Celia looked at her with an eyebrow raised. "It's not all about you, you know. Remember Evan? The guy I'm dating?"

Dimple felt like she was in the twilight zone. "You feel guilty about letting Evan down. Evan, who was trying to force you to dance in a bikini with his *cousin* as the highlight of your part in the talent show?" *Evan, who's had a thousand hookups with other girls since you guys got together?* she didn't add.

Celia shrugged and fiddled with the thin gold bracelet on her wrist. "It's complicated."

Dimple opened her mouth to say that, yeah, in her opinion misogyny *was* complicated. Mainly because of the way it was integrated into the very fabric of society, which made it hard to see when a guy was being a total d-bag to you. But she closed her mouth again. "Mmm," she said instead, hoping the lilt could be mistaken for sympathy instead of wryness. "So what are you going to do?"

"I don't know," Celia said. "I have a feeling . . . like, even last year, when Ashish and I spent time talking and stuff, I got the feeling that it was more than just a hookup thing for him. Like, maybe he had a crush on me. So it just makes me feel crappier, that I took advantage, you know? He's just a high school kid."

"Well, don't make it sound like you're robbing the cradle or something," Dimple said. "You just graduated high school. You're seventeen, he's sixteen. That's not such a big difference."

"There's still a big difference in where we are in life. I'm getting ready to start SFSU in the fall, and he's going to go off and play on his high school basketball team." She made a face.

Kind of unfair, Dimple thought. If Evan was the yardstick for what made a "man," then she'd rather just meet boys the rest of her life. But she held her tongue. "Then just be honest with Ashish," she said. "I mean, he's a nice guy. He deserves to know he doesn't have a shot with you at all. And then maybe you guys can move past the awkwardness."

CHAPTER 45

Rishi

"Avoid the topic at all costs, Ashish." The boy was lucky he had a *bhaiyya* like Rishi, who was willing to look out for him. "Seriously. If she tries to bring it up, just change the topic. Walk away. I can run interference for you at the table too. It'll blow over."

"Really?" Ashish said a tad dubiously, which was pretty ungrateful, Rishi thought. "Wouldn't it be better just to talk to her? See what she thinks about all of it?"

"Mistake." Rishi shook his head. "Big mistake. Look, Ashish, you may be a player, but it sounds like you really like this girl." His brother blushed—actually *blushed*—so Rishi continued. "And that's where I know what I'm talking about." He gestured to Dimple's empty seat in a *need I say more?* way. "Girls don't want to see a lot of neediness. They want to know you're confident, secure in yourself. Celia will come around when she sees that. All of this awkwardness will be gone." He saw a flash of fuchsia on the other side of the pillar in the center of the restaurant. "Okay, here they come. Remember what I said: Avoid the topic."

Ashish sighed and looked upward, like he was asking the gods for guidance. *He doesn't need them,* Rishi thought. *He has me.*

Rishi got up so Dimple could slide back into her old spot, and Ashish slid over so Celia could sit on the outer edge of the booth. Celia smiled hesitantly at Ashish, and he smiled coolly back. Rishi gave him a mental thumbs-up. He couldn't believe the boy had texted Celia nonstop since she'd left his room. If Rishi had known he was being so uncool, he would've trashed his phone. It just went to show, you could be a player, but really connecting with a woman took smarts. Which, obviously, Rishi had. He squeezed Dimple's hand under the table, and she stuck her tongue out at him and crossed her eyes.

"Um, so, I'm guessing everyone here knows what happened," Celia said, looking from Ashish to Rishi. Rishi nodded. "Okay," she said, turning back to Ashish. "Look, I'm sorry I ignored your texts. I was freaking out. Maybe we could talk about all of this later, after dinner?"

Ashish met Rishi's eye, briefly, and Rishi lifted his eyebrows and surreptitiously shook his head. Ashish cleared his throat. Shredding the paper coaster, he said, "Ah well, maybe there's no need for that."

Rishi bit on the inside of his lip to keep from smiling with pride. His little brother—all elbows and knees and Adam's apple, and still learning so much from his *bhaiyya.* Dimple shifted beside him, and Celia frowned at Ashish. "What? Why not? You texted me that you wanted to talk."

"Well, yeah," Ashish said. "But I was just worried about you. I'm over it now."

Ha! Ha ha ha. Rishi was so proud of Ashish. And, to be honest, of himself.

Dimple

"You're . . . over it?" Celia looked a lot more hurt than someone who didn't really want to be with a "high school boy," Dimple thought. Her cheeks were flushed and her eyes were bright, like she might actually cry or was seriously considering it. She swallowed and looked at Dimple, who gave her a sympathetic nod. What the heck was wrong with Ashish? If he really liked Celia—and she'd read some of the texts; it seemed like he really did—why was he being so aloof? He kept darting these subtle glances at Rishi too. Dimple looked over at Rishi, frowning a little. He was nodding surreptitiously at Ashish, his eyebrows high. What . . .

"You wouldn't have something to do with this, would you?" Dimple said, louder than she'd intended.

Rishi jumped and looked at her, the tips of his ears turning pink. He darted a glance at Ashish and then looked back at her. "Uh, what? With what? What are you talking about?"

Dimple raised an eyebrow and looked at Ashish, who looked back at her with an agonized expression on his face that pretty much yelled *HELP*. "Oh, for . . . Ashish, if you want to talk to Celia, you should. Right now. You should both go somewhere, by yourselves, without any interference"—here she looked sternly at Rishi, who hung his head and muttered something—"and just talk." She felt maternal toward them, she realized, which was a shock. Dimple hadn't felt maternal toward anybody in her life, except maybe Papa.

Gratefully, Celia and Ashish scrambled out of the booth and out the door.

When they were gone, Dimple turned to Rishi and tilted her head. "Really? You gave him dating advice?"

Rishi's mouth fell open. "I resent that!"

She continued staring at him until he conceded with a "Yeah, okay. I really thought it'd work, though."

Dimple laughed and rested her head on his shoulder, reveling in the hard musculature under his skin. "At least your intentions were good."

The waiter came over, and Dimple ordered *Bacalhau à Gomes de Sá,* salted cod with onions and potatoes, while Rishi asked for *Caldo Verde* without the sausage. When the waiter was gone, Rishi wrapped a hand around Dimple's on the table. She heard the smile in his voice even though he kept his face turned away, his gaze locked on their enmeshed hands. "I can't believe we're going to make this work long-distance."

Dimple snorted. "Why? Because I'm such a pain in the butt?"

He looked at her, his eyes shining. "No, because I . . ."

The pause went on.

Oh my God. He . . . what? Was he going to say . . . *that*? Those three little words? "You . . ." Dimple stared at him, urging him with her mind. Poke, poke, poke. Say it, dummy. Because I . . . do too.

I do too, she thought again, her world exploding in color at the sudden realization. *I really, really do.* It took everything Dimple

280

had to not burst into a grin and launch herself into Rishi's arms.

But Rishi cleared his throat, took a sip of water. When he spoke again, he said, "I'm just really happy we're going to make it work."

Dimple smiled halfheartedly, disappointed but eager not to show it. Maybe it was for the best that he hadn't said it. That just complicated things, didn't it? Made them so much more serious? It was crazy enough they were going to do this long-distance after knowing each other six weeks. "Me too. It's going to be hard, though, you know."

He squeezed her hand. "I know. But we can do it. I mean, we started out this whole thing with you determined to hate me."

She laughed. "True. I totally thought you were going to hold me back from winning."

"But now?" He looked at her from under his lashes, smiling crookedly, and her heart skipped several beats.

"Now I know how lucky I am to have you on my team."

His smile turned full force then, like he knew she was talking about more than just the web development aspect of it all. "Your papa is going to be so impressed when you win."

She took a shaky breath. "I hope so. I really want him to be able to use it, you know? I want him to know how much it means to me, all the sacrifices he's made."

"Like what?" Rishi said, and it was clear he wasn't just being polite. He really wanted to know more about her papa.

Dimple leaned back in her booth. With her free hand, she played with her napkin. "He had a tough start to his life, but he never talks about it. Mamma told me that apparently his dad used to drink and go into these rages. His mom, my *daadi*, would purposely anger him so that he'd beat her and spare Papa. When Papa was older, he tried to get her to leave, but she wouldn't. And when he got married and he and my mom decided to come to the States, he tried to get Daadi to go with them, but she refused. He didn't make very much money at first, but he still sent about half of it home to her. I guess he was hoping she'd sock it away and finally find the courage to leave his dad. But Daadi died when I was a baby. No one would tell him for sure how, though. The party line was that she slipped down some stairs." Dimple shook her head. "Papa is this soft, gentle soul, you know? The exact opposite of me and Mamma. I could see how an experience like that could change you, harden you, make you into the monster you hated. But not Papa. If anything, I bet he used it to become a better husband and father."

Rishi raised her hand to his lips. "He sounds incredible."

Dimple smiled at him, reveling in the delicious shiver rolling up her spine at the touch of Rishi's lips. "He is."

"And what about your mamma?"

Dimple shrugged, the shiver winking out instantly. "She's . . . Mamma. She believes my worth is directly tied to my beauty and my ability to land a husband. She doesn't give a crap about my personality or my brains."

"That can't be right. There's no way she sees what I see and thinks that about you."

Dimple smirked. "Maybe you need to have a talk with her. I'm sure I'm in for an earful when I go back home."

"Because we're not getting married, you mean?"

"Yeah." Dimple sighed, her mood darkening at the thought of that conversation.

"I'll bet there's a part of her you haven't seen yet."

Dimple looked up, frowning. "What do you mean?"

Rishi rubbed his thumb over the back of her hand. "I don't know; she's your mom, you know. I feel like if you were really hurting or really needed her, she'd be there for you without question. And maybe there's a part of her she hasn't shared with you yet that's totally not what you expect."

Dimple thought that was likely utter BS, but instead she said, "Yeah, maybe. But tell me about your parents now."

The waiter set down Dimple's steaming, fragrant plate of cod and potatoes, garnished with halved boiled eggs. Rishi's soup looked delicious, too, though Dimple thought she might've preferred it with sausage. Keeping their hands clasped between them in silent agreement, Dimple and Rishi began to eat.

"Hmm, let's see. My dad, Pappa, he had a tough start too. His parents died in an accident when he was six or seven, so he was raised by this series of relatives who treated him badly. He basically put himself through college, and when he saw Ma, he knew he wanted to marry her. He didn't have parents to go ask her parents for her hand in marriage, so he had to do it himself. And he knew it was unlikely that her parents would go for him—poor, with no family to speak of—so he just went in there and told her dad how much he cared for her. He promised to one day make enough money to give her the lifestyle she deserved." Rishi smiled and ate a bite of potato. "Her dad, my *nana*, became Pappa's biggest fan after that speech. He's the one who helped them come to the States. He even gave them seed money to get Pappa's first business started. It went bust, but the relationships he made there led to him coming in on the ground floor of Global Comm."

"A true story of the American dream," Dimple said, smiling and taking a sip of her water.

"And the Indian dream," Rishi said. "Pappa gained a real family, which is what he'd wanted. They stood by him from the beginning. He and Ma have this fairy-tale marriage."

"Is that what you want?" Dimple said softly, her palms going sweaty. "A fairy tale?"

He glanced at her, his ears pink. "I'd originally wanted a practical partnership, but now I think I'm getting the fairy tale anyway."

Dimple felt the heat bloom in her cheeks. When she smiled up from under her eyelashes at Rishi, she found him pink-cheeked and grinning too.

The waiter tried to foist *Toucinho do Céu* and *Mousse de Chocolate* on them, but Dimple declined for the both of them. "I have something for us instead," she said after Rishi had paid the bill. (He'd insisted, even though she'd tried her best to split it evenly.)

They walked out into the fog, Dimple's belly heavy and full of hot food. She zipped up her hoodie just as Rishi buttoned up his coat, both of them retreating a little farther into the warmth of fleece and heavy cotton. Dimple reached into her bag and pulled out a red cardboard box.

"What's that?" Rishi asked, squinting to see in the haze of street-lights the fog had smeared.

"These, my friend, are Pocky sticks." Dimple smiled as she

opened the box and the foil package inside, sliding three of the chocolate-covered sticks onto Rishi's palm. "Delicious, just the right amount of biscuit and chocolate, light as air."

She watched as Rishi bit into one, her gaze automatically riveted on his mouth, her cheeks heating. Blinking, she forced herself to look away. That had been happening more and more now, her noticing the sheer physicality of him, how he was so different from her, how his jaw had that beautiful smattering of stubble on it, how rough his skin was compared to hers. . . .

"Wow, these are good!" Rishi ate the remaining sticks in a couple of bites.

Dimple smiled, swallowing to dispel the warm, liquidy feeling in her bones, and handed him the box. He ate three more before holding it out to her. "Oops, sorry. Want some?"

"No." She waved a hand. There was no way she could eat now, not when her stomach was so flippy and her eyes kept latching on to details like how much bigger Rishi's feet were than hers, or how broad his shoulders were beneath that coat. You'd think she'd never even seen a boy before.

"Hey, you okay?" Rishi asked, dropping the box into a trash can they were passing.

She looked up to see him frowning slightly, watching her face. "Yeah, fine. Why?" She was still having trouble meeting his eye. She felt shy suddenly, like . . . like there was something new between them, something different. Now that they'd agreed to make this work long-term, it felt heavier, more serious. And she was allowing her brain to go places it hadn't quite gone before.

Rishi reached over, grabbed her hand, and pulled her into the darkened alley between a shuttered jewelry shop and clothing store. Dimple leaned back against the wall, and he braced his palms on either side of her. Her heart thundered in the best way, her breath quickening.

"What's wrong?" Rishi asked, searching her face. "Is it . . . because of what we talked about before? Doing this long-distance?"

Dimple started to shake her head and then stopped. "Um, sort of." She was having trouble getting the words out with his woodsy smell swirling all around her, with his heat pressing closer to her than the fog.

"So, what is it?" Rishi reached out and casually tucked a strand of her hair behind her ear, and without meaning to, she sucked in a breath and leaned in to his touch.

His brow cleared, and his eyes turned to honeyed fire as they drifted down to her lips, which, she noted, were now parted. It was like her body was this traitor, acting without her brain's permission. *Especially considering what you were thinking earlier,* that annoying voice tried to interject. *Are you seriously going to let hormones get the best of you when there are important things to consider?*

But when Rishi dipped his head down and pressed his mouth to hers, his rough stubble scratching against her chin in the most delicious way, her brain shut up entirely. His arms wrapped around her waist, cinching her to him, and she put her hands in his hair, feeling the silken strands between her fingers.

When his hands slipped under her hoodie and shirt to rest against her bare back, her blood caught on fire. She did the same to him, reaching up under his coat and his shirt, to feel the muscled firmness of his lower back. Rishi made a sound deep in his throat, and she pushed herself closer to him, feeling the way he definitely, desperately wanted her. . . .

And then he stepped back, panting. "We . . . uh, we shouldn't, can't, do this."

Dimple stopped, blinking, wanting him to come back and pick up where they'd left off. Her knees felt weak, like they might buckle. She wanted to sit. On his lap. Or lie down. With him. "What? You mean here? We can't do it here?"

"Yeah, well, here." Rishi pushed a hand through his hair. "But also, we need to stop and think about what we're doing. Where this is leading. We don't want to go too far, right?"

Dimple stared at him. "Too far. Meaning . . ."

Rishi nodded, his ears and cheeks pink. He was still panting a bit, clearly trying to calm his body down. She wanted to jump on him. "Sex. We need to talk before we go further."

"Right. So . . . I think we should go further."

Rishi laughed and groaned simultaneously, rubbing a hand over his face. "Dimple, believe me, I do too. But this is not a conversation to have when we're both . . ." He made a vague gesture between them. "We need to think this through and talk it through with more rational minds. At least, I'd like to." He raised his eyebrows pleadingly.

Dimple sighed. "If you're doing this because of some old-school concern for my 'honor,' you don't need to."

He came forward and took her hands. "It's not about your honor or mine. It's just something I feel we should think about beforehand. Instead of just doing it, I'd like to have some time to really decide if we want to take that step now."

It made sense, what Rishi was saying. This would be her first time, and, she was pretty sure, his, too. They definitely shouldn't do it up against a grotty wall in an abandoned alley with feral cats watching judgmentally from a trash can. And she still needed to think about that voice, about what it had said. About whether any of those things had merit. If they did, sex would only complicate things further. But still . . . a part of her squirmed, frustrated at being thwarted. Her desire was like its own person, pushy and bossy as heck.

Dimple took a deep breath. "You're right," she said, pushing herself off the wall. "Let's think about it and reconvene at a later date."

Rishi laughed and reached for her, snaking a strong arm around her waist and pulling her snug against him. They walked back out toward the sidewalk together, Dimple feeling confused and frustrated and all manner of things she couldn't even begin to untangle.

On Tuesday evening Ashish set the camera on a little tripod he'd bought and looked through the screen. He'd gotten even more serious now that (a) the performance was only four days away and (b) the conversation with Celia had not gone well that night after Rios. Not that either Celia or Ashish had discussed anything with Dimple (or Rishi). But their refusal to discuss it beyond an *Everything is fine* said volumes.

Dimple and Rishi posed in their final outfits, grinning as the opening strains of "Dance Pe Chance" began to play.

Dimple wasn't even that nervous anymore. Okay, that was a lie. Every time she thought about dancing in front of an audience full of strangers in four short days, she wanted to throw up or die. Or leap from tall buildings. Anything that would require her to not perform. But she kept thinking of the end goal. The prize. The money that would enable her to build a better app, which would be so much better in the long run. It'd make her—them—that much more likely to win Insomnia Con.

"Did you know seventy-eight percent of the winners of the talent show have also gone on to win Insomnia Con?" she said, pausing the laptop to adjust her headband.

"Yes, I did know, my sweet," Rishi said, kissing the side of her head. "You've told me about seventy-eight thousand times."

Ashish snorted from behind the camera, but Dimple silenced him with a glare. "Are you still recording? Shouldn't you pause when we're not dancing? Aren't you running out of space?"

Ashish looked at her quizzically. "You ask a lot of questions when you're nervous."

"What do you mean?"

He smiled and shook his head. "I'm uploading all of these to the cloud, so they're not being stored on my phone. We have a megaton of video, so that was the best option."

"'A megaton' is right." They'd spent a good four hours the night before watching videos from their "training sessions," as Ashish was calling them, or "torture sessions," according to Rishi. He insisted Ashish had gone all Coach Taylor/*Friday Night Lights* on them.

But Dimple liked the amount of effort Ashish put into coaching them. He had a natural eye for choreography, and everything he said sort of clicked for her. She knew they had a much stronger routine now than they'd had at the beginning. It was funny and fun, quirky, and just cool enough to get the votes they needed.

Rishi ran a hand along her cheek. "It's going to be okay. Even if we don't win, we'll have tried our hearts out. That's all we can do."

She put a hand over his. "I know. But I want it so much. We have to win this, you know? Not just this talent show, but Insomnia Con. We *have* to."

He shook his head, a little bewildered. "But why? You're so talented, Dimple. Even if you don't win this one contest, you're going to go on to do amazing things. This app is going to change lives."

"I know. That's why I want it to get the best possible chance it can." She looked deep into his eyes, trying to get him to see what she saw. "This app can help people like Papa—I have no doubt in my mind. That's not me being arrogant; that's just what living with someone with diabetes has taught me. I've seen it encroach on his life. I've seen what it did to him. He tries to hide it, but the anxiety is real. And winning Insomnia Con is going to help me get to Jenny Lindt, the one person I *know* can help me get it out to a wider audience. She's amazing, Rishi. You guys are probably tired of hearing me say it, but she is. I feel like just being in her presence will help me make my app better, let alone if she decides to help us build and market it." Dimple laughed, realizing how intense she'd gotten, like she always did when she talked about coding or Jenny Lindt. She was even clutching Rishi's arm in a death grip. "Sorry," she said, loosening her stiff fingers.

"That's okay, it's my left arm," he deadpanned. "Don't need it anyway." He began to dance around to the steps of "Dance Pe Chance," his left arm stiff against his body. "See? It works either way."

Dimple laughed and threw a pillow at him. "Stop it." She took a breath. "Let's practice."

"Finally," Ashish said from behind the camera, "I thought you two were never going to get serious."

CHAPTER 46

Dimple

About an hour and a half later they'd been through the dance once, watched the video once, and then done the dance again. Dimple stretched out her sore muscles. There was a light coating of sweat all over her. "I'm going take a shower. I think we're well rehearsed, don't you?" she asked Ashish.

"Yes," he said confidently. "You don't want to overdo it. I think now you guys just need to relax."

"Thank gods," Rishi groaned, falling backward on the bed.

Dimple laughed and poked him on the knee with a toe. "Gross. You're all sweaty and now your sheets are going to smell like sweat."

He sat up and grabbed her wrist, pulling her down on top of him. "You know you love it," he said, nuzzling her neck. Goose bumps sprouted all over her body as the conversation they'd had last weekend after Rios floated into memory.

"All right, I'm out," Ashish said, behind them. "You guys need to get a room."

Dimple looked over her shoulder at him, one eyebrow raised. Rishi laughed in her ear, his breath tickling.

"Oh, right," Ashish said, looking around, running a hand through his rumpled hair. "This is your room. Whatever. I'm hungry. I'm going to get lunch at that taco food truck. You guys want anything?"

They shook their heads at him, and he left, shutting the door behind him.

Dimple turned back to Rishi in the silence. She was still lying on top of him, her soft lines molded to his hard ones. She could smell him, warm and soapy, with just a hint of musk. She shifted a little, and he made a noise in the back of his throat. Dimple was acutely aware that she could feel . . . something. Against her thigh. The realization made her joints feel warm and loose, liquid. She leaned up and kissed Rishi, her tongue falling against his with a fervor that surprised her.

After a minute of his hands on her back and bottom, and hers wherever she could find space—on his face, in his hair, on his amazing shoulders—Rishi pulled her back a little. "Wait, wait, wait," he said, breathing hard. His eyes were deep and dark, nearly all pupil.

She put her mouth on his again. "Why?" she said against it.

He turned his head and groaned. "We haven't finished our discussion from Rios. And you're driving me insane. It's going to be hard to stop if we keep going. I mean, it's already hard." Rishi turned to her suddenly, studying her smile. "That's not what I meant."

She laughed and stroked his jaw with a finger, reveling in how his eyelids fluttered close. "We don't need to talk. I've thought about what you said that night."

He looked at her again, serious. "And?"

"And . . . I want you, Rishi. Now." Dimple couldn't believe the words had actually left her mouth. Was this what lust was? Did it turn you into this brazen, dauntless person who asked for what she wanted in spite of usually being racked with social anxiety? Maybe Dimple ought to spend more time in a state of frenzied desire.

Rishi stared at her. "You want . . . so are you saying you want to have sex?"

She put her mouth on his earlobe, feeling it with her lips. "I mean, why not? We're consenting adults. We've thought about it. We have a room to ourselves. We like each other. . . ." Dimple pulled back and looked at him sternly. "Right? You like me? This isn't just an elaborate ploy to get into my pants?"

Rishi looked actually offended. "What? Of course not! You know I would never—"

Dimple laughed. "Relax, I'm just kidding." She put her head on his chest, listening to the *thump-thump* of his heart. It was solid, strong, trustworthy. She traced a finger from the hollow of his throat to his breastbone. "I'm ready if you are."

His hand moved to her hair, gently cupping the back of her head. "What about your parents?"

She made a face that she was sure he would be able to see in her tone. "Um, I'd rather we left them out of this."

He laughed, the sound rumbling in his chest. "No, I mean, won't they be disappointed? My parents would be. They're huge on not having sex until you're married. Once a cousin of mine was visiting with his fiancée, and they asked to sleep in the same room. I thought Pappa would die of an apoplectic fit. He gave them this huge lecture on how they were letting down their parents, him and Ma, and all of the gods and goddesses."

Dimple snorted. "That was probably an interesting conversation to overhear. How old were you?"

"Like eleven or twelve. I was just disappointed I wouldn't get the chance to press my ear up to their wall to hear something good later."

"Ew." Dimple slapped him lightly on the chest, and he laughed. "Well," she said, "Mamma has always talked to me about the evils of boys. I don't think she was ever too worried though. I never had a legion of guys coming around. If anything, I think she's always been worried that I'll end up alone with a herd of cats." She leaned up on one elbow and looked Rishi in the eye. "But it doesn't matter to me anyway. This is between you and me. This is *our* decision. Why should we think about our parents?"

Rishi kissed her forehead. "Because it's what we do."

Dimple opened her mouth to argue, but then closed it because she realized he was right. Whether she liked it or not, she did think of her parents when she wanted to make big decisions. They mattered to her, however much she wished it weren't true.

Rishi pulled back and looked at her. "In this case, in this *very specific* case, though, I agree with you. I think we should make the decision for ourselves."

Dimple grinned and leaned in for a kiss. "Good. Then my decision is that you should take off your shirt."

This moment felt both hard to believe and completely inevitable, if such a thing were possible.

They were each kneeling and facing the other now. Dimple's eyes were wide, her lips slightly parted. "Do you have . . . ?"

Rishi looked at her, waiting. "Have?" And then realization dawned. She meant a condom. Rishi felt his face flush to match hers. "Yeah, I do."

When she nodded, Rishi unbuttoned his shirt, his fingers trembling slightly. It wasn't that he was nervous for Dimple to see him unclothed. It was that this felt like a solid, intractable line they were crossing. There were no take-backs after sex; there was no way to undo how much deeper they were falling into it.

As he let his shirt fall, as he watched Dimple's eyes rove over his chest and stomach, with her small hands following haltingly close after, Rishi wondered if he should be hesitating more. Should there be more doubt? Should he have argued with Dimple more, to see if this was something she really, really wanted, and something she wouldn't regret later?

She looked up at him. "You're unbelievably beautiful," she whispered, her eyes shining like twin stars.

And all his doubts vanished into the ether.

Rishi took off her glasses with a gentleness that made her want to cry; his fingers barely grazed the sides of her face. Folding them, he set them neatly on the nightstand before turning back to her.

Reaching behind her, he gathered her close and unzipped her

kurta top. He paused, hands on her shoulders, and looked at her, a question in his eyes. Dimple nodded, biting her lower lip, her heart thundering so hard she was sure her chest was jumping with each beat.

When her bra lay beside Rishi's bed, her jeans and underwear on top of them, all in a tangled, warm heap, she looked up at his slightly blurry form, trying to read his expression.

It was . . . reverential. There was no other word for it. He was looking at her like she'd stepped out of the pages of his comics, a living, breathing soul mate to Aditya, that wild, curly haired girl come to life.

"Oh . . ." The sound had escaped without Rishi seeming to notice. He leaned down and swept her hair aside with just his fingertips, gently kissing the side of her neck, her shoulder, her collarbone. "*Lajawab*," he murmured against her skin.

Dimple breathed out, her body turning to liquid gold under the slow fire of his lips. She closed her eyes, letting him guide them both downward onto the bed.

CHAPTER 47

Dimple

When Dimple let herself into her dorm room around dinnertime, she was still smiling. Her bones felt warm and flexible; her joints were held together with laughing gas. Everything felt brighter, shinier. And she didn't even care if that was a cliché.

She was humming "Dance Pe Chance" to herself when the lump of covers on Celia's bed moved. Dimple jumped. "I didn't know you were napping in here! Sorry. Was I too loud?"

The face that poked out had a goatee. Dimple shrieked.

"Chill, dude," Evan said, rubbing his face grumpily as he sat up. The covers pooled around his waist; he wasn't wearing a shirt. In spite of his six-pack, Dimple couldn't help but think that she much preferred Rishi's solid body to his. It just felt more . . . honest somehow.

"Where's Celia?" she asked, but the door opened and Celia walked in dressed in a lime green bathrobe that barely covered her butt.

"Um." She looked from Dimple to Evan and back again, her cheeks flushing. Water dripped from her curls to the carpet. "I thought you were going to be with Rishi till late."

"Yeah, I came to get my wallet." Dimple picked it up from her dresser and waved it around like proof. She looked at Evan. "So."

To Evan, Celia said, "You should probably go. I'll talk to you later."

"Aight." Aight? Dimple didn't know anyone in real life who said it like that, unironically. He seemed to be pulling on his boxers under the covers, for which Dimple was grateful. He slid out, pulled on his pants and a shirt, and ran a hand through his hair. The silence was deafening. Dimple stood there, fiddling with the zipper on her wallet. Celia stared blankly at Evan. Finally, he nodded at them and left, without saying a word.

They both exhaled at the same time when the door closed. Dimple looked at Celia, trying to keep her expression as non-judgmental as possible. Celia's mouth was hard, defensive, and her hazel eyes flashed. "What?" she asked.

Dimple held up her hands. "I didn't say anything."

"Yeah, but you're thinking it." Celia walked in and opened her closet door, then let her robe slip off. Dimple looked away. "Just say it."

Dimple sighed and walked over to her bed. She sat, holding her wallet between her knees. "I don't want to say anything judgy, if that's what you're afraid of. I'm just . . . he's made you so unhappy. I don't want you to be hurt."

"I won't be," Celia said, her voice muffled as she pulled some article of clothing over her head. "I'm a big girl; I can handle it." She shut the closet door and leaned against it, dressed in skinny jeans and a dolman sleeved indigo blue top that showed her belly button. "Which brings me to another thing—I decided I'm going to do the dance thing. With Isabelle and the rest of them."

She looked at Dimple from under her eyelashes, like she was waiting for an outburst. Which Dimple was determined not to give her. "Right," she said carefully. "With the . . . with the dancing in bikinis and stuff?"

Celia rolled her eyes and walked to the dresser, where she opened up various pots of makeup and began putting them on. "Yeah. It's really not a big deal, okay?"

Dimple chewed the inside of her lip, wondering if she should just let it go. Probably. But that had never stopped her before. "It seemed like a big deal when he first told you about it that day in class. Remember? You left the lecture hall crying."

"Yeah, but I was just overreacting. Look, you have a conflict of interest in this thing."

Dimple stared at the back of her head, frowning. "What do you mean?"

Celia looked at her in the mirror as she pressed on her eyelashes using what must be a curler, but looked more like a medieval torture device. "You obviously want me to get together with Ashish."

"I don't! I mean, that's not why I . . . I admit I think Ashish and you make a better couple than you and Evan." She tried to say his name without gagging and mostly succeeded. "But that's not why I'm saying this. You genuinely seemed upset—which you had every right to be. This isn't you, Celia. I know you want to fit in with the cool kids like you couldn't in high school and everything—"

Celia turned to her, her face remote and blank. "You've known me a month, Dimple."

Dimple felt something cold close around her heart. She stood up slowly. "No, you're right. I know if I was going to make a mistake,

I'd want my friend looking out for me, but maybe that's just me. And anyway, it's not like you can be friends with someone you've lived with for less than a month, so okay. I get your point."

Celia's face flashed hurt for a second, but she just turned back to her makeup in silence. Dimple walked out without saying bye.

Rishi

At dinner Rishi glanced at Ashish, who made a *who knows?* face and went back to eating his chicken and dumplings. (Their entire family was supposed to be vegetarian for religious reasons, but Ashish—of course—ate meat whenever their parents weren't around.) Rishi tried to catch Dimple's eye, but she kept shoveling in French fry after French fry like she was punishing them with her teeth. For a small second his gaze focused on her mouth, and he remembered . . . things. But then, cheeks flushing, he pushed the thought away. Now was definitely not the time, Patel.

"Everything okay?" he ventured, waiting for an outburst.

Dimple had been waiting for them in the lobby, and when he'd reached for her, she'd patted his back perfunctorily, with way more force than necessary, and then proceeded to fume the entire way to the dining hall.

"Yeah," she said, gnashing her teeth as she chewed on a fry. "Fine. Just great. Fabulous." She sipped from her glass of Coke and glared at the ice cubes when they rattled. Then, looking at Ashish, she said, "You need to forget about Celia. It's never going to happen."

Rishi watched his little brother's face fall and then settle into its usual nonchalant mask, and he felt a tug of sympathy. He turned to Dimple. "Why? What happened?"

She stabbed a fry into the little plastic ketchup pot on her plate. "She's an idiot." Dimple looked back up at Ashish, and her eyes softened. "Sorry, man, but she's just too into Evan for anything to happen between you guys. For no reason I can fathom. I mean, you're clearly the better choice, but try telling her that." She set her fry down and sat back in her chair, sighing. "Love just makes idiots of people."

Rishi grinned. "Yeah, but that's not always a bad thing."

Dimple smiled reluctantly, and his heart soared on gilded wings. He had the power to do that. To make her smile even when she was upset. She felt the same about him as he felt about her. The thought still made him giddy. Then, remembering his little brother's pain, Rishi put a hand on Ashish's shoulder. "Sorry."

Ashish shrugged and took a sip of water. Then he pushed his chair back. "I'm going for a walk. I'll see you back at your room later."

As they watched him walk away, Dimple said softly, "Do you think he's going to be okay?"

"Yeah," Rishi said, watching his brother's retreating form. "He'll be fine. Ashish always lands on his feet."

CHAPTER 48

Dimple

Saturday night came hurtling with the speed of a thousand maglev trains. Dimple did not feel remotely ready.

It was dark backstage, darker than she'd anticipated. Dimple hadn't been in a backstage area since elementary school. It was too big, too serious, too heavy. Everyone was speaking in hushed voices, racing back and forth from the dressing room, even though the audience hadn't even begun to gather yet. Max flitted around, talking to people encouragingly, one hand on the shoulders of those especially nervous.

She swallowed and turned to Rishi in the wings. "I don't think I can do this." She clenched her hand around her tote bag that held her costume and makeup. "Seriously. Maybe we should just back out now."

He smiled and kissed her on the forehead. "No."

She raised an eyebrow. "Did you just say 'no' to me?"

He looked sheepish. "No?"

That made her smile. For a second. "Look, maybe we can tell Max I'm sick. He can't dock points for that, right? It's, like, an act of God or nature or something. Even insurance companies realize those are—"

Rishi put both hands on her shoulders and took a deep breath. She copied him without even thinking about it and felt instantly slightly calmer. "We're going to be fine," he said, his voice low and rumbling and soothing. "I promise." His honey eyes didn't lie.

She nodded, and, hand in hand, they walked to the dressing rooms in the back.

If backstage had been heavy with hushed silence, the dressing rooms were mirthful, dizzying chaos. The smell of hairspray and cologne was like a physical presence, pressing itself between people, wrapping its arms around Dimple. People peered in mirrors that had big, round lightbulbs studded around them, putting off enough heat so that the light hoodie Dimple wore began to feel like a snowsuit. She unzipped it and took it off, looking around at the various stages of costumed finery. "Wow."

"No kidding," Rishi said, looking around. His eyes sparkled in the lights. "It looks like a bunch of theater majors in here."

A boy dressed like a mime—his face white with makeup, lips done in rosy red—turned to them from the next chair. "Hey."

It took Dimple about ten full seconds to realize it was José. She laughed. "Hey! Nice costume."

He grinned, his teeth slightly yellow against the white paint on his face. "Thanks. This is nothing, though. Apparently some of our classmates got the hookup from some theater camp peeps. That's why some of the costumes are so amazing." He waved his hand over at a brown-haired girl, Lyric. She wore a long-sleeved leotard, with a big plume of peacock feathers fanning out from her butt area, studded with glittering blue and green sequins and trailing black-sequined feather boas from her wrists. She looked ethereal.

Dimple looked around. Celia wasn't anywhere; none of the Aberzombies were. She wondered what was going on. Then she was distracted—some of the guys had whole cases of professional-looking makeup and actual rolls of makeup brushes. Dimple had her Covergirl stuff she'd had since ninth grade, when Mamma had forced her to buy some for the Diwali celebration. She looked in alarm at Rishi. "How do they even know how to use this stuff?"

He leaned toward her. "We don't need that," he said confidently. "We have sheer talent. They're obviously overcompensating."

One of the übercostumed guys passing by threw them a dirty look, and Dimple pursed her lips to keep from laughing. "Well, I guess I'd better get started." She sat on the stool nearest her, setting her bag on the table. Rishi took the stool next to hers.

They were already wearing most of their costumes. Luckily, Anushka Sharma and Shah Rukh Khan wore pretty simple outfits in the official "Dance Pe Chance" video—athletic clothes for her, pants and a jacket and shirt for him. It was just another reason Ashish's idea to use the song had been so genius. Now Dimple could focus on not blundering the steps and falling off the stage.

"Celia isn't here," Rishi said simply.

Dimple didn't answer the question he wasn't asking. "Nope." She concentrated on plugging in her hair straightener—which she'd borrowed from a girl down the hall who was going to be wearing a wig tonight anyway—and laid out her makeup. Powder foundation, eyeliner (not *kaajal*; Mamma would be so disappointed), and lip gloss. She tried not to think about what was probably happening out there: The show didn't start for another forty-five minutes, but some of the early birds in the audience would be filtering in. Each segment was supposed to be no longer than five minutes, and Dimple and Rishi didn't come on till the middle, so they probably had close to two hours of waiting left. Urrrrgh.

"I heard the audience is supposed to be a mix of art and theater students attending summer camps," Louis, a quiet, blond boy said. He was sitting on Dimple's right, dressed in a suit with a red handkerchief poking out from his pocket. A black top hat, white gloves, and a bouquet of colorful plastic flowers sat on the counter at his elbow.

"Magic?" Dimple guessed, nodding toward his accoutrements.

He nodded. "I've been doing it since I was seven." He nodded toward his partner, who was sitting beside him, playing on his phone. "Connor's my assistant. I'll saw him in half at the end. I think we have a real shot at winning."

Dimple's spreadsheet said otherwise. Magic was a notoriously poor performer. "Cool."

"What about you guys?" he asked, glancing over at Rishi, who, totally unself-consciously, was practicing a few moves in front of the mirror.

"We're doing a dance to an Indian song," Dimple said, feeling a flurry of nerves in her belly.

Louis's eyes drifted to Rishi's gyrating form. "Oh," he said slowly. "Good luck."

• • •

Max stood between their stools and smiled at them. This was their second visit in ten minutes. Ashish had been in before Max, to assure them that he was armed and ready with the music. He kept saying, "Chill, dudes, you're going to be great." Dimple knew he was trying to be helpful, but at the end she'd wanted to bash him over the head with her stool. She'd been glad when he left. Honestly, with her nerves the way they were, the only person she could stand to be around right then was Rishi.

"You guys ready?" Max asked, looking from Rishi to Dimple. His smile, hidden snugly behind his beard and mustache, faded slightly as he took in her face. Placing a hand on her shoulder, he said, "You're going to be great. You're rehearsed. Just go out there and have fun."

Oh great. She was one of the *hand on the shoulder* people. Dimple nodded, gulped, and smiled.

"Two minutes, okay?" He patted Rishi on the back and turned on his heel to wait for Louis and Connor to finish their magician's act. From the scattered applause, it didn't sound like it was going so well so far.

"Oh God," Dimple said, clutching her stomach. Her newly straightened hair fell into her face. "What if they start booing us? Should we finish? Or should we just bow and walk out? I mean, it's so undignified to keep performing while people boo, right? Or what if they throw stuff? I've heard those theater students can be heartless because their standards are so high. . . ."

"Don't worry," Rishi said, stretching his arms above his head. How the heck did he look so relaxed? *How?* "I'll be your body shield."

She glared at him. "Not funny, Patel."

CHAPTER 49

Rishi

Rishi didn't understand how Dimple could be so nervous. They'd watched the rehearsal videos together. She was amazing, so *apsara*-like, he felt bad for the other performers. They may as well just pack up and go home now.

He ran a finger down her arm and reveled in the way goose bumps sprouted on her skin. She was so incredibly beautiful, even then, with that frenzied, nervous energy emanating from her. Her eyes were wild behind her glasses (she'd refused to consider taking them off for the dance, afraid she'd tumble right off the stage, even though her eyes weren't that bad), and she kept swallowing compulsively. She was probably so full of air she'd lift off the stage like a balloon, Rishi thought with a smile. But he probably shouldn't tell her that.

He wrapped his hand around Dimple's as they walked to the wings. They heard Louis and Connor finishing up, the audience clapping halfheartedly. Max turned and winked before walking out onstage to introduce them.

"There are so many people here," Dimple murmured, peeking through a little opening at the audience.

Rishi took the chance to steal one last look at her. He didn't care about this whole talent show thing very much, not beyond the fact that it mattered to Dimple. He was lucky; his lack of caring made him supremely un-nervous. He watched the tiny pulse fluttering at Dimple's neck, the way her shoulders were bunched up around her ears. She wanted this so much. So, so much.

He leaned in and kissed her temple. *"Tujhme rab dikhta hai,"* he whispered, an over-the-top line from the movie their song came from. It meant *I see God in you*. He watched her smile and roll her eyes. And then he said, "I love you."

She jumped and turned to look at him, eyes wide, just as Max announced their names. Rishi grinned and pulled her onstage.

Dimple

It was dark while they took their positions. Dimple looked at the outline of Rishi next to her. She heard the near absolute silence of people in the audience. A few shifted; someone coughed. She felt herself breathe.

I love you.

He'd really, finally said the words. Rishi loved her. When the lights came on, Dimple was smiling.

The music began and Dimple started to move. She knew Rishi was doing his part, but she wasn't focused on him. She wasn't focused on what the audience was looking at. She just kept moving the way she'd been practicing all week, the way her body knew she should move. And mixed in with the music and the beat, she kept hearing, *I love you. I love you. I love you.*

Then the song was over. She and Rishi came together to bow. And the theater cracked open with applause.

Rishi

They ran offstage together the moment the spotlights went off. Dimple was giggling so hard, Rishi was worried she'd keel over. They were holding hands again, but this time, she was the one pulling them offstage.

"Oh my God," she said. "Oh my God, oh my God, oh my God. We did it."

He smiled and wrapped an arm around her waist. "*You* did it. You were incredible."

She turned to him as they made their way to the dressing room, stopping right beside a couple of people stretching their hamstrings, who paused to give them thumbs-up signs before resuming their stretches. "I love you." Her eyes were emitting so much light they'd gone supernova.

Rishi's heart exploded into a thousand colors. The world was on fire. He put his hands on her face and kissed her like he might never have the chance again. Dimple kissed him back, mouth pressed against his with a fevered hunger. He tasted salt from her sweat. When they broke apart, Rishi grinned. "I knew, though."

She laughed and clutched his arm as they walked back and entered the dressing room. "Do you think we might win? Everyone seemed to love it. I really think we have a chance."

"We totally have a chance. A really good one."

"Great job, guys!" It was Ashish, loping toward them, grinning.

Dimple spun around. "Did you really think so? Was it good?"

"Was it good?" Ashish held out his phone. "Check it out for yourselves, dudes. You guys looked just like Anushka and Shah Rukh out there." He played them a snippet.

Rishi was astounded. He'd known Dimple had looked good, but he'd been distracted by his own steps. Now, seeing it like Ashish had, he was blown away. She looked like a *professional*. Not like someone who'd decided to do this for a talent show, but like someone who did it all the time. Every step was fire; her hips were magic.

"You should be a dancer," he said, and then whistled. "I mean, wow."

She smiled and blushed adorably, swatting at him. "I'm so glad it looked okay. I really want to win that money."

"You will," Ashish said with absolute sincerity, and Rishi's heart surged with love for his little brother.

Dimple

Dimple was giddy with glee. She stood in front of the mirror, wiping her makeup off with remover José had given her. He seemed genuinely excited for Rishi and her, which she thought was sweet. Dimple could see, flush from the endorphins of a great performance,

310

why actors and performers got addicted to this kind of thing. It had always seemed unfathomable to her, choosing a career where all you did was put yourself out in front of hundreds or thousands of people and risked rejection in real time. But if they felt even half of what she was feeling now when it went well . . .

Cackling laughter broke Dimple out of her reverie. She looked in the mirror to see Isabelle and Celia stumble in behind her, arms around each other, laughing and swaying, clearly drunk on something besides life. Celia's face was red and sweaty, her usually buoyant curls stuck to the back of her neck and her forehead. She was wearing a hot pink leotard with a cotton ball tail and a headband with pink, glittery ears. She looked like she'd been dipped in body glitter. Isabelle was dressed in a black bikini that showed 98 percent of her skin, but she kept holding her arms in front of her chest and stomach, like maybe she wasn't the one who'd chosen that particular outfit.

"Oh dear gods," Rishi muttered next to her, his mouth twisting into a mixture of distaste and pity. "Celia's trying to be a sexy bunny."

"I wonder what the guys are dressed like," Dimple said just as Evan and Hari walked in. They were, no surprise, both shirtless. Their six-packs (collective twelve-packs?) had been coated in bronzing oil. Dimple got a whiff from where she stood—it smelled like the word "tropical." They wore surf shorts and their hair was carelessly bedheady.

Evan caught her eye and flashed her a thousand-watt grin. "Nice stretchy pants," he said, half leering. "Too bad you got no booty to fill them out."

Rishi stood up, hands balled at his sides. "What did you say?"

Dimple put a hand on his arm. "Not worth it," she said, looking straight at Evan, who laughed and bumped fists with Hari before they kept moving.

Celia didn't even spare her a glance. Dimple wasn't sure she'd even seen her, but it still stung.

"Man, those singer guys just bombed so hard. I mean, they utterly and totally butchered 'Hotel California,'" Ashish said, walking in with two bottles of water. He stopped when he caught sight of Celia and the Aberzombie group, his smile slowly fading.

Dimple walked up to him and took the bottles of water. She spoke quietly, looking at him, though his eyes never left Celia. "She's just doing this because she wants to finally have that high school experience she never had. It means nothing."

Ashish swallowed, his Adam's apple bobbing slowly. He looked down at her. "That just makes it worse," he said, and walked out just as Evan picked up Celia with one arm and she began squealing.

Dimple walked back to Rishi and handed him one of the bottles. "That sucks," she said, sighing. "I think he really likes her."

Rishi hadn't opened the bottle. He was looking out toward the hallway where Ashish had disappeared. "Yeah," he said, sort of wonderingly. "I think he really does."

"What?" Dimple asked. "Why do you have that look?"

Rishi turned to her after a long pause, as if just realizing she'd asked a question. He shook his head, like he was trying to clear it. "I need to go talk to Ashish for a second."

CHAPTER 50

Rishi

Rishi found Ashish sitting by a huge stack of folding chairs in a dark, dusty corner of the backstage area. He had his hands between his knees, fingers laced together, and was staring out into the middle distance. Rishi cleared his throat softly, and Ashish looked up at him. It struck Rishi how soft and vulnerable and hurt his little brother looked in the instant before his defensiveness came back. *I did that,* Rishi thought, and the idea stung like nettle. *I've made him defensive by constantly judging his choices because they aren't the ones I'd make.*

He pulled out a folding chair from the pile and sat next to Ashish. "You really like her."

"Yep." Ashish shifted. "And I don't need a lecture about how she's not 'suitable' or whatever."

Rishi raised a hand. "I wasn't going to say that."

"Well, that's a change," Ashish mumbled sarcastically.

They were quiet for a moment, watching a small group of guys talk excitedly about their chances. The guys didn't seem to notice them, sitting in the dark about ten feet away. When they disappeared into the dressing room, Rishi turned to Ashish. "I'm sorry."

Ashish's eyebrows shot up. "For?"

"You've been really supportive with this whole talent show thing. You've really helped Dimple—and me—a lot. And I appreciate it. I'm sorry I didn't say anything before."

Ashish nodded and looked away. "Yeah, no problem."

"But also . . ." Rishi looked down at his hands and then up again, waiting till Ashish met his eye. "I'm sorry I haven't always supported you. I've judged you instead of just being there for you. You're different from the rest of us, and I was always trying to get you to change to be more like us. That wasn't fair." Rishi paused and looked out into the dark before continuing. "The truth is . . . I've always been slightly envious of you. You've always been so sure of yourself, of what you want, even if it wasn't anything Ma or Pappa ever encouraged. Even when they—or I—actively discouraged you from doing something you really wanted to do, you did it anyway. I've always envied that courage." He smiled. "I see it in Dimple, too. That's probably why you guys get along so well."

Ashish stared at him and rubbed his jaw. "Wow. I, uh, don't know what to say."

Rishi shrugged. "You don't have to say anything. I just wanted to tell you that. And this girl? Celia? If you really like her, you should fight for her. Because I don't think she and Evan are going to last. I don't think she even really likes him."

"Yeah, but I'm not sure she even likes *me*."

"So what are you going to do?" Rishi asked. "Just sit back and do nothing? That doesn't sound like you." He waited a few seconds and, when Ashish didn't say anything else, stood. "I guess I'll get back to Dimple."

"Rishi?"

He turned.

"Thanks." Ashish smiled a little, and for the first time since he'd come to SFSU, his jaw was relaxed. "For what it's worth, I really like Dimple. I was wrong about her."

Rishi grinned. "I know." And then he walked back to the dressing room.

Dimple

Max looked concerned. Even his beard and mustache were aquiver. "You guys can't perform like this."

Dimple was sipping her water, trying not to look like she was eavesdropping, but it was hard to do when the conversation was taking place literally two feet from where she sat.

"We're fine," Evan said, looking right at him. "There's nothing wrong."

Max leveled a look at Isabelle, who was trying hard not to laugh. She had both hands pressed up to her mouth. Beside her, Celia was grinning loosely, like her jaw muscles had all liquefied. "Really."

"Really." Hari crossed his arms and waited till Max looked at him. "We're cool. I mean, I could get my parents on the phone, but I don't think that's necessary, do you?"

There was a tense moment when Dimple didn't know which way this would go. Who were Hari's parents? It was clear he'd just pulled rank with Max, but Dimple had no idea what it really meant.

Finally, Max let out a slow breath. "Fine," he said, in that über-calm voice older adults used when they were trying not to lose their cool. "I'm going to announce your teams, then."

Evan and Hari fist-bumped, and Evan said, "Bro, that was epic. That wing your parents donated to the computer science department must be something else."

Oh. Max's reaction made more sense now.

Hari shrugged nonchalantly at Evan's comment, but his chest was puffed out, like being rich was something he'd built with his own two manicured hands. The Aberzombies began to make their way out of the dressing room. At the last minute Dimple pulled Celia aside, which wasn't hard to do because she was trailing behind the three of them. Her skin had taken on an unhealthy pale green cast.

"You don't have to do this," Dimple said quickly. She could hear Max introducing them onstage. "You can still back out."

Celia's bloodshot hazel eyes met hers. For a second she looked like she might cry or throw her arms around Dimple's neck or ask to be taken home. But then she wrenched her arm out of Dimple's hand and stalked out behind the others.

Rishi walked in, looking over his shoulder at the group. "They smell like armpits and rubbing alcohol." Then, catching her expression, he said, "You okay?"

Dimple nodded. "I want to go out where we can watch their performance."

"Yeah, sure."

They walked out together to the wings. Ashish was there too. The stage was dark, but the four of them had already gone out to take their places.

The spotlights came on, and the guys in the crowd began cheering Celia and Isabelle, both of whom were at center stage, their arms around each other, gyrating to "Sexy Heat." There were some hoots from the women in the crowd too, especially when Evan and Hari began their bit, slapping the girl's butts and mouthing the lyrics.

"This is awful," Rishi said. Dimple noticed that, like her, he was having trouble looking away from the unfolding train wreck.

She glanced at Ashish, who looked pale. The corners of his mouth were tight, and a muscle jumped in his jaw when Evan pretended to yank on Celia's hair.

"Maybe you shouldn't watch this," Rishi said, looking at his little brother in concern.

"No," Ashish said, taking a deep breath. "I want to see."

Celia and Isabelle were getting closer and closer onstage, and Dimple knew the part where they were supposed to dance close together must be coming up. But when Isabelle put her arms around Celia's neck and pulled her close—to the thunderous applause of most of the guys in the audience—Celia stepped back.

Dimple's heart stuttered. A look of confusion passed over Isabelle's face. She stopped and blinked, as if she were wondering how she'd ended up on that stage. Evan jogged forward and whispered something to her and Celia, his face tight and furious. Hari crossed his arms. The crowd fell silent, watching.

And then—Celia pushed Evan.

He barely moved, but she stumbled with the effort. Ashish moved forward, like he wanted to run onstage. Then Celia was yelling, "Screw you!" and running offstage, right toward them.

The song stopped. After an intense moment of silence, the audience began to boo.

Celia came bursting through the wings just as Dimple moved out of the way. When she saw Dimple, she began to cry harder. Without thinking, Dimple wrapped her arms around Celia and pulled her close. Even though Celia was wearing six inch heels, she managed to fold herself down and put her face in the hollow of Dimple's neck.

Dimple patted her back. "It's okay," she said. "You did the right thing. I'm proud of you."

The Aberzombies burst through then. Hari hollered, "You totally screwed it up, Celia!"

Isabelle said, quietly, "Don't yell at her."

"Back off!" Dimple said, glaring at Hari.

"Or what?" Evan crossed his arms and stepped forward so he loomed over Dimple and Celia. "How about you stay out of this?"

Rishi put himself between Evan and Dimple. "How about you step back?"

Evan glared at Rishi, and then Hari said, "Is there a problem?"

Suddenly, Ashish was by Rishi's side. Dimple pulled Celia farther back, away from the crowd. Isabelle followed them.

Celia said, her voice tiny, "They're not going to fight are they?" just as Evan said, "It's not my fault the bitch couldn't follow through."

And then Ashish punched him.

CHAPTER 51

Dimple

It was chaos for a few minutes as Hari lunged at Rishi, and Evan and Ashish went at it. Dimple looked around, her throat tight, her heart racing. She waved to Max, who was walking toward them, his eyes widening at the sight. He and a couple of the bigger Insomnia Con students pulled the guys apart. "Break it up!" he yelled. "Right now!"

When the four guys separated, Dimple noted with horror that Rishi's nose was bleeding. Celia whimpered when she saw Ashish's lip was cut, the front of his T-shirt splattered with blood.

"I can't believe this," Isabelle said from beside them where she'd been standing. She turned toward Celia, her cheeks red. "You were right to stop. I didn't want to do this either, but they . . ." She swallowed, the blush in her cheeks deepening.

Dimple looked from Isabelle to Celia. It had always been clear that Isabelle wasn't completely on board with Evan and Hari. But this open admission was more than Dimple had expected.

Celia swiped at her eyes and nodded. "It's okay. I almost went along with it too. I guess sometimes it's just hard to find that line and stick to it, even when something feels totally wrong to you."

Isabelle let out a breath. "Yeah. I'm sorry, Celia." Then, turning to Dimple, she said, "I'm sorry . . . for everything." And then she walked off to the dressing room without looking back at any of them.

"Get out of here right now," Max said, glaring around at them. "All of you. Just go."

Rishi and Ashish walked toward Dimple and Celia. "Let's go," Rishi said, his voice low and tight.

And they did.

Rishi

The women set up a makeshift clinic in Dimple and Celia's room, with Rishi sitting on Dimple's bed and Ashish on Celia's. Rishi's nose wasn't bleeding anymore, but Dimple kept insisting he put an ice pack on it. (She'd gotten one for each of them from the first aid kit at the front desk.) Rishi wasn't even sure an ice pack was how you treated a bloody nose, but he was enjoying the attention too much to tell her.

Across the tiny room Ashish grinned at him. Celia was hovering near him, dabbing at his cut lip with a wet washcloth. She'd scrubbed her face free of the thick makeup, changed into shorts and a T-shirt, and pulled her voluminous hair back into a ponytail. She looked much more like herself, and Rishi was glad.

"Totally worth it," Ashish said.

Rishi laughed. "Yep."

Celia groaned. "No, it wasn't." She dabbed at Ashish's lip with an increased vigor, pulling back when Ashish winced. "Sorry. But seriously, you guys could've gotten really hurt."

"Fighting's never the answer; hasn't anyone ever told you dorks that?" Dimple sighed and took a seat next to Rishi. "Even if those jerks totally did deserve it."

Celia bit her lip, balling the washcloth in one fist. "Guys, I'm . . . I'm really sorry. I shouldn't have gone off with them. I'm not even sure what I was trying to prove. They were terrible friends—not really friends at all—and I was just sacrificing everything I was to be a part of their group. I guess I wanted a high school do-over or something." She shook her head and stepped toward Dimple, and, smiling, Dimple stood and wrapped her up in a big hug. "You've been such a good friend to me," Celia said, her voice high and shaky. "And you were right. I was uncomfortable, and I hated that whole thing, so I shouldn't have done it."

"Eh." Dimple pulled back and tugged gently on Celia's ponytail. "I'm proud of you for having the guts to just walk off the stage like that. Right in the middle of the performance." She grinned, a twinkle in her eye. "Plus, you pretty much decimated their chances of winning, so, you know. Thank you."

Celia laughed a watery laugh and pressed a finger to the corner of her eye. "You're welcome." She turned to Ashish next, and they looked at each other silently. There were so many unspoken words in the space between them that Rishi had to look away.

"Want to go for a walk?" Ashish said softly.

"Please," Celia replied, and they walked off together, the door closing behind them.

Dimple sighed into the silence. "They make a cute couple." She wrapped an arm around Rishi's waist and rested her head on his shoulder.

"Not as cute as you and me."

There was a smile in her voice. "Obviously."

Rishi lay down on Dimple's pillow and pulled her against his chest. "Take a nap with me?"

She snuggled in, her hair tickling his nose, flooding him with the scent of coconuts and jasmine. "Okay," she said, yawning. "We've earned it."

Dimple

The jangling of Dimple's phone woke them. Rishi sat up and rubbed his face. "Who is it?"

"I'm not sure." It was a number she didn't recognize. She cleared her throat and slid to answer. "Hello?"

"Dimple, hi. This is Max, your instructor."

"Oh. Hi." She sat up straighter in bed and looked over at Celia and Ashish, who had obviously come back at some point during Rishi's and her nap and were now lying together on Celia's bed. She grasped Rishi's hand, her eyes wide, her heart hammering in her chest. Max wouldn't kick her out, would he? She hadn't even been involved in the fight, not directly. . . .

"I know you left early, and I wanted to tell you in case you haven't heard already—you and Rishi won first place."

The words landed in the shells of her ears, but didn't really hit her brain. "We . . . what now?"

There was a smile in his voice. "You guys won first place. Congratulations. You've got a thousand dollars to put toward the development of your app. It's a step in the right direction."

"Oh my gods." She clapped a hand over her mouth, feeling like the smile was going to explode off her face. Ashish and Celia were making *did you win?* faces across the room, and Rishi was staring at her. "Thank you. Thank you so much."

"You're welcome. And . . . you can tell Rishi he isn't going to be kicked out. I'm willing to look the other way so long as this doesn't happen again."

"Great. That's great." Her ribcage expanded, as if she'd suddenly acquired the ability to hold more air. "Thank you. Again."

"You're welcome again. I expect great things from you guys now."

Dimple laughed, feeling like she might float off the bed. "Got it." She hung up and looked around at her friends. "We did it," she said softly. "We won."

Another three weeks passed way, way quicker than Dimple would've liked. She would've wanted another thousand, give or take, to tinker with the wireframe prototype. Still, she knew it was more polished than she'd hoped it would be at this point, thanks to the talent show money. The designers had taken Rishi's sketches to the next level and made the whole thing come alive.

And now . . . now it was time to let it go. The judges would be in to look at all the prototypes. There was nothing more to do. They were supposed to just go by the lecture hall later for the big announcement.

"Two more hours," Dimple said, leaning back in her chair. They were at You Gelato Be Kidding!, a sketchy little shop that had somehow become their favorite place to get dessert in the intensity of the last three weeks. Dimple had a giant bowl of cherry gelato she had had exactly two bites of so far.

"You really must be feeling sick." Rishi raised an eyebrow. He was tucking into his second bowl of gelato like he hadn't eaten in four days.

Celia giggled. They both looked at her, and she looked up from her phone and blushed when she saw they were watching her.

"Ashish?" Dimple asked, waggling her eyebrows.

"He just said the *funniest* thing about peanut butter gelato. . . ." Celia trailed off when she saw the looks on their faces. "Never mind." She put her phone down and sighed. "I'm so ready for this all to be over. Three more days."

"So they really don't care that you've dropped out?" Rishi asked, licking his spoon.

"No." Celia shrugged. "I guess there really isn't anything they can do about it if I want to waste my money like that. I'm glad they're letting me stay in the dorms till after the Last Hoorah party."

The Last Hoorah party was their chance to celebrate and let off some steam after the intensity of the last six weeks. After that it was good-bye, San Francisco. Dimple wondered if Rishi was dreading it as much as she was. They were pretty much avoiding talking about it.

"Too bad they let Evan join Hari and Isabelle's team though," Celia continued. "I was sort of hoping they'd make him drop too. Instead, they're combining their ideas or something. Whatever. Like they can do that in three weeks."

"Well, I hope it sucks," Dimple said, more loudly than she'd intended. A few people around the small store looked up at her.

Celia smiled gratefully at her. "Me too."

Rishi sat up suddenly. He looked pale and sweaty. "Um . . ."

"Are you okay?" Dimple asked, frowning, reaching over to put a hand on his arm. He pushed the chair back and ran to the bathroom.

Dimple jumped up and followed him. When he came out, he looked like he'd been run over by a trolley. "Are you okay?" she asked, rushing up to him.

He clutched his stomach and groaned. "I don't feel so good."

"Oh no. I wonder if the gelato was bad."

Celia raced up to them. "What's up? Everything okay?"

"Might be food poisoning," Dimple said, her arm around Rishi's waist. "I'm going to take him back to the dorm."

"Okay. I'm going to tell the fourteen-year-old behind the counter she might want to throw out her banana chocolate swirl," Celia said, gesturing at the kid in glitter lip gloss texting behind the counter. "I'll come up and check on you guys later. Just text me if you need anything in the meantime."

Rishi was pretty sure he was going to die. His skin was cold and clammy, his stomach kept heaving even though there was nothing left in there to come up, and he was pretty sure he could see the veil of the afterlife lifting. "I'm . . . so . . . sick . . . ," he whispered.

Dimple rolled her eyes. Actually rolled her eyes. The girl had no sympathy. "You ate too much," she said, mopping his forehead with a wet paper towel she'd gotten from the dorm bathroom. "Should've stopped at one bowl, like normal people."

"Food . . . poisoning . . . ," Rishi managed, though just saying the words made him feel like he was going to throw up again.

"I'm not convinced." Dimple straightened his pillow. "I mean, all I know is you ate like six servings of the stuff. And Celia and I didn't feel sick."

"You guys barely ate anything," Rishi countered. "It wasn't enough to get sick on."

"Exactly." Dimple grinned, victorious. "It's your own fault."

Rishi groaned. "Meanie," he whimpered.

"You're such a baby." But Dimple caressed his cheek with a fingertip, smiling. "What can I do for you, oh ye of voracious appetites?"

Rishi looked at her, an eyebrow raised, smiling in what he hoped was a dashingly lascivious manner.

She swatted his chest lightly. "Not that."

"You said I have a voracious appetite," he said, laughing, and then groaned again when his stomach spasmed.

"Okay, no more laughing," Dimple said. "I mean, I love you and all, but if you barf in here, I am not cleaning it up."

She was smiling, but Rishi could tell by the way her hands were fidgeting with the wet paper towel that she was worked up. "How're you doing?" he asked, lying on his side to see her face more easily.

Dimple sighed and hung her head. "Ugh, not well. I'm so not good at waiting for things."

Rishi wheezed a laugh, careful not to upset his sore stomach. "No way. You strike me as such an easygoing person."

Dimple glared at him. "I *am* easygoing," she snapped in the least easygoing way possible, and then they both laughed. "Okay, so I guess you're right. But this time things feel even more . . . fraught than usual. It's just so important to me, you know? Jenny Lindt. Changing people's lives. All of it."

Rishi sat up, ignoring the lurching of stomach acid and the slow roll of the wave of nausea washing over him, and grabbed her wrists. "You *are* going to do it. Change lives. Jenny Lindt would be lucky to meet you, Dimple. You're amazing."

She laughed and rolled her eyes, and he wished he could make her see it—the way he saw her, the dazzling beauty that was her glittering soul.

Dimple stood. "Okay. I'm going to get some more paper towels and another bottle of water from the good vending machine at the end of the hall." She pointed at him mock sternly. "No throwing up while I'm gone."

Rishi lay back, groaning. "Scout's honor."

CHAPTER 52

Dimple

Dimple was attempting to balance two water bottles and a pile of dripping paper towels when Celia ran up to her and took a few things. "Thanks! I really should've planned that better."

"Ah well," Celia said. "How is he?" They began to walk back down the hallway toward Rishi's room.

"Better, I think. These paper towels seem to help with his nausea."

"Ministering to his fevered brow, how romantic," Celia said, laughing.

"Shut up," Dimple replied. "It's just so he wouldn't puke on me."

"Yeah, right. I expect you to be making soup from scratch next, with organic vegetables you grew in your garden out in the country." Celia flashed a mischievous grin at Dimple. "If you don't watch out, he's going to turn you totally domestic."

Domestic.

The word echoed in Dimple's head. Was Celia right? She *was* turning domestic, wasn't she? She was becoming everything she'd said she didn't want to be. She had a boyfriend—a pretty serious one—going into freshman year. Everything the voice had said that night in Rios? It was all true, wasn't it?

And gods, he was so traditional. So trustworthy and practical and stable. He was a savings account. Dimple was eighteen. She didn't need a savings account. She needed adventure and spontaneity and travel. She needed to make a few bad decisions and have a few boys break her heart. Wasn't that what she was after? Living life on her terms? So how had she gotten mired in the same pit of domesticity as her parents?

Dimple pushed open Rishi's door feeling hot and cold, the paper towels like wet lead in her hands. When she looked at Rishi, her heart didn't bloom like it usually did. Suddenly, she wasn't sure what she felt, what she was supposed to feel. She wasn't sure of anything anymore.

But Rishi didn't seem to notice her inner war. He was sitting up in bed, his phone in his hands. "Just got a text," he said, looking up at her. "The judges are done. They've picked the winner of Insomnia Con."

Celia gasped as Dimple rushed to her phone; she'd left it on Rishi's nightstand. Max's text simply said *Announcement time.*

Everyone sat in their usual places, even though there really wasn't any reason to anymore. (Except for Celia. She was waiting in their room with Ashish, who was finally finished with the campus tour some guy on the basketball team had given him.)

Dimple found a comfort in her old seat, her arm pressed up against Rishi's, everything like it had been for the last six weeks.

For the moment she forgot all the thoughts that had been tumbling through her head back in the dorm. The judges had come to a decision early. What did that mean? Something good? Something terrible? She'd never heard of this happening before.

There was a preternatural hush all around the room. Even the Aberzombies in the back were uncharacteristically quiet. It felt like the walls were holding their breath, like they'd inhaled but hadn't exhaled yet. Dimple felt the pressure on the top of her head and along her spine. Rishi squeezed her hand, his own cool and dry. He looked like he was feeling better, though he still clutched his water bottle in his other hand.

"Where is Max? And the judges?" she mumbled, more to herself than anything, her leg jittering up and down. "Shouldn't they be here by now?"

As if he'd just been waiting for her to ask, Max walked onstage. He'd dressed in a sports jacket for the occasion, his hair somewhat neatly combed. He was followed by a man and a woman who looked to be in their midsixties, fragile and birdlike in their movements. The woman wore huge diamonds at her neck and ears—they blinked and flashed even from this distance—and the man wore boat shoes and cuff links that winked under the recessed lighting. Dimple wondered if they were related or just came from the same factory that manufactured indecently rich people.

Max stepped behind the podium. "Thank you all for coming so quickly. I know this is earlier than we'd said, but the judges both agreed on the winners so quickly. Before we go into it, I'd like to take the time to both introduce and thank them." He half turned and smiled at the couple. The woman was Anita Perkins and the man was Leonard Williams, and they both had fancy pedigrees and degrees and obviously tons of connections everywhere. That was about the gist that Dimple got. She felt her fingers squeezing Rishi's tighter and tighter as Max kept talking, until finally he leaned toward her and whispered, "That's my drawing hand, you know," so she let go and forced herself to take a few deep breaths.

"And now, the moment you've all been waiting for. . . ." Max paused dramatically. "I'm going to let Leonard and Anita do the honors."

There was groaning from around the lecture hall, and Max laughed as he stepped back and Anita took his spot.

"This was a very hard decision to make," she said in a slightly quavering voice. Dimple wondered if she was nervous, and why. It was the students who had the most to lose. Or gain. "As you all know, this year's prize includes a chance to work with Jenny Lindt, one of our talented past winners, which makes it even more excit-ing." It sounded like she was reading from a prefabricated script. A bad one. "This year's prototypes were all top-notch. However, only one winner can emerge, and this year, Leonard and I have had the great honor of bestowing that title upon Hari Mehta, Evan Grant, and Isabelle Ryland for their prototype, Drunk Zombies!"

There was thunderous applause—or Dimple's ears were roaring. Rishi was saying something to her, but she didn't hear. She saw the male Aberzombies lurching down the aisles, ironically zombielike, to collect their trophy. Isabelle glanced at Dimple and Rishi as she walked silently by. Her eyes were dark and hooded, her mouth unsmiling. She shook her head slightly—to apologize? To say she thought this was total BS? Dimple didn't know. She found herself standing, and on legs that felt weirdly like rubber mallets, transporting herself up the other aisle and out the doors.

It was quieter in the hallway. Dimple sank onto a bench a dozen feet away, by the water fountain. "It's over," she made herself say. She forced herself to really hear the words. "You tried, but you didn't win. It's over." But some small part of her insisted on asking *why* she hadn't won. Why did she find herself here now, after all the passion, all the hard work, she'd put in? Was it Rishi? Had he somehow diffused her energy, the energy that was meant to go into this project? Had she had so much passion, so much energy, for him that she'd sidelined the main thing in her life, the one thing she wanted more than anything else? Had she done exactly what she'd been afraid she was going to do and let herself get distracted by a boy? Her chest was tight with remorse; her mouth was full of a chalky, bitter regret. *Domestic,* she heard Celia say. *Domestic.*

Dimple heard the lecture hall doors open and footsteps come toward her. She felt Rishi before she saw him. He sat next to her. "That's total crap," he said, his voice low but furious. "They only won because of who Hari's parents are."

"You don't know that," Dimple said, staring straight ahead. She would not cry. She would *not* cry. She tried to put a lid on her simmering resentment. Sure, it was easy for Rishi to blame Hari. But what about *him*? What about the fact that, right at the beginning, she'd told him that she didn't want him there? Why didn't he even question what part he might've played in it, what part their relationship might've played?

"*Drunk Zombies?* I mean, come on." He pushed an agitated hand through his hair.

Dimple bit her lip and forced herself to say the next part. "Their app's going in front of Jenny Lindt. Maybe she'll love it."

"Unless Jenny Lindt is secretly a frat boy, I seriously doubt it. They're going to flop. This thing isn't going to go any further." Rishi turned to look at Dimple, his hand at her elbow. "Hey, look at me."

She did.

"This doesn't take away from how amazing your idea is. We have to continue to try to get it out there. Okay? We aren't going to stop here."

Dimple wanted to believe him. She wanted to accept what he was offering her—hope. But she knew she couldn't. She blinked and looked away. "Yeah, maybe. I think . . ." Dimple stood. "I'm going back to my room."

"Okay." Rishi stood and began to walk to the exit. "Let's binge-watch something on Netflix. And we're totally skipping that stupid Last Hoorah party tomorrow too, by the way." He stopped and looked back at her when he realized she wasn't walking with him.

"I just . . . I want to be by myself," Dimple said, not quite able to look him in the eye. "Please."

"Oh." The hurt flashed just for the briefest moment across his face but was replaced by understanding and concern. "Sure. Text me later?"

She nodded and walked quickly to the door, her eyes filling fast.

Nothing was going right. The world was falling to pieces.

CHAPTER 53

Dimple

Dimple sat in her room, staring at the wall. It was too much effort to even look outside. Twenty-four hours after she'd heard the news—she'd lost to the *Aberzombies*—everything was still a mess.

What the heck had she been thinking, wasting Mamma and Papa's money, coming out here on basically a whim and a wish to meet Jenny Lindt? She felt utterly stupid, like a dumb kid who thinks she actually has a chance at turning her home into a gingerbread house (something Dimple actually used to aspire to do when she was little; she'd thought it was simply a matter of growing up and gaining the skills).

She gripped her cell phone in her hand; Mamma and Papa had already called three times just today to find out the results. In the third voice mail, Papa had simply said, "It's okay, *beti*. Just phone us." So obviously they'd guessed. The understanding and kindness in Papa's voice was too much. Dimple didn't know if she could talk to him stoically, without bursting into tears. The worst part was that she was letting Papa down. He would've really benefited from this.

Her phone rang again. *Home,* the display said, which meant it was Papa and Mamma's landline.

Dimple took a hitching breath and answered. "Hello?" Ugh. Her voice sounded all watery even to her own ears.

"Dimple?" It was Papa, sounding concerned and fatherly and soft and all the things that made her want to cry even more. Her throat hurt with the effort of holding it in. *"Kaisi ho, beti?"*

"My idea didn't win," she sort of whispered, just wanting to get it out of the way. A tear dribbled down her cheek and she brushed it away with a fist.

"Oh, *beta* . . . these things happen, hmm?"

She shook her head, more tears falling, her face screwed up with the effort of trying not to cry. "I'm sorry, Papa," she said finally, her voice breaking.

"Sorry? *Kis liye?* For what?"

"I let you down. I asked Mamma and you for the money, and then I totally just blew it. I don't even know what I did wrong, so I can't fix it. They didn't give us any feedback, and this was all such a bad idea, all of it. . . ." Dimple dissolved into sobs, her glasses fogging over, snot leaking from her nose.

"Dimple," Papa said, his voice quiet and firm. "This was not a bad idea. It was a great idea. You went there and you did what you are passionate about. Don't be sorry. Be proud, like I am."

Dimple sniffled. "You're . . . proud? You don't think this was all a colossal failure?"

"No, no, no. Absolutely not." She heard the smile in Papa's voice, and it made her smile too. *"Ab tum ghar kab aa rahi ho?"*

"I'll drive home tomorrow morning. I told Mamma." She frowned.

"Where is she, by the way?" She would've expected Mamma to wrench the phone from Papa and deliver unneeded advice. She'd probably have told Dimple to pack it in and get married, to take this as a sign from the gods. The gods. She was starting to sound like Rishi. Dimple closed her eyes at the thought of him, at the thought of the decision she had to make that she didn't want to.

"Oh, she went to Seema and Ritu's house to watch *Mahabharata*. But actually I think she wanted to see Ritu's new curtains. She was telling me Seema hates them, but Ritu forced her to buy them anyway."

Dimple rolled her eyes and tried not to laugh. "Great. Well, I guess I'll be hearing about all that soon enough."

She hung up and sat in the silence again, the temporary lightness she'd felt from the conversation already receding. Papa could say he wasn't disappointed. It didn't matter. Dimple was disappointed with herself. And she was mad.

She set her phone down so she wouldn't be tempted to fling it across the room. The shock of losing to those idiots had tempered her rage yesterday, but it was back now, full force. It was so *unfair*. Hari, Evan, and Isabelle had not deserved to win. Yesterday, Celia had told Dimple her theory: that the founders of Insomnia Con had been in Hari's dad's pocket from the beginning. Apparently Hari knew them all by their first names; they'd all been to his house for dinner just a few months before the contest began.

It made sense. Dimple remembered hearing Evan say at the talent show that Hari's parents had donated the new computer science wing. They hadn't gotten kicked out for fighting. And the most telling of all—they'd won Insomnia Con with their stupid frat boy drinking game idea. Dimple's app would've changed lives. Well, their app might too, she thought wryly. Getting rushed to the hospital in the back of an ambulance for alcohol poisoning was life changing, right?

Her phone beeped with a text, and she peeked at the screen.

Pick you up for brunch in thirty minutes?

Rishi. Dimple hung her head, guilt and resentment jostling for space in her chest.

Something had changed. Ever since Celia had made that comment yesterday . . . but no, it had started before that. Things were fine when she and Rishi were just dating, when there were no boxes around their relationship. But the moment he'd asked for a commitment to try and make this work long-distance . . . something had shifted.

And now she'd lost Insomnia Con. There was no doubt about it—if they hadn't been going out, she would've spent almost all of her free time working on her prototype. Tweaking it. Making it better. And maybe one of those tweaks would've sent her over the edge. Maybe she would've been so good that they couldn't have ignored her, not even for Hari.

She picked up the phone and keyed in, *No, have a headache. Napping instead.*

! But Jenny Lindt will be in at noon. You could talk to her.

Jenny Lindt would be at the Spurlock building speaking with Hari et al. about their stupid winning idea. Dimple had no desire to meet her now, rank with defeat. Seeing the Aberzombies gloat would likely send her sailing off the edge, and she didn't want murder on her conscience.

Nah, think I'll skip. Talk to you later.

She hadn't spoken to Rishi face-to-face since the results yesterday. He'd been good about giving her space, but she knew he was probably starting to wonder. Guilt clutched at her as she thought of his open, honest brown eyes. His sweet, goofy smile. His hands on her waist.

The truth was, maybe they'd come to the end of their path together. Maybe it was time to say good-bye.

Rishi

Rishi watched Celia inhale another doughnut. Ashish reached across her and pulled a cruller onto his plate. How could they eat like that? Rishi's own stomach felt like *khishmish*—a dry, desiccated, shriveled raisin.

They were at the cafeteria, as were pretty much all of the Insomnia Con participants, eating brunch before Hari, Evan, and Isabelle's meeting with Jenny Lindt. Afterward, other people who wanted to speak with her could have a few minutes too. Rishi had been looking forward to it for Dimple, but now he wasn't so sure. He patted a USB stick in his pocket, wondering if what he had planned was a good idea after all.

"Are you sure she's just depressed about losing?" he asked for the eighteenth time.

Celia wiped pink icing off the corner of her mouth with a napkin, and Ashish's eyebrows knit together sympathetically. This was something he could get used to—a brother who actually felt something for him other than dismissive exasperation. Celia put a hand on his. "I really think so," she said. "She's barely said a word to me, and I live with her. She's taking it hard, but she'll bounce back. You know how she is. This isn't going to hold her back."

From the far end of the cafeteria, they heard a whoop and then guffaws of laughter as Hari got on the cafeteria table, stripped off his shirt, and twirled it around. Evan clapped and cheered him on. Isabelle was nowhere to be seen.

"Idiots," Celia muttered. "I can't believe they won."

"Me either." Ashish reached out and squeezed her hand. After a moment, he turned to Rishi. "*Bhaiyya,* I feel like Dimple and I are pretty similar in some ways. So just give her some time. I think she probably needs to lick her wounds for a bit before she gets back up."

Rishi nodded and took a sip of his tea. He could do that. And, in the meantime, he'd move forward with his plan.

CHAPTER 54

Dimple

There was an almighty bang as the door opened. Dimple groaned under the covers. A moment later, she felt the bed shift as someone sat down.

"Dimple?" Celia's voice behind her was soft but firm. "It's time for you to get up now. We're all worried."

She opened her eyes a touch. It was gloomy in the room, either dusk or dawn. "What time is it?" she asked, her voice just a croak.

"Seven p.m. How long have you been napping? You missed lunch."

Dimple turned over. Celia looked down at her, her hazel eyes worried. Her hair was held back by a cloth headband with sequins sewn in. "Couple of hours."

Celia smoothed a curl off Dimple's forehead, her face full of compassion. Dimple swallowed so she wouldn't tear up. Taking a deep breath, Celia sat up straighter. "All right. It's time to get up and get dressed. We're going out."

Dimple frowned. The thought of getting out of her warm, quiet room and into the buzzing, chaotic world sounded about as appealing as going *salwar* shopping with Mamma. "Why? Where?"

Celia cocked her head. "Why? Because you've become incapable of responding to my questions in more than little nubs of sentences. And where? To the Last Hoorah party."

Dimple groaned and burrowed back into the covers. "No."

There was silence for a moment, and she thought Celia was mad. But then her friend spoke in a quieter voice. "Is this about having lost Insomnia Con? Or something else?"

Dimple's heart began to thud. "Like what?" she said after a pause, her eyes wide under the covers in the dark.

"I've noticed you haven't been speaking to Rishi. Or about him. He's noticed too, you know." She said it without judgment, but Dimple's chest constricted with that familiar guilt.

"Has he . . . what has he said?"

"He just wants to know what's going on. He's such a good guy, Dimple. He really cares about you. No, scratch that. He really loves you."

Dimple took the covers off her face and looked at Celia. "I know he does." And it was true; she did. The thing was just . . . she'd met him too early in her life. That was the cruelest of things. It wasn't that Rishi was wrong for her. It was that he was too right.

Celia looked at her for a long moment and then nodded. "If you're going to break his heart, do it now. Don't stretch it out. It's not fair to him."

Dimple sighed. "I don't know what I'm going to do yet." Although that wasn't quite true. She was pretty sure. She just didn't have the courage and energy to admit it to herself yet.

Celia stood. "Well, I do," she said. "You're coming to the party with us." She shrugged when Dimple made a face. "You may as well face him. Maybe it'll help you make up your mind, move on from this weird limbo you're in."

Rishi

Rishi hung up the phone and paced the floor, his heart jittering in his chest. He ran a hand through his hair and grinned. "Oh my gods."

Ashish looked up from where he was reading one of Rishi's old issues of *Platinum Panic*. "What?"

"Do you know who that was?" Rishi felt like his face was going to split in two, he was grinning so hard.

Ashish put the comic down and sat up slowly. "No . . . who?"

Dimple

Dimple walked into the main lobby of the Spurlock building with Celia. It had been decorated for the Last Hoorah with balloons and confetti, and a local restaurant was even catering a big buffet. People were already lining up for the free food, piling their plates high. No one seemed especially sad to have lost, except maybe José Alvarez. He sat with his partner, Tim Wheaton, both of their shoulders hunched, their faces slack and lifeless. Dimple felt a twinge of sympathy. If the pain weren't so raw, she'd go over there to commiserate.

She scanned the room, her stomach lurching. Where was Rishi? He'd texted her to meet up with him here, which actually worked out well. It would be like a Band-Aid, she thought. Just rip it off.

"Where is he?" she asked Celia, tapping her sweaty hand against her thigh. She hadn't explicitly told Celia what she was going to do, but she thought maybe her friend had guessed. How could she not? Dimple shut down every time Celia said Rishi's name. It was easier that way, less painful.

Then she saw them, Ashish and Rishi, pushing through the clusters of students. There was a barely suppressed, excited energy about them as they walked, both of them bounding on the balls of their feet. Ashish's eyes were on Celia, though they kept darting to Dimple. Rishi looked straight at her.

Her stomach lurched again. Dimple felt another major prickle of misgivings. Was she really going to do this? When just looking at him made her feel like this? This rush of love and companionship and friendship and happiness? Was she just going to extinguish it all because of timing?

But she knew the answer. Yes, she would. Yes, because this was not the plan. Yes, because the last thing she wanted was to break it off five years down the road, when the two of them would be in so much deeper, it'd be like cutting off a limb. It would be painful now, but nothing compared to what it could be like. So the answer was yes.

Ashish pulled Celia close and kissed her, and Rishi stood in front of Dimple. Somehow, he instinctively knew not to pull her into his arms. Had he guessed? She took a deep breath, and said, "I have to talk to you" at the same time that he said, "Come with me."

They both paused, and then Dimple said, "Where?"

Rishi's eyes were shining as he reached out and took her hand.

343

"You'll see, my friend," he said as he began to tug her toward the hallway that contained their lecture hall.

Rishi

Rishi could barely keep himself from sprinting through the crowd of Insomnia Con students to the hallway and the lecture hall. He knew now why people said love gave you wings. All he could think was how Dimple was going to feel in a few minutes.

She was so beautiful and so brave. Just coming here, to the Last Hoorah party, was an act of courage. He knew how much this had meant to her, how crushed she was, though she was trying not to show it. It was there, in the lines around her mouth, in the furrow in her brow. Even her usually buoyant curls looked a little wilted.

He put his hand on the handle of the door to the lecture hall and turned around to glance at her. She looked thoroughly confused. His heart lifted and he grinned. Ha! Ha ha ha. This was going to be epic. "Ready?"

Dimple nodded, and Rishi pushed the door open.

Dimple

Dimple walked in, wondering what the heck Rishi Patel was up to now. If this was some kind of pity party he'd arranged for her, she

344

really wasn't in the mood. And anyway, she really wanted to just get it over with, tell him what she'd decided, and go home. But the way he'd basically just run here . . . she'd let her curiosity get the best of her.

She walked into the quiet, empty lecture hall and looked around. "What? Why are we—"

And then Dimple saw her, up at the head of the room. Sitting there in the front row, like a student, turned around and smiling slightly.

Jenny Lindt.

Dimple's mouth legit hung open. Her knees felt weak, like they might buckle at any moment.

Jenny Lindt raised a hand. "Hi, Dimple."

Dimple nearly fell over. She would've, if Rishi hadn't grabbed her elbow and very firmly steered her forward.

"Go," he said softly in her ear. "You deserve it." And then he slipped out, leaving her with her idol.

Dimple walked forward on wooden legs. It was her. It was really her, with her teal mermaid hair in an angled bob, her quirky retro clothes (right then she was wearing a blue polka-dotted circle skirt, a shirt with a Peter Pan collar, and jeweled cat's-eye glasses), and her incisive gaze. Her brown eyes looked like they could cut right through you. "Hi," she said again when Dimple was within talking distance. "Have a seat." She gestured to the chair next to hers, and Dimple sat, aware that her every muscle seemed to be vibrating.

"This is . . ." Her voice came out a husky whisper, and she cleared her throat and tried again. "Um, I don't even know why . . . or how . . ." Dimple made a vague circling gesture with her hands, like that would make what she was trying to say clearer. Gods, why had she saved her inarticulate seal act for now, when she was face-to-face with Jenny freaking Lindt? Idiot.

But Jenny's smile just got wider, like she was used to this reaction. She probably was, come to think of it. "Your friend." She gestured at the door to the back of the hall. "Boyfriend? Anyway, he came to see me when I was here earlier, meeting with the winners of Insomnia Con."

The words were like an ice water bath. *The winners of Insomnia Con.* That should've been her. Then what Jenny Lindt had just said came seeping in. "Wait. Rishi came to see you?"

"Yeah, waited in line about an hour so he could catch me after everyone else had melted away." Jenny raised her eyebrows. "That's some serious dedication."

"But . . . why? What did he say?"

Jenny reached into her pocket and held up a little USB stick. "He showed me all the work you put into the talent show. There was even a part where you were talking about how important your app was to you, and why you wanted me to see it. He attached your wireframe prototype, too." She shook her head. "It's a solid idea. You're very good."

Dimple's breath caught in her throat. She'd waited years, *years*, to hear that. All those times she'd considered giving up but hadn't because maybe one day Jenny Lindt might tell her she had what it took—that day was here. Dimple blinked, hard, and tried to ignore the goose bumps that ravaged her arms and legs. "I, um, wow. I can't believe this is happening."

Jenny laughed, a throaty, sophisticated sound. "Well, you should. You're the real thing. Not like those idiots I met with before. Drunk Zombies." She snorted. "What a joke."

Dimple felt a gleeful grin spread across her face. "But they won Insomnia Con."

Jenny's chair let out a plaintive squeak as she leaned back, steepling her fingers in front of her, serious now. "Yeah," she said, looking right at Dimple. "And I'm going to have a talk with the organizers about conflicts of interest. If your parents donated the new computer science wing?" She shook her head. "You shouldn't even be allowed to participate." She fixed Dimple with a serious look. "I wish I could say stuff like that's a one-off, but it's not. You're going to see a lot of it. People getting ahead unfairly because of the category into which they were born: male or white or straight or rich. I'm in a few of those categories myself, which is why I make it a point to reach out and help those who aren't, those who might not necessarily be seen if I didn't make the effort. We need to shake this field up, you know? We need more people with different points of view and experiences and thought processes so we can keep innovating and moving ahead." Jenny Lindt smiled a little. "Which is why I want to talk to you about partnering together to get your app market ready. What do you say?"

Dimple was fairly sure she was going to burst into tears. She counted to three, took a breath, and said, "Yes, please."

CHAPTER 55

Rishi

Rishi paced outside, feeling like someone waiting on life changing news from the doctor. Dimple had looked so utterly discombobulated, he hoped he'd done the right thing by surprising her. He'd figured with how depressed she was, she might argue against meeting with Jenny Lindt—that she wasn't ready, or didn't feel up to it. He'd wanted her to just do it, to see how impressed Jenny had been by her. The woman had called Rishi personally to say she'd been totally bowled over by both the video and the code.

Rishi felt a glow of pride at the memory. He'd spent almost the entirety of last night glued to his computer, editing the videos Ashish had taken of them practicing, and then splicing them together to create a five-minute montage to share with Jenny Lindt. The idea had come to him after Dimple had gone to her room. *If only Jenny could see how much time and effort she's put into this, how good she really is*, he'd thought. And then Rishi had realized he could make that happen for her. Ashish had helped him for the first hour or so, and then he'd gone to bed. But before he had, he'd looked at Rishi and said, "Man, *bhaiyya*. You've got it bad, huh?"

Rishi took a deep, shuddering breath. Yes, he did.

He'd paced to the opposite end of the long hallway when the door to the lecture hall opened with a great bang. He spun around and found Dimple striding toward him, practically running, her hair streaming behind her. He walked forward to meet her, and she slammed into him, wrapping her arms around his neck.

He held her tight, feeling her heart pound against his chest, hearing her breathing rapidly, furiously. He was beginning to worry that the meeting had gone really, really badly when she pulled back, her eyes wet, a small smile playing at her lips. "Thank you," she whispered.

All the breath exited his lungs in a great whoosh. He grinned. "So it went well?"

Dimple stepped back, out of his arms, and folded her arms against herself, unsmiling now. Rishi frowned a little. Something was off. She should be cheering, running madly around, but she wasn't. His smile faded.

"Let's talk outside," she said, gesturing to the side door behind him, beyond which lay the darkness of night.

They stepped outside just as a silver Porsche went flying by, honking its horn. Dimple raised a hand, and he saw genuine joy in her eyes, and pride. So the meeting *had* gone well. Rishi held his questions as they walked a few yards to a small patio area swathed in mist and sat on one of the damp benches. Light from the interior of the building lit the ground and table in fat yellow stripes. He looked at Dimple, across from him, and waited.

She pulled her hoodie sleeves over the tips of her fingers, still not meeting his eye. Something began to squirm in the pit of his stomach. The Pocky sticks he'd inhaled earlier in his room threatened to make a comeback. Something was wrong. Very wrong. He reached for her hand across the table, and she jerked back. His heart froze, encased in a block of ice.

Dimple looked up at him then. "Thank you," she said quietly. "That was . . . an incredible gift. Making the video, contacting her, all of it."

Rishi nodded, though everything seemed to be happening from a great distance, like he was viewing his own life through a telescope. "You deserve it."

"She wants to partner with me to finish and market the app, so . . ." She smiled and bit her lip, as if to contain it.

He grinned. "That's great. I knew it. How could she have any other reaction?"

"I have a confession," Dimple said in a rush.

Rishi's heart thundered. "What sort of confession?"

"I . . ." She pulled the hood of her hoodie up, as if to ward off the fog. "I did something similar for you. Or, I tried to."

He frowned, not understanding.

Dimple scratched at the paint on the wood table with a fingernail, sending green flecks flying. "I sent your sketches to Leo Tilden."

Rishi stared at her, not fully able to grasp her meaning. "Sent him my sketches?" He shook his head, like that would make this congeal a bit more. "How? When?"

"The day Ashish came. You stepped out of your room to talk to him, and I took pictures of your sketch pad. And then I e-mailed him." She met his eye, looking equal parts defensive and nervous.

disappointed and defiant. "He . . . he hasn't e-mailed you yet, I'm guessing. But he will. I know he will."

Rishi shook his head, trying to dislodge his feelings. Anger at her. Disappointment at the silence from Leo Tilden. Embarrassment. Betrayal. He set his elbows on the table and put his head in his hands. "Why . . . how could you do that?" he said softly, afraid that if he raised his voice, he'd never stop shouting. "After I *told* you. After I explained why I couldn't do this."

"Because!" Dimple said, and her voice did echo around them before getting swallowed by the unforgiving fog. "Because you're being . . ."

Rishi looked up sharply. "Being what?"

"Cowardly," she finished, her chin thrust out. "You're being cowardly. You have a real *gift*, Rishi. You can't let your parents or anyone else dictate what you do with it."

Rishi swallowed, willing his heart to stop pounding, his blood to stop boiling. "Cowardly. Right." He jumped up and began to pace, running a shaking hand through his hair. He didn't know if he was more hurt or more angry. "And I guess talking to you about obligations and duties would do no good. Just as it did no good the first few times." He stopped pacing and glared at her. "Speaking of cowardly . . . you sneaked into my bag and pulled out my sketch pad. You e-mailed Leo without my permission! How's that for cowardly?"

"I was doing you a favor!" she said, her hands forming fists on the table.

"A favor!" he thundered, throwing his hands up. "Do you know how condescending you sound right now? So you were just doing the cowardly idiot who doesn't know what's good for him a favor, right?"

"That's not what I said!" Dimple glared at him, eyes sparking behind her glasses. "How is what you did for me with Jenny Lindt any different?"

"Because you've been telling me for six weeks now how much she means to you and how much you want to meet her! Because you came out to Insomnia Con specifically to have her see your work! That's the difference—you wanted this and I didn't! I specifically told you I didn't!"

"And I specifically told you I didn't want a relationship! I don't want this!" Dimple yelled, her voice crashing into him, reaching into his chest, and pulverizing his heart.

Dimple

She sat there, panting, unable to believe she'd just yelled it out at him like that. "I'm sorry," she said immediately, her voice shaking. "I'm sorry. But I . . . this isn't working for me anymore."

Rishi stared at her like she'd just told him a giant meteor was headed for the Earth and there was nothing to be done about it. He walked forward on shaky legs and fell onto the bench. He stared down at his hands and then looked up at her. "How long have you known you wanted to break up?" The fog curled around his words.

"I didn't know," Dimple said. "I mean, I was having all these doubts weeks ago . . . but . . ." She took a deep breath. "I wasn't really sure till a couple of days ago. When they announced the winners."

Rishi was quiet for a long time. Then he said, "Why?"

She thought about telling him the truth for a split second: How he was too right for her, how she was afraid they'd just met too early, how she was terrified she was giving up an essential part of herself or forgetting the reasons she hadn't wanted a relationship in the first place. But Dimple knew he'd talk her down, that he'd have a good counterargument for every one of hers. She'd end up wanting to be with Rishi again, and she didn't want that. A clean break, that's what she was after. "We're too different," she said finally, choosing a half-truth. "I can't . . . I can't be with someone who cares so much about what his parents want from him. You lack courage, Rishi. And I can't be with someone like that." She was being so cruel. But she couldn't pull any punches. "I want so much more from my life than what you seem to want."

He looked at her, his eyes hollow, empty, like she'd never seen them before. Her heart hurt, physically, truly hurt, but she forced herself to keep her expression firm, unmoving, as he spoke. "I've changed so much for you. I know it doesn't seem like it, but I have. I just wanted to be with you, Dimple. I was even willing to put aside my parents' wishes. I was willing to follow you around the world, wherever you wanted to go, wherever your career took you. But you're right, I don't have the courage you seem to have to buck every tradition and just do what I want. I actually care what my parents think of me, I care about what they want."

Anger began to simmer in Dimple's veins, even though she knew she'd provoked him. "Are you calling me selfish?"

Rishi stood, his fingertips pressed against the table. "I'm calling you unkind. You're right; we are too different." He turned and walked away, the fog swallowing him whole.

CHAPTER 56

Dimple

"But can't you wait till tomorrow morning?" Celia asked. She was sprawled on her bed, her legs in Ashish's lap. They were both exchanging worried glances that Dimple pretended not to see.

She threw her clothes in her suitcase without bothering to fold them. She'd spent the first hour after she and Rishi broke up crying alone on the bench, wrapped in the fog. But then she'd wiped her eyes, marched to her dorm room, and taken a long shower, scrubbing her hair until her scalp was raw. That's when she'd decided she wasn't going to wait till the next morning to leave. What would be the point?

Celia and Ashish had just walked in ten minutes ago. Dimple got the feeling Rishi had told them what happened from the very obvious way they were *not* asking about him. "No. I need to get out of here now."

Ashish cleared his throat. "But what about Jenny Lindt? The meeting went well, right?"

So they had talked to Rishi. Dimple paused for a moment as the pain washed over her, but then she continued as if nothing had happened. "Our work is mainly going to be over the computer. I'll be at

Stanford in a few weeks anyway, and it isn't too far from here. I can always make the drive." She snapped her suitcase shut and turned around.

Celia hopped off the bed. "I'm going to miss you," she said.

"Me too." Dimple stepped forward, and they hugged. "But we'll keep texting. And we'll be driving distance apart starting in the fall."

Celia nodded furiously, and when she stepped back, her eyes were all misty. "I feel like no matter what roommate I get now, I'm going to be disappointed," she said. "Because it won't be you."

Dimple swallowed the lump in her throat. "Ditto. You know, you could change your mind and decide to transfer to Stanford. . . ."

Celia rolled her eyes. "Yeah, right. Like they'll ever let me in that place."

Dimple laughed and turned to Ashish, who was standing by Celia now. He smiled down at her, but it was coated in sadness and it made her chest tighten. His eyes reminded her so much of Rishi's, she had to blink and look away. "It was nice to meet you, Ashish," she said, rubbing at her nose. "Thank you for your help with the talent show."

She held out her hand, but Ashish ignored it and pulled her into a hug instead. "You would've made a great *bhabhi* someday," he said, and that, more than anything, drove it all home with an ironclad finality. She and Rishi were over.

Dimple swallowed and stepped back, smiling brightly. "Okay, I'm out. You guys are leaving tomorrow, right?"

They nodded. "Want me to help you with your suitcase?" Ashish asked, but Dimple shook her head.

Celia reached out and grabbed her in a hug again and then

stepped back and put an arm around Ashish's waist, swiping at her eyes with her free hand.

Dimple took a deep breath and squared her shoulders, determined not to shed another tear on this campus.

Rishi

Rishi sat on the edge of his bed, his head bent as the phone at his parents' house rang. It seemed a lonelier sound than usual, as if it were echoing around an empty home.

He felt like he'd been struck by a freak flare of lightning on a sunny, blue-skied day. He had not seen that coming. He'd thought maybe she was unhappy, but that it had to do with losing, with not being able to see Jenny Lindt. Rishi had no idea she . . . that Dimple . . . that she didn't love him anymore. Had likely never loved him.

All those things she'd said—was that how she saw him? As some big coward, too afraid to stand up to his parents, too afraid to really live life? Someone who wanted to cower and be sheltered from every storm in life, someone who wanted an easy, placid, dull, nothing existence?

Was she right?

"Haan, bolo, Rishi beta!" Pappa's happy greeting came down the line, startling him out of his cold, tumbling thoughts.

"Pappa . . ." His voice came out husky, unpolished. He cleared his throat. The words were gone.

"Rishi?" Pappa sounded a little concerned. *"Kya baat hai, beta?"*

"Am I making a mistake, Pappa?" he said, his voice just barely above a whisper. He rubbed the back of his neck, feeling a sudden surge of frustration he couldn't explain. Rishi hopped off his bed and began to pace. In a louder voice, he continued. "I mean, MIT? Engineering? You're the one with a mathematical brain, not me. I couldn't even fix the laptop when it broke last year, remember?"

There was a moment of silence, and he knew Pappa was hurrying to catch up. "But, Rishi, there are many different types of engineering degrees," he said finally, a little wondrously. "*Tumhe patta hai*, you don't have to fix computers to be an engineer. You know this."

Rishi kicked at the foot of his desk, making the whole thing shudder. "But it's not about fixing the laptop!" He threw his free hand up in the air. Why couldn't his father see? "It's . . . it's everything. It's my brain, Pappa. It doesn't work like yours. I'm not interested in mathematics and business and, and everything else that you do. Do I want to spend fifty or sixty years of my life stuck at Global Comm, doing stuff that bores me now, at eighteen? I mean, what will my life look like at that point? Who will I even become if I do that?"

"But there are many good companies besides Global Comm, Rishi," Pappa said, still sounding bewildered. "You don't have to work here. You can go to Google—they're progressive, *na?* Many young people enjoy working—"

Oh gods. He just wasn't getting it. "No, Pappa," Rishi cut in, standing still in the center of his room, looking at the bed where not too long ago he and Dimple took things to another level. Where he realized he couldn't live without her, no matter what. The bitter burn of rejection flared in his chest. "What if I want to do my comics instead?"

There was a long beat of silence. Rishi waited, his heart hammering. "C-comics?" He'd never heard Pappa stutter like that before. "Rishi, why are you saying all this, *beta*? Where did you get these ideas? Plan *sub change kar rahe ho*—you're changing all your plans. For whom? *Dimple ne kuch kahaa?*"

Did Dimple say something? Rishi wanted to laugh. *Yeah,* he thought. *She said a lot of things.* But instead of getting into that, he said, "Yes. She said something. But I was feeling it before that, Pappa. I was . . . engineering doesn't feel right for me. It feels right for you. I'm an artist in my soul. Not an engineer. Not a corporate machine."

Pappa exhaled, the sound long and reaching for a patience it currently lacked. When he spoke, his voice was low and controlled. It was the voice Rishi had heard him use in phone meetings when he was trying not to lose his temper. "*Ghar aao,* Rishi. Then we'll talk about it. *Aur Dimple . . .*"

"There's no Dimple," Rishi said softly. Pappa and Ma didn't know the extent to which they'd moved their friendship forward, and now Rishi was glad he hadn't told them. "And yes, I'm coming home."

He hung up and stood in silence for a full minute. Then, grabbing his bag, he thought, *Semper sursum. Always upward.*

Was it possible to expire of boredom? Dimple was pretty sure she was close. Her heart rate was way down, her body temperature had dropped. She was going into standby mode.

For the past hour—sixty full minutes (she'd been keeping track)—Mamma, Ritu auntie, and, to a lesser extent, Seema *didi*, had been sitting in the living room talking about pregnancy.

Yes, it was true. Silent Seema and Ritu auntie's spawn, Vishal, were on their way to producing spawn of their own. Dimple shuddered to think what the creature might turn out to be. Would it come into the world gossiping and nattering on about inconsequential nothings? Or would it come out hidden behind a curtain of black hair, watching the doctors with its inscrutable dark eyes?

To be fair, Seema *didi* did look fairly happy—happier than Dimple had ever seen her. There was a hint of a smile about her mouth as she looked down at her ultrasound picture at the grainy blob/glorified amoeba.

"But *jo bhi kaho*, delivery is one of the most painful experiences of a woman's life!" Ritu auntie proclaimed, jamming another

Milano into her mouth. "I screamed so much when I was having Vishal *ki* I couldn't talk for two days afterward!" She sprayed bits of cookie crumbs everywhere. Seema *didi* was cringing beside her, but Dimple couldn't say if it was because of the projectile partially digested food or that encouraging wisdom about childbirth.

"Haan, bilkul sahi," Mamma said, nodding with a martyr-like look on her face. "They had to extract Dimple with the forceps, you know. Very painful. I couldn't go to bathroom without screaming after that." She sipped her chai and then sighed, looking at Dimple. "And they're so ungrateful after they come out."

Dimple rolled her eyes to herself. "So sorry to disappoint," she mumbled too softly for anyone to hear. She thought, anyway. But when she looked up, Seema *didi* was chewing on her cheek to keep from smiling.

"But still, Ritu, you're so lucky, you know," Mamma said, smiling wistfully at the ultrasound picture, which was now in her hands. "In eight months you're going to be a grandmother! *Tum kitni khush kismet ho.*"

Khush kismet. Lucky. Which, of course, implied that Mamma was unlucky. She'd gotten a dud of a daughter who ripped her way out in the world and had done nothing but disappoint her ever since.

Dimple and Mamma hadn't had a real conversation about any of what had happened over the summer at SFSU with Rishi. Papa had reassured Dimple that he supported her decision to sever all ties with him, even if he didn't know all the details. He'd just wanted to make sure that Rishi hadn't hurt Dimple. Papa told her to focus on her app and her relationship with Jenny Lindt. He told her she'd make new friends and have new things to look forward to at Stanford, that all of this would be a distant memory soon. All the things that parents say to their kids when life deals them lemons.

And then there was Mamma. She'd looked at Dimple with reproachful eyes ever since she came home from Insomnia Con. She hadn't said anything outright, but she'd sighed so much, Dimple was afraid the house was on the verge of collapse. And she loved to talk about Seema *didi*'s new pregnancy. Incessantly. Mamma talked about domestic life, and how much it suited Seema, and how happy Ritu was. And in the empty spaces between her words, Dimple heard how disappointed Mamma was in her. How much she wished she and Ritu could swap lives.

Dimple stood abruptly, tears threatening. That seemed to happen without warning now, like severing ties with Rishi had left her emotions raw and vulnerable to the elements. "Excuse me," she said, aware that her voice was trembling. "I should finish packing."

Ritu auntie beamed up at her from her wheelchair, oblivious, though she saw Mamma in her peripheral vision, frowning. "*Haan*, you're leaving tomorrow, *na*? Stanford!"

Dimple tried to smile and failed, so she settled for a nod.

Ritu auntie reached in her bag and handed a dollar bill to Dimple, a common practice for elders when younger people were entering a new stage of their life. "Oh, auntie, I can't—"

"Yes, you can, and you must," Ritu auntie said, pressing it into her palm. "*Khush raho, beti.* And best of luck."

Dimple managed a half smile then, thinking, *It's a nice sentiment, but happiness is way too tall an order.*

Dimple sat on the edge of her bed, staring at her suitcase and pillow and her lone box of books. She wasn't taking much else with her on this trip. She'd managed to convince Papa and Mamma to let her drive up there alone, but they'd only agreed because she'd promised to come back down for the long Labor Day weekend. Dimple figured she'd get anything else she really needed on that second trip. There was no need to overdo it; all she really wanted were her laptop and books.

She purposely didn't glance over at the bookshelf where she'd left the graphic novels Rishi had given her in Two Sisters. She'd read one of them before she left Insomnia Con. It was full of love and magic and the promise of new things. Dimple couldn't handle that right now. She'd wanted to donate them, but hadn't found it in herself to do that yet. Maybe when she came back home.

Dimple looked around at her room, wondering if Mamma would even notice she was gone. Maybe she'd be happier without having to think about Dimple every single second, without Dimple's many disappointments in her face all day, every day.

Mamma entered her room without knocking, just like usual, and set a glass of *haldi doodh* on the nightstand. Dimple looked away. She couldn't bear to see more disappointment or reproach. She was so done. Things were hard enough—her own doubts were hard enough—without Mamma's constant pressure.

"You told me you finished packing," Mamma said, sitting on a wicker chair Dimple had bought at a flea market years ago.

"I did," Dimple replied. "I just wanted to get out of there. Couldn't stand the baby talk anymore."

Mamma chuckled. "*Haan*. They're very excited. First child and grandchild, *na?*"

"Did they leave?"

Mamma nodded. After a pause, she said, *"Sab theekh hai?"*

Dimple looked at her, feeling a lump in her throat rise. "No, everything's not all right, Mamma."

Mamma frowned, confused. God, the woman was clueless. "*Kyon?* Rishi—"

"It's not Rishi," Dimple snapped. Then, more calmly, she said, "It's not *just* Rishi. It's you, too." She took a shaky breath. "Your . . . your disappointment is like a cold, heavy blanket around my shoulders, Mamma. You can't even look at me without showing it."

"Dis . . . disappointment?" Mamma said, leaning forward in her chair. "*Hai Ram,* Dimple, I am *not* disappointed in you."

Dimple felt a tear drip down her cheek and wiped it away roughly. "Yeah, right. You wish I were more like Seema *didi*. Quietly get married to someone you choose, quietly have a baby, accept my path without a fight. Right? You'd love that."

"I would love that no more than I love this." Mamma took a deep breath and adjusted her peacock blue sari. "Dimple, you are my *beti*. The only thing I want is your happiness. *Bas. Aur kuch nahin.*"

The tears were falling more quickly now. "But you sent me to Insomnia Con to fall in love with Rishi Patel. You want me to get married young and have kids, and I'm giving you none of that. Instead, you have this headstrong child who's determined to be alone. . . ." Dimple began to cry, her breath hitching, her nose plugged.

"Oof oh, Dimple . . ." Mamma came and sat next to her on the bed, putting her arm around her. "I am not so old. I understand; *aaj kal* eighteen is very young for *shaadi*, for marriage. I want you to have a happy home one day." She squeezed Dimple. "But only when you are ready. *Beti*, I am not disappointed. I am sad for what I see in your eyes, in your silence. Very deep sorrow. *Tum usse pyaar karti ho, na?*"

You love him, don't you?

Those words were the key to the floodgates Dimple had kept tightly shut for the past month. She turned, and burying her face in Mamma's neck like she hadn't since she was in elementary school, Dimple wept.

She wept for the moments that she and Rishi would never have. She wept for the love that had just blossomed and would never ripen. She wept for how mean she'd been, the names she'd called him. She wept for her hardheadedness, and for a world that couldn't just let her be both, a woman in love and a woman with a career, without flares of guilt and self-doubt seeping in and wreaking havoc. No one she knew had balanced both. There was either work or love. Wanting both felt like a huge ask; it felt like wishing for hot ice cream or a bitter sugar cube. And so she'd pushed Rishi away. She'd broken his heart and decimated her own.

"I do love him, Mamma," Dimple said when she was able to catch her breath. She sat up straighter and wiped her eyes with Mamma's *pallu*—the loose end of her sari. "But there's no way to make it work without one of us sacrificing something big. And you know how it is. It's usually the woman who ends up sacrificing. And I can't do that. I won't."

Mamma sighed and rubbed her back. "You're right, Dimple. Usually it's the woman who sacrifices. But, *beti*, looking at your unhappiness. . . . I wonder, aren't you sacrificing now? Either Rishi or career, this is the way you see it. But to me it seems cutting off either is like cutting off a part of yourself. Hmm?" Mamma kissed the side of her head.

"Whatever you do, Dimple, I am your mother. I will always support you. I am always proud of you. Okay?" She handed the *haldi doodh* over.

Dimple looked at Mamma through watery eyes, and saw nothing but love and patience in her smile. Something hard and painful in her chest loosened. Taking the milk, she whispered, "Okay."

Rishi

Rishi stood in the driveway with his parents and Ashish. He had only a small duffel bag with him; the rest he'd worry about later. He couldn't help but draw a parallel to the day he'd left for Insomnia Con. The thought pulled forth unbidden memories of Dimple— her sparkling, watchful eyes, her frown with the crease between her brows, her curly, wild hair. He struggled to push them away.

He smiled at Pappa, and Pappa smiled back. There was no hint of tension. They'd worked it out. Somehow, two divergent points of view hadn't resulted in yelling and screaming and hurt feelings. Somehow, they'd been able to sit and talk about it.

And Rishi had come to understand Pappa's point of view. He hadn't asked Rishi to give up comics from a sense of arrogance or pride or feeling ashamed of his oldest son's artistic proclivities. Pappa was just a deeply practical man, which Rishi could appreciate.

Pappa had taken a while to convince, but once he got it, he *got* it. He realized asking Rishi to commit to an engineering program was like asking him to live in a nicely decorated cage for the rest of his life. And when Rishi had sent in his late application to the art program and withdrawn from MIT's engineering track, Pappa had actually clapped him on the shoulder, smiled, and said, "I used to paint when I was your age. Sometimes I dream in watercolor. You're brave in a way I could never be, Rishi."

In the driveway, Ma had already performed the *puja* with the silver tray, just as she'd done before his trip to Insomnia Con. Now she grabbed his arm and looked up at him, tears sparkling in her eyes. "Call us soon, *beta*."

"I will, Ma." He hugged her tightly, feeling a heaviness in his throat. This was really it. He would see them only rarely for the next four years. This wasn't his primary residence anymore. He reached down and touched her feet, and then Pappa's, asking for their blessings.

As soon as he was done, Ashish grabbed him in a bear hug and clapped him on the back. The phone in his back pocket jangled. Rishi pulled back and raised an eyebrow. "Celia?"

Ashish nodded, blushing a healthy pink. He and Celia had gotten more serious over the past month. Ashish had made several trips up to San Francisco to spend time with her. Pappa and Ma were letting it slide for now, but he'd heard them discuss having Celia over for dinner one day soon.

"*Bhaiyya,*" Ashish began, itching his jaw. "Are you sure?"

They'd touched on this conversation so many times over the past month, and every time, Rishi had put a stop to it. Rishi sighed. "Yeah, I'm sure." He looked at Pappa and Ma, too, although they were pretending they had nothing to do with this conversation. "Dimple made it clear she wanted nothing more to do with me. She said I was too afraid to live life, to take risks."

"*Lekin, beta . . . ,*" Ma started.

Rishi held up a hand. "We've talked about this. Did she have some good points? Maybe." He shrugged. "Did she always encourage me to be my true self? Sure. But ultimately, she called me a coward." He looked around at them. "A *coward*."

Pappa and Ma sighed, but Ashish grabbed the back of his own neck and huffed. "Look, I think that's totally idiotic." He glanced at their parents. "I'm sorry, Pappa, Ma. I know you guys don't want me butting in and upsetting him." He turned back to Rishi. "But Dimple wanted you to be your *true self*, Rishi. She saw who you really were and she pushed you to be that person. I saw how she looked at you. She loves you. She may have had a temporary freak-out, but she *loves* you.

"I told you what Celia said—Dimple hasn't seemed the same for the last month. Like she's in this depression or shock or something. And we all know"—he gestured at Pappa and Ma—"that you've been the same way. You've only been half here. You're like a freaking ghost, barely eating, barely sleeping. You guys both love each other. You need to stop being so freaking stubborn and go tell her how you feel."

Rishi silently stared at his little brother and then at his parents. Something in his chest hitched, a seedling of doubt that was rapidly beginning to grow into a proper tree. "Ma, Pappa? Do you think this too?"

Ma looked uncomfortable, and Pappa shrugged. "Rishi, it is your decision. But . . ."

"But you seem so unhappy, *beta*," Ma finished softly. "So unhappy."

Rishi thought he'd been making the healthy choice, not pining after her. Well, not visibly pining. Trying to move forward. Get past all the heartbreak. But they'd still noticed. They'd seen how miserable he was. How truly miserable. It was a battle he'd raged internally every single day, trying to forget the woman who so obviously had forgotten him. When Ashish told him what Celia said, he hadn't paid attention. They were obviously just trying to make him feel better.

But what if it was actually true? What if Dimple really did still love him? What if maybe she'd only said those things in anger and regretted them? Maybe she'd seen to the core of his soul and truly liked what she'd seen.

Looking at the faces of his family, Rishi knew one thing: He had to find out. Now. Oh my gods, he'd been so stupid. So very stupid.

He straightened up and threw his duffel bag in the backseat of his convertible. "I'm going," he said, jumping into the driver's seat.

"Where?" Ashish asked, his face both hopeful and wary.

"To try and win your *bhabhi* back," Rishi said, grinning.

He raced down the tree-lined driveway, the sound of his family's whoops and laughter cheering him on.

Dimple

Dimple was nearly to the Stanford campus when her phone buzzed. She reached into the console, only to realize she'd stuck it in her purse at her last rest stop. Reaching into her purse, she riffled around until she felt the hard edge of her phone underneath a pile of papers. She dumped her purse out on the seat next to her, looked down to see Mamma's face flashing on the screen.

Dimple laughed; Mamma had called her three times already, just to make sure she was awake. She didn't get the concept that driving while talking on the phone was almost just as dangerous as falling asleep behind the wheel. She pressed the reject button to send it to voice mail when her eyes caught on a piece of paper that had fallen from her purse.

Glancing back up at the road to make sure she wasn't going to drive off, Dimple smoothed out the piece of paper. It was the twenty-five expressions exercise Rishi had done on the night of their non-date-turned-date, at the top of Bernal Heights Hill. Dimple's breath hitched as she caught sight of the fluid lines, when she remembered how perfectly honestly he'd captured her, how she'd been sure he'd been watching her, studying her.

And then their summer together began to come back to her in blinks and flashes—the way Rishi stood up to the Aberzombies for her; the way he'd worked tirelessly to help her make her prototype the best it could be, even though he didn't really care about web development himself; how he'd been willing to make a fool of himself dancing so she could win the talent show; how he'd set up the meeting with Jenny Lindt because he knew how important it was to her. And, in a wave, it came to her: the realization that Rishi Patel loved her so deeply, so truly, that she'd never find that again, no matter how long or hard she looked. For the rest of her life, she'd be comparing men to him. He'd be the yardstick of the perfect relationship, the truest love.

Dimple found herself bypassing the exit that would take her

to Stanford University. Instead, she kept her eye out for the SAN FRANCISCO INTERNATIONAL AIRPORT sign. If she hurried, she could get to him before he boarded his flight to MIT.

Rishi had told Dimple during their time at SFSU that he was going to MIT on the twenty-seventh of August. She'd remembered because it was the day she'd planned on leaving for Stanford too. There could be only so many flights from San Francisco to Logan Airport, right? And it was still early in the day. He probably hadn't left yet.

She pulled into the airport parking and rushed inside, scanning the monitors for the next departing flight to Logan. There was one leaving in forty minutes, at Terminal 2. Perfect. Dimple ran to the terminal, hoping he'd be there. Her heart was in her throat, pounding a frantic rhythm. She should've texted him first. Or, or e-mailed him. Something. What would she say if he looked at her blankly? Or what if he looked horrified? Maybe she should've thought this through a little more.

But Rishi wasn't in Terminal 2. Dimple scanned the crowd twice, three times, but he definitely wasn't there. She walked up to one of the waiting passengers, a young woman reading, and tapped her on the shoulder. "Hi," she said. "Is this the terminal for people going to Boston?"

The woman nodded briefly before going back to her book. Dimple looked around, her heart sinking. She was turning around, wondering what to do, when the woman said, over her shoulder, "There's another flight to Boston in ninety minutes. Terminal 1."

Dimple waited just outside Terminal 1, but he never came. She was sure he'd said his flight left before lunchtime, which meant this was the only other possible flight. Maybe he'd changed his ticket for another, earlier day. He definitely wouldn't leave later—classes started soon, and he'd want to be ready. So he'd gone across the country without even trying to reach out. And Dimple was an idiot.

She walked back out to her car and got in, steeling herself against the pain of a twice-broken heart.

Rishi

Rishi found himself on the Stanford campus at the biggest freshman residence hall, where Dimple had told him she was going to be staying. He'd waited in the lobby for thirty minutes, trying to see past the streaming lines of freshmen and their parents, looking for her wild hair, her petite body.

But she wasn't here. She'd said she was coming on the morning of the twenty-seventh, he was sure of it. He'd made a reminder in his phone when they were at SFSU, because he'd wanted to send her a bouquet of flowers for her first day.

Forty minutes.

Fifty.

He'd texted her about ten minutes into his wait (*I'm in the lobby. I'm sorry.*) and she hadn't responded.

Sixty minutes.

She wasn't going to respond. Dimple wasn't feeling any confusion, clearly. She'd made her decision and stuck to it.

And Rishi was an idiot.

He got up and walked out to his car, his steps plodding, weighed down with misery.

Dimple

Dimple walked toward the Starbucks on the SFSU campus. Maybe she should've just gone straight to Stanford, but she couldn't leave without saying a formal good-bye to this place. Maybe seeing it, touching that fountain, would help her put it—put him—behind her, once and for all. The sun was a bright ball of glittering fire; there was no fog in the air today. Even Karl was keeping his distance.

Rishi

Oh, what was he doing here? Was he really that much of a sentimental fool? Why hadn't he just gone where he was supposed to go?

But as if his brain were completely disconnected from his legs, Rishi found himself being transported to the Starbucks on the SFSU campus. As if he was dumb enough to hope she'd be there, perched on that fountain like last time, an iced coffee in her hands. . . .

He blinked.

And blinked again.

"Dimple?"

Dimple

Her eyes flew open at the voice, her heart constricting painfully, her brain telling her it was stupid to hope, so very stupid. But—

It was him. Rishi Patel, staring at her with his mouth hanging open.

Dimple stood on shaky legs, her breath ragged, disbelief and hope mixing, swirling, bursting in her chest. Her hands were shaking so hard, the coffee threatened to fall to the ground. "Rishi?"

Rishi

He stood there, staring at her. One word echoed in his brain, over and over, like a songbird's call: "Kismet." He was sure he looked deranged, the way his heart was hammering in his head and his chest and his throat all at once, the way his mouth felt dry, his entire body stiff and cold with shock. He reached out to her and then dropped his hand midway. "I texted—"

"I went to—"

They'd both spoken at the same time, and Rishi stopped and made an *after you* gesture with his hand. "Go ahead."

Dimple bit her lip. Gods, she was beautiful. So, so perfect. His chest felt warm and way too tight. There was intense yearning inside him; he needed to tuck her head under his chin and smell her shampoo. That was the only thing he wanted right now, the only thing. But he kept himself rigid, held himself at an angle so as to not get too close.

"I, um . . ." She tucked a curl behind her ear, and he saw her hand shake a bit. "What are you doing here?" Her eyes searched his, trying to find answers.

Rishi tucked his hands into his pockets so he wouldn't be tempted to reach out and stroke her cheek. "I, ah, I go here."

Her eyes widened almost comically. Gods, she was cute. "You're an SFSU student now? What about MIT?"

Rishi shook his head and smiled. "I had a long talk with Pappa about how I'm an artist at heart."

He caught a glimpse of Dimple's full throttle smile, just for a second, before she put it away. "And he was okay with that?"

Rishi shrugged. "Eventually. He's still getting used to the idea, but I think he wants me to be happy more than anything."

Dimple nodded, like she got that. "But weren't you too late to apply for admission?"

He rubbed a hand through his hair and forced himself to hold her gaze. "Leo Tilden spoke to them. They're big fans of his, so . . ."

"So he e-mailed you?" That big grin was back, but then she tamped down on it again, cheeks flushing a deep burgundy, and looked away. "That's great."

"Thank you," he said quietly.

Dimple

Dimple looked at Rishi. "For what?"

He was still looking at her in that unfathomable way. His honey eyes were speaking volumes, but she was too afraid to guess what they were saying. "For sending him my pictures. He e-mailed me a couple of weeks ago. He was actually the one who helped me show Pappa how important this is to me. And he helped bolster my courage so I could take this leap. That was an incredible thing you did for me. And I'm sorry I didn't see it before. I didn't see a lot of things."

Did he mean . . . ? Was he talking about . . . ? No, of course not. Dimple blinked, her throat tight. "It's okay. It would've been a disservice to the world if you hadn't pursued it, you know?"

He smiled, a gentle, soft thing like fading light. "And what about you and your app?"

"Jenny's been incredible. We're nearing completion; maybe another month or two." She adjusted her glasses. "Thank *you* for doing that for me. I don't think I was very grateful at the time, and I'm sorry too."

Rishi nodded slowly, sadly. "Maybe we were both too caught up with other things we needed to sort through." He took a deep breath. "What are you doing here, by the way?"

Dimple flushed and looked away, hands tightening around the iced coffee cup. "Nothing," she said quickly. Then she took a breath and tried again. She'd come all this way. She'd wanted a chance to make this right. Well, this was it. This was her chance. Maybe Rishi didn't feel the same way anymore, but she still owed him an apology. "Actually, the truth is, I, um . . . I went to the airport first. I thought you'd be there."

Rishi

Rishi's heart began to trip along in his chest. She'd gone to the airport to find him? "I wasn't there," he said, stupidly.

Dimple smiled a little. "Yeah, I see that. You weren't going to MIT after all."

"But why . . . why did you want to find me?" he asked, his breath speeding up. He tried to calm his pulse and was only marginally successful.

"I . . ." She swallowed, an audible gulping sound. She looked into his eyes. "I . . . made a mistake, Rishi." Laughing a little nervously, she held out the iced coffee. "And if you want to throw this at me, I'll totally understand." Then, softly but firmly, she added, "I was a total idiot. I love you." There was a pause, because Rishi couldn't think of a single thing to say. His brain had iced over or overheated or something. "I get it if it's too late," Dimple hurried to add. "I just wanted to say I was sorry. And that, you know, I should never have said all those things to you. I was afraid, and . . ." She shook her head and looked away, biting her lip like she was afraid she might cry.

Was this real life? Was this really happening? Surely this was a dream. . . . Rishi pinched his forearm, hard. "Ow!"

Dimple frowned and looked back at him. "What the heck are you doing?"

Rishi shook his head a little, still utterly in shock. "Wait, but . . . but I texted you from the lobby of your dorm. And you never texted me back."

Dimple looked startled. "I . . ." Then she hit her forehead with an open palm. "My phone fell off my seat while I was driving, and I couldn't get to it, so I left it. It's on vibrate, so I didn't even hear it. And when I got here, I was in a hurry to see this place, and I totally forgot." She smiled suddenly, big and wide and bright, as if she'd just realized what he'd said. "Wait. You waited for me in the lobby of my dorm? Why?"

Rishi stepped toward her, his heart pounding like it was trying to make an escape. He circled his arms around her waist. "Because, Dimple Shah, I am stupidly, idiotically, annoyingly in love with you. You were right about so many things. I *was* afraid. I was terrified of doing what I wanted and of hurting my parents. I was carrying this huge weight on my shoulders without even realizing it—without even needing to. You've made me braver. It's like you have this paintbrush, dipped in brilliant mauves and teals and golds, and you just totally redid my monochromatic life. I need you; I need your paintbrush." He pushed a shaky hand through his hair, terrified and exhilarated and breathless. "Wow. I'm not even sure if that made any sense."

Dimple tipped her head back farther and smiled up at him in a way that made his heart do some very interesting things. "It makes total sense. I was the same way. I said you were cowardly, but I was just as terrified, Rishi." She shook her head, sunshine glinting on her glasses. "I was so afraid of going down the same path as my parents, of ending up in the same domestic life, that I forgot to consider one thing: This is *our* life. We get to decide the rules. We get to say what goes and what stays, what matters and what doesn't. And the only thing I know is that I love you. It hurts too much to be apart from you." She stopped, her eyes glittering with tears.

Rishi breathed deeply, the loneliness and the doubt and the brilliant pain of the last month finally dissipating. "Same," he whispered. And then, louder, "I'm sorry it took me the rest of the summer to realize it and come after you. But I'm here now. You're here now. So what do you say we do this the right way this time around?"

Dimple grinned, her ears pounding with the rhythm of a thousand Bollywood love songs. "Yes, please."

And she closed the gap between their lips.

Acknowledgments

This book would never have happened without my amazing editor, Jennifer Ung. Not only is Jen a talented editor with an uncanny ability to mind-meld, she's also working tirelessly to bring diversity to children's book publishing, an undertaking near and dear to my heart. And as if that weren't enough, she's also the master of sending relevant dog memes via e-mail. Thank you so, so much for all you do. I'm beyond excited that we're going to be continuing to work together!

To my indefatigable and completely lovely literary agent, Thao Le, thank you for bringing this opportunity to me. I was in a complete writing slump until I got that e-mail from you—on my birthday, of all days.

To the entire Simon Pulse team, from my exceptional designer, Regina Flath, to the publicity and marketing team, and everyone in between—thank you, thank you for this wonderful opportunity. Pulse has been like a warm and welcoming family. I couldn't have asked for a better house!

To my family, who support me without question and with unbridled enthusiasm always, I want to say, you guys are my lobsters. I love you, and I can't wait for more mountain adventures!

And last but definitely not least, I want to thank YOU, dear reader. You, who felt moved by Dimple and Rishi's story, who rejoiced with them through the joyous moments and cried alongside them through the hard ones. I hope you were able to see yourself in this book, no matter who you are or where you come from. I'm pretty sure kismet led you here—and I know Rishi would agree.